MASTER ALVIN

TOR BOOKS BY ORSON SCOTT CARD

ENDER SAGA
Ender's Game
Speaker for the Dead
Xenocide
Children of the Mind
Ender in Exile
The Last Shadow

ENDER'S SHADOW SERIES
Ender's Shadow
Shadow of the Hegemon
Shadow Puppets
Shadow of the Giant
Shadows in Flight

Children of the Fleet

THE FIRST FORMIC WAR
(with Aaron Johnston)
Earth Unaware
Earth Afire
Earth Awakens

THE SECOND FORMIC WAR
(with Aaron Johnston)
The Swarm
The Hive

ENDER NOVELLAS
A War of Gifts
First Meetings

THE MITHERMAGES
The Lost Gate
The Gate Thief
Gatefather

THE TALES OF ALVIN MAKER
Seventh Son
Red Prophet
Prentice Alvin
Alvin Journeyman
Heartfire
The Crystal City
Master Alvin

HOMECOMING
The Memory of Earth
The Call of Earth
The Ships of Earth
Earthfall
Earthborn

WOMEN OF GENESIS
Sarah
Rebekah
Rachel & Leah

THE COLLECTED SHORT FICTION
OF ORSON SCOTT CARD
Maps in a Mirror: The Short Fiction of Orson Scott Card
Keeper of Dreams

STAND-ALONE FICTION
Invasive Procedures
(with Aaron Johnston)
Empire
Hidden Empire
The Folk of the Fringe
Hart's Hope
Pastwatch: The Redemption of Christopher Columbus
Saints
Songmaster
Treason
The Worthing Saga
Wyrms
Zanna's Gift

ORSON SCOTT CARD

THE TALES OF
ALVIN MAKER VII

MASTER ALVIN

TOR PUBLISHING GROUP
NEW YORK

This is a work of fiction. All of the names, characters, organizations, places, and events portrayed in this work are either products of the author's imagination or used fictitiously.

MASTER ALVIN

Prayer on page 117 based on "The Most Powerful Healing Prayer of St. Padre Pio" from the website TheCatholicCrusade.com.

A Tor Book
Published by Tom Doherty Associates / Tor Publishing Group
120 Broadway
New York, NY 10271

www.torpublishinggroup.com

EU Representative: Macmillan Publishers Ireland Ltd, 1st Floor, The Liffey Trust Centre, 117–126 Sheriff Street Upper, Dublin 1, D01 YC43

The Library of Congress Cataloging-in-Publication Data is available upon request.

ISBN 978-0-7653-0018-8 (hardcover)
ISBN 978-1-4299-4350-5 (ebook)

First Edition: 2026

Printed in the United States of America

10 9 8 7 6 5 4 3 2 1

To Beth Meacham
Thank you for Octagon Mound
For decades of trust
For helping Alvin talk like Alvin
For being a friend to every writer
And to every reader

MASTER ALVIN

ARTHUR GOT HIMSELF up a tree because he was still young and spry and because he couldn't see heartfires clearly from afar off, so if he was going to keep a lookout, he had to be where he could see into the distance. And he saw them, a party of five men and one woman, leading a two-mule cart through a narrow trace in the woods.

This part of Irrakwa country was still forest, but they allowed Arthur's friend and brother-in-law, Alvin, to use the old trace, because the Irrakwa didn't like Puritan New Englanders any more than any other citizens of the United States of America. Looking to kill folks for no other reason than they had them a knack seemed as wrong to the Reds as it did to any Whites. Or Blacks, for that matter, seeing how Arthur himself was half Black—or half White, depending on which way you looked at it.

So Peggy Larner told them a party of knackers was coming out of West Hampshire by way of Rutland, and they'd need some protection. That's why Arthur had run behind Alvin all the way through the wooded land from Crystal City to the state of Irrakwa, where there was still a lot of primeval forest where the Greensong was so strong Arthur could hear it. Not like Alvin, of course, and it wasn't singing *to* Arthur, he was just overhearing it. But it was beautiful and he wished everybody could hear it so they'd be gentler to the living things of the Earth.

Arthur didn't know the names of the folks who were making their way up the trace, nor their faces, but they were the ones. Peggy had said they'd be pulling a heavy mule cart, which Arthur thought was plain stupid—what possessions did they have that was so precious they had to slow themselves down to bring it along by cart through a forest? But when knacky folk were trying to get away from witch-hunters they needed help even if they was stupid. Maybe *especially* when they was stupid.

He could hear Peggy Larner's schoolroom voice saying, "Maybe especially when they *were* stupid." And Arthur saying, "Alvin talks like I do." And she said, "Making you brothers in ignorance. Learn to think to yourself with proper grammar, and then when you speak, respectable language will come out of your mouth without your even having to think about it."

"Thought you didn't like me to talk without thinking," said Arthur on one such occasion, and Miz Larner laid a ruler atop Arthur's head right sharply, making him glad she didn't use a thimble but not making him regret his impertinent remark very much, since it was true.

The knackers were moving again, but faster, having left the wagon behind. Arthur shinnied down the main trunk of the tree and set himself down on the ground in front of Alvin. "They're no more than five minutes away," he said.

Alvin nodded. "I hear them."

"Left their wagon off the trace in the trees," said Arthur.

Alvin nodded again. "They think nobody can see it there."

"Unless somebody clumb up a tall tree and could see down through the branches cause the forest is only just coming into leaf again."

"I'm glad you still like to climb trees so high you could kill yourself just *thinking* about jumping down."

"Never been injured by thinking of something stupid," said Arthur.

"Good thing," said Alvin. "But a lot of misfortune comes to folks as think of something stupid and then they do it."

"I didn't even think of jumping down," said Arthur, "and so you shouldn't be surprised that I didn't land dead at your feet."

"I wasn't surprised," said Alvin. "And I'm happy you're not dead."

The first of the knacky people came into the small clearing. It was the woman.

She stopped, and Arthur looked at her, and she looked at him and then at Alvin and then back at Arthur again. "Who am I talking to?" she asked.

"Both of us," said Arthur. "But I reckon I'm likely to do most of the talking back." And as he said it, his voice slid into sounding just like Alvin's voice, because that was Arthur's best knack, being able to imitate voices perfectly. He lost it for a while, but Alvin and Peggy helped him to learn it back again, and he was almost as good as ever.

The woman didn't know Arthur sounded like Alvin, though, because Alvin hadn't said a word in front of her. Hadn't even looked her in the eye.

The woman turned to Arthur, took a step toward him. "I was told that someone from the Crystal City would be here to meet us. Meet me."

"Oh, I know there's five men as well as you, ma'am," said Arthur. "And you left your mule cart hid up in the trees just off the trace, about a quarter mile back."

The woman took a step back. "You been spying on us?"

"Well of course," said Arthur. "You think we'd let somebody get this close without knowing who they are and what they're here for? You rather we *didn't* watch out for you, and so when you came over the border you'd meet up with Irrakwa border scouts instead of us from Crystal City?"

"Watching out for us," said the woman. "Not spying. I get it."

Arthur doubted that she got *anything* right yet, but . . . no reason to argue the point. If he was going to imitate Alvin, he should say only things that Alvin would say, and picking an argument about nothing was something he'd never do, not with good folks, anyway.

"I bet you have a name," said Arthur.

"I bet you do, too," she answered.

"You're the stranger," said Arthur.

"I'm not a stranger to *me*," she said, "but *you* are."

"I'm Arthur Stuart, reckoned by most people to be the cleverest boy in Crystal City, though I'm over twenty and have a man's height."

"I'm glad you're so highly thought of," said the woman. "At least by yourself."

"Everybody agrees with me," said Arthur. "You'd be amazed."

"My name is Goody Sower," she said. "Even if they weren't nobody looking to kill me, I'd be glad to get shut of New England. Hardly any honest soil in the whole country, just stones and smaller stones."

"You got you a husband, Goody Sower?" asked Arthur. "Just wondering if there's a Goodman Sower among the five men standing just out of sight among the trees."

A man stepped out from the wood. "That's me," he said.

"The rest of you come out, too," said Goody Sower. "They know you're there. These men are from Crystal City."

"How do we know that's true?" asked a suspicious-looking man.

Arthur laughed. "Who else is going to be waiting here to welcome knacky folks from New England and take them west?"

The men looked a little uncomfortable. Then Goodman Sower walked to her and put an arm around her waist. "If you're here to take us west to the Crystal City, can you lead us to a wagon road?"

Arthur grinned. "Now why would we do that?"

Goody Sower said, "Because you already know we have a wagon."

Arthur nodded wisely, still grinning. "To be precise, ma'am, you *had* a wagon. Now you're just six people standing in a clearing with us."

The other men reacted abruptly—two of them turning around to head back toward the wagon, the other two to step forward and demand an explanation.

"Rest easy, merry gentlemen," said Arthur. "Your wagon is where you left it. The contents are undisturbed."

"I bet you got it surrounded with armed men. Or Irrakwa warriors."

"Not yet," said Arthur. "Which would you prefer?"

"Neither," said Goody Sower, preempting them before they could say something dangerous. "But we worked hard to get that wagon where it is, and if we can find an easier path, that would be . . . helpful."

"We're here to help," said Arthur. "So, what's in this wagon that you can't bear to part with even to get to the prairie by the Mizzippy?"

"It's everything we own," said Goodman Sower.

"Well, now," said Arthur, "I think you're making fun with me. Because you own the clothes you're wearing, and the guns some of you are carrying. The shoes or boots on your feet. And every thought inside your head. Ain't none of those in that wagon."

The men looked nervously at each other, but Goody Sower was unfazed. "You know what I meant to say," she said.

"I also know what you meant *not* to say," said Arthur. "I'd say there's about four thousand dollars in gold in that wagon, in two chests and three heavy cloth bags."

"Who's been spying on us!" demanded the largest of the men, looking as if he wanted to rassle the culprit to the ground there and then.

"Just think a minute," said Arthur.

The men paused. The big one said, "Think about what?"

"Think about where you're going."

This time they thought. Goody Sower, who seemed to be the sharpest blade in the knife drawer, finally said, "You're a city full of people with knacks. Maybe one of you can see afar off. Maybe this fellow." She indicated Alvin, who wasn't looking at them or at Arthur.

"Close," said Arthur. "We've got one farseer who maybe could spot you and the gold from Crystal City all the way to the bank you just come from."

"What bank!"

"Who said anything about a bank!"

Arthur held up his hands to quell their outrage. "Every citizen of Crystal City is free to look into the crystal walls and floor and see what's there to see. You folks were there to see. All the way here, trying to get them mules to stay in order and not hang up the wagon on a stump."

Some of the men nodded—no doubt the ones who had to help the mules get the wheels over those stumps.

"And those same folks also saw you rob the Whitman Bank and Trust and fill your wagon up with other people's gold."

Now the men stiffened up and a couple of them clenched their muskets and one of them made as if to run off, but Goody Sower stopped them all. "Forgive my companions," said Goody Sower. "They weren't none of them chosen for their wits."

The men glowered, but kept still.

"I can assure you," said Goody Sower, "that nobody saw us enter the bank or load up the gold. There's no pursuit behind us."

Arthur laughed. "Well, I sure know what your knack *ain't*," he said. "There's a posse comitatus tracking you through the woods not two miles back, and having an easy time of it, your wagon tracks being mighty easy to see."

"Then we've got to get that wagon moving right now," said the big man, and he and another fellow took off running back toward the trace in the woods. Or so they thought.

Alvin looked up and called out to them. "The trace you came through is over there," he said. "That's the path to your wagon and its cargo of contraband."

The two runners corrected their course and disappeared into the woods.

Goodman Sower stepped closer to Alvin. "Are you the one in charge of this party?"

Alvin shrugged. "Arthur and I travel together and we make decisions pretty much at the same time. Nobody's in charge, not officially."

"I'm in charge," said Arthur, "on account of I got more common sense."

"While I have some uncommon senses," said Alvin.

"Here's the thing," said Arthur. "That wagon's already gone as far as it's going to go."

"Is that a threat?" asked Goodman Sower.

"It's a fact," said Arthur. "Because you ain't getting no further without our help, and we ain't going to help you bring stolen gold into Crystal City."

"Then I guess we'll have to go somewhere else," said one of the other men, looking angry but also scared.

"I doubt it," said Arthur, "since your wagon wheels are buried up to the hubs in squishy mud."

"There wasn't no mud where we—"

Goody Sower held up a hand again. "So you ain't leaving us no choice," she said.

"You got several choices," said Arthur. "You can run back to the wagon and try to kill all the men who are coming after you, so you can take the wagon further along one trace or another."

"I'd like to hear another choice," said Goody Sower.

"You could leave that wagon and all that gold behind, so that the good folk of Whitman can take it back to the bank and no harm done."

"I'm hoping there's a third choice," said Goody Sower.

"I'm thinking," said Arthur.

"Here's what I'm thinking," said Goody Sower. "Crystal City's growing by leaps and bounds, we hear. It's got to be expensive, feeding and housing all them folks. This gold isn't for us, no matter what some of these clowns might think. We mean to contribute all of it to Crystal City, to the Maker and his people. What we've got is prosperity."

Arthur laughed. "Don't you know that Maker fellow can turn iron into gold whenever he wants?"

They had nothing to say to that—they had all heard the stories.

"Iffen you bring that gold to Crystal City," said Arthur, "then the law's going to follow you all the way, and then if they find the gold *in* the city, they'll be arresting a lot more folks than just you."

"Don't you people have hexes to conceal the gold?" asked Goodman Sower.

"What gold?" asked Alvin.

Goodman Sower stammered a little. "The gold back in our wagon."

"Ain't no gold there," said Alvin. "Just bars of tin and little tin disks. Like a tinker tripped and dropped all his kit in that wagon."

The men were outraged. "Tin!" "We hefted it and it's gold." "We know the difference between tin and gold!"

"And so do we," said Alvin. "But I can promise you—if the posse from

Whitman finds that wagon, it'll be full of gold, just how you left it. But the minute you try to defend it or conceal it or transport any part of it away from here, it'll be tin."

"We can use tin in Crystal City," said Arthur helpfully. "You can probably sell it for enough to rent some houses long enough to find work and earn your way."

The tall man came back into the clearing. "We earned our way," he said. "Gold enough to let us *buy* houses and hire workers to till our fields. Gold enough to keep carriages and fine horses, and china plates for our wives."

"Wives that none of you got," said Arthur, "not even Goodman and Goodwife Sower, who are no more married than this tree to that stump."

"How can you know anything like that?" said Goody Sower. "Specially on account of it's a lie."

"Why did you come back?" Alvin asked the big man. His erstwhile companion emerged from the trace.

"The posse got to the wagon before us," said the big fellow. "And the two of us were outnumbered by a few."

"Well," said Arthur to Goody Sower, "you got fewer choices than you had awhile ago. I'm thinking, you can take off running down one of these forest traces and hope you reach some town before you run into Irrakwa who might not appreciate your trespassing."

The men said nothing to this.

"Or you might just come along with us," said Arthur, "which was what we came for, to guide you and protect you all the way to the Crystal City, where the Maker's likely to try to teach you to use your knacks for something better than stealing other folks' gold."

"You two, protect *us*?" asked the big guy.

"I reckon so," said Arthur. "For instance, that posse saw you take off running this direction. They tried to follow, since they didn't know all the gold was still on the wagon. But they haven't been able to find any trace that leads to this clearing. Isn't that protection?"

The men looked at each other, at Goody Sower.

"You can lead us to safety?" Goodman Sower asked.

"Only a couple of conditions," said Arthur. "And don't worry, it's not payment the Maker asks for. It's honor."

"I think that's in short supply in our company," said Goody Sower.

"First, he expects folks to tell us their right names, and some of you been passing by other names so long it might be hard for you to remember the name your mama called you."

"I really am named Sower," said Goodman Sower. "Robin Sower."

"Robert," corrected Goody Sower.

"Robin is what my mama called me, and that's what he said they want," said Robin Sower.

The big man allowed as how his nickname had been Tiny for so many years that he wasn't sure if his original name was Cincinnatus or Hobb. Or Cincinnatus Hobb?

"Cincin Hobb," offered Arthur. "Sounds like the devil's work, though—Sin-Sin."

"That's what they called me," Hobb said, nodding.

They all had names, though Arthur figured that two of them having no real knack, just a lust for gold, they'd peel off from the party and go their own way pretty soon.

"Goody Sower," asked Alvin. "We're eager to learn your name."

"Ain't Sower," she said.

"Figured that," said Alvin.

"What's *your* name first?" she demanded.

Alvin rose easily to his feet, showing he was taller even than Hobb. "My father was a miller, and so I grew up with the name Alvin Miller. But then I was prenticed to a smith, and took that name, Alvin Smith."

Her eyes widened. "Alvin Maker," she said softly.

"The same," he said, bowing and doffing his cap.

"I don't believe it," said Robin Sower. "Alvin *Maker*, come all the way here to meet a party of six travelers?"

"Bank robbers," murmured Arthur.

"The bank got their gold back," said Hobb, "so they ain't no robbers here."

"I'm Alvin Maker, right enough, though I don't use the Maker name much outside the city. It makes some folks kind of agitated. I'm Alvin Miller or Alvin Smith, as suits your fancy."

Goody Sower stuck out her right hand.

"You mean me to shake that hand?" asked Alvin.

"Kiss it," said Arthur. "Be a gentleman."

"Or plant your foot and see if you can throw me," said Goody Sower.

Alvin put his right foot next to her right foot, and held her right wrist as firmly as she held his.

"What should I do here, Mr. Miller?" she asked. "Better to beat you or to let you beat me?"

"Nobody ever let me beat them before," said Alvin.

"Because you got plenty of knacks to trick them or overpower them, I wager," said Hobb.

"I never use a knack to win at wrestling, unless my life's in danger."

"I don't kill folks," said Goody Sower.

"Then when do we start?" asked Alvin.

She gave a mighty tug on his arm and tripped him over her right knee so he was flat on his back in the meadow.

From the ground, Alvin said, "I wish you hadn't plunked me down in a meadow so full of bees."

"They stinging you?" she asked.

"No, they pretty much leave me be. But they're annoyed, and I'm afraid of what they might do to you when I get up."

"*If* you can get up," she said.

"You owe me a name," said Alvin.

"Eliza Nutbutter," she said.

"Your real name," said Arthur.

"My father was named Nutbutter and my mam called me Eliza, so if my name ain't Eliza Nutbutter, I don't know what it is."

"Miss Nutbutter," said Alvin, "you got the first throw on me, and that's good enough for now. We'll finish this best-of-seven rassling contest another day. For now, we've got a powerful lot of walking to do today."

"Used to have a wagon," said Robin.

"A wagon you stole, mules you stole—I don't think you're going to get much sympathy," said Arthur.

"But we're going to come into the city with Alvin Maker himself," said Robin Sower.

"Unless you try some nefarious trick and he has to sink you into the bedrock somewhere," said Arthur. Arthur noticed that the two men who had no knacks were no longer in the clearing. He spotted their heartfires, since they weren't far off—but on a road that would take them south, into Irrakwa country for sure. Maybe they figured to catch a ride on a train to some place where they weren't known as thieves. No longer Arthur's business, though, so he no longer tried to keep track of where they were. He wasn't like Miz Larner, able to spot heartfires halfway across the country. Arthur's range wasn't even a mile.

"Don't fret," said Alvin to Robin Sower. "I haven't put anybody inside stone in a while. I said you'll have my protection all the way to Crystal City. That means protection from the Puritans, the Irrakwa, the people of every town that hates knackers, and all the folks who want to keep anybody from getting to Crystal City. It even means protection from any knacker who thinks to play pranks on you."

Arthur cried out, "Hey! Including me?"

"Especially including you," said Alvin. "You know I brought you along because you're so pretty, not to have you making our fellow travelers miserable with your shenanigans."

"I never done a shenanigan," said Arthur, "let alone more than one."

And with that Alvin led the way forward into a barely visible trace. With only a bit of hesitation, Eliza Nutbutter followed him, and Robin Sower right behind. The two thieves with knacks came next, bringing up the rear. Arthur wondered if they might slip away like the other two, but then he realized that knacky men from New England would expect to be accepted in Crystal City.

As soon as they started going in earnest, packs slung on their backs, Arthur heard the Greensong coming up faintly all around them. Not like the powerful music when Alvin took Arthur running faster than any deer. But enough of the Greensong that the way was smooth and there were no rocks or roots to trip them, and they came to clear running water as often as they needed it, but never a stream too big to jump over. Arthur still hadn't figured out whether the land changed because of the Greensong, or the Greensong simply led them to where the land offered the most ease and bounty.

"Try to keep up," said Alvin, and Arthur almost retorted, "I'm keeping up just fine." But then he realized Alvin was talking to the others, who didn't none of them have an affinity for Greensong, and wouldn't understand why the walking was so easy now, after the hard trail to where they dragged the wagon. If they even noticed how easy it was.

"Glad we don't have them mules anymore," grumbled one of the men.

"No shortage of mules in this party," said Eliza Nutbutter.

Nobody set out to spread the word. They just went about their business, looking to buy something here, looking to sell something there, getting to work on building a house, getting to work on draining a swamp, and caring for crops and gardens because it was already spring and coming on summer and anything you didn't plant now would have a much harder struggle come August.

Every time they'd come upon somebody they hadn't seen yet that day, they'd lead off with, "Heard the Maker's back in town," or "Alvin's home again, and Arthur with him," or "The Maker's brought him a passel of knackers from back East." And a few more cynical souls saying, "So Al's found him some new friends, including a woman, and brung em along, cause we didn't have us quite enough mouths to feed."

Not everybody's heart was right with the other folks in Crystal City. That would've been too much to hope for. Most everybody cooperated and did business and got along, trying to avoid doing anything to get em hauled into court. And most people were pure in heart, or at least enough so to gaze in one of the crystal rooms and see things in the walls and ceiling and floor.

Them as couldn't see anything useful in the Crystal kept their lack to themselves. No reason to advertise that the Crystal hadn't judged you ready, or worthy, or meek enough to be given vision.

The word reached Margaret Larner in the schoolroom as she dismissed her college preparation class for the noon meal. It was Narth Pew, the principal teacher, who was nominally her boss, but this was the Maker's wife, so let's be serious about who was in charge. "I thought you'd want to know," Narth said, "your husband's back in town. Unless you already knew."

"I knew he was close," she said, "but your news that he's already here is good and fresh."

"Will you be wanting the rest of the day off?"

"I do not believe so," said Margaret Larner—once called Little Peggy Guester, when she first laid eyes on the baby that would grow up to be Alvin Maker. "If Alvin needs me, he knows where I'll be, so if he doesn't come to me, he doesn't need me to go to him. I have a few more hours of teaching this afternoon, since half my class is heading off to college in other states and colonies."

"You done a good job preparing those children for college," said Narth.

"They did a good job of preparing themselves," said Margaret. "But I was glad to help."

"Too bad most of the good colleges are in New England," said Narth.

"Can't be helped. As soon as Puritan schools like Harvard learn that a student applicant comes from Crystal City, they'd only grant them admission in order to arrest them, try them, and either hang, drown, or burn them."

"And without giving them a diploma first, or a single hour of teaching," said Narth.

Margaret was never sure if he was joking when he said absurd things like that. Was he being ironic?

"But the other schools are good enough," he said. "I never heard of a Harvard engineer's bridge standing up stronger than a bridge built by an engineer trained in Irrakwa or Williamsburg College, or in Appalachee University."

"Haven't had a lot of bridges falling down lately," said Margaret. "So far as I've heard."

"Wish we had us a good college a little closer," said Narth.

Margaret sighed. "I'm not ready to desert my students here in order to gallivant off to try to make friends with students and faculty at Northwestern."

"A teacher like you is needed wherever you go," said Narth.

"But not wanted in half so many places."

Narth chuckled. "Well, you're sure wanted here."

Then Margaret saw Narth notice someone behind her. Without turning, she said, "Well, my love, you came to me almost as soon as you arrived."

"I've repented of the madness of thinking that anything was more important to me than you," said Alvin.

She turned, and there he was, still dirty and bedraggled from the journey. But he was holding Vigor by the hand, the boy looking up at his father with sheer adulation on his face.

"I see you found the young lady who was watching our boy," said Margaret.

"She surrendered custody of him reluctantly," said Alvin. "I believe she enjoys her job." Alvin sat down on the edge of the teacher's table, then hefted Vigor up to stand on the table, Alvin's arm around his waist.

Margaret looked at the boy. "Have you discovered anything interesting since I saw you this morning?" she asked him.

"Other dogs keep trying to climb onto Canna," said Vigor, "but she's too small and I think they might crush her."

Alvin spoke up. "Right now, Vig, she's giving off a smell that just drives the boy dogs crazy."

"I don't smell it," said Vigor

"Are you a boy dog?" asked Alvin.

"I'd druther be," said Vigor.

"Why?" asked Margaret, a little concerned about where this conversation started and where it might be going.

"I don't like having to go sit with Missy Wander because all she ever wants to do is read."

"You know how to read," said Margaret.

"I like to do stuff," said Vigor. "Dogs get to do stuff all they want and nobody minds as long as they don't dig in the garden or pull food off the table."

"And Miss Wander doesn't let you do . . . anything?" asked Alvin.

"She wants me to read to her," said Vigor. "But I don't know the words. I sound them out and she either corrects me or lets it go but I still don't know what anything means."

"The classic complaint of students everywhere," said Margaret.

"Isn't that what teachers are for?" asked Alvin.

"Miss Wander is not a teacher or a tutor or a governess or anything else, I'm afraid," said Margaret. "She was all I could find last month after Missy Harborlight left to become Mrs. Blue."

"Blue is a stupid name," said Vigor. "She isn't *blue* and neither is her stupid husband."

"I take it Miss Harborlight was a favorite?" asked Alvin.

"And after Missy Wander leaves, I think Vigor will like her better than whoever her replacement might be."

"I don't like her at all," said Vigor.

"I remember you saying that about Missy Harborlight," said Margaret.

"Have you ever thought of letting Vigor sit in on *your* class?" asked Alvin.

"No," said Vigor, "and I hope she never *does* think of it. Missy Wander says Mommy talks as if she's getting paid by the letter."

Alvin whooped with laughter, and Margaret soon joined in. "Lots of long words, eh?" Margaret asked her son.

"I don't know how many letters there is in a word," said Vigor, "less'n you spell it out."

Margaret embraced Vigor and then lowered him down from the table to the floor.

"What am I sposed to do now? You and Papa always talk about stuff I don't understand and I think you do it on purpose cause you don't *want* me to understand."

"You're exactly right, Vigor," said Alvin cheerily. "You're a very clever boy."

"Donny says I'm a smarty-pants and then all the girls call me that over and over."

"Donny Crassum says that because he's a dummy-pants," said Alvin, "and you being so clever makes him feel bad."

Margaret escorted Vigor to a corner with a book and a slate in it. "You can draw with the chalk, Viggy, or you can read a book. Your father and I will finish our conversation very quickly."

As Margaret returned to the table where Alvin sat, she could see in his face that he expected to be told off. And she probably should do exactly that, but she thought "dummy-pants" was a pretty good name to use for Donny Crassum, especially since "Dummy" could be a nickname for "Donny."

"Where's Arthur?" she asked, when she sat on the table edge next to Alvin.

"He had two offers of lunch and accepted them both, so he's getting what he needs."

"Did both of those offers come from families with nubile daughters?" asked Margaret.

"I believe so," said Alvin, "though I can't keep up with who's wooing and who's betrothed."

"Do you really believe you know everyone in Crystal City by name?" asked Margaret.

"I recognize near everybody I see, and everybody I don't recognize, I introduce myself and they always just got here."

"Alvin," said Margaret, "I'd like to know about the woman who was with those knackers."

"Says her name's Eliza Nutbutter. Also pretended to be married to the fellow named Sower, so she was using his name when we first met. He wasn't happy about it, so it's as well she goes by Nutbutter now. I think Sower will be out of Crystal City as soon as he discovers his knack don't amount to much around here, and there's no way for him to steal anything."

"What's to steal?" asked Margaret. "If he steals a block of Crystal it stops working and within a week it melts back to water."

"There are other things to steal," said Alvin. "If stealing's what you want to do."

"And no way to get out of town without somebody giving the alarm or spotting the contraband or just seeing the theft in a Crystal wall."

"So maybe Sower will stay. The other two won't."

"You're sure?"

"So are you," said Alvin. "They want three things: women, money, and prestige."

"They can make money here," said Margaret.

"But here's the one place in the United States or any of the English-speaking countries on this side of the Atlantic where having money does *not* bring prestige."

"Oh, Alvin, I wish that were so. Or that money didn't attract women."

"I never noticed that," said Alvin.

"Because you've never had money," said Margaret.

"I think that's maybe my best virtue," he said. "I have an affinity for metal, yet it always seems to be repelled from my hands as soon as it becomes coins."

"We're not so pure in heart here, Alvin," said Margaret. "Rough men can get everything they want here."

"Don't even have to be rough," said Alvin, and Margaret immediately knew he was referring to Calvin, Alvin's younger brother, an envious and frustrated young man. Calvin was nothing if not smooth.

"He will never have the dominance he craves," said Alvin. "Not as long as I'm alive."

"Do us all a favor, Alvin, and stay alive."

"If man and nature will cooperate, I plan to do just that."

"I have a class to teach this afternoon," said Margaret.

"There's no 'husband-just-came-home' holiday?"

"It was offered, by Narth," said Margaret, "but my students need teaching."

"So that's even more important than a meeting between two leading citizens of the Crystal City?" asked Alvin.

"I want to hold that meeting tonight over supper. Or if we have guests—and I'd wager you've already invited at least three people—then our meeting can take place in bed."

"Only if you keep the minutes," said Alvin.

"There will be no minutes," said Margaret. "We both have nearly perfect memories, among our other talents."

"Or maybe we just have congruent memories, so anything I forget, you have also forgotten so we are never confronted with our forgetfulness."

"Go talk with all the people who have petitions or suggestions or who are looking for a job."

"Why is that my duty?"

"The rest of us try to deal with things as they come up, but there are many people who won't accept a verdict from, or even tell their problem to, anyone but you."

"Have they never read what Jethro said to Moses in Exodus?" asked Alvin.

"Part some big lake, Alvin, or walk across the Mizzippy, and they might start comparing you to Moses."

"I already did as much," said Alvin.

"But the people you brought from Nueva Barcelona, they're the only ones who saw it, and when they tell it to people here, folks only half-believe it at best."

"Miracles don't make people faithful or obedient," said Alvin. "They make them jealous or frightened."

"You're so cynical," said Margaret.

"You taught me that word, Miz Larner," said Alvin. "You know that I'm not cynical."

"Don't you 'Miz Larner' me, Alvin Miller," said Margaret.

Alvin smiled and then kissed her. "I'm glad to be home." Then he went and took Vigor's hand, and swung him up to perch on Alvin's right shoulder.

"Oh, Mister Smith," said Margaret in a swoony voice. "Your arms are so strong."

Alvin laughed and carried Vigor on out of the school.

But being home didn't even begin to suggest Alvin's being in their house for more than a few minutes at a time. While she was teaching, he brought Vigor along with him on all his errands and to all his meetings. When Alvin let somebody challenge him to a stick-pull in the market square, Vigor didn't just stand and watch, he managed to get into a wrestling match with a six-year-old with six inches of reach on him. An onlooker might be forgiven for thinking Alvin was an inattentive father, letting his son get into a fight, but Alvin was plenty attentive. After pulling the other fellow right over the stick and throwing him onto the ground behind him, Alvin went over to pick up the stick and shake hands with the young man he just beat—but on the way he paused and held Vigor and his opponent apart while he said, "Hey little feller, you might think because you're bigger, you're probably going to lick Vigor here."

"He's not," said Vigor.

"What you don't know about little guys is they just pile right into you, so close that your long arms can't land a blow. So if this boy"—indicating Vigor—"cares enough, he'll whup you right down to the ground."

"Will not," said the boy.

"Don't complain that nobody warned you," said Alvin. Within a couple of minutes Alvin had another opponent across the stick from him, and Vigor had the six-year-old on his back calling out, "Uncle! Uncle, dang you!"

By the time Margaret got home from school, she had already heard of Alvin's and Vigor's shenanigans, including Vigor beating up a boy two years older than him. "You know I don't like him fighting," she said to Alvin softly after Vigor had proudly told her about his victory. Vigor went right to the kitchen for a pitcher of lemonade from the icebox, and didn't show any interest in what Mommy was saying to Papa. But he was listening. Sharp ears, that boy.

"If Papa doesn't let me fight," said Vigor, "then someday when I'm big and married and have little children of my own, I won't know how to protect them."

"From whom will you protect your family?" asked Margaret.

"Bad men," said Vigor. And then, practicing a new word, he added, "Hooligans."

"That's not a bad ambition," said Margaret. "But the boy you defeated today, was he a hooligan?"

"He was bigger than me, just like most of the hooligans are."

"Aren't you afraid a bigger boy will hurt you?" asked Margaret.

"Well he *did* hurt me," said Vigor, pulling up his shirt to show off some bruises. "But that don't make me *afraid.* Why should I be afraid if this is the worst he can do?"

Margaret had to laugh along with Alvin, and when Vigor ran back outside to look for friends to play with, she said, "Alvin, I don't know what kind of father you're trying to be. Isn't it our job to civilize our children?"

"I reckon that's what *you're* best at. You civilized *me*, didn't you?"

"Obviously not, or at least not enough," said Margaret.

Alvin took her by the hands and looked into her eyes. "My love, is our son a good boy?"

"Yes he is," she answered forthrightly. "But your teaching doesn't contribute to that as far as I can see."

"Then see farther," said Alvin. "I'm doing what looks like good fathering to *me.* I'm helping him get ready to live in the world he's going to have to live in, not the world we wish would come to be."

Supper was a maelstrom of visitors and conversations, with some guests sitting at the table with Alvin and Vigor, and Margaret and the kitchen girls going from room to room, handing platters of food to whoever was sitting in whatever place. When Margaret passed Alvin a new plate at the table, she said, "Every one of these people said you invited them to come celebrate your homecoming."

"I was feeling festive," said Alvin.

Margaret rolled her eyes and moved on. Fortunately, Alvin didn't set up a free-for-all supper very often, and just as fortunately, Margaret had already set up a posse of helpful women in the neighborhood who would bring over food as soon as word spread that there was a mass meal at Alvin's house. With Alvin away for a couple of weeks, suppers at Miz Larner's house were modest, respectable affairs, with only the guests that Margaret had invited, plus whatever kids Vigor was playing with who came with him when she called him to supper. And even when Alvin was at home, these big chaotic celebratory feasts were pretty rare—every few weeks or so. She thought it was one of the best things about her husband, as well as one of the worst, that his generosity knew no bounds.

And it's not as if they couldn't afford to reimburse their friends for the food they brought over. Alvin's smithing and repair business was always booming when he was in town. He'd up and follow anybody to where they needed something fixed, and when he left everything worked perfectly. He never told anybody a price for his work, or asked for payment in advance—this was Alvin Maker, after all. But most of the people would bring things to the house in payment, or in gratitude, or just to share their best. Foodstuff, mostly, and handmade items—furniture large and small, a free tuning of their piano, two doghouses though they had only the one dog, bookshelves though they didn't have near enough books to fill them, and little carved soldiers and nutcrackers and wooden spoons and pottery bowls and jars. Whoever had a craft wanted their work to be displayed and used in the Maker's home.

Every time Vigor saw the two doghouses, on opposite sides of the house, he would demand to know who the second dog was and when he would get there. Margaret always assured Vigor that there would never be another dog, because Canna was already more work than she was worth, especially considering the litter of puppies she dropped at least once a year—or once a week, Margaret would claim when she was annoyed enough to exaggerate the situation.

All through the chaotic supper, people would try to get close enough to Margaret to tell her of some remarkably kind or remarkably powerful thing Alvin had done for them just that very afternoon. Margaret silently wondered whether Alvin even had time to void himself—did his knacks include the ability to make urine vanish from his bladder? But he seemed to have time for everybody, and a way to help anyone in need. There were diseases whose causes he didn't understand, and therefore he couldn't cure them. But there were many broken bones he could knit right up as good as new, and some illnesses that he called "easy," which he could heal in just a few minutes of quiet conversation.

Margaret couldn't help but be reminded of the scripture, "Whoever would be the greatest among you, let him be the servant of all." That was Alvin, never telling other people what to do, just asking what they needed. Was he mayor of the city? He didn't need a title. A handyman of all trades? Not all, but pretty near. She knew the spectacular things he had done at times in his life, the power in his hands and in his mind that was almost terrifying if you didn't know how adamantly Alvin refused to do harm.

How easily Alvin could have chosen to be aloof, to make people come to him to beg for favors, how easily he could withhold his help, his gifts, until people did his bidding. He could command and people would obey. But the only time he did that was on the days when more crystal blocks were needed for the walls and towers of Crystal City. Then, at the water's edge, he would first purify the water, then drip a tiny bit of his blood into the water as he formed a block with his hands. When it was done, when it was solid, then he would tell one of his helpers to take it away. "Where should I take it?" they would ask, and his answer was always the same: "Go where they're building and see where you think it fits."

Margaret had been to the building site—sometimes on the third story of a tower. Sometimes near the ground, forming the foundation. The workers there, all of them approved by or hired by or solicited by Alvin, would place the blocks one way and then study what the crystals showed, then change it up, a complete rearrangement or one block swapped for another. Only when they thought that the messages in the crystals were coherent and useful instead of chaotic and confusing, they would say, "Let's show this to Alvin."

And when Alvin saw what they had built, he would sit staring into it, sometimes for hours. The longer he gazed, the prouder the builders were. Alvin was finding truth and beauty in the crystals. The city had grown by just this much, and they had helped each other build it out of the crystals Alvin made.

But today, one of the guests at supper whispered to her, there had been a difference. "Your husband went into the new part of the high tower and he walks around the walls of the highest level, and he stops at this one block. And it was a block that caused us fits, but we thought we finally found the right place. But Alvin looks into that block for only a few seconds and then he reaches out and touches it and it just dissolves into water, it stops being crystal at all. And he won't tell us why, what we did wrong. He even said, 'You did the best you could. It was the crystal that was wrong.' And we still don't know why he broke that part of the wall."

Margaret stayed long enough to ask, "Did the wall collapse? Was anything else damaged?"

"No, it was just wet. With a gap in the wall."

"Did you put another crystal block into the gap?" asked Margaret.

And the builder looked abashed. "We didn't try," he said. "If Alvin makes a gap, who are we to—"

Margaret didn't let him finish. "Alvin didn't make a gap. He undid a block that he felt was somehow wrong—not wrongly placed, just wrong. So he didn't want a gap there, he just wanted true crystal."

Not that Margaret understood the whole business of crystal-making or any part of it. But she knew that Alvin did not make by unmaking. For him to unmake a crystal block was a strange and powerful thing. She would have to ask him about it.

But not that night. She had to think about it herself for a while. If it was important, he'd tell her without her needing to ask. Otherwise, she'd bide her time and try to understand a few things for herself.

Vigor was finally bathed and in bed.

When Margaret had taken care of a few personal chores, she returned to the parlor. Alvin was sitting on the settee, perusing several old maps. Her physical longing for him had been on her mind all afternoon, probably making her lectures disjointed and unhelpful, but now that they were actually alone together, she was exhausted from teaching. She wasn't sure she could stay awake long enough for conjugal cooperation, but she didn't want to disappoint Alvin about his homecoming. He seemed fresh as . . . well, there was nothing daisy-like about Alvin. Fresh as a cucumber?

Not everything would be difficult for her tonight. There were many personal services she could offer him. "Would you like me to draw you a bath?"

Alvin said, "You know dirt doesn't stick to me if I don't want it to."

"What about food? Plenty of bread and cheese, or I could cook you a few eggs."

"On my trek, I was moving slower than usual, so there was time for all the fruits and berries of the woods and croplands to offer themselves to me. You don't say no to such offers, not inside the Greensong, so I'm still plumb full up. So full that I didn't eat anything at supper tonight."

"I noticed that," said Margaret, "which is why I thought you might be hungry."

"If I'd've been hungry," he said with a grin, "don't you think I would have et?"

She rolled her eyes at his use of that old word. "What about you just go to bed in the nice new bedstead that Darn Dammer made for us, the best in town?"

"It's still early, Margaret," he said. "For me, I mean. And you know I don't get tired walking with the Greensong. In fact, I feel as rested as if I'd had a fine night of sleep."

"Or is that a night of fine sleep?" she asked.

"Now I can be happy. I haven't had anybody twist my words around since I left here a couple of weeks ago."

"I suppose you think two weeks apart from me is nothing," said Margaret.

"Indeed I do," said Alvin cheerfully, "and you feel the same about me. What's a brace of weeks to people who know each other like we do?"

"Knowing your heartfire doesn't mean I'm pleased to be apart from it for days on end."

"Margaret, are we quarreling?"

"A little," she said. "I want to take care of you, I want to welcome you with the pleasures of home. A hot bath, a fresh-cooked meal, a nap on a soft bed. And you don't want anything that I can offer you."

"Is the city peaceful?" asked Alvin.

"Mostly," said Margaret. "A few rowdies, but the Whittlin and Whistlin Brigade encouraged them right out of town."

"And nobody more dire than that?"

"I'm not pleased about the people you brought with you into town today," said Margaret.

"Now, see? This is going to be much more important than my getting to bed."

"The two men who left you right away, back in Irrakwa, they were worse than scamps. It was in their heart right from the beginning to use the woman and the other three men to steal the gold and transport it beyond the reach of the posse, but then they were going to kill the others and take the wagon on by themselves."

"So I saved the ones who are with us, saved them from murder."

"The men I told you about, they've killed before. I believe one of them has a knack of getting smart, suspicious people to trust him."

"Don't think there *is* such a knack," said Alvin.

"Which is why you're going to be taken in by rapscallions your whole life."

"What about the three men and the woman I brought here?"

"Alvin, I know you didn't choose them as companions—I did, I believe—but the only difference between them and the killers is they haven't got around to killing anybody yet. They have the pleasant philosophy that when they steal, the only thing they're taking from people is their possessions. They leave their victims alive and undamaged, if possible."

"So . . . scamps," said Alvin.

"Worse than scamps," said Margaret.

"All the way to being scoundrels?"

"Sneakthieves because their knacks make it easy."

"Then it's a good thing nobody in Crystal City has anything worth stealing."

"Do you really believe that?"

"It's one of the principles of the city," said Alvin. "Property owns us more than we own property."

"Then why do we give people deeds to their land and houses?" asked Margaret.

"So that outsiders can't come in and claim land that we happen to be using," said Alvin.

"It's still property."

Getting a little heated, Alvin quickly resorted to the dialect of his childhood. Margaret knew that education was only a thin veneer over his language, so she had to trust that he'd keep from sounding hill-country when he was out in the city.

"If those fellows what stole the gold and lost it again, if they try such nonsense here—"

"You'll just sneak whatever they stole out of their possession," said Margaret, "and then let them go on their way."

Alvin looked even more solemn. "Of course we let them go, if we can. We don't want to have no prison in Crystal City. The walls we want here should be made of crystal and show visions to people with good hearts."

"There are people in the world who shouldn't be walking around loose," said Margaret.

"I've had people hold *me* in jails from time to time," said Alvin. "I didn't like it."

"You're not supposed to like it," said Margaret.

"Of course not, I was innocent."

"And we'd use our jail to lock up miscreants until we can turn them over to authorities in some other county."

"Because we don't need a sheriff."

She wasn't sure if he was mocking the idea. "We have the Whittlin and Whistlin Brigade," said Margaret. "Why give somebody the kind of authority that makes them feel like they're in charge?"

"I agree with you," said Alvin. "But usually jails and sheriffs go together. Who decides who gets locked up and when they get let out of jail? I'm against it from beginning to end. I don't want Crystal City to be a place where we forbid some folks to leave."

"I know their hearts," said Margaret.

"But we never punished anybody for the desires of their heart," said Alvin. "Only for the actions they chose to take as harmed other folk."

"I know, Alvin, I'm the one that taught *you* that people have to be free to choose right from wrong."

"But after they've chosen to do wrong, you'll know which ones we need to lock up?"

"I suppose I'd be the best choice for that job," said Margaret. "Given my knack."

"Even though you don't want to do it."

"I do not. But the job, if it is done at all, should be done fairly and rightly."

"Which you are best equipped to do," said Alvin.

"Why do I think you're saying these things sarcastically?"

"I'm telling the honest truth," said Alvin. "The problem is that it's the nature and disposition of almost all humans that, when you give them a little authority over other people, they begin to grab for more and more, power that they shouldn't have, that wasn't given to them."

"You think I would become an unjust judge?"

"I don't think that would happen to *you* at all. But when you travel, when you're doing another task, you're going to want to assign your magistrate duties to someone else, and whoever that is, he's going to keep finding new emergencies that he needs to deal with in order to keep the peace."

Margaret sighed. "Why couldn't you have just eaten some bread and cheese?"

"When I'm gone," said Alvin, "you always govern the city wisely. Nobody challenges you because you always choose rightly and most often kindly as well. So kindly that they aren't even aware that they're being governed."

"Thanks for noticing," said Margaret.

"Neither of us was meant to govern a city," said Alvin. "We can only do our best."

"You were born to do it," said Margaret.

"I was born to *build* the city. With my blood and the water of the Mizzippy. But governing it? I don't have the desire."

"But who else? Who else do the people come here to meet, to be led by, to be protected by?"

"Protected from what?"

"From bad, selfish government," said Margaret. "From people who care only for gold, for the wealth they can take from those who earned it, for the control they can exercise over the weak."

"I think it's a shame," said Alvin, "that the only way to ensure government that is, in our opinion, good and just, is for you and me to do the governing."

"So you're aiming to retire?" asked Margaret.

"The only job I really like is bringing knacky people to the city."

"Too bad it's not the only job that must be done, which only you can do."

"What about the woman I just brought here?" asked Alvin. "You didn't say a word about her. Is she a murderous scoundrel, too?"

"No," said Margaret immediately. "Of course I looked into her first, to make sure she wasn't one of the women who thought you needed a better wife than me."

"I don't think there's any such women, but go ahead. What about Eliza Nutbutter?"

"She's not falling in love with you, though she admires you greatly," said Margaret. "Her knack is mysterious to me. Usually a person's knack floats in the midst of their heartfire, plain for me to see, but she has considerable power and doesn't really understand what it is or how to use it."

"I imagine that means you're going to make friends with her," said Alvin.

"If she's willing," said Margaret.

"She is," said Alvin.

"You discussed it with her?"

"Of course not. I just know that she's very interested in how the Crystal City works, not as an architectural marvel—which I happen to think it is, what with being made out of water with a speck of blood—her interest is in how the *people* work together. That's all she asked about, when we talked at all. How do people with all these powers get along? Do they agree not to use their knacks on each other without permission? And while she was asking I thought, How *do* they all get along?"

"They're just normal people. The normal envyings, resentments, longings, hurt feelings."

"Yet nobody's putting curses on people."

"Alvin, a few people *have* tried to put a hex on somebody, but I always detect it."

"And what, you go beg them to take it off?"

"Your very talented brother Measure removes any hex that I don't approve of. So if somebody is cursed with, say, irresistible flatulence—"

"Arthur swears he didn't know that's what would happen."

"But he swears so hard that I know he was pleased with it, or at least I'm pretty sure," said Margaret.

"Arthur is pleased with himself almost all the time," said Alvin, "and he's usually right to be. I let him do almost all the talking when we met Robin Sower and his pretend wife and their shady friends."

"So Eliza Nutterbutt is interested in how our community manages to get along with so much power floating around."

"Nutbutter," said Alvin.

"What difference does it make if I mix up her name?"

"To her, the difference between being your friend and being a target of investigation," said Alvin.

"Everybody gets investigated whether I want to or not. It's not something I can forgo with no sheriff and no jail."

"And do you think that's close enough to the truth that it doesn't count as a lie?"

"I must look into everybody's heartfire," said Margaret. "If I don't do it, who will? Even though it's as unpleasant as coughing your guts out when you get a bit of liquid in your lungs."

"You said 'guts,'" said Alvin.

"It's a perfectly acceptable word," said Margaret.

"The Bible says 'bowels.' I prefer guts to that," said Alvin.

"As do I, which is why I used it."

"If I had taken that bath you offered," said Alvin, "I'd be out of the bath and toweling off by now."

"But if you had accepted my food, you'd still be eating."

"I'm a slow eater," said Alvin.

"And a fast bather," said Margaret.

"I only bathe when I'm too lazy to chip all the dirt off my body myself."

"Alvin, tomorrow, when you go out to find some boys in the street who want to pull sticks with you, would you be so kind as to find Eliza Nutbutter and invite her to luncheon at our house?"

"It would be rude not to invite Robin Sower along with her—I daresay he's just as hungry."

"But not those two thieves," said Margaret.

"They were all thieves, carrying their contraband through the woods on a stolen wagon pulled by a couple of stolen mules."

"I'm a thief at heart, too, Alvin," said Margaret. "I believe that in your place I might have admitted that gold gratefully into the city, because we're so short on specie."

"I'm thinking we should start a bank, so we could print our own paper," said Alvin.

"You have to have the gold to back up your paper."

"I heard to the contrary. I heard that as long as your assets are held in mortgages on the houses in the community, a bank can get by with much less gold."

Margaret shrugged. She didn't want to argue finances with Alvin. He just didn't have that much regard for gold, considering that he knew how to make it from iron or granite or limestone.

"I will go and invite Mr. Sower and not-so-goodwife Eliza Nutbutter. Should I tell them what we're eating?"

"It depends on what the catch is tomorrow from the river."

"Really? Can't we afford beef?"

"It's still spring, and nobody's been butchering, except for a few geese, and goose is hardly the nicest meat we can serve."

"Duck?"

"Sparrow? Crow?" Margaret grinned. "Fish cooks the quickest, so if we have more guests than we planned, I can dress and cook another round of fish in ten minutes, if I keep the fire hot."

"Just remember," said Alvin, "mustard doesn't belong on fish."

"*Anything* belongs on catfish."

"You're not serving that bottom-feeding water-scab, are you?"

"Not everyone shares your distaste for it."

"Margaret, please don't embarrass me with catfish tomorrow. Because I won't stay to eat, if it's catfish."

"I was just teasing, as you well know. Try not to invite every boy who challenges you to a stick-pull."

"The only person who still owes me a wrestle right now is Eliza Nutbutter."

Margaret looked at him through squinting eyes. "Threw you, did she?"

"I let her," said Alvin.

"Meaning you didn't break the leg she tripped you over," said Margaret.

"You know I don't fight like a riverman."

"You learned fighting from Mike Fink, my love. There's not a way to cheat that you don't know."

"And I choose to fight fair whenever there's absolutely nothing at stake."

"But with the Buttnutter woman," said Margaret, "your honor is at stake."

"She threw me," said Alvin. "In front of witnesses."

"You don't care about the witnesses or the rumors about it in the town, how a woman threw you."

"I have my honor to uphold."

"So something *is* at stake," said Margaret.

"I can't very well take her on in the street—she's not much of a lady, but she deserves better than to take part in a wrestle, which would make her socially unacceptable to a good number of folks."

"You like her," said Margaret. "You feel protective."

"Are you suspicious?" asked Alvin. "I feel protective about everybody."

"And I feel suspicious about any woman you feel obliged to grapple with."

Alvin rolled his eyes and headed for the door. "Taking a walk before it's full dark," he said

"Try to be home before breakfast," Margaret called after him.

The door closed behind him. He wasn't really angry, she knew, but he did hate it when she kept him from being careless about engaging the affections of women. He did not understand how he was admired in the Crystal City, and, by many, worshiped.

She went into the kitchen and then into the pantry, where she opened the icebox and took out a couple of fine fat catfish, which she believed God had created just to frighten small children. She had served catfish at table more than once when Alvin was home, and he never realized that's what it was, because she had learned some pretty good tricks from Mistress Modesty, about how to cook any fish without confessing its ancestry or natural domicile. Not many knew how to do it, and other people had served him catfish and he detested it; how could he recognize *her* catfish, seeing how it was delicious?

Am I a disobedient wife? Margaret wondered. Deceiving my husband?

Yes, she told herself. I obey him whenever it matters, but I choose to be the judge of when it matters. It's part of my responsibility as magistrate in this semi-organized community to keep Alvin Maker happy and keep everyone else happy with *him*.

And sometimes that required her to reinterpret his instructions so that she could follow them without alienating too many people in the town.

3

ELIZA NUTBUTTER WASN'T sure what to make of this Crystal City. She had seen the big cities of the East, but she was sure none of them was in the same league as the European cities that she had always intended to see before she died. She had tried more than once to save enough money to cross the Atlantic, but something had always blocked her.

Getting robbed and left penniless.

Having her ticket of passage on a trans-Atlantic ship stolen and the captain refused to recognize her even though he had personally given her the ticket.

Being accused of witchcraft, which really infuriated her because those fools didn't understand that knacks didn't come from the Devil—if there even *was* a devil, he didn't have anywhere near the powers of some of the knacks she had seen. As her own knack, for that matter. She was able to escape—of course, because that was what she did—but she had to leave things behind. Money she had earned legitimately, not stolen. The daguerreotype of her mother. She was sure that the landlady of her tiny attic apartment would keep the money. But would she keep the picture? *Why* would she?

No matter. She ran into Sower then, and figured that her share of the gold would easily buy her, not only passage to Liverpool or Nantes, but also the trappings of wealth, including hired bodyguards.

And if these sneakthieves she was with were caught, one thing Eliza was sure of: She could get away.

But she hadn't gotten away. She was going along with their plan of hiding out in that haven of knackery, the Crystal City, but only until the gold was divided up, and then she'd have been out of there.

Instead, they had their wagon taken out from under them by Alvin Maker himself. Without the gold, she had no more reason to head for Crystal City. But Alvin Maker intrigued her. So quiet, able to be silent while his partner did all the talking—a lippy, obnoxious, absolutely delightful Black man—and yet the Maker was able, from a distance, to change their gold into tin. Or so he claimed.

Europe would still be there next year, she decided, right then while Arthur and Alvin were questioning them. She could go to Europe any time, but the Crystal City might be the most exotic place she could go.

How could people inhabit one city whose citizens all had one inhuman power or another? Some were trivial, some were valuable, but some were irresistible, like Alvin Maker's gifts. Some of the stories about him were nonsense—that he could fly, that he carried slave children from Southern plantations to free soil in the North, or to Canada, places where no man was a slave, no matter who thought they owned him. A worthy, noble undertaking, Eliza was sure. But no human being could fly. How did stories like that arise?

Still, he was a man of confidence and strength, the kind who did not need to boast or present himself as more than he was. A man who was so powerful he did not feel any need to show off his power or assert his abilities. Eliza was drawn to such men, the handful of times she had met one.

A politician who pulled a lot of government strings. But the government itself wasn't all that powerful, so he was a disappointment in the end.

A very, very rich man, so rich that he could dress in common farm clothes and still be served in the finest gentlemen's clubs. She liked him, but he was a Puritan, and she realized that if he really understood who and what she was, he would certainly denounce her as a witch. Better not to involve herself with true believers in the Puritan brand of Christianity.

Nobody else came close to being what she was looking for, till Alvin Maker.

But on the long trek from the borders of Irrakwa country to Crystal City, Eliza had learned that Alvin was not susceptible to her charms. Leaving her blouse open a couple of buttons did nothing—she looked down and found that instead of being buttoned, the neckline of her blouse had been sealed together as if both sides had been woven that way. The power of making women more modest than they wanted to be—a mighty yet delicate power indeed, but in her experience, a knack that no red-blooded *man* would even aspire to.

Why was Alvin immune to her charms? Uninterested in her conversation, her wit, her sharp tongue, Alvin would not even banter with her. Was he not clever enough to know sarcasm and irony when he heard them? No, it wasn't that he didn't understand her wit, or that he was offended by it. He just didn't care how she talked or what she said or how she dressed or undressed.

It was Arthur Stuart who enlightened her, though he didn't know it. He was talking to Sower, explaining why a young man like him hadn't yet found a feminine companion for his life. "Many men don't marry until their late thirties or into their forties," Arthur said.

"True, but they're fools," said Sower. "The joy of marriage comes from children—from making them, and then from having them. But if you don't have babies until you're forty-five, then you're too old and feeble to play with them. Romp with them. Children are more frisky than randy squirrels, boy. You need to have them when you're still young, in your early twenties, as I perceive you to be."

"Being married is no guarantee that you'll have children," said Arthur. "Alvin and Miss Margaret lost their first little one, then had a fine boy named Vigor. But no baby for the longest time."

So, thought Eliza, Alvin is a married man who, unlike many such, took his vows so seriously that he did not respond to temptation at all, except to set it aside. A very, very married man. Which was honorable and Eliza respected him for it. After all, if he could seal up the neckline of a woman's blouse, he could unbutton it, too, at his leisure, irresistibly. He would have to pick his time—nothing good would come from undressing a woman when other men were present—but Alvin could have his pick of women, Eliza was sure. But he was true to the one he had already picked.

On the journey to Crystal City, they had stopped only once a day, for dinner, so there wasn't all that much time for talk and no time at all for flirting. Not that Eliza would be above winning the heart of Arthur Stuart, but she suspected that Alvin's protectiveness would keep her from taking *that* flirtation very far at all. She would find it very uncomfortable if Alvin stymied her by making sure *all* her clothes were sealed together.

Still, she gravitated toward Arthur Stuart because she already knew the men she had traveled with, and had nothing to gain from them. But Arthur knew Alvin. It would be good to have him as a friend. And he appreciated her cleverness and gave better than he got.

On their last meal stop, somewhere in Noisy River or maybe the western edge of Wobbish, she and Arthur were chatting about, of course, marriage. "Sower told you to marry young," said Eliza, "and that *can* be good advice, if you're able to support a wife. You're a charming lad, Arthur Stuart, and a good-looking fellow, but I wonder at the trouble you'll have finding a wife. Your unique heritage will make you a social dilemma for any woman, no matter her color."

Arthur shrugged, then gave her a little half-smile. "And yet *you* flirted with me, Goody Sower." He called her that even though he well knew that she and Sower had no connection, that they had only pretended to be married to make the group look more respectable. A woman traveling alone with five men, or even three, could not have any surviving reputation. Goody Sower. Goodwife Sower.

"I did," said Eliza. "But you know it would have led nowhere."

"I think you were just afraid of what Alvin would do if you really made a try for me," said Arthur. He glanced over toward Alvin, who was demonstrating a wrestling hold with one of the other men.

Eliza smiled. "What would he do?"

"Take away your ability to do anything at all with me," said Arthur. "Because he thinks I'm still naive and need to be taken care of."

"And if Alvin hadn't been with us, and I made you the same offers, would you have taken them then?"

Arthur suddenly looked uncomfortable. "I think this salt pork isn't sitting well with me," he said.

"If I asked you to give me a baby, would you?" she asked, pushing even harder.

"With you not married to me?" asked Arthur. "I would not."

"Nobody is born married," she said. "Marriages can happen even between strangers—that's how kings do it."

"Are you proposing marriage to me?" asked Arthur.

"Keep your voice down, Arthur, please," said Eliza. "I'm only talking about supposes."

"Hypothetically," said Arthur, "if a woman as pretty as you told me she wanted me for a husband, I would have to think, why? Does she hope that as my wife she'd have better access to Alvin Maker, because he and I are such friends?"

She said nothing. She was ashamed of herself, that Arthur had seen through her so easily.

"Oh, don't be embarrassed," said Arthur. "You're far from the first woman to have that plan in mind, though none of *them* even hinted about marriage."

"More fools they," said Eliza. "It's obvious that you're very smart, very honorable. You'll make a fine husband."

"But not for a woman who only has eyes for my friend Alvin," said Arthur.

And that had been the end of the conversation, as Arthur turned his attention back to his plate.

The rest of the way into the city—which they reached the next day around noon—Arthur never happened to be near enough to Eliza for them to talk. She was sure that this was by his design, that he was shunting her over near Alvin, as if saying to her, if he's the one you want, then he's the one you should talk to.

Or maybe he was saying, I will never marry a woman, I will never have carnal knowledge of a woman, without the approval of my friend. So if you really do have designs on me, persuade him first.

Or maybe he was just trying to avoid her. That would be the simplest explanation.

When they reached the city, there was no wall, just well-planted fields coming up green, orchards coming back into leaf and blossom. They passed between two masts and a sign suspended between them:

CRYSTAL CITY
A HAVEN FOR THE TALENTED

A haven. Talented. To come here was to declare that either you have a knack, or you liked the company of people with knacks, and that you wanted to be protected from a hostile world.

Is that me? thought Eliza. I have never needed protection—I get away clean, every time. What do they offer me here that I really need?

No, I'm here for something else. Or somebody else.

Eliza was surprised that they had gotten here, walking, in only . . . four days? Or was it three? She should be exhausted. But it felt as if she had floated here like a leaf in a stream, with Alvin Maker as the current. Yes, her legs had taken every step, but her feet were not sore, her calves were not painfully tight, her hips had not worn down to have bone scrape on bone. How did they travel so fast, yet not be in pain?

Alvin Maker, of course, thought Eliza. That or fairies, and she didn't believe in fairies. Or magic. Whatever knacks were, Eliza didn't believe that anything magical was involved. It was all science that nobody had figured out yet. Her knack for escaping never involved anything supernatural. She just knew, looking around her, where she could go to get herself out of sight, hide, and then continue her escape as soon as a way opened up. It was all keen observation, stealthy movement, and maybe some knack for averting the attention of anyone seeking her.

Maybe that was magical.

No, it wasn't. There was no magic. Everything she could do, anyone could learn. The others just hadn't bothered to learn it. Maybe, as children, they didn't have such a motive for staying out of sight as she had.

After her father had killed her little brother, still a baby in the bassinet, by throwing him drunkenly at his mother, who could not catch him, Eliza had decided that theirs was now a murder house, and instead of helping them conceal the crime—or accident, as Mother called it, when she wasn't saying, "I'm so clumsy, dear God, why am I so clumsy?"—Eliza made her escape from the house, unnoticed by her sisters or her father, who wasn't up to noticing anything, though Mother seemed to glance toward her and nod. Wishful thinking?

She went straight to the sheriff's office, found a deputy asleep at the table, woke him, and told him of the crime that had just happened. "My father was drunk and he threw the baby at my mother, but she didn't realize what was happening, it was so unbelievable, that she couldn't catch the boy, and his head banged against a chair and I think it snapped his neck, too. If you hurry there, you can catch them before they figure out how to hide the body."

The deputy just sat there, looking dumfounded.

Fourteen-year-old Eliza leaned on the table, putting her face right in front of the deputy's face, and said, crisply, "A baby was murdered at the Nutbutter house. Mr. Nutbutter did it. He's drunk and probably dangerous, but if you don't arrest him right now, they'll find a way to hide the baby's body."

"Yes," said the deputy. "Yes, terrible."

"Tonight you are the law," said Eliza. "Tonight you are the hand of justice. Stand up from your chair, take your gun, take some armed men with you in case Mr. Nutbutter decides to fight you, and arrest him. Or kill him, if he resists arrest."

The deputy nodded.

"Stand up now," Eliza said, "or I'll have to tell the sheriff you were too drunk to do your job tonight."

The deputy looked deeply offended. "I never touched a drop."

"How could you, when you just poured it straight down your throat?" said Eliza.

The deputy stood up. "Got to get me a posse right now. With guns."

Now that he was finally moving, Eliza's job was done. She headed on out the main street of town, as the deputy was knocking on doors to get the men to help him arrest that miserable drunken baby-killer, Mr. Nutbutter, her father.

From then on Eliza lived on the move. She dressed above her age, and she learned to imitate the way ladies walked and talked—doctors' wives, lawyers' wives, preachers' wives, merchants' wives, even schoolteachers—who by law could not be anybody's wife, but who had been reared with the same gentility as the wives.

In each new town, she would throw herself on the charity of one of the local churches—never the finest church in town, but maybe a humbler church, a Methodist or Baptist congregation, where someone always gave her housemaid employment or, sometimes, gardening work. The humbler congregations seemed always to have more food to spare, more room to offer shelter, more money to offer wages than the richer congregations.

Before she was sixteen, she was regularly accepted as a young lady of eighteen, and was even invited to apply to be a teacher at a high school in Appalachee, though some of the students were older than she was. She declined the offer and left the town fairly quickly, because she feared that if anyone found out how little education she actually had, some men might take her imitation of a mature woman far too seriously. Appalachee could be rough country.

Crystal City wasn't London or Paris, she was sure of that, but neither was it rough country. Everybody was polite, and instead of going to a church to find charity and perhaps employment, she simply walked down the main street of town. Without meaning to, she had slipped away from Alvin, Arthur, and her thieving companions, so she was a lady walking unescorted out in public. Yet there were no catcalls, and no men to solicitously offer her their protection while she walked. She knew from experience that the ones who offered protection were exactly the men she needed protection *from*.

There didn't seem to be anybody on the street in Crystal City who posed any threat to her. She was tempted to let a couple of buttons fall open, but no, this was no place to get a reputation like *that*. It was almost never hard to get men to be attentive to her, but in this town she wanted the friendship of the women, which could not be had if they thought their husbands would find this girl attractive and available.

It turned out, though, that her first friend was *not* a woman.

He was a tall man, obviously, judging by how far his legs reached out beyond the rocking chair he was sitting in on the raised wooden sidewalk in front of a tailor's shop. He looked as if he bought his clothing there, handmade to fit him perfectly, though he looked a little rumpled now. His legs were *so* long that when Eliza reached him, she could not continue without either stepping over his legs, which would require an indecorous amount of skirt-raising, or walk out into the street, which was nearly paved with old horse dung and other effluvia. If they had a street-cleaning crew in Crystal City, it hadn't gotten to this part of town recently.

She stood, waiting for the man to notice. To move his legs.

He was concentrating on the block of wood he was whittling with a knife that looked big enough to scare a bear. His hat brim was low, so that it was possible he hadn't seen her arrive.

"Isn't that an awfully big knife to use on a sculpture so delicate?" she asked.

He startled and immediately drew his legs back and sat straighter. "Beg your pardon, ma'am," he said. "I didn't mean to be an obstacle."

"You're carving the image of an elephant," she said.

He feigned mild surprise. "I had no idea," he said. "Is that what elephants look like?"

"Very amusing, sir," said Eliza. "Thank you for moving your . . . lower limbs."

The man hooted with laughter. "Are the prudes finally coming to town?"

Eliza had to smile. "I spoke ironically, sir. I'm perfectly capable of saying 'legs' in polite company."

"And I was ironic when I pretended not to know I was carving an elephant. I doubt there are three other people in town who have ever seen one."

"Where did you see an elephant?"

"Not at Bailey's menagerie," said the man. "I saw two elephants at the zoological gardens near Paris."

"You've been to Paris?" asked Eliza, unable to contain her admiration.

"Several times, for several months at a time," he said. "But the voyage there and back is such that you really don't want to waste so much time in your limited mortal life, on the ocean looking at the ocean with nothing else to draw the eye."

"Except that on the return trip, you could remember seeing elephants."

"Just another animal, saggier than most, bigger than anything else on land. When they walk, the ground shakes a little. But they're not beautiful enough to *daydream* about on the voyage home, especially when the sea is as gray as the elephant's hide."

"Are the elephants in cages at the Paris zoo?" she asked. "I hate to think of large animals cooped up in a small space."

"Not cages, but not a huge area, either," said the man. "Enough room for them to walk around, trumpet loudly to make sure nobody accidently falls asleep, and do the robust baby-making dance."

Eliza knew instantly what he meant, and there were two schools of thought, she knew, about how she should respond. The best way was to look at him quizzically and say, "I do not understand you." The second way was to put on an offended, snooty face and without a word walk away.

But he was far too interesting for her to leave him now, and she was quite sure he would see through the ruse if she pretended not to understand.

"Do I take it, then, sir, that the elephants were of two different sexes?"

"The one in front was female, it seemed to me, but the one trying to climb over her was in such a position that I could not be sure."

"You speak rather rudely in front of a lady," said Eliza.

"Is that what you are?" he asked. "It's good of you to tell me."

"What grounds have I given you to speak to me this way?" asked Eliza.

"It's a simple enough test. I've said enough rude or crude or lewd things that a *lady* would have walked away long since."

"Yet by staying, I learned that elephants mate rather as horses do," said Eliza. "I've seen enough of that in my native village to be no longer shocked to hear, think of, or even see it."

"You speak of animals in your native village," said the man.

"The village was far too small to have any population of hack women who would perform coitus on the public street."

"I apologize for entertaining such a thought, even momentarily."

"You are not forgiven, you are not excused."

"Yet you are still not leaving," said the man.

"Because I do not know your name," she said.

"So you can tell the deputy about my crime?"

This hit a little too close to home. He could not possibly know that she had denounced her murderous father to a deputy. Could he? Was that his knack? She had thought it was doing delicate carving with a too-big knife—which he had continued to do, the whole time that they talked.

"My name," she said, "is Eliza Nutbutter."

"Not 'Missus' something?" he asked.

"Neither widow nor fiancée," she said.

"Unattached."

"Except to myself and my dignity—very much attached to both."

"And my name, my lady Nutbutter, is—"

She interrupted him. "Please call me Eliza. I want you to use that name. The other is the name of a detested drunken murderer of a father, as I think you knew already."

He looked hurt and puzzled. "How could I be privy to such information, having never seen you before in my life?"

"I heard that in Crystal City, people could look into the walls and see stories about other people, far away or in the past. When you spoke of telling a deputy about a crime . . ."

"Oh," he said. "Yes, I did see that, and I wondered why at the time. So that was you? The deputy seemed awfully stupid, refusing to get up for so long."

Had he really seen that day? "Mr. Nutbutter had a fearsome reputation. The deputy would have stood bravely beside the sheriff, but to take action on his own—that was a lot to ask."

"Your father," said the man.

"I have no reason to doubt my mother, though I hope to heaven that I bear him no resemblance."

The man looked up from his carving, then set the wood and the knife in his lap as he regarded her. "I can assure you that your mother was an honest woman."

"That was not in doubt," said Eliza, finally getting offended and showing it.

"You were the one who cast her chastity into doubt," said the man, "by insisting that you bear no resemblance to your father."

"A rude man might have construed it that way."

"Every man would construe it that way," said the man, "but only a rude one would mention it to you."

"Think what you want, say what you want, I don't care."

"Because you mean to leave this haven for the overknacked too soon for gossip to be a problem for you?"

"If I want to leave, I will," she said. "But will I have to leave still ignorant of your name?"

He hooted in laughter once again. "Calvin," he said, thrusting out his hand.

She looked at his hand. "Isn't it customary for a gentleman to rise when greeting a lady?"

He did not get up. "Yes, I'm quite sure it is."

"Do you imply, sir, that I am not lady enough to deserve such dignity?"

"Miss Eliza," said Calvin, "I only meant that I, as you should know by now, am no gentleman."

She couldn't help but smile.

He began to rock the chair a little. Then he held out both knife and wood to her. Without even deciding to, she took them both.

"Rising from a rocking chair," he said, "is more labor than I usually undertake in a day, and I need a few feet of room directly in front of me."

Not moving out of his way, she said, "What *for*?"

He bounded forward out of the chair and immediately ran into her. He reached around her in a tight embrace, carrying her backward several steps, but not allowing her to fall and not causing them to have to step off the wooden sidewalk.

"I warned you that I needed space," said Calvin.

"And then left me no time to make way," said Eliza.

"Perhaps I hoped I could catch you in my arms and never let you go."

Eliza didn't actually mind being in his arms, but she knew her role. "Whatever your intention might be, I do not approve of nor appreciate your embrace."

"I think you do appreciate it," said Calvin, "and I don't give a fig for anyone's approval."

"Why don't you let me go, sir?"

"Because I'm afraid that if I do," said Calvin, "you will take a step backward and wind up sitting on your bottom in the city street."

Eliza glanced down and saw that only the toes of her boots were on the sidewalk. She really was relying on his embrace to remain standing.

"Please step back and bring me away from the precipice," said Eliza.

Holding her even more tightly, he took two steps back. Now she touched her feet to the wooden sidewalk. But he immediately leaned back enough to raise her feet off the sidewalk again.

"You are holding me so tightly," she said, "that I cannot even set my feet on the ground."

"You're not barefoot," he said, "and the ground is a good two feet below the level of the sidewalk."

"Why do you insist on holding me like this?" she said, getting a little irked now.

"Are you embarrassed to be seen like this on a public street? Because I can assure you, no one is looking at us."

"So this behavior is not for show?" she asked.

"This behavior, as you call it," said Calvin, "is because I very much like the feeling of your breasts pressed against my upper abdomen, and your belly against—"

"Do you *like* being offensive? Speaking of my breasts like that?"

"I wasn't going to leave my own sacred anatomy out of the discussion," he said.

"I wish you would," she said. "Delightful as our dance has been till now, I no longer hear the music. Let me go."

Immediately Calvin let her go—and plunked himself back down into the rocking chair.

"I can take back my knife and elephant now," he said, reaching for them.

While he was holding me, thought Eliza, I was holding a big hunting knife. I didn't even think to threaten him with it. Well, better late than never. "I would have stabbed you with it, sir, except it would be impossible to get the bloodstains out of my blouse and skirt, and using it for stabbing would dull the edge so that carving with it would be out of the question."

She relinquished both his wood and blade into his hands.

"None the worse for wear," he said, spinning the knife like a baton.

"Be careful with that."

He continued twirling it. As he did, she took a good look at him. A manly face, slightly bearded, as if he had only decided to grow it out three days ago.

"You don't need a beard. Your face is comely enough without it."

"I'm not seeking comeliness," said Calvin. "I'm seeking to reduce my resemblance to my older brother."

Now she looked at him with new eyes. "Good heavens, is Alvin Maker your very brother?"

"You see my problem?" asked Calvin. "The resemblance."

"But you don't resemble him at all in character," said Eliza.

"Let me guess. On your entire trek here to Crystal City, he never once showed the slightest interest in your charming self?"

She said nothing.

"And not because you didn't try to interest him," said Calvin, letting a smile creep onto his lips.

"What do you mean by that?" she said.

"I mean that I think you found ways to offer yourself, and he did not even notice."

"Offer myself? As his maid?"

"He could have almost any woman in the city, and yet he withholds himself from *you*," said Calvin. "Of course you resent him."

"Then why are you trying to *not* resemble him?" asked Eliza. "If he's so irresistible to women, and you look so much like him, how is that not a *good* thing for you, since I take it you wouldn't be averse to making use of almost any woman in the city?"

"It isn't his fine looks that attract these women," said Calvin. "It's his power. His knack. His prestige."

"Have *you* no knack, then?" asked Eliza.

"I am very knackered," he said.

"A pointless pun," she said.

"Being pointless is the whole point of puns," said Calvin. "I have every knack he has. I am also a seventh son of a seventh son."

And at that moment, Eliza realized that she had very much enjoyed having her breasts press against Calvin's body, and that Alvin's chastity was not going to be much of a problem to her, if she could attract the attention of a less chaste copy of himself.

4

ALVIN WALKED THE corridors within the Crystal City. Of course, the whole town was called "Crystal City," but everyone knew that the real Crystal City was this mansion of ice-that-was-not-ice—the blocks of crystal water that were neither hot nor cold, but were as solid as steel. Alvin had made all these blocks himself, and they contained the Red power that he had acquired from Tenskwa-Tawa, the one the Reds called "the Prophet."

Tenskwa-Tawa had taken Alvin up into a tornado, not one that dropped down from the sky, but a tornado Tenskwa-Tawa had brought up out of the water. And the water was touched with the Prophet's blood, and the tornado turned into a wall of glass, or so it seemed. And in the glass, in the solid water that was not ice, he saw things—Alvin saw them, and the Prophet saw the same. Things near and far, things past and present, and perhaps future things. Sometimes future things.

That was when Alvin was a boy. In the years since then, Alvin had turned iron into gold, cut stone out of the mountain without hands and rolled it down a hill. Alvin had liberated some slaves and saved some lives and, to his sorrow, taken some others. He had learned much of what the world had to teach, and had learned much that no one else in the world had ever known.

But here amid the crystal walls of the mansion house he could come to learn things that could be discovered no other way. His wife Margaret could not see it all in the heartfires, nor could Alvin discover it by sending his doodlebug out into the world. He could find it here. Not everything, but the most important things.

Which block of not-ice should he look in? Sometimes it didn't matter—whatever he needed to see would follow along beside him until he stopped and looked at the wall. Other times, the wall's visions would be frozen, and all very small, a separate image in each crystal block, and he had to look at them one by one until he understood something.

That was how it was today. Random-seeming images. People traveling. Perhaps coming to Crystal City to gain the protection of this place where knacks were not crimes or sins, but gifts, perhaps from God, which could be used to build and create and protect. Come one, come all, there is room enough and to spare. We need every head, every pair of hands, every idea, every knack, so that Crystal City's safety can reach farther and farther from this town by the Mizzippy until the peace and freedom here fills the whole land, from the mighty river to the ocean in the East. Not to rule, because coercion could not forge a community or a nation. They all had to desire it, work toward it together, like the people in the wall who might be coming here, or why else would the crystals show them?

Alvin walked very slowly, looking at each crystal block, seeing its image, wondering why it was being shown to him. (And wondering, as he sometimes allowed himself to do, who controlled this wall, these blocks, and who or what decided which images Alvin would see.)

He worried that he could not see the images he needed if there was someone with him who should not see them. So he came alone. After dark, deep into the morning hours after midnight. And now he saw something that surprised him. Up near the top of the wall, there was a block with no image in it at all.

A shadowy misty swirling, so it was not empty and it was not still. But it showed no *thing* and it showed nobody and Alvin knew at once that this crystal block was not of his making.

The block on either side *was* alive with images. Only this one defective block at the top of the wall where it could have been set in without having to reconstruct anything. Just remove one of Alvin's blocks and replace it with this counterfeit, this defective crystal.

Defective, but also a genuine block of water made solid with blood. Could someone have poisoned one of Alvin's own crystals and killed the images inside? No. Alvin had not made this crystal block. It had none of his blood in it. It was not a *part* of him.

Some other Maker who could shape water into solid crystal blocks just by adding a drop of blood.

Not Alvin's blood, but like it. Near it. Blood like his own blood, but not his own.

Calvin, thought Alvin. My envious little brother, who wants so badly to be a Maker because he is a seventh son of a seventh son, just like me.

Only he's actually the eighth son. Alvin was seventh, born before his oldest brother Vigor died on the Hatrack River's flood, saving their mother so she would live to give birth to Alvin. Vigor, whom I never met but who saved my life and made me what I am.

With Vigor dead, Calvin was the seventh *living* son in the family, when he came along not that many years after Alvin. But the eighth son overall. No one knew the rules of these things. Calvin certainly had many of the knacks that Alvin had accumulated. And he could demonstrate some powers that would impress people with the idea that Calvin was a younger Alvin, also powerful, also a Maker.

He could fashion blocks of crystal out of the water of the Mizzippy, clarify it, make it show something moving inside. Not an actual image. Nothing *true.* But he must have proved to someone that he could make a crystal and set it into Alvin's wall and nothing bad happened. I'm a Maker, too, Alvin could imagine him saying. I'm also the seventh son of a seventh son. There's healing in *my* hands, too, and wood bends in my hands without breaking, if I want it to.

Calvin, don't you know that your foolish ambition will destroy you? I wanted to teach you, I tried to teach you, you wanted what I had but you didn't want me to give it to you. You wanted to take it yourself, untaught, with none of the experiences that shaped me.

Alvin thought of taking the block out of the wall. Then he decided to leave Calvin's shoddy work in its place. No one would ever see anything useful in it. But I see the future in it, thought Alvin. I see the destruction of this city.

Calvin has done nothing treasonous yet, nothing outright destructive. He's not a tempest that can knock over walls, he's a spider weaving little webs here and there and coming back to check on them. He'll be back to look at this block. He's proud of it, because it *is* crystal and he *did* make it with a drop of his blood.

Alvin looked down from the defective block, down three ranks and over two columns and *there* was an image worth looking at. It was a man in a canoe, paddling through the fog. Crossing a river without being able to see either shore, and not knowing if there were shoals or eddies that could capsize him.

But then the fog cleared, and fifty yards away, standing on the far shore, was Tenskwa-Tawa, the Prophet.

The Prophet did not shout, though he raised a hand in greeting. When the paddler got close enough, Tenskwa-Tawa spoke. He did not shout, but his voice was as clear as if the water had carried it out to the canoe. "Alvin," said the Red Prophet. "You came when I called. Thank you for such respect."

And then the image froze: A man on a canoe, a man on the shore, one White, the other Red. Then the fog flowed back into the scene, and now there was only a man on a canoe, lost in the fog. Alvin was there in that canoe. "Thank you," said Alvin quietly.

Alvin wakened Margaret, not by climbing into bed, but by kneeling beside the bed and taking her hand.

She opened her eyes and smiled a small but beautiful smile. "He called you."

"That's how I interpret what I saw in the wall."

"And you're worried about Calvin," said Margaret.

"I love you, you know. We were young together. If only he had not always been so envious. I could have taught him everything I know."

"No you couldn't," said Margaret.

Alvin thought a moment. "I could have *tried*."

"You *did* try."

Alvin shrugged. "You think better of me than I deserve."

"Sometimes, no matter how hard you try, the right thing cannot be done."

"Not going to stop trying, Miz Larner."

"That's why you're such a good pupil, Mr. Miller," said Margaret.

He knelt up and leaned over and kissed her. That was one of the nice things about being so tall. Alvin could reach things kneeling that other men would have to stand to do. But for Margaret he would stand, jump, run, leap, fall, if she needed him to do it. Here he could kiss her without standing up. She was the one who could look into his heartfire and know what he worried about, what pain he felt. Knew that Calvin was foremost in his thoughts, but he had no idea how to help the boy. Knew that the summons from Tenskwa-Tawa was important, and Alvin would go. In the crystal Alvin had seen himself rowing alone in a canoe, so that is how he would go. He would trust Tenskwa-Tawa to provide a way for Alvin to cross the Mizzippy, to break through the Red Prophet's wall that protected all the free Red nations that had crossed the river after the massacre at Tippy-Canoe, the people Tenskwa-Tawa now protected by covering the Mizzippy with perpetual fog and laying currents and eddies and shoals to spin and capsize the boats or send them to the bottom with broken hulls.

Or let them go back to the White man's side of the Mizzippy, arriving in boats that sank as soon as they got to shore. No one bothered to keep boats now on the White shore, because they were useless. Couldn't go anywhere. Damned lucky if you got back alive. Not a good place to take out a fishing boat.

Alvin stood on that shore, walked along the low rise just back from the river. He was looking for the canoe the crystal showed him. He needed a canoe, and *nobody* kept boats on this shore.

Except there it was, bobbing up and down in the lapping wavelets at the shoreline. Not tethered, not anchored. Just waiting, floating, going neither upriver nor down.

"You know something about this?" asked a man.

Alvin found the source of the voice. A middle-aged man with a knack for . . . for . . . oh yes, for only falling asleep when he wanted to, and sleeping only as long as he wanted to. Alvin didn't envy many gifts that he didn't have, but he could sure use this one. "Dinny," said Alvin. "Why you down here by the river?"

"Your brother Measure set me to watch here," said Dinny.

"Watch for what?"

"I asked him the same," said Dinny. "Didn't even answer me, just rolled his eyes."

"So . . . in all your watching, what did you see?"

"You mean, besides yourself just now?" asked Dinny.

"Measure didn't set you here to watch for *me*."

"No, I think I was here to see that canoe."

"Who brought it here?" asked Alvin.

"Brother Fog," said Dinny.

Alvin let him see his puzzlement.

"Or Sister Mist," said Dinny. "That canoe came all by itself, across the river from heaven knows where. No one paddling, just floating in a straight line, not getting caught by any current."

Alvin nodded and smiled. "So he sent me transportation."

"He?" asked Dinny.

"The one who called me to a meeting," said Alvin.

"My but you know how to keep your mouth shut and your friends confused," said Dinny.

"Practiced both for most of my life. Not good yet at keeping my mouth shut *every* time I should, but at least I can say my friends are all confused."

Dinny grinned. "I spose you're getting in that canoe."

"Spose I am," said Alvin.

"They's a two-spoon paddle laying in there, but no place to sit."

"This kind of canoe you paddle on your knees," said Alvin.

"How do you know that? Sounds uncomfortable."

"Saw a man paddle a canoe exactly like this one, and that's how he done it."

"Talk to a rough man like me for too long, Master Alvin, and you'll forget all the fine grammar Miz Larner taught you as a lad."

"I like to forget it sometimes," said Alvin. "But then it all comes right back into my head the next time I see her."

"Doesn't work that way for me," said Dinny. "None of it stuck in my brain. Fell right out, replaced by gravel."

Alvin wondered just how well Tenskwa-Tawa had prepared for this crossing. Would Alvin be able to walk on the water and keep his feet dry?

Nope. Water sloshed up over the tops of his boots and soaked him to the thighs before he was able to roll himself over the gunnel and plop down into the canoe. The little boat rocked side to side as if it wanted to turn over and spill him out, but that didn't happen.

Alvin took off his boots, which wasn't easy, and poured the water over the side, back into the Mizzippy.

"Better wash those feet next time you come to land," said Dinny from the shore. "All kinds of sickness and sores come from the river water."

"Thanks for the caution, Dinny, my friend."

"Should I keep watch here till you come back?" asked Dinny.

"I wish I knew. Tell you what, go home and get a good night's rest, come back tomorrow about noon. I promise I won't be back before then."

"You want me to tell Miz Larner where you are?"

"She knows," said Alvin.

"Yep, I reckon she does."

"I'd ruther you didn't tell a soul where I am."

Dinny laughed. "It's an easy secret to keep, since I got no idea this side of Hades where you're going and what you're gonna do."

"Hoping to stay this side of Hades for a few more days, at least," said Alvin. Then he picked up the paddle, knelt up in the boat, waggled goodbye with the paddle, and then began pushing it into the water and pulling back, then doing the same on the other side of the boat. In a few minutes he was swallowed up in the fog.

He wasn't worried. He wasn't going to fall into any of Tenskwa-Tawa's traps. He wasn't going to be led astray by any wayward currents. He didn't *need* to see through the fog because he knew the Prophet was guiding his canoe.

It was maybe an hour, maybe ten minutes, who knew, who cared, when the fog thinned and opened up, and there was the western shore of the Mizzippy, and standing right where he was supposed to be was Tenskwa-Tawa, who raised a hand in greeting.

THESE DAYS THE tribes of the prairie rode horses and jabbed with spears to bring down buffalo. Tenskwa-Tawa told Alvin that a few Reds from several different tribes had brought guns to the prairie for the hunt. "They said the muskets would make the hunt safer," Tenskwa-Tawa explained. "They said it would be more merciful to the buffalo. All of this was told to me by the leaders of the hunt, and I sent word for the musketmen to come to me."

A group of six Reds were arriving over the brow of a low hill, riding fine horses, bareback in the Red manner. "They had to ride horses," said Tenskwa-Tawa softly, "because they have lost the ability to run with the Greensong."

Alvin was surprised by this. "On *this* side of the Mizzippy?" he asked.

"Just because Whites cannot come here does not mean that we are safe from that influence," said Tenskwa-Tawa.

The men were carrying muskets, pointing them upward, which was a sign that they were probably loaded. They were an intimidating group, and for about half a minute Alvin wondered if the Prophet were in danger. There were other Reds nearby—strong men, some with bows—but nobody had an arrow nocked or a hatchet or a knife in hand.

Alvin knew, of course, that with *him* there, no ball of any metal could strike Tenskwa-Tawa or harm him even if it did. Alvin had long since learned how to soften and melt and evaporate metals instantly in a bullet's flight, and how to knit together torn flesh, even the muscle of a beating heart punctured by a metal ball. And Tenskwa-Tawa knew this. But Alvin also understood that Tenskwa-Tawa would have been just as calm if Alvin had not been there.

The six musketmen brought their horses to a stop six steps away from the Prophet. The men looked at the Prophet. The horses also, insofar as Alvin could tell where horses were looking. No one spoke.

The men dismounted—awkwardly, because they did not let go of their guns.

Still looking at the silent Prophet, three of them laid their guns in the grass at the Prophet's feet.

The other three stood intransigent, their faces showing nothing, as was to be expected with Reds who had strong feelings. In this case, Alvin could guess shame at having been summoned to the leader of all tribes, and maybe fear, but more likely anger. Reds did not commonly make decisions based on fear, but on rage, that was far more common.

Tenskwa-Tawa merely looked at the three still holding their guns. There was no hint of the men preparing to aim or fire; they held the guns barrel-up, but their fingers were not within the trigger guard. Alvin recognized the make of the rifles—three from a Noisy River foundry with a poor reputation with their firearms, the others from an Irrakwa manufacturer whose muskets were fashioned with such precision and regularity that you could take any part from any musket of that make, and put it on any other musket, and it would fit as if it had been made for it. It was called the Mohican Foundry, though its owners and workers represented most of the Irrakwa tribes.

The guns on the ground were from Noisy River, and therefore had little resale value, thought Alvin. Few prosperous people would ever buy one new; nobody would buy one used, since they didn't hold up well, and old ones were always closer and closer to the fizzle—or the explosion.

The guns still in their owners' hands were from the Mohican Foundry, and Alvin was reasonably sure that they had been purchased rather than commandeered. They were an investment, and they had great value.

Finally one of the recusants spoke. "What will you do with our muskets?" he asked.

"When you lay them on the ground," said Tenskwa-Tawa, "they will no longer *be* your muskets, and so you will have no more reason to be concerned with them."

Alvin waited for one of the recusants to point a gun at the Prophet. None of them did. One of them laid down his very expensive musket in the grass and, hanging his head, he knelt in the grass before Tenskwa-Tawa.

"Let me see your face," said Tenskwa-Tawa.

"The White man," he said softly.

"This is Alvin Maker, my friend and savior," said Tenskwa-Tawa. "There is no shame in his presence. He is me and I am him."

The kneeling man raised his face toward the Prophet, not even glancing in Alvin's direction.

"I will hear you," said Tenskwa-Tawa.

"A great buffalo dragged my father from his horse and dragged him long enough that he died."

"I knew your father," said the Prophet. "A good man, a brave man, but also a stubborn man. Why didn't he let go of the spear?"

"The spear was deep in the buffalo's body, and I think my father might have imagined that the buffalo would weaken and stop."

"As I heard it, the spear was only in the hump," said Tenskwa-Tawa.

"The hump is pure muscle, the strongest of the buffalo's meat," said the kneeler, allowing himself to show a bit of pride in his knowledge.

"It is very strong," said Tenskwa-Tawa, "which is why your father's spear did not come loose. But it also does not contain any vital arteries or veins, so the buffalo that dragged your father was not seriously wounded. Your father would know this."

The kneeler bowed his head again. "My father was very proud of that spear."

"He died for it," said Tenskwa-Tawa. "The buffalo who dragged him was killed later that day, and you were given the first choice of his meat. You refused to eat it."

"The buffalo was the victor. Only the meat of the defeated may be eaten."

There was a long silence. Nobody moved.

"My young friend," said Tenskwa-Tawa, "I know you do not carry a musket because you fear a buffalo killing you or hurting you."

No answer.

"Nor do you seek vengeance," the Prophet continued.

Silence.

"Tell me why you spent so much to buy this fine weapon."

"I earned the furs I traded," said the kneeler. "They were mine to use as I wanted."

"So you are without a clan?" asked Tenskwa-Tawa.

Silence.

Tenskwa-Tawa spoke to Alvin. "Everything we own belongs to the clan."

"I have no clan," said the kneeler.

"They weep for you every day," said Tenskwa-Tawa.

"They should mourn me," the kneeler said. "I died with my father, and I am now a ghost."

The Prophet took a few strides forward and shoved the man by the shoulder. He toppled over into the grass, and made no effort to rise.

"You are a living man of flesh and blood and bone, but apparently very little brain. You will return to your clan, but speak to no one there. You will lie in your mother's house like a dead man, saying nothing, eating nothing, drinking nothing, until you are truly dead, or until you decide you want to be alive and a part of your family, whereupon you may speak to your mother and beg her to forgive you. Then you will be alive again. And you will never touch a White weapon again as long as you live."

The kneeler rose to his feet and walked toward his horse.

The horse shied away, then ambled toward the river.

The former rider walked off to the southwest.

"So he's lost everything," said Alvin.

"He lost his father, and stopped caring for anything. He will care again. He will belong again. He knows that his punishment is really his reward."

Two men still held their muskets. Tenskwa-Tawa looked at them expectantly. Meanwhile, the three who had laid down their cheaper muskets followed the example of their companion, and knelt beside their guns.

"Did a buffalo kill your father? Someone you loved? A favorite horse?"

No one answered.

"Then you are not the same as Mud-in-the-Ear," said Tenskwa-Tawa, "and you will not receive the same merciful judgment."

Alvin wondered if it was wise to be threatening serious punishment while two men were still armed.

The Prophet called out to four of the men waiting nearby, who hurried to stand before him. "Take the guns from the ground," said Tenskwa-Tawa. "Then take these three to the river and carry them across in the canoes you find there. When they are on the White side of the river, return their White weapons to them. Sell the Mohican musket for whatever a gunsmith will pay, and return with as many iron pots and long spoons as you can buy with the money."

Tenskwa-Tawa turned to Alvin as the men walked away. "You wonder why I will buy pots and spoons of White manufacture. The reason is simple. Earthen pots break easily. Iron pots do not. Long spoons can reach to the bottom of those pots."

Iron weapons were also less likely to break than bows and arrows and spears, Alvin thought. Then he understood the Prophet's wisdom. He will use items of White manufacture if they have real value, and do no harm. Alvin nodded.

Two recusants still stood there holding Irrakwa muskets.

"You paid dearly for those weapons," said the Prophet.

The recusants said nothing.

"They do not belong to you," said the Prophet. "They belong to your clan."

One of the men finally spoke. "My clan don't want it."

"Then no one in your clan may claim it," said Tenskwa-Tawa. "That means that these fine Mohican muskets belong to all the people of the prairie and the mountains."

A long moment of waiting.

At last one of the men threw his weapon to the ground. The other did the same. Then they stood expectantly. Alvin thought, They imagine that they, too, will have their weapons returned to them on the east side of the river.

"Now you have a choice, each of you separately. You can be exiled to the east side, the White lands, and you will never cross the Mizzippy again."

The men said nothing.

"No, you will not have these fine weapons returned to you."

The men still said nothing.

"Exile, or . . . you can remain on the Red side of the river. But you are dead to your own tribe and your own clan. They will never recognize you if they see you, or they will run from you as they would from a ghost. Instead, I will assign you to two different tribes and you will each be given to one of the clans to raise as a child who is not yet old enough to speak their language. You will learn the language of your new clan, and learn whatever skills they choose to teach you, and on a day they will bring you back before me to tell me you are ready to become a man—a man of that tribe, that clan."

Did they understand how merciful Tenskwa-Tawa was being? thought Alvin. Maybe. These were not stupid men. They knew that if the Prophet had given the word, they would have been cudgeled to death within a minute. They were traitors, and they had known they were traitors when they brought the muskets across the river.

The men did not even look at each other. "I will stay," said one. And the other said, "As a newborn child I will stay."

"Not that young," said the Prophet. "Your new clan needs you to be able to walk and feed yourself and carry out useful tasks. Do not imagine that you will be permitted to suckle at anyone's pap."

Then Alvin realized that Tenskwa-Tawa knew these two men. They were the kind who would try to turn every situation to their advantage, and find a way to subvert every rule. If they did not change, their new clans would never declare them fit to be men, and they would die as children.

Since Alvin lived on the White side of the river, he knew that exile was not such a bleak existence, especially for a Red who had already decided to adopt White ways. There would be Cherriky or Irrakwa who would take them in at first, till they could learn a trade. They would survive.

And if they stayed, they would still never return to their right families and clans.

Even so, the two of them walked away from the river. They were not going to go into exile. Maybe they would become loyal men of the West. Maybe they would stir up trouble or try to go east again. Maybe they would get themselves executed for treason after all. But Alvin thought that right now, at least, they thought they would easily learn the new language and be accepted by the nations as men before very long at all.

"Their horses?" asked Alvin.

The Prophet beckoned to one of the men-in-waiting. "The Pawnees are providing me with aides and escorts this year," said Tenskwa-Tawa. "Nobody wants to tangle with a Pawnee, so they are invariably obeyed."

"You gave them all choices," said Alvin.

"They already made choices that could have cost them their freedom or their lives," said the Prophet. "I dealt as kindly as I could within the range of choices they had given me."

The Pawnee man the Prophet had summoned arrived.

"There are six horses here that belong to the prairie," said Tenskwa-Tawa. "Take them to see which tribe they want to join, or whether they wish to fend for themselves on the open prairie."

The Pawnee walked toward the horses, and they immediately shifted position to follow him. Not a word, not a sign was given.

"Those are very good horses," said Tenskwa-Tawa. "Animals are not property. We don't decide for them how they will live."

"There must be a lot of free-range horses, then."

"Some. Several herds. Most stay where humans make sure they are fed through the winter and train them to work and earn their living. The wild ones are always free to join us. The working horses are always free to go out on the prairie. Like many people, some poor horses can't make up their minds."

"I don't understand," said Alvin. "You control who crosses the river."

"Reds are always free to move East, and Reds are always free to come West."

"Even carrying White weaponry?" asked Alvin.

"If I make it so they don't have the power to break the law," said Tenskwa-Tawa, "then how is it a virtue for them to obey it?"

Alvin smiled a little. "I'm glad you called me here."

Tenskwa-Tawa showed no emotion when he said, "I didn't call you."

"I saw myself crossing the river in the canoe you sent," said Alvin.

"So the Crystal City called you."

"Did it send me the canoe?" asked Alvin.

"That canoe goes where it's needed," said Tenskwa-Tawa. "It doesn't consult with me."

"Then why am I here?"

"Exactly my question, Alvin. Why are you here?"

6

Alvin was confused, of course. If Tenskwa-Tawa had not called him, why did he see the images he saw in the crystal blocks? Why was it a vision *of* Tenskwa-Tawa? What purpose would be served by Alvin's being on the western shore, with the Prophet, at this time?

Meanwhile, the Prophet seemed to think this was an opportunity to show Alvin Maker the West country, which Whites were no longer able to see. "I could take you to mountains that would make the Appalachees look like a child's sand village at the beach."

"When have you ever seen *that*?" asked Alvin.

"I wasn't always the leader of a great people," said Tenskwa-Tawa. "And White children are not the only ones who pile up sand."

"I don't think I'm here to see mountains," said Alvin.

"Ah, but are you here to see mounds?"

"You know I'm familiar with Eight-Face Mound," said Alvin, "because you took me there."

"That was one kind of mound, true, and an important one. But that's in the East now, and I won't be returning to it soon. Maybe ever."

"Show me whatever you want me to see, while we *both* try to figure out why I was sent here."

It wasn't a long walk, because the Greensong was immediately accessible on this side of the river. They ran and with little effort beyond sloshing through a half-dozen rivers and streams, they reached the mound that Tenskwa-Tawa wanted Alvin to see.

"All right, yes, this is something," said Alvin.

It wasn't that the edge of the mound was exceedingly high. On the contrary, it wasn't quite as high as Alvin remembered Eight-Face Mound to have been. It was the mound's breadth that was astonishing. "How big *is* this mound?" asked Alvin.

Tenskwa-Tawa smiled. "Come," he said. Then he took Alvin's hand, and together they walked up a ramp built into the side of the mound. It was easier than going straight up the face would have been, but it was still a steep climb, and there was no Greensong to help here, since absolutely nothing was growing on the steep slope.

"Why isn't there any grass here?" asked Alvin. "And when it rains, why doesn't this whole edge of the mound slide on down?"

"There are many strange things here. But I like to say to curious children like you, Alvin, 'This mound was made for many purposes, but maybe growing grass was not one of them.' "

"You're sure this mound was *made*? Couldn't it be natural?"

"Oh, we know it was made, because our people made it. Carried every bit of this soil up from the riverside in baskets."

"That must have taken—"

"Several years in the building, but the original mound was finished four hundred years ago."

"Then how do you know—"

"Alvin, why do you think that nothing can be known without being written down? The songs of building Cahokia Mound are often sung, and memorized by young singers, so we can continue to remember our stories as they are sung to us. We have a history and we know it and treasure it because we have to work harder to keep it alive."

"I agree, my assumption was wrong. Of course you know."

"Cahokia Mound. Perhaps Whites would call it New Cahokia, to emphasize that it is not the original. But to us, it is Cahokia, the same place, simply relocated to the other side of the Mizzippy. Here we are."

Alvin noticed that when he was dealing with Reds, the Prophet was taciturn, and when he spoke at all his messages were terse. Now, though, he was talking to Alvin like a White man would—almost garrulous with his information, and saying needless things like "Here we are," a statement that is invariably true and almost invariably uninformative.

Then these thoughts faded, because now Alvin could see the scope and scale of Cahokia Mound. From east to west it had seemed very large. But now he could see north to south, and he could not detect the end of the mound to the south.

"How big—" asked Alvin.

"No one has measured it in White miles. Early White explorers—Spaniards, I think—who visited Cahokia about three hundred years ago, they had their estimate, but none of my people knew or cared what the numbers meant. What the people knew was that more than fifty thousand Reds lived in a dozen villages—no, towns, I know the difference. Not a tent city, but mud and daub buildings that remained winter after winter. Roads leading from town to town. Storehouses of maize to eat during winter, and pemmican and smoked buffalo meat. Whatever anybody needed, that we had, they could have it. No one could possibly be poor, because we all owned everything and nobody took more than their share."

"How old *are* you?" asked Alvin.

"They were *my* people, so I say 'we,' but of course I wasn't there. Remember that I know the stories. We all listen to the songs as if we were inside them. We *are* inside them. They are stories of us."

"Fifty thousand?" asked Alvin. "There's not a city that big in the White lands."

"Nor is there a city that big here and now. So much space between villages. And not everybody stays. You can see some of the villages are abandoned. Look at the collapsed roofs, the tilting walls, the unused streets. But up ahead, see the smoke of the cookfires. That village is alive."

"If the original was east of the river—"

"The mound is still there," said Tenskwa-Tawa. "White people don't usually notice it, because it's so large. It's just part of the landscape, a stretch of land higher than the surrounding prairie. It's in what you call Noisy River country."

"Where did all the people of *that* mound go?" asked Alvin.

"Into the ground," said the Prophet. "The Spaniards who first visited Cahokia Mound brought diseases. I don't think they knew they had these diseases in them. We don't blame them for what happened after they came through. But half the people of Cahokia were sick, and most died, and the others fled, until the villages were empty, except for the dead and dying, and the handful of brave souls who carried water to the sick so that if they died, it would not be of thirst."

"Do you know what disease it was?"

"Do you want to know the name because you and the sickness are already friends?"

"Mortal enemies," said Alvin. "But every disease is different."

"Swollen itching marks all over the body," said Tenskwa-Tawa.

"Smallpox."

"And another one, thumb-size swollen dark sores—"

"Bubonic plague," said Alvin.

"Are these diseases you know because you have a cure for them?"

Alvin shook his head. "I can cure them, one person at a time, by getting inside the sufferer's body and making changes until the disease is extinguished. But I can't *make* a cure—a potion, a poultice, that other people could use. I don't understand the diseases that well."

"I wish you had been there then. More than half the people of Cahokia died, and many of those who ran away also died, because they had already been infected. We thought Cahokia had been destroyed by the Whites—not a-purpose, we knew that—but dead of the White diseases, that could not be denied by anyone. From then on, any White hunter or explorer would be carefully guided away from Cahokia, by scouts who were quarantined before they could come home.

Most of those who ran away never came back, and those who returned could not rebuild because there weren't enough people in the surrounding country to trade with, and living on the old Cahokia Mound was impossible, without enough people to hunt and grow the maize and care for the babies that had survived. So even those who returned had to go, joining the surrounding tribes. All the tribes have Cahokia blood in them by now."

"This is not the remnant of Cahokia, then," said Alvin. "This is a new settlement built to the same plan."

"Built since the river divided White from Red. Those who fled from Tippy-Canoe and other places where Whites were trying to oust them, when they came west they didn't know how to hunt buffalo, the ground was so dry and rain so scarce that the ways of growing maize in the East no longer worked. Some experimented with irrigation, and that is working now, in more places every year. And the expert hunters took more buffalo than usual, so they could feed the newcomers. And most of the newcomers earned their food by carrying baskets and bags of earth from the floodlands near the Mizzippy and they built this mound."

"With you in charge."

"With my understanding of the old Cahokia Mound to guide us, yes. I told them how large from east to west, and how large from north to south, and I gave them the shape of the corners because this was not going to be a mathematically squared-off place, as White surveyors would have made it."

"Is it the same size and shape as the original?"

"I don't care if it is," said Tenskwa-Tawa. "The idea was not to build it exactly as it had been built in different terrain, but to fit it to the land here, creating channels for streams to flow through it or around it."

"And the city, or villages—with the mound about the same size as it had been before, how many people does it sustain?"

"We are near twenty thousand people now, including those who roam and scout and hunt, but always come back here to report, or to guide new settlers here."

"Is this your capital?" asked Alvin.

Tenskwa-Tawa looked puzzled. "Why should it be a capital? Why would we need a capital? This is the largest poblacion on the prairie—that's what the Spanish call a group of villages. Each village governs itself, and when there's a matter that involves all the villages of Cahokia, then the Council is called, each village having a vote, and we decide together what to do. But no one *has* to do it because there's no government to force them to comply."

"But what about other towns that aren't up on Cahokia Mound?" asked Alvin.

"What are they to us, unless they trade their crops or skins to us for our pottery and wattles? Cahokia does not rule over any other villages or anybody else who doesn't dwell on the mound. Throughout the whole West, no rulers force their will on others, or steal their possessions as taxes. What do you think we are, White?"

Alvin laughed, and so did Tenskwa-Tawa.

"But you are obeyed all over the Red lands, aren't you?"

"My words are listened to by some, and repeated to others, who sometimes listen. And people bring me disputes to settle, so that sometimes I'm a judge. But not a king or governor or mayor. I get no taxes from anybody, nor even any fees for my service as mediator. Why should I gain from damaging disputes, as if my income should depend on people being mean to each other? Who wants to earn money from something like *that*?"

"More than you'd think," said Alvin, thinking of his friend Verily Cooper, who had a law office back in Crystal City. And other lawyers, many of them without a knack of any kind, who depended for their income on outsiders who brought complaints against the Talented people who came to

Crystal City for refuge. But even they had their uses, Alvin knew. He'd had enough ridiculous legal trouble in his life to know that a good lawyer is as necessary as a good bowel movement—as he said to Verily more than once, until Margaret told Alvin she'd prefer never hearing that vile joke again.

Still, Alvin couldn't help but think of the lack of lawyers in Cahokia as a benefit, not because lawyers themselves caused the problems and disputes, but because their complete absence suggested that people knew how to settle their disputes in a dispassionate way without *needing* lawyers.

As if he knew what Alvin was thinking, Tenskwa-Tawa said, "In Cahokia, lawyers would starve, except that we don't let anybody go hungry here."

"How do you get people to act that way?" asked Alvin.

"We Reds have *always* lived that way. Maybe it's our knack as a people. My brother would tell you that 'our way' was the reason we could never unite to fight off the White onslaught, and yet the same reason that we could not keep the peace, because the young warriors did not have to obey the elders who had agreed to peace."

No wonder Reds had always opposed being governed by Whites in the East. No wonder so many of them—even from Irrakwa and Cherriky—made their way to the banks of the Mizzippy and then crossed into Red country. Irrakwa and Cherriky were like Whites in their government. The Red states of the East had elections, and sent electors to choose the President of the United States, now that they had joined that federation. They had deeds to their houses, factories, and lands, and they made contracts with White businesses and industries and suppliers. When you have deeds and contracts you're going to have lawyers.

No wonder Tenskwa-Tawa thought of the Cherriky and Irrakwa as not being Red at all. The eastern Reds had taken on White ways and triumphed over many of their White competitors. It was Irrakwa crews that were hired to build railroads all over the States, and Cherriky engineers that built bridges over rivers and streams of every size. They also farmed, and the Cherriky, at least, kept up some remnant of the common ownership of property, though that ideal was breached over and over as individual families obeyed only the decisions about their property that they agreed with.

They were not going to walk the whole length of Cahokia Mound. And Alvin had had his fill of touring the Red capital, for to him that's what it had to be. Instead, they returned to the northern brow of the mound and sat down and talked.

They talked about ideas. They reminisced about their own past, about Tenskwa-Tawa appearing to Alvin in his bedroom as the Shining Man, telling him how to dedicate his life. Rebuking him for his stupid mistakes, helping him discover his own rules on how to use his knacks. In return, Alvin had helped the drunken Lolla-Wossiky get over his alcohol craving so he could become the sober Prophet.

Their lives were so entangled.

"In England, where the Puritans rule," said Alvin, "they kill people who have knacks."

Tenskwa-Tawa shrugged. "It's a faraway land," he said. "Full of Whites."

"Full of *my* people," said Alvin, though until that moment he hadn't really thought of the English as being some kind of kinfolk. Whites weren't like Reds. They didn't feel like every other White was their brother or sister. But maybe that was a mistake. Maybe Whites and Reds and Blacks should all think of each other as brothers.

Impossible. Because the real division now was between people with useful knacks, and people without. That's why Alvin had built Crystal City, to be a refuge, a gathering place for the Talented. A fortress? He hoped not, hoped that such a thing would never be needed.

Then an idea struck him with great force. "My friend," Alvin said. "What if the war against knacks, against people like me, what if we lose it? What if we can see that we will be overwhelmed, slaughtered, imprisoned, my Crystal City overrun and ruled by people who thirst for our blood?"

"I know something about that," said Tenskwa-Tawa.

Alvin remembered the killing field at Tippy-Canoe Creek, where enraged Whites slaughtered defenseless Red families. Yes, Tenskwa-Tawa knew.

"My friend, Lolla-Wossiky, Tenskwa-Tawa, Prophet, ruler of the river and the fogs above it—"

"Let me think about it," said Tenskwa-Tawa.

"I didn't ask you yet," said Alvin.

"Let me think about allowing your people with the powerful knacks to cross the river and find refuge in the Red lands."

"They know nothing about the kind of society you have here. Living without government, I don't know if they'd be ready for that."

"That's why I have to think about it," said Tenskwa-Tawa. "*You* are always welcome, of course, either to visit, like now, or to dwell for the rest of your life. You and Margaret and such children and brothers and sisters as you choose to bring. But the whole of Crystal City? It's become quite large, I hear."

"Not like Cahokia," said Alvin.

"Exactly like Cahokia," said the Prophet. "Dependent on trade to supply the city with food and fuel. Too large for anyone to know everyone."

"Could we gather on the western shore, in such a case of dire need, and rebuild the Crystal City there? Or should we go farther inland, even though water for the blocks of crystal might be harder to find?"

"The farther west you go, the drier it is," said Tenskwa-Tawa. "There's no reason for you to leave the western shore, if the river lets you cross westward. If the Whites can ever force their way across, then it won't matter where you are, prairie or mountains, forest or desert, they can find you and destroy you. Unless you have knacks among you that can serve as weapons."

"I don't like them to do that," said Alvin.

"I taught you not to kill," said Tenskwa-Tawa. "But did that save us from White Murderer Harrison? So now I say that when there is no other way, what can you do but kill?"

"I have learned—from you," said Alvin, "that there is almost always another way."

"Don't bring your people across the river," said Tenskwa-Tawa. "There would inevitably be conflict between Reds and Whites—even persecuted Whites with knacks."

"I won't count on coming," said Alvin.

"You and your family are always—"

"My friend, you know I cannot come here by myself, or even with my family, while the rest of my people are being massacred."

"As I said, Alvin, my boy," said Tenskwa-Tawa, "let me think about it."

They sat in silence.

"I'm thinking that I ought to go back home now," said Alvin. "But I don't know why. Have I accomplished anything here?"

"You have a city that depends on you," said Tenskwa-Tawa. "You learned how Red people live when Whites don't impose their laws on us. Of course you feel as if you ought to go back home."

"Something called me here, sent me, *dragged* me here."

Tenskwa-Tawa shrugged slightly. "I have no answer." Then he stood up. "I know who *might* have your answer," he said.

7

It was the most permanent-looking building Alvin had seen in the Red West, very much like a log cabin that Whites might have built. Only there were no stands of trees nearby, as there were everywhere in the East, and individual trees on the prairie were all too precious to cut down to build something as transient as a dwelling-place. So these logs must have come from trees across the river.

Tenskwa-Tawa explained: "When the river became a barrier, the White settlers here all fled East, though there was no threat of violence against them. The buildings they didn't burn, they left behind, and Ta-Kumsaw saw no reason to leave the place unoccupied. For a log house, it is roomy, and now Ta-Kumsaw's daughter, my niece Wieza, keeps house here."

Alvin remembered Wieza. "When I was in Becca's house, I met her daughter Wieza. I think her Red name, her real name, was Mana-Tawa."

Tenskwa-Tawa looked at him in bemusement. "You remember both names of a woman?"

"I don't know of any women more important in all of North America than the Weavers."

"Not always women," said Tenskwa-Tawa. "My brother Methowa-Tasky has a son—"

"I know there are men among the Weavers," said Alvin.

"I forget sometimes how much you learned," said Tenskwa-Tawa.

"So this is where the Loom is kept," said Alvin.

"This Loom is only *the* Loom while it is being used," said Tenskwa-Tawa. "It's a heavy, awkward piece of furniture when it's just being 'kept.'"

"I have always wondered—if the Weavers stop their work, what happens to the lives they've been Weaving?"

Tenskwa-Tawa thought for a moment. "Let's not find out."

"You brought me here so I could consult with the Weavers," said Alvin.

"I think you should visit with Mana-Tawa."

Alvin waited for more explanation. Then he realized. "You have to be the Prophet when we go inside this house."

He looked at Tenskwa-Tawa, who merely looked back at him, expressionless.

Alvin knew this was his answer: The Prophet is taciturn, and does not say what does not need saying.

The door opened before they came to it, and a young man stood there. Alvin had seen him before. He started to say the man's name. "No," said the man. "My name is Suckling now."

It was a ridiculous name for a grown man, and Alvin turned to Tenskwa-Tawa for explanation. But it was Suckling who answered his unspoken query. "When you translate a word into another language, it can be exactly right, yet it can carry meanings that are very wrong. My name is manly and meaningful in Mohawk. Or so my father, Methowa-Tasky, told me."

Tenskwa-Tawa spoke up. "Methowa-Tasky is my brother. Suckling is my nephew."

Alvin said, "If a male Weaver is named Suckling, then it *is* a name of dignity."

Suckling smiled. "You honor this house, Alvin Maker."

"I am the one being honored, when you welcome me like this."

Suckling led Alvin into the house. Alvin turned to see Tenskwa-Tawa waiting beyond the threshold. Alvin looked at him expectantly, but did not ask.

"The Prophet druther not come near the Loom," said Suckling, "for fear a Weaver might tell him what he don't want to know."

Alvin smiled at Tenskwa-Tawa. "I thought you wanted to know everything."

"All in due time," said Tenskwa-Tawa solemnly.

Alvin turned to Suckling. "I'm not here to avoid the Loom."

"What do you want to know?" asked Suckling.

"Whatever the Weaver has to tell me."

"At this moment I'm not *the* Weaver. Mana-Tawa is at the Loom."

"Don't we call her Wieza anymore?"

"Don't be fretting about names so much, Master Alvin," said Suckling. "We saw you coming, and Wieza's eager to talk to you."

Alvin waited. Suckling remembered that Alvin had never been there before. "You don't know where the Loom is, I reckon," he said.

Alvin smiled.

"This way," said Suckling. He led Alvin to a stairway that went down into the cellar.

As they descended, Alvin said, "Can she weave in the dark?"

"She can weave in her sleep, and she does so many a night," said Suckling. "But this house is on a slope, so one end of the cellar is dark, but the other end has north light all day."

"Good choice of house, then," said Alvin.

"That's so," said Suckling. "But we could weave in a cave or outdoors on an island. Only place we can't really is underwater, because the threads don't act right, and the shuttlecock won't go far enough on one throw."

"So you've tried it."

"The Mizzippy flooded around here last spring, on the snow melt from the mountains. Wieza didn't want to stop weaving long enough to move the Loom. The rest of us stacked up baskets of dirt to make a kind of levee, and it kept the water two feet lower inside than out, but Wieza was still weaving, even with wetted strings and a sluggish shuttlecock."

"She didn't see it coming?" asked Alvin.

"We never look at our own threads," said Suckling, as if that were something everybody knew. "We never try to weave to an outcome we desire. We just weave as the threads need to go."

"You knew I was coming from my thread."

"We saw you joining with the Prophet, and we knew that he'd bring you here, and here you are."

"What else do you know?"

"A crystal vision led you to the riverside and a canoe offered to carry you west," said Suckling. "I was weaving when all that happened. I told Wieza and she said, 'Probly not till tomorrow.'"

"But this is still the very day I crossed the river," said Alvin.

"True enough, Wieza guessed wrong. But remember she said probly."

Alvin heard the sound of dishes being stacked or unstacked upstairs. "I didn't mean to come around suppertime, this is just when we finished at Cahokia Mound."

"We eat when we eat," said Suckling. "We carry food down to the Weaver, if they're hungry, but mostly when we're weaving, we don't think of food."

"I could never do that job," said Alvin. "I think of food a lot."

Suckling shrugged. "Wieza's ready for you now."

"How did you know that?"

"There was a change in the rhythm of the Loom," he said. Then he ushered Alvin through a door and there was the Loom.

It was twice as big as the one he had seen in Becca's house over in the East. And the threads were different colors, not as vibrant, more subdued, but the cloth emerging from the Loom was intricately woven with beautiful fine lines and also wide lines of many threads together for a longish time.

"Not the same Loom," said Alvin.

"No two Looms are alike, except for being looms," said Suckling. "The power isn't in the machine."

"It's in the threads?" asked Alvin.

"It's the threads and the fingers of the Weaver," said Suckling. "Took me ages to learn how to let my fingers find the way, and me not trying to control them."

"Hardest thing to learn," said Alvin, "how not to try to control what you're doing."

"What is it *you* have to not control?"

"Crystal City," said Alvin. "The scrying blocks and the people. The blocks will tell you what you demand that they show, but the more you push, the falser they get, until you ruin the block and it has to be replaced. People struggle with that one all the time."

"Reckon so," said Suckling.

"The people are the same. You can push and push them into doing something they don't want to do, but turn your back and they spring right back to their old ways."

Through all this, Wieza kept weaving, her eyes closed, her face serene.

"Howdy, Wieza," said Alvin.

"I'm surprised you didn't bring Arthur Stuart with you, Maker," she said softly.

"I didn't see him in the canoe with me, when I looked into the block."

"You didn't bring him because you didn't see him," she said, "but you didn't see him because you didn't bring him."

"Now I wish I'd've thought of it," said Alvin.

"If the crystal didn't guide you, I reckon it wasn't all that important," said Wieza. "You can go now."

Alvin was startled, but Suckling put a hand on his shoulder. "She's talking to me," he said. "She wouldn't just give a command like that to *you*."

"Wasn't a command," said Wieza. "It was permission."

"And with that permission, I excuse myself. Should I tell them you're eating with us?"

"I don't want to steal from your pot, Suckling," said Alvin.

"It's not about the quantity of food," said Suckling. "It's about the number of plates and bowls and mugs on the table."

"Set a place for him," said Wieza, "and toss a few more carrots into the pot. Or those new batata roots, but chop them up fine enough to cook quickly."

Suckling smiled. "Yes, ma'am."

"Don't ma'am me, you catfish tickling scrub of a man."

"That's Wieza's term of endearment for me," said Suckling. "She pretends to find me annoying."

Wieza gave a little sniff, which sounded like a complete refutation of his word "pretends."

Suckling left the room with a smile, but through the outside door, so he'd trudge up the hill rather than climb the stairs.

"Cantankerous boy," said Wieza. "Thinks he knows everything, most especially me."

"Annoying, isn't it?" said Alvin.

"I took you for a know-everything kind of man," said Wieza.

"No, ma'am. Miss."

"Wieza," she said, "or Mana, or Mana-Tawa, or Tawa, but no honorifics, please."

"Got it," said Alvin. "I'm a wants-to-know-everything man."

"You're never taken anyone on as a teacher."

"Tenskwa-Tawa," said Alvin. "My father. Miss Margaret Larner, who is also now my wife, and she's still teaching me. I learn from—"

"Nobody taught you making," said Wieza.

"Nobody knows how better than me," said Alvin. "But I still learned some things. 'The Maker is the one who is part of what he makes.'"

"A good maxim," said Wieza. "That helped you?"

"It helped me find my way to making gold out of iron," said Alvin.

"Where *is* that plow these days?" asked Wieza.

"Wrapped in burlap among a lot of other things wrapped in burlap."

"Think you'll ever need it again?" asked Wieza.

"Unless you tell me otherwise, no. Not after I used it to help lay out and break ground for Crystal City."

"Good plan," said Wieza. "You save yourself a lot of bother and heartache by not showing the thing to anybody, for any reason."

"I don't hide it from Margaret or Measure or Verily or—well, I wouldn't hide it from Tenskwa-Tawa or Ta-Kumsaw, iffen they ever come around."

"Listen to you. 'Iffen,' plus bad grammar. Don't you remember anything Little Peggy taught you?"

"She knows how I talk when I'm away from home," said Alvin.

"She doesn't like it, though, does she?"

"Says it reflects badly on her as a teacher."

"Why do you still do it, then?"

"Because it's a lot more fun than talking proper."

"Talking properly enhances communication and doesn't put up class barriers."

"I'll try to remember that, at least until I can figure out what the hell it means."

"Alvin Maker," said Wieza, "why have you come to me?"

"I don't know," said Alvin. "All I know is I saw myself crossing the Mizzippy in a canoe. Tenskwa-Tawa suggested I should come here."

"For what purpose?" asked Wieza.

"For me to ask you why I came here? It wasn't my idea. I didn't think it was *possible* for a White to cross the Mizzippi."

"Many things that are thought to be impossible turn out to be essential, whether they're possible or not."

"That's it, I came here for the gnomic aphorisms."

"Do you want to know how your life ends?"

"Not how, not when, not where," said Alvin.

"Sooner than I want," said Wieza. "But not right at the doorstep."

"Do the threads tell you anything I ought to know?"

Wieza thought, her eyes closed. Only after she had opened them again did she say, "Is it only in America that Puritans are persecuting people with knacks?"

"In England, under the Lord Protector, there's plenty of mercy-killing of witches, for only thuswise can they become purified and live harmlessly among their fellow men." Alvin sighed. "I think of them in England, waiting for deliverance that only I can bring, but I need to be here in America."

"Better to be needed in two places rather than not being needed in any."

"What, are you becoming an oracle?"

"Think of me as the natural successor to Poor Richard," said Wieza.

"Poor Wieza," said Alvin, "are those dangers coming up primarily in just one area?"

"It has been a nightmare in England for many decades, but all those who needed to leave because of their extraordinary abilities are gone," said Wieza. "So there are a few hundred left, and they've learned to keep their mouths shut and their knacks unused."

"That's just wrong."

"They're alive. So it *is* working for them. The real problem comes in another place, within the English Empire. A place where the people are caught between hating their English overlords, but loving the land and the people. A place where the people's religion tolerates knacks, but the religion of their overlords condemns knacks and seeks to use the death penalty to purify their church."

"It sounds to me that you're angry," said Alvin, "but you're reluctant to tell me who these oppressed people are."

"Because I know you'll immediately want to go there and help them develop their knacks and bring as many as you can to Crystal City, to be free."

"That sounds like me," said Alvin. "I want to do exactly that."

"And we want you to be in favor of living in North America," said Wieza. "Which requires that you avoid death and always return to your Crystal City."

"You're saying I shouldn't go to Ireland."

"I'm saying nothing of the kind. I'm not even saying that the threads show you *do* go to Ireland."

"Not saying it, but saying it anyway," said Alvin.

"I don't know what's best for you or for your people or, for that matter, for *my* people. I merely urge you to be careful not to die."

"You know I don't have any money for a voyage like that."

"*We* don't have any money at all," said Wieza. "So I don't think we can help."

"I wasn't asking for money. I was asking how this would be possible."

"Your people aren't rich, but they're prosperous and many of them have full enough pockets to help you on your way."

"Why would they help me to leave them?" asked Alvin.

"Because your purpose is to rescue persecuted people. People like them. Of course they want you to go—and then to come back. This much I'll tell you: Only raise enough money to pay your passage there, not back again, and live from the generosity of strangers once you're there."

"The Irish are poor," said Alvin. "How would they have anything to share with *me*?"

"Come now, Maker," said Wieza. "You know that the poor always have more to share with beggars than the rich."

"True enough," said Alvin. "I can see that I have to go to Ireland, booking passage only to get there, and bring people with knacks back to the Crystal City."

"That might be your best course, though as far as I know, it might be a terrible set of choices."

"Ambiguous answers," said Alvin, "like every wise oracle."

"I don't want to promise you certainties when I'm uncertain."

"I'm going, if we can raise the money."

"They speak English there, mostly, so you won't have to learn Irish, though I imagine they'll be gratified if you try."

"Arthur Stuart has the knack for languages, not me."

"And I say, all you need to do is learn a few words, including the words, 'I'm so sorry, I don't speak Irish.'"

"I bet I'll have to say that all the time."

"Practice is good."

"There's one barrier that you haven't mentioned. My wife, Margaret Larner, has suggested often that I should be done with traveling to bring people to the Crystal City."

"Whether she likes it or not, the threads don't say. But if you go, she'll remain close to you, and faithful, and when you come home, you'll still belong to her and she to you."

"That's quite a promise right there, with no weaseling."

"I don't weasel," said Wieza. "I don't say things because you want to hear them."

"I know," said Alvin. "I was being . . . I was jesting."

"You meant every word, and I understand why, because the threads are so nonspecific. I do know that very shortly this continent will be the host to hundreds of thousands of Irish people."

"Hundreds of thousands? With knacks?" asked Alvin.

"I don't know about knacks. I know the immigration will begin with your people, but why so many thousands more will follow I can't guess. Your charms are not infinite."

"That's the kindest way anyone has ever found to tell me that."

"Alvin, you have all the skills you need to do this work, and in my opinion it needs doing. But if you don't go, maybe they'll find their own way to Crystal City. I don't know."

"But what you see is that I go," said Alvin

Wieza looked down at her weaving once again. "I only have another hour of light, even now with longer days. And I can hear that supper is ready upstairs."

"You're sending me away."

"I've told you all that I can about what I have learned from your threads."

Alvin heard her words and parsed them carefully. She has told me all she *can*, but she has not told me all she *knows*.

He bowed to her, and thanked her, and went up the stairs, closing the door behind him. She would not starve, and he needed to eat. Her people would bring food to her, or save food for her. Whatever was needful.

To Alvin's surprise, Tenskwa-Tawa was seated at the table. He looked up at Alvin and said, "The little girl invited me."

Alvin saw that a child of about five was beaming with pride. She had asked the Prophet to dinner when none of the big people had dared. And the Prophet had come and would eat at their table, along with the Maker. It was a delicious stew, with peppers from the south to make it tingle in Alvin's mouth. I must bring some of those peppers home so we can liven up the fare at our own table.

They offered Alvin a place to sleep, and he would have taken it, but he felt a sudden urgency to get home to Margaret and let her know what the Weaver had said and what he had decided to do. So when supper was over, he went outside with Tenskwa-Tawa, bade him farewell as one of the great friends of Alvin's life, and then took off running for the shore of the Mizzippy. He got there just as the Pawnees were returning with their canoes from taking the gun smugglers across to White America.

"The canoe will go eastward with little trouble," a Pawnee said to him. "And then you can put the paddle aboard and walk away. It knows how to get back home."

As do I, thought Alvin. I always know the way home, because that's where Margaret is.

8

Lisbon

FRA ANGELICO NEVER made demands. Never asked favors, never begged for alms. He was a mendicant, and a mendicant who never begged was something of an anomaly. He was supposed to go about the world providing opportunities for people of plenty to share their wealth like good Christians. Instead he simply showed up at Father Lukasz's modest home overlooking the sea just northwest of Lisbon and, without announcing himself, sat on a bench in the garden, looking, not at the beautiful view, but at the blossoms and bees.

Eventually, the housekeeper came into Father Lukasz's office and, on the pretext of picking up empty plates and glasses and cups for washing, said, "By the way, Father, he's back again."

No need to explain who "he" was. "Bench in the garden?" asked Lukasz.

"A different one this time, Father. Straight out of the conservatory door."

"A sunny spot, this time of day," said Lukasz.

"On a cool day, perhaps the best seat in the garden," said the housekeeper. "You might try it sometime, if you should ever choose to give yourself a moment's relaxation."

"I'll rest on that bench next to Fra Angelico."

"Is he?" asked the housekeeper. "Angelic? Truly?"

"Not for me to judge," said Father Lukasz. "Only for me to be his friend when he happens to come by."

A few minutes later, his papers turned over, his books closed, Father

Lukasz made his way out into the garden and sat down beside Fra Angelico. They sat there in silence for a long time, or it felt like a long time to Lukasz, anyway. They didn't so much as glance at each other.

"Portuguese is nothing like Polish," said Fra Angelico, "and yet they say you speak it like a native."

"Portuguese is very much like Latin spoken through the nose," said Lukasz, "and no Luso has ever mistaken me for a native."

Fra Angelico gave a tiny hoot of laughter.

"I've never heard," said Lukasz. "What's your native language? Is 'Angelico' Spanish? Italian?"

"Angelico was the name I chose when I set aside worldly concerns and entered into a life of poverty."

"Then where were you born? What is your native tongue?"

"I was born a Muslim named Ali Jafar, in Lebanon, where I was converted with the help of Christian neighbors. I wasn't baptized until I made my way to Greece, and then I went to Rome—"

"Always a test of a convert's faith," said Lukasz.

"I left the Church twice during my years in Rome, but I always came back to the fold, more determined than ever to prove my worthiness to Christ and to myself. I was *not* going to be a corrupt priest, you see. If I had wanted to be rich, I could have stayed in Beirut, where my family still owns several ships—"

"Pirates, I assume," said Lukasz.

"Pirates are in Tripoli. We're the civilized part of the Levant."

"Is any of what you're telling me true?"

"I was born," said Fra Angelico. "After that I just followed the story wherever it wanted to go."

"The story I want to hear is about your most recent visit to the Holy See, and what you might have overheard from the Holy Father."

"I try not to eavesdrop, but he *will* speak quite loudly, because half the cardinals are deaf."

"Anything I should take particular interest in?"

"The Holy Father is concerned about Ireland," said Fra Angelico. "It seems the land is a hideous pit of witchcraft and conspiracy."

"Or so the English are fond of saying," said Lukasz.

"Miserable heretics, those English," said Fra Angelico. "A thorn in the side of every good Catholic."

Lukasz said, "You know that here in Portugal, I have spent many years ministering among those whom the false English church accuses of witchcraft and expels from their island."

Fra Angelico chuckled.

"I would like to be amused along with you."

"Oh, I think you won't be amused. You see, there are those who have the ear of the Holy Father who believe that we are missing an opportunity."

Lukasz already saw what was taking shape. There were reasons he didn't stay in Rome himself.

"They believe that instead of being sympathetic to the Gifted Ones, we should take the lead in purging Christianity of these traffickers with devils."

Lukasz looked down at his feet. "And the Holy Father listens to them?"

"The Holy Father listens to everyone," said Fra Angelico. "Even me."

Lukasz nodded, wondering if he could deal with whatever Fra Angelico had to tell.

"I proposed to the Holy Father that there was no evidence at all of any trafficking with the devil. I proposed that the Protestants of England are finding what they look for, whether it's there or not. I suggested that putting to the torture sinless people with gifts from God would not in the long run benefit the Church, because everyone would hate us again for the Inquisition once they realized that these people are not witches or wizards or demons from hell."

"I imagine he loves to hear the way you phrase things," said Lukasz.

"There were two Cardinals present, arguing for persecuting the witches."

"How even-handed, two against one."

Fra Angelico said nothing.

"All right, with you there, the Cardinals were outnumbered."

"It was Truth that outnumbered them, as it always does," said Fra Angelico. "I said that if we want to kill innocent people there is no shortage of the innocent in any land. They said that none are innocent, no not one, to which I speculated on when the Inquisition would be called to examine *them*, which made them livid. They raged, they shouted, and Swiss Guards rushed into the room and the Holy Father asked them to escort the Cardinals back to their chambers."

Lukasz chuckled. "Two more men who hate you with their entire soul."

"They are both very old, Lukasz. They won't have many more years of hatred for me. I intend to outlive them, you see, outlive them and all their evil ideas."

"Did the Holy Father share your view of their ideas as evil?"

"I believe he did," said Fra Angelico, "though you know that my ability to guess what other people think is very limited."

"Less limited than any other man I know. But yes, I would gladly hear your unreliable speculations about the Pope's thoughts."

"His first words were about you, and the letter you sent that reached him in the winter."

"He read it?" asked Lukasz.

"Here's my evidence. He held the folded letter in his hand, and did not open it, and quoted the entire thing to me."

Tears came to Lukasz's eyes. The Pope had read and *memorized* his letter.

"I will not bore you with the rest of our conversation," said Fra Angelico.

Which Lukasz took to mean, I am forbidden by the Holy Spirit to tell you any more about my conversation with the Holy Father. Fra Angelico never wavered, once such a decision was made.

"I will tell you his instruction to me, if you like."

Lukasz smiled. This is why Fra Angelico was here.

"The Holy Father is Christ's vicar to all the world—even to people in places where laws and false clergy believe that they, and not the Pope, rule the people's faith."

"Nobody rules anybody's faith," said Lukasz mildly. "If it *is* faith, it is held in a free heart which has chosen to follow the Redeemer."

"It is hard to find people who hold that opinion, inside and outside the Church."

Lukasz nodded. "I sometimes fear that my opinion is shared by so few that I will be labeled a heretic."

"Not while I am alive," said Fra Angelico.

"What was the Holy Father's decision?"

"He hopes that you will continue ministering to the people with Gifts and strive to protect them from the Protestants of England."

"I wish more of the Povo Jeitoso could make their way to Iberia."

"The Pope has heard your wish, and here is his hope: That you will go to a land filled with people faithful to Mother Church, who are persecuted and oppressed, and who even now are being purged of all the known . . . Jeitosos?"

"Jeitoso. It means 'one who has a way with things.'"

"What the Americans call 'knacks,'" said Fra Angelico. "Or so I'm told."

"The Americans are as bad as the English," said Lukasz.

"You are underinformed, my friend. New England is full of purifying Protestants, who have driven out or driven into hiding most of their 'Jeitosos.' But where do the ones who are driven out go?"

"Not England, I'm reasonably sure."

"They go west. There is word, I am told, of a place called Crystal City, where a great magician takes them in and protects them."

"A great magician?"

"So I am told. He is called a Maker."

"Only God is Creator," said Lukasz.

"Amen," said Fra Angelico. "I report to you what I have heard. What matters is this: There is a place in the world where the Povo Jeitoso can go and find safety, at least for now."

"Besides here in Portugal?"

"My dear friend, you know that the Portuguese are as frightened of the Gifted as anybody else. How long will this be a refuge?"

Lukasz bowed his head. He worried and prayed about this many times a day.

"Lukasz, the Holy Father told me that he would not be disappointed to learn that you had moved your ministry to that most oppressed island."

"Ireland," said Lukasz

"I believe you already know English," said Fra Angelico.

"As well as I know Portuguese," said Lukasz, "but not as well as I know Latin."

"Ireland will be dangerous for you. Catholic priests are anathema there, and are invariably killed. The Father hopes that you will be willing to travel incognito as long as you can, lest the heretics defeat your mission before it begins."

Lukasz nodded. "I will do this thing. If it is my last mission, so be it. I pray that the Holy Mother will plead for my mission. And Santiago—"

"Pray all you wish when I'm gone. For you need a boost in your authority, to give you precedence over any of our clergy who think they should be in charge of your mission."

Lukasz could not imagine any advance in his station that would not hinder rather than help him. Bishop? Cardinal? Although without a bishopric of his own, he would be as much of a mendicant as Angelico. But if he *was* granted a bishopric, he would have to find a vicar to govern it in his absence.

"He isn't going to burden you with a frivolous ordination," said Fra Angelico, "but instead, he gave me this authority for you."

He pulled out a paper from his small bag. Papers. Three of them, sealed by the Holy Father.

Angelico handed him the one addressed to him. Lukasz pulled it open gently, so that the seal was lifted off the paper unbroken. The purport of the letter was instantly clear. "He makes me an inquisitor?"

"With authority in Ireland and England, as you need. All clergy are to respect your office and obey you. No one in all the Church outranks you on this mission except the Holy Father himself."

"But . . . an Inquisition in a land where the Church is heretical?"

"In the past, Inquisitions have purified the Church by removing faithless deceivers who posed a danger to the Church."

"Tortured and wrung confessions from people that I believe were sometimes, perhaps usually, innocent," said Lukasz.

"The Holy Father said, 'Who better to entrust with this deadly power but one who has long opposed the Inquisition as an episode of shame in Iberia?' "

"I have never spoken to him of . . . my views."

"You have never spoken of them to me, either," said Fra Angelico. "But I have seen what I have seen, and so have others. You openly associate with Conversos, as if you trusted their conversion from Jewry to Christianity."

"Because I do, unless they give me reason to doubt them, which none has ever done."

"These things reach the Holy Father's ears, from those who hate you, hoping the information will lead to your downfall."

Lukasz brandished the letter of appointment. "Is this meant to be my downfall?"

"When he hears stories from your enemies, the Holy Father wisely consults your friends. I told him that your enemies were absolutely right about your beliefs, but that I thought they proved you to be a better Christian than any of them."

"So he entrusts an inquisitorial mission to an opponent of inquisitions," said Lukasz.

"Your inquisition," said Fra Angelico, "is to examine Povo Jeitoso and determine whether or not they are heretics or witches. Everyone expects that the auto-da-fé will always find guilt, so when you return verdict after verdict of innocence, as the Holy Father expects you will, then the faithful Irish will not join with the English in denouncing such people as witches."

"I imagine that some of the Irish will help protect them."

"By traveling to Ireland and asking for the help of the faithful, you will put them all in danger of death," said Fra Angelico. "They are Irish, so this circumstance will only make them more determined to help you and keep you and the Jeitoso safe."

"You know the Irish?" asked Lukasz.

"I was born in the land of Saint Padraic."

"And do you speak Irish?"

"My mother fled the country before I had time to learn the local language. Your Poland is a faithful Catholic land, even though it has no legal existence as a nation. That will not always be the case, just as the oppression of the Irish Church will not last forever."

"Is this account of your childhood true?"

"As much as possible," said Fra Angelico.

"The better I know you," said Lukasz, "the less I know."

"Such a paradox," said Fra Angelico. "Such a mystery."

"Please tell the Holy Father that I accept this burden."

"I will not be going anywhere near Rome in the near future. He will know you accept the mission when he hears that someone in Bretagne helped you slip into Ireland unobserved. He does not need *me* to tell him who you are and what you do."

"How will I find the faithful in Ireland, if they risk death just to know that I'm there?"

"The English have imposed on the Irish a church called 'The Church of Ireland,' which is merely a part of the heretic Church of England. For almost two centuries the Irish ignored this heretic church. Forced to pay tithes to the Church of Ireland, the people have long hated every false bishop and false priest that lives from those tithes."

"This saddens me, of course," said Lukasz.

"Recently, instead of trying to convert stubborn Irishmen to their heretic church, the ministers of the Church of Ireland have started persecuting the witches and sorcerers of Ireland."

"So I heard, from Jeitoso Irish who have made their way to me," said Lukasz.

"The Irish have ignored all such nonsense about witches in the past," said Fra Angelico, "but under the constant haranguing of the English ministers, many Irish have begun to denounce so-called 'witches' and turn them over to the Church of Ireland for punishment."

"The real Church of Ireland is the Roman Catholic Church," said Father Lukasz.

"You spent time in England as a young priest?" asked Fra Angelico.

"I was sent covertly into England, having memorized a long list of reliable households that had a hiding place and a few good meals for priests who came and gave Mass, baptized babies, and prayed for the souls of those who suffer," said Father Lukasz.

"Don't be modest. You speak English like a native."

"I haven't spoken it in years," said Lukasz. "But yes, if I ever sounded foreign I would have been arrested."

"Good," said Fra Angelico. "Now, when you learn it again, you can acquire the Irish lilt, for no one speaks that heretical language more sweetly than the Irish."

"I look forward to my trip to Ireland," said Father Lukasz, "where I will find many loyal Catholics to shelter me while I . . . minister to the Povo Jeitoso."

"Is that what you will do, now that your assignment in Portugal is completed?" asked Fra Angelico.

"I may attempt to establish a liaison with the Bishop of Dublin or some other heretic luminary," said Lukasz. "I may suggest to him that the Irish people are likely to be far less rebellious if the so-called witches among them are not killed, but instead are given passage to America, where witches go about without anyone trying to call them back to Christ."

"What a lovely idea," said Fra Angelico. "You would be blessing the people with Jeitos, promoting peace between the Irish and their English overlords, helping the exiles find their way safely to their promised land, and helping the Holy Father avoid the painful dilemma of either seeming to agree with the English hatred of witches, or seeming to sponsor these satanic creatures with other-worldly power."

"Do you think, then, that the Holy Father would approve of my taking such a costly journey upon myself?" said Lukasz, holding up his letter of appointment.

"I am sure that you will find that the angels of heaven will bless you and help you meet your needs," said Fra Angelico. "Not ravens, but human friends will feed you and speed you on your way."

"I know you don't see the future, my dear friend," said Father Lukasz, "but still, I seek your guidance. How long do you think I should take to wrap up my affairs in Lisbon before taking ship to Ireland?"

For the first time in all this conversation, Fra Angelico turned toward Father Lukasz, rested a hand on his shoulder, and looked him in the eye. "Oh, my friend, when I got here I was surprised to discover that you had not already gone."

Father Lukasz responded to Fra Angelico's warm and loving smile. Lukasz understood his instructions from the Pope. He was to go to Ireland, help to support good Irish Catholics who happened to have knacks, and enter into a secret agreement with the Church of Ireland to punish witches only with exile. Meanwhile, the Vatican would supply him with funds to help finance the exiles and get them safely across the Atlantic Ocean.

In all of this, he was to pretend that he chose this work only out of love for the Savior and his Irish disciples, and no one commanded him to do it, because it would not be good if rumors were to spread about the Pope once again sending Jesuit spies into the British Isles to stir up rebellion, treason, and papistry among the subjugated people of Ireland.

But at great need, he had his letter of appointment as Inquisitor of the British Isles to prove that he was not just a wandering priest causing trouble.

More troublesome was the idea of somehow winning the trust of the people with knacks. Why should they look for anything but woe from the Inquisition?

If the mission had been easy and simple, it would not have been such an honor for him to be sent.

The Pope would open the doors that were within his earthly power to open. God himself would need to make the rest of his journey prosperous and clear. Expect miracles, Fra Angelico had once said to him. Greatest gifts come to those who need them and have the faith to *expect* them.

By the time Lukasz got to the door that led into the house, he turned and saw that Fra Angelico was already gone. How he had gotten over the wall, and how he would get back over, was the mendicant's business, not Lukasz's.

The housekeeper asked, "Should I lay another place for the visitor?"

"He has already moved on," said Lukasz.

"Unfed? Are we so inhospitable in this house?"

"To eat at our ample table would feel like failure to the mendicant. He will search out a meal among the poor, and leave his blessing with them when they pray over the food."

The housekeeper raised her eyebrows. "The miracle of loaves and fishes?"

"I haven't heard such a story from a reliable source," said Lukasz, "but knowing the dear mendicant, I would not be surprised if, from time to time, a poor family's meal turned to a feast after his prayer."

The housekeeper smiled. Lukasz knew that she treasured the idea of miracles in these modern times. "Godspeed the mendicant," said the housekeeper.

"God already does," said Lukasz, "but your prayer will help him on his way."

9

Blight

ALVIN WALKED INTO the potato field with Kweeva Maloney, watching as she bent down and showed him plants whose leaves were turning brown. "It's not just my own plot, it's all the neighbors', too."

Alvin reached down and broke off the stem of the potato plant. He sniffed it, examined it, stroked it—none of which had anything to do with his real study of the plant. Instead, he had his doodlebug scooting through the stems and leaves of the living plant, and on down into the ground, where the tubers grew.

"Mrs. Maloney," said Alvin, "I don't think you understand how terrible this plague is. Please dig up some of the potatoes."

"No, it's too early! We need them to reach full grown before we harvest!"

"There will be no harvest in this field, Mrs. Maloney," said Alvin. "Dig up the root."

She did not go back for a spade. Instead, she knelt in the dirt and plunged her hands into the loamy soil. In a moment, she pulled out a spud that was covered with bluish, purplish mold.

Alvin took the potato from her hand, and using his own knack, he caused it to split right in half, though he pretended to exert some force to break it. What with the gathering talk of witches, he didn't need to have rumors of his powers spreading beyond the fact that sometimes he could heal folks.

That brought him entry into many houses, but kept the witch-hunters from the Church of Ireland from going in search of him.

Inside the potato, where the white flesh should have been, there were streaks and seams of brown, soft rot.

Mrs. Maloney gave what could have been a moan or a cry or a sob. While she did, Alvin was studying the mold as deeply as only he could. He sensed that this blight was alive, that it propagated in the wet environment of an Irish potato field, that it would not stop. But when the plant was gone, the mold would also go, because it left no spores in the soil.

"I'm sorry, but you'll get no edible potatoes from this field," said Alvin.

"Can't you do anything? They say you can heal the sick."

"These potato plants are sick indeed," said Alvin, "but it's not a disease that I can work with. It's a blight, a living thing that feeds off the leaves and flesh of the potato, and yet it's also made of many living things together, so that killing a thousand of them still leaves ten thousand to keep spreading the blight." He was reasonably sure that he was right.

"I have potatoes in yon corner that show no signs of this," said Mrs. Maloney, somewhere between hope and desperation.

"We'll examine them. Any that aren't blighted, you must dig up now and store in a dry place."

Mrs. Maloney gave a bitter laugh. "You do know that we're in Ireland, don't you? Even our dry places are damp."

"As dry as you can make it," said Alvin. "And still no surety that the blight isn't in them, lying in wait till next year's planting."

"And these? What do we do, burn the field?"

"In America, where it's much dryer, the fields might burn, but your field would no more than smolder, I think," said Alvin. "And fire isn't the solution. Every sick plant must be dug up, to the last root, and taken to a stony place and a bonfire built over it so that every vestige of every plant—root, fruit, stem, and flower—is consumed."

Mrs. Maloney took to weeping in earnest now. Alvin took her shoulder and guided her into the house where her five children, one for every two years of her marriage, looked at her in awe.

"Did you say a bad word to her?" asked the oldest, a nine-year-old girl named Rosheen.

"I try never to say bad words," said Alvin.

"Bad words make her cry."

Alvin nodded. "So do failing potato plants," said Alvin. "Hard times are coming."

Rosheen looked at him in apparent puzzlement. "All times is hard, Mr. Alvin."

"Harder times," said Alvin.

"Will we have no food for the next year?" asked Rosheen.

Alvin was both pleased and saddened that she was already so aware of the cycles of life in this country. "Only what you can buy. There'll be no potatoes this year, not in these parts."

Now the three-year-old boy piped up. "I know who did it! Witches!" he cried out.

"There are some who are going to say that, Adam," said Alvin. "But they don't know what they're talking about. There's no witch in all the world who knows how to make a curse like this blight. And you'll see—those they call witches will be hungry long with everybody else. What witch would make a curse that starves his own family?"

"A stupid one?" asked Rosheen.

"Hush this nonsense about witches," said Alvin. He did not say: Your mother would be among the first to be arrested, tried, and slain for witchery, since she has a powerful knack for keeping water from quite reaching a boil, or from boiling over—very useful in the kitchen. It was a knack that wasn't really visible, yet most of the neighbors had the saying, "Safe as a stew over Kweeva's fire." Neighbors lived in each other's kitchens, day in and day out, swapping gossip, child-tending, nursing, and cooking. Smart women could not help but notice how disaster-free the Maloney kitchen was.

"What about last year's potatoes?" asked Rosheen. "Are they going to be sick, too?"

"Let's go see," said Alvin.

Rosheen led him to a stone-lined room that opened into the kitchen. "It's warm all winter in here," she explained, "and it keeps them fairly dry."

Alvin bent over to reach into the potato bin. He pulled out many and examined them inside and out, before he said, "I see no blight on any of these," said Alvin. "Doesn't mean it can't come later, but it's not here now."

"So we're safe to eat them?"

Again, Alvin was impressed at how much the little girl seemed to understand. Was there some knack in this? Was she seeing these concerns in her mother's mind? In Alvin's? Or was she merely an attentive girl, with no knack beyond cleverness?

"Until your mother says not," answered Alvin. Then he left to go meet his traveling companions at the pub in Ballycarra, a good stiff walk that would warm him up on such a chilly day.

This had been a prosperous family, complete with an indoor kitchen with a coal stove and a chimney, and a tiled roof instead of thatch. They had every reason to expect that with hard work, they'd get more and more ahead, save up money to dower their daughters and apprentice their sons. Their absentee landlord didn't mind what they did as long as he got his bushels of potatoes every year.

What about this year? They would not be able to pay their rent. Would he evict them, because a disease came upon the potatoes? Or would he forgive their rent so they could remain on the land, perhaps plant a different crop? In his house in London or some country estate, would he even know what was happening on his Irish holdings? His agent here in Ireland would know, but would the landlord believe what he reported, or assume that the agent was getting kickbacks, or lying to cover up his own theft of rents?

I should go to London and see, thought Alvin.

And then the smarter part of his brain, the part that his wife, Peggy, had educated, thought: The most powerful Maker in the world goes to the country that is most eager to catch people doing "witchcraft" so they can be imprisoned or killed? What part of that is wise?

No part of it. But wise or not, he figured that was right likely to be the course he had to follow before this all worked out.

"What will we do, sir?" asked Rosheen.

"The best you can," said Alvin.

Rosheen glared at him fiercely. "Don't I deserve an answer, sir?"

"If I had an answer," said Alvin, "I would tell it to you. I'd tell it to all your neighbors, too, and the government."

Mrs. Maloney spoke bitterly from the corner. "Government cares nothing about us. Potatoes all die, they'll raise taxes, sure. And landlords will raise the rents."

"Talk to your neighbors," said Alvin. "They won't have a solution, either, because I think there is none. But somehow you have to stay alive. Everybody has some potatoes stored, I reckon."

Rosheen said, "Yes," as Mrs. Maloney nodded.

"Whatever you have, if you put it all together and then share it out in fair amounts, you can make it through winter, I think."

"And then in the spring, with nothing to plant?" asked Mrs. Maloney.

"I can't see the future. But if this blight affects all Ireland, how can the government fail to act?"

"Parliament off in London will debate for a year and a half," said Mrs. Maloney, "and count themselves lucky at how many of us problematic Irishmen have starved to death."

Alvin nodded. He was no expert on English government, but he did know that if there was a pro-Irish faction in the House of Commons, they had kept their heads down and their mouths shut for a good long time. "I can't contradict you," said Alvin. "It would be wicked of them to do nothing, but it would also be the lazy thing to do, and the cheap thing, and between wickedness, laziness, and parsimony, I do think you can account for the majority of lawmakers."

"And then what?" asked Rosheen. "Rise up in rebellion?"

"Putting down Irish revolts will always get approved in Parliament," said Mrs. Maloney.

"Starving people don't make good rebels," said Alvin. "They can't march far. They're too weak to fight when battle comes."

"How do you know anything about it?" asked Mrs. Maloney, bitterness in her voice now.

"I've walked a long way, and I've had my starving times," said Alvin. "And anyone with a brain knows that if you wait till you've run out of bread or potatoes, it's too late for a fight."

"Can anyone in America help us?" asked Rosheen.

"Maybe the King in Camelot could send some food, though they mostly grow tobacco and cotton there, and if they tried to bring ships to any Irish port, I expect the English would send a fleet to sink them."

"Aren't there three nations?" asked Rosheen.

"The king has Catholic sympathies. That's why he doesn't rule from London. I think you might have your best chance there, if he gets the word in time. New England is more Puritan than England, and I think Irishmen would not be welcomed in Boston."

"And the middle part?" asked Rosheen. "The United States part?"

Alvin grinned. "You've had some good schooling," he said.

"Keep your praise, sir, and answer me, I beg."

"You're not a beggar, Rosheen," said Alvin. "I daresay you're a leader. I don't know what the United States would do. They're confused themselves about who they are and who they want to be. But that's where I live, and when I go home, if this blight has not already been solved I'll encourage the United States to send food here."

"And why would they do that?" asked Mrs. Maloney.

"I don't know if they would. But there are good people among them, Christians at heart, who would hear about your plight and try to help."

They stood in silence, looking at the potatoes in the dry cupboard.

"Do you want to know what I think?" asked Rosheen.

"No he doesn't, girl, you've talked too much already," said Mrs. Maloney.

"I think that instead of bringing food to Ireland, we should bring the Irish to the food."

Alvin contemplated the girl for a good while. "That's wiser than any thought I had in *my* head," he said. "Let me see what can be done, one way or another."

"'Let me see' is how grownups tell children to mind their own business," said Rosheen.

"That's enough out of you, rude creature!" cried Mrs. Maloney. She jumped up and made as if to catch Rosheen by an arm and beat her with her other hand, but Alvin caught her wrist and sent calmness into her body, feelings of peace. Feelings of love for Rosheen.

"I don't mind," said Rosheen. "She'll only beat me after you leave, anyway."

"Liar!" The word came out as a hiss.

"Your mother knows what a treasure you are," said Alvin. "And I know, too. When I say, 'Let me see,' I mean, I will look into all these possibilities and find out which ones look the most feasible. It's expensive to transport an entire nation across the Atlantic, but maybe the whole nation doesn't have to go. Just enough that those left behind can survive on whatever food they have."

Rosheen nodded, but Alvin could sense that she still didn't believe his promise. "Is the blight only on potatoes?" she asked. "If we could find another crop, would it also die?"

"Where do we find another crop!" demanded her mother. But she made no move to strike Rosheen.

"What did you grow before potatoes?" asked Alvin.

"It's always been potatoes!" cried Mrs. Maloney. "You're in Ireland, sir!"

"Potatoes came from South America," said Alvin. "A scholar I trust has told me that there are three stories about English voyagers who might have brought potatoes to Ireland in the 1580s—Raleigh, Drake, and Cavendish—but that scholar believes that the potato first came to this land by way of Spain, which had been growing it for years."

"Your scholar is a fool," said Mrs. Maloney.

"As are we all," said Alvin, "compared with the knowledge of God and the angels, but we make do with such wisdom as we can gather. Does anyone in this island grow wheat, for instance?"

"How would I know?" asked Mrs. Maloney.

"I'll inquire, then, from people who do know," said Alvin. "You can be sure, Rosheen, that I'll be back not long from now, to give you better answers to your questions."

"You'll never be back," said Mrs. Maloney.

This was said glumly, and barely audibly. Was it a prophecy? Or a warning?

Alvin didn't bother to answer. "Good day to you, ladies. And give my best wishes to Mr. Maloney, when he returns."

Rosheen spoke, "Da is on his way to England to get work so he can save money to buy food."

Mrs. Maloney did not contradict her daughter. Alvin nodded at the mother and the daughter, and glanced at the other four children in various stages of lethargy around the room. Children should have enough energy to play.

Alvin put his hat on his head and stepped out the door into the grassy yard. It was a well-tended place, with many vegetables growing in carefully weeded beds. Alvin wondered if he was seeing the work of the parents, or if Rosheen looked after these plots, which were likely to provide the only sustenance for the family before long.

It didn't matter to him now, he told himself. Rosheen had some kind of knack, as Mrs. Maloney did. But Alvin doubted that either would consider herself to be a witch—that had to do with curses, like this blight, or babies getting sick. If the accusation was made, however, they would surely be tried and convicted by the Church of Ireland.

Alvin could still see the Maloney house from the brow of a hill when he heard, then saw, riders trotting their horses along the track before him and behind him. Why would they trot? he wondered. It was a brutal gait for a rider, and indeed these men were all standing in their stirrups to avoid the pounding of their nether regions.

Alvin stopped and stepped aside to let both pairs of riders pass. Instead they drew up and stopped near him. "Are you looking for me?" asked Alvin.

"We are if you're the American called Alvin Miller," said their leader.

"Can you tell me your name, sir, since you seem to know mine?"

"I'm Sergeant Porter of the Dublin Guard," he said. "And you are invited to come with us."

"I'm sorry that I don't have a horse, gentlemen," said Alvin. "If I come with you, won't I slow you down?"

"We'll walk our horses slowly, so you can keep up," said Porter.

The other men smiled a little, and one of them snickered. Alvin was pretty sure this would mean a very fast walk for him.

"And if I decline your invitation, because I have other places to go?" asked Alvin.

"Then you'll be bound over for resisting arrest, and brought to Dublin in chains."

"So you're arresting me," said Alvin. "On what charge?"

"We're inviting you," said Porter.

"But if I decline, I'm resisting arrest?" asked Alvin.

"He's pretty clever, for an American," said one of the other riders.

Meanwhile, Alvin realized that instead of going to England, as he had halfway planned, a visit to Dublin, to the witch-finders of the Church of Ireland, might serve his purposes as well or better.

"I'll tell you what," said Alvin. "I'll come along with you, even though Dublin is a long walk from here, provided you tell me the charges, and who my accuser might be?"

"The charge might have been witchcraft," said Porter, "if we were arresting you. But at present we only have suspicions about you, based on stories told by some of the people around here."

"What acts of witchery do they say I've committed here?" asked Alvin.

"You'll hear those accusations in Dublin."

"That will be far from my accusers, won't it," said Alvin. "Will they come and testify?"

"We have their written declarations," said Porter. He took a packet of papers from inside his coat. Alvin reached for them. Porter started to pull them out of his reach.

"Sergeant Porter," said Alvin, "I may be an American, but I'm not so stupid as to tear up witnesses' statements in front of four officers of the court."

Porter reluctantly handed down the packet.

Alvin untied the ribbon that bound the pages and handed it up to Porter. Then Alvin unfolded the papers and read the name at the top of the first sheet.

The name was Kweeva Maloney.

"I just came from Mrs. Maloney's house," said Alvin. "She did not accuse me of anything."

"She's afraid of you, as all good people are afraid of witches," said Porter.

"And here I thought good people would have the protection of the Lord," said Alvin.

"They do," said Porter. "We are his instruments in gathering the tares from amid the wheat."

"This tare is curious about how you were able to get an affidavit from the Maloney house so quickly after I left it."

"Not clever after all," said Porter to the others. Again, chuckles and smiles. "We've been gathering these affidavits for days. And when Mrs. Maloney signed her affidavit, she told me that she expected you to come by today, after the hour of the noon meal."

"Her prediction came true," said Alvin. "Doesn't that make her a witch?"

Porter frowned. "We don't accept accusations from the accused, except under questioning."

"Meaning torture?"

"This is not Spain," said Porter. "And we are not the Inquisition. We are officers of the Lord Protector, acting under the instructions of the Bishop of Dublin, head of the Church of Ireland under the authority of the Lord Protector."

"Thank you for explaining the difference," said Alvin.

At a signal from Porter, the three other men dismounted. Two of them approached Alvin from the sides, while the third brought a coil of rope from his saddle.

"You won't need to bind me," said Alvin.

"Not your decision," said Porter.

The two men took hold of Alvin's arms. Despite not having worked a forge in months, Alvin's arms were still massive, and neither man could wrap a hand around an upper arm. Alvin also made the fabric of his cloth coat slippery, and their hands slid away.

"Hold him," said the man with the rope.

Alvin looked the fellow in the eyes. "I don't need holding. I give my word that I'll keep up and won't run away."

"What is the oath of a witch?" asked the rope-holder.

"I don't know," said Alvin, "on account of my not being a witch."

The other two men, meanwhile, had tried twice more to get hold of Alvin's arms, and one of them had seized his collar, but still their hands slid away. They looked at their hands dumfounded, as if trying to see some grease that made them slippery.

"You should have brought stronger men," said Alvin. "Or perhaps their consciences rebel against taking captive an innocent man."

"You *will* have the rope," said the man who had formed a lariat at the end of it.

"Looks like a stout rope," said Alvin.

The man cast the lariat over Alvin's head.

Alvin did not move, did not dodge or shrink away. But the lariat, instead of looping his head, slid off one shoulder and hit the ground. Now the other two men snickered openly.

"This is witchcraft," declared rope-man.

"It will be reported to the prelate," said Porter.

The lariat flew again. This time it slid off Alvin's other shoulder. "In America," said Alvin, "we have a lot of men who can set a lariat on a running calf."

The men stood there, regarding him. Porter got off his horse and joined them. He held out his hand toward Alvin. Alvin took it. They gripped each other, not tightly, but not loosely either.

"Are you a man who regards an oath as sacred?" asked Porter.

"If I took that oath freely, and not under threat," said Alvin.

"Do you swear by God that you will—"

Alvin interrupted him. "The Lord said, Swear not by heaven, but let your communications be yea and nay."

"You'll swear by God or you'll wear the rope," said Porter mildly.

"God hears all things," said Alvin. "He hears me promise you that I will not try to escape you, and that I will match your pace all the way to Dublin, and I will submit to being interviewed by your prelate."

"So God is your witness," said Porter.

"As he is witness of all the deeds and words of men," said Alvin.

"Just so you know," said Sergeant Porter, "these men are all very skilled with the weapons they carry. If you should change your mind about your promise, it will not bring you freedom."

"I am always free," said Alvin. "But thank you for acquainting me with their skill, since they're bound to be better at shooting than they are at arm-grabbing and head-roping."

Porter walked to his horse and mounted it. The other men did as well.

"Well," said Alvin, "are we going north along this track, or south?"

Porter looked both ways, as if he hadn't yet decided. "I don't want to walk you to death," he said.

"Don't worry, you can't," said Alvin.

"So we'll go north to where a spur of railroad has just been built."

"Do they have seats to accommodate your horses?" asked Alvin.

"We did not ride the horses from Dublin," said Porter. "We requisitioned them from the fort at Sligo."

"A fort? But surely we are in the United Kingdom of England, Scotland, and Ireland. Why would there be a fort in this land, as if it were a conquered and occupied country?"

"It holds an arsenal," said Porter, with a bit of tension in his voice.

"Why do you answer him, Sergeant?" asked rope-man.

"He's a courteous man," said Alvin, "and I am not a prisoner."

The man wheeled his horse and started walking it northward along the track. Alvin fell in behind him, walking briskly. "I can go faster than this," Alvin offered.

"It's a long trek," said Porter, whose horse was right behind him.

"I'm a good walker," said Alvin.

Porter walked his horse a little faster, passing Alvin. Then he broke into a trot, and the other men did likewise.

Alvin jogged along, keeping pace easily. Green though the countryside of Ireland was, there was scant Greensong to help Alvin run; this once forested land had been fully cleared of all but a few trees. Still, Alvin could feel the life of the place, just as he could now feel the distress of the potato fields, responding to the death that was growing among them. From the blighted potato plants he drew no strength, but from grasses and sheep and moss and lichens he drew, not strength, but a welcoming invisible embrace. We know you, the plants and animals seemed to say. We know you have no harm in you.

It was not the way it was when he practically flew along with the Prophet and other Reds back in America, when he could make prodigious runs without wearying. But it was enough that he kept up with the trotting horses without any strain, and even increased his speed when some of the men, wearying of the trot, took their mounts into a canter. He loped along with them and, feeling a little playful, he increased his speed and passed the cantering horses.

Immediately some of them broke into a gallop to overtake him, and Alvin could hear pistols and carbines coming out of their holsters.

Alvin came to a stop.

Porter came up beside him, berating him from his perch atop the saddle. "What was that!" he demanded. "You gave your word."

"Have I escaped?" asked Alvin. "Or am I right here among you?"

"Then why did you run on ahead?" asked Porter.

"Because I could," said Alvin. "And to show you that you can't wear me down with your pace on horseback. The horses will wear out before I do. Look how they're lathering already, with only a mile's canter and three rods at a gallop."

"So you're concerned for our horses."

"They serve you," said Alvin, "but these creatures belong to themselves and to God. Of course I'm concerned for them. Aren't you? Don't you feel that you owe them consideration and kind treatment, considering all they do for you?"

"We'll walk the horses from here," said Porter. "Nobody needs to wear anybody out on this journey."

"I'm glad to hear it," said Alvin. "Walking will allow us to enjoy this beautiful countryside. I only regret that we're not in a place where we can have a view of the sea. The sight of water—even water that you can't drink—refreshes the soul."

When night fell, Alvin picked a dry place, sheltered from the western breeze by a hillock, and lay down.

The horses gathered around him.

"What now?" asked Porter.

"It's many miles till the next inn," said Alvin, "and here we have soft grass, plenty for the horses to eat, and a brook not far off when it's time to drink. Isn't this a good place to sleep?"

Porter and the other men looked at each other.

"I extend my oath, of my own free will. I will not run any farther than I need to go to micturate in privacy."

"Micatur—"

"Void my bladder. Or, to use biblical language, to piss."

"So if we see you wander off . . ."

"Follow me if you want," said Alvin. "You won't see anything unusual, because even if witches existed, I've never heard that they don't urinate and defecate like all God's creatures."

"What are we supposed to eat out here?" demanded Rope-man.

"Whatever you brought with you," said Alvin. "Or are you completely unprepared for the task at hand?"

"I have some bread and cheese in my saddlebag," said one of the men.

"So you have a loaf," said Alvin, "and we can count the cheese as fishes. Not feeding five thousand, or even three thousand. Just five grown men, and I don't eat much."

"And none of us is Jesus," said Porter.

"Don't I know it!" said Alvin. "But Jesus set the example and prayed over the food. You know how to pray, don't you, being a representative of the Church of Ireland as you are?"

Porter frowned a little. He wasn't glad that Alvin had seen through his claims and realized he represented no government authority, but the Church of Ireland alone. But Alvin thought it was better to allow Porter to lie a little less, which would be good for his soul.

Porter said grace over the bread and cheese, and then divided it out. Alvin admired him for giving him an equal share, and did not refuse it, though he really wasn't very hungry. The reward of Porter's generosity would be to have the gift accepted and used, so Alvin ate with the energy and roughness he thought they probably expected from an American.

Except for Porter, though, they ate as roughly as Alvin. And Porter's slower pace didn't amount to fastidiousness. They all ate like men, and Alvin felt good that he could use his makery to extend the bread and cheese so that all of them were truly satisfied with this supper.

10

Alvin had expected to be taken to the cathedral in Dublin, or at least to some fine building, so he was surprised when Porter led the party down ever narrower streets and past ever shabbier buildings, until he stopped and dismounted, tying up his horse's reins at a hitching post in front of what had to be a tavern. The other men dismounted and tied up their horses, and sure enough, Porter led the way inside.

Alvin made no comment, even though the tavern was even more slovenly than it had looked from the outside. This was a place that sold alcohol, yes, but it also provided solace for lonely men, renting them the use of a woman's body for a half-hour. Alvin had some idea of the level of desperation that would bring a woman to such a trade. To be a wife to one man was hard enough, even without adding children into the mix; but to be a nonce wife to a multitude, at times of their choosing, seemed unnatural and unbearable to Alvin. In such places as this, he kept picturing one of his sisters dwelling in an upstairs room. Even to imagine it made him feel like weeping—or raging.

But he calmed his temper. Of course he had the power to make this whole building crumble into dust—but to do it so gradually that not a soul would be injured. What then? How would these women earn their bread? Would there suddenly be a spinning mill to hire them? Or would they only find another place to uncover themselves for lascivious men? The drinkers would find a place to drink; the fornicators and adulterers would easily find women to meet their needs.

And this was where the Bishop of Dublin held court?

Only at night, Alvin concluded. When he could do things that exceeded his legal authority.

To Alvin's relief, Porter did not lead him upstairs, where the sole occupation was harlotry. Instead, waving away the other three, who headed directly for the bar, Porter led him through a labyrinthine corridor that Alvin calculated to have taken them not one but two buildings over. They would not meet, then, in the tavern itself, but in a place that visitors only reached through the tavern.

Porter rapped lightly on a door that looked no different from other doors. Instead of anyone answering, the door simply opened. Porter did not step through, but motioned Alvin to do so. The man who had opened the door had a sword at his side, which made him some kind of gentleman or officer.

There was a desk in the dim light at the far side of the room, and behind it sat a man of some age and even more dignity. The bishop, Alvin concluded, and bowed his head in greeting.

The bishop looked at the door guard and said, "Please wait outside until I call."

The guard silently left the room, closing the door softly behind him.

Alvin was tempted to cause the wood of the door to swell, making it impossible to open—or dry it out and shrink it, so the door could not latch and stay closed.

Not a time for mischief. He had done enough with the games he played back in the west part of Ireland, to convince Porter's squad not to try to seize him or tie him.

There was a light rap at the door. The bishop showed no sign of noticing.

Alvin, ever wishing to be polite, said, "Should I open the door, Your Grace?"

The bishop nodded.

The door guard came back in, holding a sheet of paper, and laid it on the bishop's desk. Then, having said no words, he left and again closed the door behind him.

The bishop studied the paper for about a minute. If there was writing on it, Alvin wasn't sure how the man could read anything at all in such dim light. The man was squinting and holding the paper so as to catch the faint light from a high window.

This feels like a dungeon, thought Alvin.

"I see that you led my servants on a merry chase."

"There was no chasing, Your Grace," said Alvin. "I kept up with them, and they kept up with me."

"You walked the whole way?"

"Flying being outside the range of my talents," said Alvin.

The bishop raised an eyebrow. Alvin remembered that in England, they believed witches could fly. He should have curbed his humor.

"I'm a good walker," Alvin explained, "but we kept a pace that did not strain the horses."

"And no rope could hold you," said the bishop.

"The poor fellow wasn't well practiced with the lariat, so he missed. Only twice, but then he gave up."

"And my men could not take hold of your arms."

Alvin shrugged. "I thought they should have been strong enough. You can see for yourself that my arms can easily be held." He extended an arm toward the bishop. "I'm a blacksmith by trade, so maybe my arms were too big around for them to hold."

The bishop looked alarmed for a moment—perhaps he couldn't tell the difference between extending a hand and striking a blow. Then he reached out and took Alvin by the wrist, including the sleeve of his shirt and of his coat. His grip was firm but he was not trying to grip particularly hard. "Pull your arm away from me with the same force you used against the grip of my men."

Alvin shook his head. "I don't know what's written on that paper, but I believe Sergeant Porter is an honest man, and he'll tell you that I made no movement to resist. They simply let go of me, and their hands dropped to their sides."

"You were completely compliant?" asked the bishop.

"I told them that I didn't need to be seized or bound. I gave them my oath that I would not try to escape. And I even found us a place to sleep without having to hunt for an inn along the way. We all slept very well."

"Perhaps I should have you help me find a better bed than the one I have," said the bishop.

"I'm not an expert on beds, Your Grace," said Alvin.

"But you know soft ground when you see it," said the bishop.

"I spent several months with the Reds, Your Grace," said Alvin, "and I learned to look at the ground the way they do."

"So you have been tutored by savages," said the bishop.

"They know the forest," said Alvin, "which still covers much of our part of America. A White could starve to death in a patch of woods where a Red would not only feast, but store up a good amount of food for the morrow."

"You speak their language?"

"I can understand several of their languages," said Alvin, "and say enough in their tongues to avoid needless combat and achieve cooperation."

The bishop nodded. "They don't all speak the same language, then."

"The different tribes and nations speak Nahuatl, Commanche, Shawnee, Apache, Navaho, Cherriky, the languages of the Irrakwa alliance, and others as they've sprung up all over the continent. Rather the way that Germans and Poles and Spaniards and Greeks all have languages of their own."

"But you speak only English and the Red languages?"

"*Some* of the Red languages. The most important of them. And my teacher helped me achieve some small knowledge of French, which I could have used years before when I had to converse with Napoleon, before he achieved high office."

"You met Bonaparte?"

"He would not remember me," said Alvin.

"He has a very good memory," said the bishop, "or so I hear."

"I'm afraid my curiosity is getting the better of me, Your Grace. Surely you had more on your mind than my connections with Reds and Frenchmen when you invited me here to your palace." Alvin let no trace of irony come out in his voice or expression, but the bishop knew he had been mocked and grimaced very slightly.

"If I questioned possible witches out in the open," said the bishop, "then whether I acquitted them or called them guilty, the moment they went outside they would be beaten by the mob, usually to death."

"Then you are charitable to make all such questioning a private matter."

"There's a chair," said the bishop, indicating. "Bring it closer and sit down. You make me weary, standing there."

Alvin fetched the chair. But he sat on it backward, his arms on the back of the chair, his legs astraddle.

The bishop raised his eyebrows and showed a faint smile—Alvin assumed that his rough manner of sitting in the chair amused the bishop. That was what Alvin intended. Peggy had taught him the finest manners, but in this time and place, Alvin thought it better to be seen as a half-wild American. It briefly crossed his mind to offer a stick-pull or chunkey or a wrestling match to the bishop, but it wouldn't be fair to the old fellow, and he would certainly refuse any such contest.

"I've heard you called 'Alvin Maker,'" said the bishop. "Can you tell me why?"

"I've heard that such a name is used, Your Grace, but never to my face. My father is Alvin Miller, and he gave me his same name. I'm proud of it and never looked for another. But some folks call me Alvin Smith, on account of my trade."

"I believe you call your witchery 'knacks,'" said the bishop.

"Every man has a knack at something, at least if he works at it. Every woman, too. They're just better at some jobs than other people are. A friend of mine is an English lawyer, but his real knack is fitting together the staves of a barrel. His kegs and barrels never leak."

"And you don't find that unnatural?" asked the bishop.

"I've watched him make barrels, and I've watched other coopers at their work, and he does exactly what they all do, only perhaps a little slower, and definitely with better results. I don't know how he does it though, not being a cooper myself."

"I've heard that you split a millstone in half without touching it," said the bishop.

Alvin grinned, though inside he was trying to imagine how the bishop could have heard of the incident, since it happened more than two decades ago and there were few witnesses.

As if in answer to Alvin's wondering, there was a rap on the door. Alvin rose to his feet, offering with the look on his face to admit the visitor. The bishop nodded, so Alvin took a stride to reach the door and opened it.

He stood, surprised to recognize the man at the door. It was Philadelphia Thrower, a man who Alvin knew was a servant of the Unmaker himself. Itself. A man who had tried to kill Alvin, or at least planned to.

Thrower recognized Alvin, too, but gave only a moment to regarding him. He came in and set a thin sheaf of papers on the desk, then stood waiting for some kind of response.

The bishop scribbled something at the bottom of every sheet of paper. Alvin looked at the papers, but in the dim light he couldn't read them upside down.

Thrower gathered up the papers and left, closing the door behind him. Alvin immediately sat down, but this time turned the chair around and sat on it in the civilized manner. "How well do you know that man?" asked Alvin.

"He knows *you,*" said the bishop.

"Or so he thinks," said Alvin. "He's Scottish Rite, not Church of England or Ireland."

"In the struggle against Satan, I have found that Presbyterians and Anglicans can work together."

Alvin wanted to say, I have seen Satan and this man was his servant. But he wasn't sure that the Unmaker was actually Satan, and telling the bishop that he had seen Satan would cement his fate. He couldn't do much in Ireland under sentence of death. He would only endanger the people he was here to rescue.

"Reverend Thrower thinks he knows me," said Alvin, "but all he knows are rumors, many of them started by himself. His malice isn't directed only at me, Your Grace. He has worked to promote the Property Rights Crusade, which exists only to protect, promote, and spread the practice of slavery."

"But he's a staunch opponent of witchery," said the bishop.

"It's fairly safe to oppose something that doesn't actually exist," said Alvin. "But slavery does exist, and he promotes it. When it comes to war in America, will you be happy to be on the side of men who promote slavery instead of those who oppose it?"

"I would be surprised if Parliament supported either side, and Ireland will do as London decides."

"So for you, slavery is not a moral matter, but witchery, which is only an accusation, not a fact, you will exert great energy to oppose."

"If it doesn't exist, my opposition will do it no harm," said the bishop mildly.

"But your accusations do great harm. As you said, people brought before you under a charge of witchcraft are treated harshly by the citizens."

"You say witchery doesn't exist," said the bishop, "but for some reason the people fear it and hate it."

"Because the Puritans have spent the past two centuries under the Protectorate teaching the people of these islands to fear witches and hate them and look for pretexts to bring charges against neighbors who annoy them."

"My view is that they can't help but see the workings of dark, satanic magic around them, and bravely try to bring it to an end."

Alvin nodded. "So you want to rid Ireland of witchery, such as it might be."

"You have spoken very politely, Brother Alvin—may I call you that?"

"All men are brothers," said Alvin.

"You have dealt with my observations with poise and calm, without anxiety or fear."

"I am not worried, and I fear nothing."

"Because you think your witching powers will keep you safe," said the bishop.

"Because I believe you to be an honorable man, having had no evidence to the contrary, and an honorable man will not find me guilty of anything."

"This is not a trial," said the bishop, "so there is no question of finding guilt."

"I'm glad to hear it."

"I detect doubt in your voice," said the bishop.

"The fact that Reverend Philadelphia Thrower seems to be in your service causes me to suspect that you are sometimes careless about which witnesses to believe and which to doubt."

"I doubt all the witnesses," said the bishop. "So many of the accusers seem motivated by malice or envy rather than godly service to their fellow beings."

"So you weigh their testimony carefully?"

"I am not a judge. Ecclesiastical courts can inquire, but we have no power to condemn or punish suspected miscreants."

"Not even those who bear false witness?" asked Alvin.

"Brother Alvin," said the bishop, "I can no more be certain of the falsity of an accusation, merely because I suspect that the accuser has a low motive, than I can be certain of the truth of an accusation merely because the witness seems to be a person who genuinely believes in the accusation."

"I've seen enough of courtrooms," said Alvin, "to believe that it is impossible for mortals to know the heart of any other person, and to judge them on their motives is to judge them on what we imagine their motives to be."

"And yet we must have a judicial system, which must do its best to discern truth, falsity, error, prejudice, malice, deception, and, yes, the heart of a witch whose soul belongs to the great enemy of God."

"Do you keep a tally of those who are killed as witches, who were not in fact witches?" asked Alvin.

"How could such a tally be kept?" asked the bishop.

"Doesn't the fact that they were killed suggest that they had no satanic power?" asked Alvin.

"Satan is as treacherous as he is sly and deceptive," said the bishop. "His servants should not be surprised when he abandons them in their hour of need."

Alvin nodded, then smiled.

"It seems that you have judged me," said the bishop.

"Not at all," said Alvin, "except to admire the ease with which you explain away your irrationality in rational ways."

"We are none of us rational, compared to God," said the bishop. "As you said, we have to muddle through with whatever sense we have, and whatever information is conferred upon us by the Holy Ghost."

Alvin nodded. "So the Holy Ghost communes with you."

"And with all whose souls are not trapped behind the walls of Satan's power."

"Yes, always an answer," said Alvin.

"I don't think that my having an answer is proof that my views are incorrect," said the bishop.

"Always an answer that retreats from the brink of declaring yourself an angel of death in the service of the Holy One of Israel."

"Nor any other kind of angel," said the bishop. "Only a man who tries to discern the will of God and does his best to serve God in the position he has placed me in."

Alvin realized that nothing he could say would cause this man to admit the slightest doubt about his war on witchery. "You didn't bring me here to try me, or even to inquire about my supposed witchery."

"I have no need to inquire. Your use of magic is attested by the soldiers who brought you here, and by many affidavits brought from America."

"So why am I here?" asked Alvin. "Captain Porter said there were complaints from the local citizens, including the ones that I counted as my friends. Yet you sent for me before receiving any of their accusations."

"Captain Porter is skilled at turning people's words into much stronger statements than they intended."

"So you disregard any such accusations he relays to you?" asked Alvin.

"I weigh everything in the balance," said the bishop. "Captain Porter is a reliable servant of God. I don't believe he would lead anyone to bear false witness."

Alvin stopped himself from pointing out that the bishop had just stated that Captain Porter did exactly that.

"He kept his oath to *you*," said the bishop.

Alvin bowed his head for a moment, in acknowledgment. Then he said,

"Your Grace, if you have finished with your inquiries, may I make some inquiries of my own?"

"I'm not sure about the propriety of allowing you to question *me*," said the bishop.

"I have no power to compel you to answer," said Alvin. "But if you choose to respond, I would be grateful."

"Ask what you like," said the bishop.

"Your Grace, what if the people accused of witchery were able to leave Ireland permanently? Not to England or Scotland or anywhere on the continent of Europe, but rather to a part of America where nobody treats knackery as a crime or a sin."

"If I understand you, are you asking if my goal is merely to cleanse Ireland, but allow the wickedness to be transferred to a place where wickedness already rules?"

"If we discount the word 'wickedness,' then yes," said Alvin.

"How would this be different from sending them to the fires of hell?" asked the bishop.

"When the Savior was tempted by Satan in the wilderness," said Alvin, "did he slay Satan? Or did he cast him down to his dwelling place in hell?"

"We know he will not slay Satan until the end of time," said the bishop. "But neither does the scripture say he cast Satan down to hell."

Alvin nodded. "I see your wisdom there, Your Grace. Even Milton shows that Satan can freely leave hell and walk upon the Earth, where he tempts and tries the souls of men."

"Milton is not scripture," said the bishop.

"Just as many Catholics believe Dante's Inferno is a faithful representation of hell, so many Puritans believe that Milton has given a faithful representation of the war in heaven between Michael and Lucifer."

"I wish you would not use the term 'Puritan,'" said the Bishop. "That is a name of derision applied to the most fervent Christians by those who gloried in paying no attention to righteousness."

"I intended no derision. In New England, the people generally call themselves and their government 'Puritan' with pride."

"They put you on trial in New England, didn't they," observed the bishop.

"I was acquitted," said Alvin.

"The Devil has many clever lawyers in his employ," said the bishop.

Alvin smiled. "I'm sure he has," said Alvin. "But I have never hired a lawyer who already had such an employer."

"As far as you knew."

"That's a caveat that can be added to almost any statement of fact made by anyone ever," said Alvin. "The sun will rise tomorrow . . . as far as I know. I will someday die and be judged for my sins and forgiven as Christ sees fit—as far as I know."

It was the bishop's turn to smile. "All of us judge according to what we know, or think we know, or know that we do not know but merely believe."

"Back to my question, Your Grace," said Alvin. "Suppose someone were to organize voyages to carry away accused witches to the New World? Would you oppose this?"

The bishop thought for a long moment. "Is it cowardly for me to be attracted to the idea of purging Ireland of witches by such a method, which would make it so that any errors of judgment did not leave blood on the hands of the Irish people?"

"If you're afraid of what people think, how can you make righteous decisions?" asked Alvin. "I think you are afraid only of what God would think of you, and I can't imagine why he would call you a coward."

"Perhaps because I am one," said the bishop. "It's so hard to pass just judgment on yourself. Either I will be too harsh on myself, or too lenient."

"If it is a mistake to permit suspected witches to leave Ireland and go to a land where they will not be condemned, then God can find other ways to punish the unrighteous. But if you set these people up to be killed, then you take the matter out of God's hands."

"Nothing is out of God's hands," said the bishop.

"He has sent back only one man from the dead," said Alvin, "and even he did not stay long or tell us all. So God seems to follow the rule that once people are murdered unjustly, he will not vindicate them by unslaying them."

"Has the word 'unslaying' ever been uttered before?" asked the bishop.

"Because the thing rarely happens," said Alvin, "the word has not been much needed."

"You believe," said the bishop, "that if I turn accused witches over to the unforgiving mob, I am foreclosing God's mercy toward them in this life. But if I let them go, God can take whatever vengeance or make whatever judgment he desires."

"It seems reasonable to me," said Alvin.

"Oh, your logic is sound," said the bishop. "But Jesus said that the devil can quote scripture to promote his wicked plans."

"And yet we all quote scripture, on both sides of every dispute."

"God does not need my permission to do what he will," said the bishop. "He does not wait on me, I wait on him."

"I am having a little trouble deciphering your meaning, Your Grace. But I think you're saying that you will pursue witchery in whatever way you please, and you will not cooperate with my plan of evacuating these supposed witches from Ireland."

"That is a fair summary," said the bishop. "I didn't bring you here to bargain with you for the lives of the darkest sinners."

"That is your privilege," said Alvin. "And in reply, I remind you of Pharaoh, who sent his chariots to prevent the Israelites from crossing the sea to safety."

"The chariots were swallowed up in the sea," said the bishop.

"Nobody uses chariots anymore," said Alvin, "and it is wasteful and unrighteous to kill animals that are only doing as their masters require."

"I'm not sure how to take that," said the bishop. "Are you comparing me to dumb horses?"

"Absolutely not," said Alvin. "I'm comparing you to Pharaoh, and anyone you send against me to the dumb horses who do not deserve to be drowned in pursuit of a foul cause."

The bishop nodded. "You will not attack me, then. But you will destroy anyone I send against you?"

"I won't destroy anybody. I only reminded you of the Book of Exodus because Pharaoh believed he was a god who had the power to decide who should live and who should die, who should be slaves in Egypt and who should live free in another land."

"Your America is the land of slavery."

"The crown lands in the South are the land of slavery. Where I live, no man can buy or sell another."

"Here is my dilemma," said the bishop. "You have sworn to me that you have no powers at all. That the slipperiness of your arms and the impossibility of binding you with rope were completely natural events, and that no satanic power allowed you to cross the breadth of Ireland at the same pace as horsemen. Yet you seem to contradict yourself by implying that any soldiers I send against you will come to grief—specifically, the same fate that met the soldiers of Pharaoh during the Exodus."

"I don't see the contradiction," said Alvin. "Did Moses cause the waters to close over Pharaoh's chariots? Or did God?"

"You think you're Moses?" asked the bishop.

"I think I'm Alvin Miller, Junior, who has never served Satan in his life, and whose talents, such as they are, came as a gift from God."

"Or as the magical result of your being a seventh son of a seventh son," said the bishop.

"We're both grown men here," said Alvin. "You don't believe in childish superstitions, and neither do I."

The bishop said nothing to that.

"I also don't believe that we are not being listened to. You're a careful man, Your Grace, and so I think you have scribes working in a room where every word spoken by us is completely audible. It's quite possible that they are making faithful copies of our words. But what if they believe that it would serve your cause if they were to write down only *my* words, and only the words that can be made to seem as if I am confessing my guilt."

"That is not happening," said the bishop.

"I'm glad to have your witness to that effect," said Alvin. "But will you join with me in a prayer?"

The bishop stiffened.

"I pray to the Heavenly Father," said Alvin, "the God to whom Jesus prayed in the garden of Gethsemane, that if there is anyone transcribing our words spoken in this room, then words faithfully taken down in their right context will be preserved. But if there are words selected deceptively, or altered from what either of us truly said, may God strike out those words, without causing any harm to the scriveners. In the name of Jesus. Amen."

Alvin looked at the bishop. "Is that not a prayer to which you can add your amen, spoken with the authority of the Bishop of Dublin?"

"I don't take my religious instruction from you," said the bishop.

"I'm only asking," said Alvin, "if you can say amen to those words spoken to God. If you can't, then don't forswear yourself. If you can, though, I beg you to add your faith to mine."

The bishop hesitated, glowering at Alvin until he finally looked away. He looked to the right, toward the secret room in which Alvin knew three scribes had been working the whole time, taking down words—but not all the words.

"Amen," said the bishop, clearly and firmly.

Immediately Alvin caused the letters on their papers to burst into flame. He made sure none of their sleeves or collars caught on fire. He also made sure that not just the top sheet, but all the sheets with writing on them, were burnt, while the blank sheets were kept from any flame at all. Fire was an element that Alvin was comfortable with; how could it be otherwise, with his years of training and practice as a smith?

From the hidden chamber there came muffled shrieks and a tumult of furniture being overturned.

Alvin could see, using his doodlebug, that all three scribes had fled the room. He immediately quenched the fires, since the written-on pages had already been consumed.

"Your Grace, I hear a sort of noise," said Alvin. "Is it something you need to attend to?"

"No," said the bishop.

"Isn't it possible that it was God's response to our prayer?" asked Alvin.

"Your prayer," said the bishop.

"When you said amen, Your Grace, it became our prayer, isn't that right?" asked Alvin. "Your amen was an honest one, wasn't it?"

"Yes," said the bishop.

"How could it be otherwise, from a man who has such trust within the Church?"

The bishop glowered even more. "I'm done with you," he said.

"I'm not sure what that means," said Alvin. "Are you dismissing me to return to the west of Ireland, without hindrance or harm?"

"Do you always speak in this high-sounding way? I thought you were a frontier bumpkin."

"I was educated by a fine schoolmistress who taught me to speak like a gentleman, in spite of the poverty of my family. Will I be able to go on my way unmolested?"

"Of course," said the bishop.

"Let me expand my question. Is there a mob of Irish citizens outside, waiting to punish me for being accused of witchcraft?"

The bishop said nothing.

Alvin waited.

"I do not assemble mobs or spur them on," said the bishop.

"Is there a way out of this place that will not cause me to emerge from a brothel to reach the street?"

"Yes," said the bishop.

"I pray that you or one of your servants will lead me by that passage, to a place where no one is waiting to punish me."

"That is not my responsibility," said the bishop. "I have not set anyone there to harm you."

"Can you promise that none of your associates have done so, either? Reverend Philadelphia Thrower has set traps for me before."

"I cannot guarantee your safety," said the bishop. "Few of the native Irish have any respect for my authority."

"Whose authority do they respect?" asked Alvin.

The bishop didn't answer.

The man must still be planning something, and was reluctant to deny it outright, especially since his amen to Alvin's prayer had apparently yielded real results.

So Alvin would need more of a demonstration that Pharaoh's power should not be extended to reach for him. It was a simple matter to weaken the boards under the bishop's desk and chair. Alvin checked beneath the floor and saw that there was only a crawl space a few feet down, and no occupied cellar. No one would be in much danger.

"Your Grace," said Alvin, "my knack—a talent I've worked on since childhood—includes the ability to sense when nails and wood no longer hold on to each other. The floor beneath you is in a weakened state. It would be wisdom if you got up and moved to the edges of the room."

"Are you threatening me?" asked the bishop.

"The weakened wood is threatening you," said Alvin. "I am giving you fair warning that you can't rely on this floor."

"Then why are you still sitting on your chair on that same floor?"

"The floor under my chair is strong. It will hold, at least until I leave the room. If I go out the door I came in through, will there be people on the other side waiting to arrest me?"

Since Alvin knew that there were four such men, he was not surprised when the bishop paused a long moment before saying, "I don't have any reason to believe that you are in any danger of being arrested."

"But the secret doorway behind that bookshelf—there is nobody waiting for me there, right? And that passage is the one you use to enter this place unseen, so when I come out into the open air, nobody will see me, right?"

The bishop rose to his feet. "Take whatever route you choose. All I ask is that you leave this room immediately."

"I had hoped to see you move away from this perilous part of the floor before I left you. What if you need my help when the floor collapses?"

"If I need any help, I won't want it to come from you," said the bishop.

"Ah. Just as the wounded traveler on the Jericho Road refused to allow the Samaritan to help him."

"That was a parable, not a historical incident," said the bishop.

"A story made up by Jesus, so perhaps we can still take it seriously as a guide to our behavior."

"Get out," said the bishop.

Alvin rose from the chair, and lapsed right back to the homespun accent of his childhood in Vigor Church. "I reckon you'll do what *you* do, and I'll do what *I* do, and we'll both figure out who made the best choice."

The bishop caught the change. "So you've set your education aside?"

"As so many of us do," said Alvin.

He walked to the bookshelf, and instead of looking for the hidden latch, he simply pulled forward and the bookshelves glided open, revealing a passage behind. It also revealed the cubbyhole where three scribes had watched their writing burst into flames. They were long gone, but the unburnt blank sheets and the inkwells and quills still sat there on the table, undamaged.

Alvin caused the boards and nails under the bishop to creak and tremble, giving him plenty of time to get away to an edge of the room. Meanwhile, Alvin continued down the passage until he came to the door that he knew would lead out into a courtyard, where nobody would see him because no one was there.

Behind him, the floorboards in the bishop's chamber gave way, and he dropped four feet straight down into the crawlspace. Alvin made sure that the bishop was uninjured. He also made sure that the door to the chamber was stuck fast and could not be opened, no matter how much the bishop's men, frightened at the crashing sound, might strain to pull the door open. The bishop was crying out for help, for someone to come to him, what are you waiting for, somebody tried to kill me!

I have given him only a taste of what the power of my knack can do, Alvin said inwardly as he walked out into a small courtyard and onward to a cobbled Dublin street.

In Alvin's mind, he had a clear memory of the route he had taken into the city, and without going near the entrance to the brothel, Alvin picked up the path farther out and began his long walk back to the west.

But because he had no horse and did not have to keep pace with any soldiers or bishop's men, he moved off into the fields and began to hear the feeble Greensong of meadows. He stayed away from fields of rotting potatoes—the blight was already prevalent on farms not far from the city—

and was able to draw strength from the plants and the few untamed animals that lived in this country. Soon he was running, not full out, but gently, causing no harm to the grasses and plants he ran on, for they stayed away from his light footfalls and sped him on his way.

If the bishop sent anyone after him, they would not believe he could already have come this far; the searchers would be looking far behind him, if there were any searchers.

Meanwhile, Alvin could only hope that the bishop would think twice and yet again before he sent anyone to interfere with Alvin's work in Ireland. Right now, the bishop was undoubtedly feeling triumphant about the fact that he had firm confirmation that Alvin's powers included dropping him through the floor and opening the secret door without finding the latch first.

But on sober reflection, the bishop would probably realize that Alvin could have killed him by having the ceiling above him collapse, or by causing his desk to catch fire, or by sealing him inside the room and starving him to death. He would realize that, like Pharaoh, he was being granted his life, and that this would continue to be the case until he reached out to harm Alvin or anyone under his protection.

Maybe this would keep Alvin safe for a while. But not forever. Pharaoh always forgot the power that was against him, and mistook the mercy shown to him for weakness. The bishop will think that I'm weak. He'll get more and more daring.

I'll try not to kill anyone, Peggy, he said silently. But I *will* protect my people.

If I *have* any people willing to come to me and sail west to America.

Will the story of what I did to the bishop's scribes and to the bishop himself become known? Or will the bishop keep it a closely guarded secret? Only the latter made sense—the bishop would hardly want to have it known that he was defeated but *not* killed by one of the very people he had vowed to destroy. But there were too many people inside that building who had heard and would see the damage to the bishop's secret chamber, and there was no reason for the scriveners to keep secret what happened to the papers they were writing on. The story would get out. Alvin wouldn't have to tell it to anybody himself, except to correct any errors that might have been included in the rumors.

Is this what you sent me to do, Crystal City? Or was I a fool to go to the bishop to give him a chance to cooperate in a bloodless exodus of people with knacks? Was I wrong to demonstrate a bit of my power to him? Was I wrong to use the power so destructively? Is that what I was given it for? It should be only the power to heal and protect, to empower good people and enfeeble the evil ones.

If Peggy were here, with her gift for seeing into people's heartfires, she could have told Alvin what kind of man the bishop was, and what he now intended to do. But she wasn't here, and so the bishop's mind and heart remained closed to him. Either Alvin's ploy had worked, or it hadn't. Or maybe it had worked, but not for long, or not as Alvin intended.

Are you watching all this from afar, Peggy? Am I doing well? What did you see in my heartfire, before you said that I should go? Are you saving me from some nasty doom in Crystal City? Or is my future as much a blank to you as it is to me?

As Margaret had said several times before, sometimes knowing some things is worse than knowing nothing, because if you turn aside from your path to avoid a bad fate, you may find yourself on a path to meet a worse one.

My path must be the wine-dark sea, the vasty deep, the whale-road, because only by crossing the jagged Atlantic can I return to you, dear Margaret Larner, my Little Peggy.

11

FATHER LUKASZ SLOSHED through the water onto the shore of County Waterford in the southeast of Ireland. He would have preferred to arrive in the west of Ireland, the part most staunchly Catholic, but the ship's captain, who had some experience smuggling, told him that a shallow-water landing at this particular spot would shelter him from the view of passing strangers.

"If you were unloading a cargo, you'd choose a different place," said Lukasz.

"It is against the law to unload cargo except at the designated ports," said the captain. "That is called smuggling, and by act of Parliament the penalty is death."

"By hanging," said Lukasz.

"God has sent me harsh dreams of my neck in a noose," said the captain. "I take it as an admonition to live my life entirely within the law. Except for delivering a servant of God to the land of his ministry."

Lukasz bowed his thanks and pressed a coin into the captain's hand. The Holy See had already paid Father Lukasz's passage, but the captain would not mind a bit of extra compensation.

His trousers soaked, Lukasz walked over the low hill that hid the beach from view and found himself in a land of lush grass being consumed by languid sheep. He sat down in the grass, took off his boots, poured out the water, and wrung out the bottoms of his trousers. He laid his stockings on the grass to dry. He had no luggage, and carried not even the Holy Book, because he had long since committed the entire Douai translation to memory, where it waited for him to need it, alongside St. Jerome's Latin Vulgate version. The English heretics had it so much easier, having jettisoned the apocrypha from their King James Version. But if memory could not flawlessly hold the word of God in more than one language, what was memory for?

It was a day bright with sun, once it had fully risen, and before long his stockings were wearable again. He gartered them at the knee and pulled his trousers down over the tops. The boots, however, got no sunlight inside, but at least no water came out when he tipped them over. This would have to be dry enough.

In all the time he sat there, no one came by on the grassy track that showed signs of being used as a wagon road. Perhaps wagons only came along here during shearing or haying.

His boots were ice cold and a little squishy, but if that was the worst thing that happened to him today, he would be relieved. He had half-expected that someone would betray him and he would be met on the beach by English soldiers. So being met by no one made him feel more optimistic about his chances.

When he set foot on the wagon track, though, he did not do it as Father Lukasz. Now he was Brother Luke, an itinerant lay preacher of the Methodist persuasion. It was well known that Methodists had won the right to be considered as members of the Anglican church as far as the law was concerned. They were no longer classed as Dissenters, so they could hold public office and their ministers could draw upon a small emolument from the fund of the Established Church.

Luke's story would be that he had served as a missionary in Brittany, though he never learned their crude version of French and made not a single convert among the stubbornly Catholic Bretons. Now he was new-arrived in Ireland, and glad to be back among people who spoke English. He would soon discover why Fra Angelico praised the Irish pronunciation of English—Luke would test himself by trying to learn to speak like them as quickly as possible.

It was a long walk on a warm day, but Luke was still a healthy man and walking had always been his exercise of choice. Keeping a horse was too much trouble, and if he hired a stableman to take care of a horse, then keeping the stableman would also be too much trouble. I will serve God best if I don't require a noble animal to serve *me.*

The wagon track led past several farmhouses, but Luke had drunk a good draught from the freshwater barrel on the boat that carried him, and he was not yet thirsty. Best to get to an inn, where the news and the gossip would be much fresher and, perhaps, somewhat accurate.

In his coat pocket he had a small loaf of bread wrapped in an old towel, along with a miniature wheel of Azeitão cheese, made from sheep's milk, in a town about forty kilometers from Lisboa. It was clotted with thistle flowers instead of rennet, so no sheep had to die in order to make this cheese. And the flavor was exquisite. It was a vanity to spend money to acquire the cheese in the first place, and even more vanity to bring it with him for his noon dinner on this journey, but he hoped God would not hold it against him, this taste for luxury, because if a poor person came upon him now he would share it all, including the finest cheese he had ever eaten in his life. He would not withhold his luxuries for his own use, if another child of God had need of it.

If a rich man asked him for a bite of cheese, Luke would smile and say, "I doubt you would find this Breton sheep's cheese much to your liking. It isn't even aged enough to be hard." Calling it Breton sheep's cheese would be a lie, but he needed to seem to be recently arrived from Brittany. And he would not give up a single bite of it to a rich man. He'd rather cast it in the dirt.

You are a rich man, Father Lukasz, said the soft voice of the Jesuit conscience that dwelt always in his mind, judging him.

"I have lived on whatever stipend the Holy Father gave me," whispered Luke aloud. "And I have given more than half of that to the poor."

"Thus you try to bribe the poor to lend you the keys of heaven."

This dialogue had to stop. He didn't want anyone to see him talking to himself.

His belly full—the Portuguese could make cheese, and the Bretons could bake bread—Luke arrived at a town and looked for a public house. It wasn't hard to find, and at this hour it had no customers—the men would be working and the women would be tending to dinner and the children.

The publican greeted Luke without a smile, and Luke took the cue and did not smile either. But he nodded in greeting, and the Irishman nodded back, and Luke walked up to the bar. "After a mile or two of walking, I could use a sit-down," said Luke, remembering the English used by working-class men he had known and ministered to in England years before.

"English," said the publican.

"Methodist," answered Luke. "And I have money to pay."

"Not a beggar, then?"

"A man who wishes a bed for the night and a meal before sleeping," said Luke. And he produced a coin of much smaller value than what he had given the boat's captain, and laid it on the counter.

"That will buy you two nights' lodging and meals for two days," said the man.

"I commend you for your honesty," said Luke, though he knew it was enough for four days' lodging or more. He wasn't here to catch Irish publicans overcharging their guests—especially English ones. He would not begrudge the man his bit of extra income. The money came from the donations of Catholics throughout the world, the rich man's largesse and the poor widow's farthing. All gave their money to Christ, and Christ would give this man his extra payment and then forgive his sins. Even so do I forgive you, my son, thought Luke.

If you knew who I really was, would you beg for a Mass and several baptisms in this hamlet? Or would you surreptitiously send word for soldiers to pick me up?

This is not the place to make such a test, Luke told himself.

"Mayhap I'll need two nights," said Luke. "I confess to being right weary from my day's walk, and at my age a man needs his sleep and profits from sleeping late some mornings."

"We break our fast in this public house right after Prime. If you don't come down about then, the next meal is right around Sext. But it's a good one. Stick to your ribs."

"I hadn't heard that the Church of Ireland kept the old Catholic hours," said Luke. "Some days it's good to remember the old ways, I think."

The publican cocked his head, apparently sizing up this Methodist named Luke. "I think maybe it's good to remember them on all days," said the publican.

"So memories are long in the county of Waterford," said Luke.

"Have Methodists forgotten?"

"We have been persecuted for many years, and even now we are not invited into the best houses. But this does not compare to the persecution of the Irish," said Luke.

"Are you here to convert good Irishmen to your strange new faith?"

"We don't think of it as a new faith," said Luke. "We think of it as a purifying of the ancient faith. What I teach will bring people closer to Christ, whatever doctrine they profess."

"What about those who dare not profess their doctrine, since it is forbidden by law?" asked the publican.

This was an invitation—or a provocation.

"They call me Brother Luke. I'd wager good money that you also have a name."

The publican smiled. "A gambling Methodist, are you?"

"I didn't say I'd collect the money if I won."

"But you'd pay it out if you lost?" asked the publican.

"The outcome of this wager is in your hands."

"My mother gave me a name, my father being away on business at the time."

"Did she name you for a bird? A flower? A season?"

"Finchie Rosie Spring," said the publican. "A much finer name than my own."

"I look for truth, not flowers," said Luke.

"Brother Luke, will you pray for me?" asked the publican.

"What is your need?" asked Luke.

"I have a constant pain in my elbows, and for a man who pours drinks and serves them, it's an inconvenient malady. I go to bed at night in agony from the day's work. Is there a prayer for that?"

"I can pray for you, if I know the name that was given to you at baptism, for that is the name God knows you by."

The publican nodded gravely. "I am Simon Peter O'Reilly."

"Your mother had high hopes for you, I think," said Luke.

"I fear I've disappointed all her hopes, for I have no children for her to dote on."

Luke saw real sadness in the man's eyes, and concluded that he was married and no child had come to them.

Luke reached out and took Simon Peter by the hands and then leaned closer and held onto his elbows. "Heavenly Father," he said, "Simon Peter and I thank you for loving us, and for sending your Son, our Lord Jesus Christ, to the world to save us and set us free of our sins. We trust in your power and grace that sustain and restore us."

"Amen," whispered Simon Peter the publican.

"Loving Father," Luke went on, "touch Simon Peter now with your healing hands, for we believe that your will is for him to be well in mind, body, soul, and spirit. Cover him with the most precious Blood of your Son, our Lord Jesus Christ, from the top of his head to the soles of his feet. Cast out anything that should not be in him. Find every part of him that is not obeying your will in creating him, and teach his body to do its rightful duty, to serve a good man well, and give him many days without pain until the end of his life."

Luke opened his eyes to see that the snuffling sound he heard was Simon Peter weeping.

"Touch Simon Peter in the deepest recesses of his heart, so he can feel your presence, love, joy, and peace, which have drawn him ever closer to thee every moment of his life. Grant the prayer in his heart, for the blessing of Abraham. And Father, fill me also with your Holy Spirit and empower me to do your works so that my life will bring glory and honor to your Holy Name. We ask this in the name of the Father, and the Son, and the Holy Ghost. Amen."

Simon Peter was openly sobbing now, as he bent over Luke's hands and dropped many tears on them. "Thank you, Father," said Simon Peter. "No one will hear of your presence here, not from me. You are safe in my house."

"I am called Brother Luke," said Luke, "not Father anything."

"I know," said Simon Peter. "And so I shall call you."

"Is anyone else sleeping upstairs now?" asked Luke.

"It will be only you, so take your pick of the beds. I promise that the linens are clean and the mattress has been aired this very day, though bedbugs can be resourceful and sly, so I can't promise you'll pass the night unbitten."

Luke smiled. He liked this Simon Peter. And, up to a point, he trusted him. He was Catholic enough that he knew, from Luke's prayer, that Luke was a priest. Simon Peter could not guess the mission that had brought Luke to Ireland. To him, Luke was no more than a simple Catholic priest walking about in disguise, to minister the true rites to those who still had allegiance to the Pope. That would be enough to get him killed, of course, and in whatever gruesome ways the local heretics preferred. But the Inquisitor of Ireland? *That* would be a prize for the heretics to get their hands on.

As Luke climbed the stairs, he softly echoed sentences that Simon Peter had uttered, with the lilting, musical tones of his Irish accent. Fra Angelico was right. Even saying quotidian things, this Irishman has a poet's voice.

12

Rosheen Maloney was digging up potato plants from her family's field, more than a furlong from the house. She tossed them into the sledge, so she could drag it to the burning place, where the Maloneys and five other families burned what should have been the crop that would feed them through the coming winter.

She had long since stopped thinking about the fact that they had no money to buy grain, and nothing to trade for it. It was too late to plant wheat or any other useful grain. The small store of potatoes in the dry place off the kitchen was diminishing too quick, despite how fine Rosheen and Mam sliced them for frying or boiling. Onions and leeks they had, so the potatoes could have some flavor, and their small supply of salt, laid by in more prosperous days, helped the food remain savory and somewhat satisfying.

But Rosheen knew her numbers well enough to calculate how much the family ate each day, and how soon they would run out. Rosheen also knew who the biggest eaters in the family were. There was Da, but now he was gone to England looking for work to send them money for food. This greatly decreased the rate at which the store of potatoes was depleted.

Now Mam should have been the biggest eater, because she was still nursing the Worm, as Rosheen called the wriggling little one-year-old who did not yet have a real name, there having been no priest to baptize him. But Mam did not eat enough, so the Worm also went hungry, and kept up a half-whispered whimpering through day and night, waking and sleeping. He should be crawling by now, but when Mam set him on the reed-covered floor he just lay there, whimpering.

He was probably going to die without ever being baptized, which would put him in Limbo awaiting the mercy of the Lord, though the Church of Ireland preached that unbaptized babies who died would go to hell. Rosheen no longer spent much thought on that, either.

Instead, she calculated how long the potatoes would last if Rosheen herself was no longer at home. She did not gorge herself, and was always hungry when she stopped eating, but she ate enough to give her strength to continue her work of obliterating the blighted potato plants. But if her portion was no longer being taken from the store every day, there would be many days more.

Still it was not enough, even if Father came home with money. Because what could he buy, with the whole country blighted? The English corn merchants would puff up their prices in such times as these, so a man's work for a year would not buy enough to feed himself, let alone a wife and five children.

Rosheen had decided a few days ago that when she left, she would need to take one more child with her. Not Worm, obviously, and not Adam, the boy, because Da would be murderously angry if she took *him* off. So it was her next younger sister, Love O'Jesu, that she would take. Lovey would come, yes, and though their going would deprive Mam of her two best and most reliable helpers, it would give Mam and the remaining children enough food to eat whether or not Da came home with money or flour.

The only thing Rosheen fretted about now was whether to tell Mam that they were leaving, so she wouldn't worry and get up a search party among the neighbors, or leave a note for Mam to take to one of the neighbors who could read, that not being part of her upbringing. It would be wrong to sneak away at night like escaping burglars.

She started pulling the sledge toward the firepit when she caught movement out of the corner of her eye and saw that Alvin Miller was walking up the road that ran along the top of the hill. She stopped her pulling and watched him. He did not seem to have been maimed or injured by the men who arrested him there a few weeks ago. Nor did he so much as look at the Maloney house, a place where he had several times been received with friendship. So Mam's affidavit to the bishop's soldiers had been part of the basis of Alvin's arrest, though Rosheen had heard the captain swear to Mam that Alvin would never know of it. He knew of it.

How angry was he? He could have avoided their house altogether, simply by walking in the field below the brow of the hill. So he was showing himself. To reassure his friends that he had suffered no serious harm, that he was still a free man? Or to strike their consciences for having been so faithless as to betray him to the witch-hunters?

He could not have come back to lay a curse on us, thought Rosheen. What curse could he have within his power, that would cause more harm than the blight was already causing?

As Alvin Miller came nearer to where she was standing, Rosheen reached a sudden and impossible decision. She let the sledge rope drop and stepped over it. She ran back to where Love O'Jesu was also digging at the blighted potatoes, while watching over Worm in the nearby grass. As Rosheen approached them, she saw Worm roll himself from his back to his stomach, and reach out his hands and curl up his legs to creep forward. So maybe the baby wouldn't die after all. I'll give you a better chance for life, lad, if I leave so that your mam can eat more, and fill her paps with milk for you.

Lovey looked up at Rosheen as she arrived. "What?" she said testily, because she expected Rosheen had seen her doing something wrong and was here to rebuke her.

"Pick up the baby, Lovey," said Rosheen.

"What for?"

"We need to bring the lad to Mam."

"Did she signal or wave?" asked Lovey. "I didn't hear her call."

"I'm glad you didn't hear it, because she did *not* call," said Rosheen. And when Lovey was slow to get up off her knees, Rosheen bent down and picked up Worm and started striding boldly toward the house.

"Wait! Mam put me in charge of the baby, Sheen!"

When Rosheen reached the door of the house, Lovey was right behind her, starting to remonstrate again, but Rosheen turned on her and with her fiercest face whispered harshly, "Be still. Say nothing. On your life, say nothing, but obey me."

Lovey moved past her and opened the door. Rosheen strode through and gently laid Worm onto the patch of cloth that served as his sleeping place during the day. Again the baby immediately started to try to creep. But he wouldn't be able to open the door and there was nowhere for him to fall, so let him practice moving himself.

Rosheen turned and held out a hand to signal Lovey to stay at the door. Rosheen then walked into the room where Da and Mam always slept, with the baby between them. Mam was inside, lying down with a cloth over her eyes. Standing in the doorway, Rosheen said, "When Lovey and I are gone, there'll be enough food to sustain you all through the winter."

Mam's hand came up and drew the cloth off her eyes.

"We'll be under the protection of Alvin Miller," said Rosheen. "He's up on the road."

"And whose protection will *he* be under?" whispered Mam.

"God's," said Rosheen, though she had no idea if this was true. God hadn't protected him from getting arrested.

Rosheen closed the door behind her and strode quickly to the door where Lovey waited. Rosheen opened it and drew Lovey after her. The younger girl came willingly enough—if she had resisted, Rosheen would have let her stay. Lovey followed her closely up the hill toward the road.

Alvin had stopped walking. Did he guess what Rosheen intended? Or was he merely resting? Though his back was to the girls, Rosheen did not call to him, because she could sense that he already knew they were there.

When they were within a rod of him, and on the road, he began to walk away from them, farther down the road in the direction he had already been going. Rosheen sped up to overtake him; Alvin also sped up. When Lovey dragged behind and Rosheen had to wait for her, Alvin also waited. He never looked back to see them; he simply seemed to know where they were and how fast they were going.

Only when they had passed beyond sight of the Maloney house did Alvin slow down and let himself be overtaken. "Are we journeying together today?" he asked.

"God willing," said Rosheen.

"You're a fast walker," said Lovey.

"Fast as I need to be," said Alvin.

"I'm sorry Mam swore against you to the captain," said Rosheen.

"I forgive her," said Alvin. "She owed me no allegiance."

"I'm sorry, too," said Lovey.

"Just so you know," said Alvin, "I'm bound for a town up ahead to meet with some of my American friends, and from there we're walking on to the sea, to look at boats. It's a long way."

"That's just where we're going," said Rosheen.

"Then let our paths keep us traveling together," said Alvin. "Did you happen to bring food and water with you?"

"Slipped my mind," said Rosheen.

"Meaning that there's no food to spare in your house about now."

Rosheen said nothing, just started walking along, expecting Alvin and Lovey to come with her. They did.

"I only asked about food and water because when we get to the village and meet my friends, if they're there, then we'll all eat together at the inn, and I'll pay the publican for all."

"That is kind of you, sir," said Lovey. "How long will that be from now?"

"A good walk," said Alvin, "but I'll help you bear the distance as best I can." He reached out his hands, one to Rosheen, one to Lovey, and they took his hands, the callused strong hands that had held hammers, tongs, and iron of every weight. His hands did not crush theirs, but only held them.

At first Rosheen could feel Alvin dragging her a little faster forward than was really comfortable for her. Then it *was* comfortable, so he must have slowed down. Faster and faster they went, until Rosheen was barely aware of setting one foot in front of the other. She heard a thin melody like a wee piper in the grass, and now and then the faint sound of a horn. It was the music of the green fields of Ireland, she somehow understood. It was the life of the land bearing them along.

Rosheen did not look toward her sister, on the other side of Alvin; she knew that if Lovey was lagging, Alvin would bear her up.

And then Rosheen felt as if she were waking up out of a light sleep—alert and aware all at once, yet she knew that she had slept an hour or two while her feet continued to bear her along, keeping up with the music.

There was a village and they were entering it. The music instantly faded, and Rosheen slowed down to her natural walking pace. She did not feel as if she had just walked hours along the track; she felt ready to take on another journey twice as long, if Alvin would hold her hand and the music would sustain her.

Alvin told the girls to count to a hundred and then come into the public house. He went on ahead to prepare the way, he said. By which he really meant to see if his friends were there, and if there were rooms to let for the night. Even with their drifting along in the Greensong all the afternoon, they had to be weary from much walking, on too little food.

At the start of their journey together, Alvin had sent his doodlebug into their bodies to see about their health. They were sturdy enough. Even in this wet and cloudy land, they had plenty of sunlight, which he knew was important for health, though he wasn't sure how it worked. We're not *plants*, after all, he told himself. But we need sunlight too, just like trees and grass.

There were weaknesses in the girls that would come to the surface in time, if they continued to starve, but right now, a few good meals would fix them up right. They were strong, with wiry muscles. Alvin could not help but wonder if they had knacks of some kind, so he could justify taking them to America. For now, though, he had to deal with the problems of taking care of two girls who were not his own daughters, on a trek as long as he intended to take.

The publican gave him a nod when he came in, but the man was busy with wiping down the bar. The smell of a good strong stew filled the place, and Alvin could tell from the scent that it contained mutton and potatoes, carrots and leeks, and, from the best he could tell, sage.

Alvin looked around and did not see the friends he had expected. John Binder should have been there, but at this hour of the day he might be purchasing materials to make rope. Alvin's older brother Measure was there, however, with his long legs propped up on a bench while he sprawled in a chair that looked like it came from a dollhouse, he was so tall.

Measure looked up as Alvin saw him, but gave no sign of recognition. Then Measure glanced over at an oldish man sitting by a west-facing window, so that in this late-afternoon light his face was only a silhouette. So Measure was warning him—a stranger not accounted for, no idea if he could be trusted.

Alvin walked up to the publican. "Excuse me, friend," he said. "I got me two nieces waiting outside for me to find out if you got a room for them tonight, and another one for me."

"Don't need no little girls loose upstairs," said the publican.

"I vouch for their good behavior."

"We get men in here sometimes whose behavior can't be vouched for by anybody short of Satan himself," said the publican.

"I'll make sure nobody troubles the girls," said Alvin. "What matters is, you got rooms for us?"

The publican nodded. "These aren't prosperous times, my American friend. We're glad for the custom."

"How'd you know I'm an American?" asked Alvin, pretending to be a little hurt.

"Because you don't sound Irish, so I know you're not a native of this land, nor any part of the island. And you don't sound English, so I'm willing to rent you a room and sell you some bowls of stew. But what you do sound isn't Scottish or Welsh, and yet not foreign like Germans or Dutch as comes through here on rare occasions."

"Well, a man talks how he talks," said Alvin.

"Aye," said the publican. "And stays silent when he wants, as well." The publican nodded his head toward Measure, or maybe toward the man by the window.

"I reckon I can get that long fellow to jump to his feet and shout," said Alvin, knowing perfectly well that Measure had enough of a makering knack in him to hear every word he said.

"I saw him look at you when you came in, and I figured you for friends, so I'm not taking your wager."

"Wasn't a wager," said Alvin. "It was a boast."

The publican smiled for the first time. "So I've heard about you Americans. Always full of brag."

"I'm proud to say I'm not the worst braggart in America, but I can safely say I've met several who were in the running."

"Go talk to your friend. And those girls standing in the doorway, bring them in, we have a room for them tonight, next to the room you'll be in, so if they need anything they can call out and you can come protect them."

"Please promise me that you don't have ruffians who come here regular to frighten children," said Alvin.

"I don't think anybody needs to be afraid with you and your brother watching over them," said the publican.

"Who said anything about brothers?" asked Alvin.

"Who needs to say it, unless they're blind?" said the publican. "You don't seem twinny to me, but if you have a different mother or father I'll give you a double portion of stew."

"Let me taste it before you start doubling up on me," said Alvin.

Measure chuckled as he rose to his feet. "He's figured us out, Al," he said. "No secrets from *him*, not today."

"Can't help it that we both got beat by the same Ugly Stick," said Alvin.

"You took the worse licking," said Measure.

Alvin led him over to the girls, Rosheen and Love O' Jesu, and introduced them to his older brother. Measure showed his best manners, bowing over their hands when they offered them to him. "My brother seems to have acquired two nieces from the pretty side of the family," said Measure.

By which he was telling them, We're pretending you're our nieces and don't you contradict us.

"Uncle Alvin didn't pick us," said Rosheen, the elder one.

"We picked *him*," said Lovey.

"You're the only ones on God's green Earth who ever would," said Measure. "'Lessun they was drinking. Here, come set at my table and let's make friends. I think the publican is just about to dip a bowl into his stew for each of you."

Alvin saw the publican head back into the kitchen, where he was no doubt complying with Measure's implied request.

Alvin did not join them at Measure's table, though, even when the publican came back with bowls for the girls and a bowl each for Measure and Alvin. Instead, Alvin set his bowl on the table, took a few steps toward the old man at the west window, and sat down across from him.

The old man looked at him, and nodded.

"I see your nod and raise you a grin," said Alvin. Then he grinned.

The old man smiled at him. "I call your grin, my friendly traveler," said the man. "Show me what's in your hand, sir."

Alvin cocked his head. "I never thought a priest of the Church would be one for gambling games, least of all poker. That's a game for ruffians and rivermen."

"I'm lately come from Portugal," said the man, "where the game is played under another name but still impoverishes men with no skill for bluffing."

"I think you can bluff the antlers off a mule," said Alvin.

The old man looked startled, then grinned. "I must have bluffed them off of all the mules I've seen around here," he said.

"My name's Alvin Miller," said Alvin. "Or, rightly, Alvin Smith, since smithery is my trade, while milling was my father's."

"I've heard stories about a wandering American smith or miller named Alvin," said the man. "I'm glad to make your acquaintance."

"I'd wager that somewhere along the line, a body gave *you* a name, too."

"In my native land, I was named Lukasz, after the evangelist. But people here call me Luke, because it sounds more natural to them."

"But they never call you by the name of your trade," said Alvin.

"Not often," said Luke.

Alvin leaned forward and spoke more quietly. "I think nobody would give you a surname, like Priest. I think they'd be more likely to call you Father Luke, except that name might get you arrested and killed."

Luke showed no sign of startlement. "I didn't expect to fool you, Alvin Smith, because from what I hear of your knacks, you already knew before you sat down that I have worn the vestments of my trade."

"You're a brave man," said Alvin. "These are parlous times."

"As much for witches as for priests of the Church," said Luke.

"What do you tell folks you're doing here?" asked Alvin.

"I'm a Methodist preacher, now that the Archbishop of Canterbury has declared us to be members of the Church of England, and not heretics or dissenters."

"Do you know anything about Methodist teachings?" asked Alvin. "Cause we got a powerful lot of Methodists in my part of America, and they can't stop preaching except to teach, and don't stop teaching except to preach."

"The only people who talk more than Methodists are Quakers, but the Church of England has no patience with *them*, since they go out of their way to point out the hypocrisy of the English Church."

"Why are you here?" asked Alvin. "Surely you're not joining in the witch hunting of the Church of Ireland."

"I can't stop fools from dancing, but I don't have to join their jig," said Luke.

"Now, you sounded almost Irish when you said that," said Alvin.

"I'm working on trying to acquire the lilt of their language."

"And the native accent of every language you speak, as well, I think," said Alvin.

"I can only do it if I live in the country with native speakers for a while," said Luke. "I'm glad to know that I'm progressing a little in Ireland."

"Let me guess other languages you speak," said Alvin. He thought through what he knew about Catholics from Peggy's teaching. "You were in Portugal, and I assume you also know French and Italian, since they're close kin of Latin."

"Do you speak Latin, sir?" asked Luke.

"Not a lick of it," said Alvin. "My wife would tell you—she's a schoolteacher—my wife would say I'm still only halfway to learning English."

"Me too," said Luke. "But it's coming back to me."

"You spoke it before," said Alvin.

"I go many places," said Luke.

"But not just following your nose," said Alvin.

"Sometimes a godly man will come to me and give me ideas about where I might be able to do some good."

Alvin nodded. "So the Pope sends you on errands," said Alvin.

Luke winced. "Best not to mention his holy office aloud in this place."

"You're on his errand here, right now, waiting for me to arrive at this public house," said Alvin. He was only guessing, but Luke's reaction told him that he was right.

"How would I know you would come this way?"

"Because my brother was here," said Alvin.

"And how was I to know he was your brother?" asked Luke.

"Because he was waiting for someone, but showed no impatience or urgency. He knew I would come, so you knew I would come."

Lukasz just smiled.

"We both know more about each other than is good for us," said Alvin.

"Alvin Smith—or, perhaps I should say, Alvin Maker—have you heard of the Inquisition?"

Alvin's heart sank. "I heard of Jews being put to the question, and dying no matter what they said."

"Father Torquemada made the name of the Inquisition stink throughout Europe," said Luke regretfully. "That was well before my time, but we still pay heavily for his excesses."

"He did to the Jews what the Church of England does to the witches," said Alvin.

"He thought he was purifying the Church in Spain," said Luke. "And I notice you didn't ask me if I spoke Spanish."

"Didn't cross my mind," said Alvin. "But I've seen enough Portuguese and Italians, French and Croatians in Nueva Barcelona, to know that you aren't native to any of those lands."

"Another land, farther east and north, where snow covers the ground all winter."

"Bohemia," said Alvin.

"Good guess. If your wife taught you geography, she did well."

"Poland," said Alvin.

"The language that terrifies foreigners because it has few vowels," said Luke.

"I wouldn't know about that," said Alvin.

"But it's not as bad as Hebrew and Arabic," said Luke, "because they never write their vowels at all, just the consonants."

"Brother Luke," said Alvin, choosing a title safer than Father, "why did you want to meet me here?"

The priest took a deep breath, then let it out in a sigh. "I have been appointed Grand Inquisitor of Ireland." Alvin got the sense that he was the first person the priest had told of his office. Alvin gathered that he was *not* an Inquisitor in order to persecute people.

"Are you going to rouse the people in rebellion against the Church of Ireland, so called?"

"So many of the Irish would die, and still not have their freedom at the end of it."

"When has that ever stopped a crusade?" asked Alvin.

"I was sent here to save the witches," said Luke.

Alvin sat back on his bench and grinned. "You're funnin' with me now," he said.

"Here's my plan. See what you think of it."

Alvin listened with growing understanding when Luke explained that he would hold Church trials of witches, find them guilty of something, and then sentence them to transportation to America. "To the part of America where knacks are welcome, or at least tolerated."

"What shipmaster would take a witch aboard?" asked Alvin.

"A shipmaster who has knacks of his own," said Luke.

"I have no power over the sea, and precious little influence over anything else."

Luke grinned. "I admitted *my* power and authority, my friend. Be honest with me, and admit your own."

"I have no ecclesiastical authority, either, except what I officiously take upon myself, and I try to avoid that."

"You aren't here to make war on the Church of Ireland, either," said Luke. "From all I've heard of you warning people of the famine and how to rid their land of the blight, you're here to carry away to America as many Irishmen as are in danger of dying here."

"I don't know how I'll do it," said Alvin. "The miracle of the parting of the Red Sea isn't in my power, and it would be a long walk in any case, crossing the Atlantic that way, with miles of water looming above us on both sides."

"I assumed," said Luke, "that you would search for Irishfolk with knacks to stay afloat, and knacks for navigation, and the skill to make boats."

"How could I hope to find them, when everybody is so fearful to be caught out as a witch?" asked Alvin.

"That's how I thought we could help each other. When people know I was sent by the Holy Father in order to find the so-called witches and sentence them to exile in America—"

"They'll step forward and face your Charitable Inquisition."

"They trust the Mother Church," said Luke. "I won't betray that trust."

"Nor will I," said Alvin.

Luke grinned. "I think that stew is calling our names louder and louder."

"I think we can make a good meal of this," said Alvin, "by eating it together."

"Christ redeems the people from their sins. But perhaps the Inquisition and the Master of Knacks can save at least a few of the people from the pious ministrations of the Church of Ireland."

Alvin rose to his feet, and gave Luke a hand up, too. They walked over and joined Measure and the girls at their table. The publican rushed over with freshly served bowls of stew, steaming so much that Alvin knew it would be a while before either of them could take a bite.

"Measure, my brother, let me introduce you to my friend Luke, who plans to make common cause with us."

Measure smiled at Luke. "If Alvin sees that you'll be a help to us, then I'm your friend, too."

Luke reached out his hands and covered one hand of each of the brothers. "God bless you," he said. "And if it doesn't offend you, as heretics, I will pray to the Holy Mother to take you under her protection."

Alvin nodded. "I'll take all the protection we can get."

Rosheen cocked her head. "What by all the saints are you going on about?"

"We're working out how to be friends," said Alvin.

"You don't work things like that *out*," said Rosheen. "You just say you're friends and then live up to the covenant."

"An educated girl," said Luke.

"An eager learner," said Alvin.

"I'm sleepy," said Lovey.

"Try to stay awake till I've eaten my stew," said Alvin, "and I'll take you up to your room."

"No need to wait," said Measure. He stood, scooped up Lovey into his arms, and then followed Rosheen as she led the way, even though she had never been inside a public house before.

The publican's wife intercepted them at the top of the stairs and showed the girls to their room. "I'll tuck them in," she said. "And see to other matters as they come up."

Measure was a little surprised when Alvin came upstairs soon after.

"I thought you and Luke would have more to discuss," said Measure.

"Oh, we have plenty to talk about. But the good Father can't bless folks and say Mass and baptize babies while an American is sprawled all over the chairs downstairs."

"I didn't think you held with all that Catholic mumbo-jumbo," said Measure.

"I hold with the folks who believe in it, and I show them respect."

Measure nodded. "Good enough for me."

13

ALVIN SURVEYED THE Quay in Westport and was astonished all over again about how quickly word of the lenient Irish Inquisition had spread through western Ireland, and how many people were showing up. Most of Alvin's time was taken up with teaching people how to strengthen and control their knacks. But he was aware of how John Binder and Father Lukasz spent their days, finding housing for these "witches" and bringing food into Westport so they could eat.

Naturally, the food was also intended to provision many boats large and small for the long voyage across the Atlantic. Sometimes Alvin wished that they could arrange some of the new steamboats that were beginning to brave the ocean swells, but so far it took so much coal to get across the ocean that the ship had little room for cargo and passengers. Pretty soon they'd find a way to make the ships a lot bigger and the paddlewheels more efficient. But for now, the wind was the best and cheapest tool for moving ships across water.

One of the people Alvin was working with most closely was Jedediah O'Something—Alvin could hardly tell an O' from a Mac with the Irish names, since almost everybody had one or the other. Jedediah's knack for clearing the air showed potential for the voyage. Not that smells would be a problem. But however he managed to keep smells in one place and not another had to have something to do with moving air around, and air that moved was called "wind."

There were too many people for Alvin to know all their names, but he remembered many and never forgot a knack or how much progress had been made with it. Parents with knacks would let their children sit in on their sessions, and Alvin figured that even though it was pretty unlikely that they'd develop the same knacks as their parents, they might learn something about how to *think* about a developing knack.

Father Lukasz learned all their names and never forgot them or made a mistake. Alvin challenged him once, sure that this was Lukasz's knack.

"Oh, no, my son, that's nothing I was born with," said Lukasz. "When I joined the Jesuits, one of the first things we did was construct a memory palace."

Alvin immediately wondered if such a thing could be built out of the blocks of water that made up the walls of the vision building in Crystal City.

"It's not a physical palace," said Lukasz. "I saw that glint in your eye. It exists only in your own mind. You build it with lots of details, so that no two rooms are even similar to each other. You learn the plan of it, which room leads to which others, and what you can see from all the windows."

"Sounds complicated," said Alvin.

"Very," said Lukasz. "But you don't have to do it all at once—it keeps growing your whole life. And with practice it becomes almost automatic. There are times I sit back and simply wander through my memory palace, seeing all those familiar rooms and sights, and remembering all the things I've put in there so I'll never forget them."

Alvin thought he understood. "So when you learn somebody's name, you put your memory of their face and name into that palace?"

"Close," said Lukasz. "But the idea is to make it so you don't have to imprint them on your memory, you have to involve them in a room. So I took your name, Alvin, and I broke it into 'all the vines.' That would make me think of 'Alvin,' so I had you in my palace. I have a room with all kinds of machinery in it, a thing I saw in a factory in Bretagne, a candy-making factory. So I had your vines of every different kind growing and twining around the machinery. The machinery reminds me that you're a smith and as the machine plops out candy onto trays, I think of you making the world a sweeter place."

"I'm afraid you give me too much credit."

"I don't publish such things, Alvin. They exist only in my memory. But you see how it works, não é? Vines of every kind, twining around steel machinery as the machine is plopping out candies. 'All vines, smith, maker.'"

"That's clever. And I'll never get that image out of my mind, so I can see that it works. I just wonder if I'm seeing the same kind of candy you're seeing."

Lukasz laughed. "Does it matter?"

"I first thought of horehound candies, cause that's all we could get in the first few years of my life," said Alvin. "I learned soon enough that horehound makes you need to piss, and as a child, when I overindulged in horehound I'd pee so much I got so thirsty that I drank all the water I could get and then I needed to piss even more. Taught me that I should suck on one horehound candy all day, and not take another till the next day."

Lukasz laughed again. "Sometimes you have dignity, and sometimes you talk about things that would get you thrown out of any drawing room in England."

"Good thing I'm not in any drawing rooms."

"The candy I think of is nougat, soft yet firm, formed into tubes. It's laid down on the tray, the candymaker slides the tray along, as the machine pours out warm chocolate onto the nougat to enrobe it. You must enrobe it three times before it has the right balance with the nougat."

"Wish I knew what nougat is," said Alvin. "I never heard of it."

"You will. At least if you ever get to the continent. The Swiss and the Dutch have different processes, but I imagine you'll understand the recipe at once and never forget it."

"If that's true," said Alvin, "why does Peggy always throw me out of the kitchen when she's working?"

"I believe that's frontier humor. She never does any such thing, does she?"

"I wouldn't know," said Alvin. "We're never in the same house more than a few weeks at a time."

"I don't know much about marriage," said Lukasz, "but when people spend too much time apart, friends or spouses, their affection cools, or turns toward others."

"What good is a promise if you don't stick to it even when you don't feel like it?" asked Alvin.

"I wish more people understood that," said Lukasz. "So many promises barely outlast the desire."

"There must be a thousand adults in our little community, Father Inquisitor. You have objects standing for all of them in your memory palace?"

"And many more besides," said Lukasz. "The exact number of convicted witches in our seaside encampment is eight hundred and forty-five."

"Only that many?"

"The confessed witches awaiting trial are another hundred, and friends and relatives who are just glad to be in a place where there's food, they bring the total over a thousand. Your estimate was solid enough."

What Alvin hadn't yet brought up with Lukasz was the issue of money. Lukasz did disappear from time to time—long enough to take the train to Dublin, meet with somebody, and come back. When Alvin or one of the other Americans found a boat or talked about materials needed for the voyage or food that was needed, the money Lukasz handed over was always in florins or doubloons.

"Lots of horehound grows around where I grew up and pretty much everywhere. When folks came over from Europe and Britain, a lot of them brought horehound with them as a medicine. Trouble with horehound is, it's a kind of mint, so once you plant it, there'll be new plants springing up all around till the Second Coming."

"Wouldn't it be good if potatoes grew the same way," said Lukasz.

"It would," said Alvin, "but better if you know how to cultivate them. To get any use out of potatoes, though, you got to dig them up. But if you leave them alone, they spread all right, though not as fast as horehound. Problem isn't that potatoes don't grow all right. Problem is there's a blight grows faster."

"I wish there was something you could do about the blight," said Lukasz.

"I remember what I saw when I looked deep into it, and I'm still trying to think of a way to get at it. I don't usually look for ways to kill something, because the blight is as alive as I am, and it's only filling the measure of its creation. I just want to persuade it to stop eating potatoes."

"Unless that *is* the 'measure of its creation,'" said Lukasz.

"How did things go with the Bishop of Dublin?" asked Alvin.

Lukasz smiled. "I haven't met with him, probably never will. He can't officially know that I exist, though stories about our Inquisition are spreading."

"So who do you meet with?"

"Other missionaries," said Lukasz. "Hermits and flagellants. And now and then a priest of the Church of Ireland who hates what folks keep doing to so-called witches. *They* talk up their moral qualms with other priests. The idea is to make it so, if the English Church were to stop the persecution of our people, and admit there's no such thing as a witch, all the rank-and-file priests would sigh with relief and say, Thank God that wretched business is over."

"You want the members of the church to lead their pastors."

"Pastors can't lead the sheep to a place they don't want to go."

Alvin didn't tell him that he shouldn't use sheep as examples, because it was obvious Lukasz had never worked as a shepherd. Of course, Jesus told stories using sheep all the time, and the Bible didn't say he was ever a shepherd. Sure, lambs were gentle, but grownup sheep were not. Especially not rams. Couldn't get a flock to do anything, if the ram doesn't agree with you, plus the ram will knock you over like a ninepin. Which was Lukasz's point, after all, wasn't it? Yes, flocks with rams in them weren't so easy to lead.

Yet I need them to be a flock with a lot of rams—so that every ship and boat and barrel that would be used for crossing the Atlantic could have a leader, someone whose knack allowed them to keep the passengers in their craft safe until they got across.

I can't send them separately. There are no knacks except mine and Measure's that I can count on to keep people safe. Jedediah might be able to whip up a wind on demand, but what if he couldn't control the direction of the wind? Westerlies prevailed in these latitudes, he'd been told, so if you let a ship in these waters have its head, the wind and currents would carry it right back to Ireland. Had to go west, relentlessly west. Do that long enough, and even though you might end up in some godforsaken corner of Canada, you'd reach land, North American land.

"You're thinking worrisome thoughts," said Father Lukasz.

"I am indeed." And then an unexpected thought. "You don't happen to have a knack for—"

Luke waved off the question. "I cannot read minds, Alvin. I read faces, I read posture and gestures, I read actions and choices. That usually tells me what I need to know."

"My Margaret can see into people's heartfires. She doesn't read their minds, not like letters on a page. Most people think that they do all their thinking in words, but that just isn't so. Margaret says—and I've done enough with heartfires to know she's right—she says that the important thoughts don't have words at all. After all, babies know how to think before they're even born. They know what they want, they don't know how to say it, so they cry till some adult gives it to them or does it for them. And they know when they got it, and they lie there practicing the use of their limbs until they can balance sitting up, and then they practice grasping and also cooing and making other noises, and the adults say, 'Oh how cute, did he just say—' and the baby knows that whatever sound he made pleased the adult. And they learn language."

"And immediately begin using it to deceive," said Father Luke.

"Of course," said Alvin. "Manipulation of other people is what language is *for*. Little children have no idea what truth is—you mean I'm only allowed to say words that correspond with what actually happened? No! Says the baby, I need to say whatever it takes to get you to do what I need you, what I want you to do."

"So lying comes first."

"Trying to control what happens to you and around you, that's why learning language is worth the effort."

"And from what philologist did you learn this?" asked Luke.

"I don't know a philologist from a frying pan," said Alvin.

"I don't want to be around you when you're cooking!"

"You're a philologist?"

"You know my trade," said Luke.

"Smuggler."

Luke hesitated, then smiled. "Bringing in illegal stock to supply a desperate need. I accept that title."

"At the prices you charge, you'll never break even."

"My account book is kept in heaven, and enumerates a different coin. 'Even as ye have done it unto the least of . . .'"

Alvin almost finished the quotation himself, but instead asked, "Why have you stopped?"

"I find myself quoting the Protestant translation."

"I imagine it's safer for you to quote from the King James Version. If you quote from the Catholic Bible, it might be a hint that you have actually read the Catholic Bible, which is a serious crime in England and, therefore, in Ireland."

"Yes," said Luke. "It's hard to *not* use what you know."

"I do that all the time—not using what I know. And when you add in all the things I don't know that I should know, I'm surprised I can chew my own food without help."

"I like you, American Wizard."

"Just a man with a knack."

"American *Maker*. I like you. You are able to jest about your own vast abilities—"

"Which you know about only by rumor," said Alvin.

"I know people who have seen what you can do, and I can't doubt their solemn testimony."

"Have you been gathering testimony about me?" asked Alvin. "You're not going to Inquisit *me*, are you?"

"You *are* a heretic, aren't you?"

"Because I got me some knacks?"

"Because you're not a good Catholic."

"I'm not a bad Catholic, either."

Luke laughed. "I believe, Alvin Maker, that you will find a way to get your ragtag fleet and these Children of Ireland across the wide Atlantic and safely to America."

"I hope that's a prayer you say often, because I don't see an open road to that result."

"I believe you're doing God's work, Alvin," said Luke. "So the way will be opened to you."

14

Calvin tried not to make a count of how many spectators had joined him and Goody Lamb and her husband at the shore of the Mizzippy. Naturally, the fogs of the river obscured everything to the west of them, but here at the shore, Calvin was fulfilling a promise.

"What will we see in the crystal?" asked Goody Lamb.

"I don't know," said Calvin. "I have nothing to do with what you see or don't see. All I can do is help you make a crystal that truly belongs to you."

Her husband, Plato Lamb, thrust his hands into his pockets. "If this can be done, why hasn't Alvin been doing it?"

"Alvin doesn't report to me, just as I don't report to him. He makes crystals that can be looked into by anyone. He doesn't think it matters to make crystal blocks for individuals, to see what *they* need."

"But you can't say if we'll see anything," said Goody Lamb.

"Indeed I cannot," said Calvin. "All I can do is make the crystal using a few drops of your blood and water from the river. What it does or does not show you is dependent on the blood you contribute and what you look for when you gaze into the crystal."

"Sounds like hokum-pocus to me," said Plato Lamb.

"Sounds the same to me, too," said Calvin. "Except I'm not going to say any magic words cause there's nothing magic about it. Doesn't Alvin say that all the time? No such thing as magic. Everything has a natural explanation. We just don't know all the explanations yet."

"Hokum-pocus," murmured Plato.

"Then let's not do it," said Calvin. He stood up from his place at the water's edge.

The onlookers murmured and sighed.

"Please," said Goody Lamb.

"I can't predict what you'll see or promise anything at all. That's not how it works. You know how it is, inside the Crystal City. You look at the crystal blocks, you see what you see. Someone right beside you won't see the same thing at all. Who controls that? Not me. Not Alvin. Not you. Images simply appear. Scenes like in a play."

"With singing and dancing?" asked Plato wryly.

"I didn't say it was a musical revue," said Calvin.

"So there's nothing to see or do in Crystal City except go looking into blood-crystal blocks and try to make sense out of the random things they show."

Calvin chuckled. "Brother Plato," he said.

"Not your kin," murmured Plato.

"Brother Plato, because that's what folks call each other here, where knacks abound. Brother Plato, are you already bored with the fact that when you look into those crystals, you actually see things? Real-looking things?"

"They don't all look real," said Plato.

"My dear," said Goody Lamb.

"They don't," he said to her. "And I don't know if anybody in Crystal City is one lick smarter or wiser or better-informed because of anything they saw in the Crystal."

"They're free to stop looking," said Calvin, "just as they're free to *keep* looking, if that's what suits them."

"You're as vague as your brother," said Plato.

"I'm as clear as my brother," said Calvin. "He won't, and I won't, ever promise anything we don't *know* we can deliver. For all I know, when your wife puts her blood into the water, we'll end up with a solid crystal block that shows nothing but the fog on the river. If that's too vague for you, *don't* look in the crystal."

"I don't want my wife shedding blood into this filthy muddy river hoping to get a clear crystal out of it."

Calvin sighed. "Don't you think you should have settled *that* between the two of you before you asked me to come out and make you a crystal from your own blood?"

"I want you to do it, and if Plato Lamb makes a fuss about it *that* is between him and me, and won't reflect bad on you at all." She turned to her husband. "I wouldn't give a fieldmouse's fart over whether you want me to drip some blood in the river. It's my blood, not yours, and my body and soul are not your property."

"I think we made some vows that kind of say—"

"If they only 'kind of' say something, then they aren't vows, are they? Our vows did not make me your property. I'm not a slave, am I? In the Crystal City, am I not a citizen with a vote, just like any man? May I not own property that does *not* belong to my husband?"

"I can see the two of you should be talking to a lawyer," said Calvin. "Settle this matter of who gets the say about Goody Lamb's blood."

In reply, she pulled a long pin out of her hat. Immediately the hat blew away, even though there wasn't much of a wind. Calvin raised his eyebrows, making sure he looked as surprised as anyone, even though he made the hat fly away.

Everybody was watching the hat, except Calvin, who watched Goody Lamb jab herself in the wrist so hard he was sure it had gone all the way through.

She turned her hand over, and indeed, the sharp end of the pin was sticking out of her wrist a good two inches. Goody Lamb made no sound of pain. Calvin looked at her in admiration.

But he had a job to do. Her blood was dripping into the murky water and Calvin had to hurry to gather it into one place with his hands *and* his doodlebug, and then swirl it like a tornado in the water.

The water clarified until it looked like pristine spring water, or the melt from winter icicles. Goody Lamb looked at it, breathing more heavily. Like a woman in the midst of lovemaking, thought Calvin. It was his favorite way to hear a woman breathe.

Plato began humming—nervously, some kind of childish song with words Calvin couldn't even make out. Plato was clearly disturbed—by his wife's self-savagery? Or by the way the river water clarified?

It took about ten minutes before the clear water with threads of blood in it began to solidify, and as it did, the blood attenuated and disappeared.

"My blood is gone!" said Goody Lamb in dismay.

"It is *not* gone," said Calvin. "It's doing its work in the water. It made the water crystal clear. Now it's making the crystal solid."

Plato wasn't saying anything about hokum-pocus, maybe because he could see it all happen with his own eyes.

And very soon after, the block was a perfect cube of crystal. "Me oh my," said Calvin. "I've never had one form up in a perfect cube before."

"What does that mean?" asked Goody Lamb eagerly.

"Like I said, Goody Lamb, I've never seen one come out as a perfect cube before, so how am I supposed to know what it means?"

"Don't be short with my wife, sir," said Plato Lamb. "She only wants to know what it means."

"And I want to tell her, but I can't tell her what I don't know. Should I make up some lies—of the sort sometimes referred to as hokum-pocus—so I can satisfy her curiosity for a moment, only to have her be sad because whatever I said didn't come exactly true?"

"No lying," said Plato.

"You can see by this crystal in my hands that I haven't lied to you at all, not at all, so stop fretting about whether I'm lying or not."

"You're the one who talked about things you said not coming true."

"Is the almanac lying when it doesn't rain on a day it called for rain? Or was it simply wrong? Being mistaken isn't lying."

"I know that," said Plato.

"Then indeed you have the wisdom of Socrates."

There was not a sign that Plato knew who Socrates was, let alone that he had anything to do with the ancient Greek Plato he had been named for.

Calvin held out the cube of crystal to Goody Lamb.

"Is it heavy?" she asked.

"Do I look like a massively strong fellow to you, ma'am?" asked Calvin. "Whereas you are well-muscled and strong."

"Are you talking about my wife's body, sir?" asked Plato.

"Indeed I am, because I can see that she is strong enough to carry this crystal, as can any man. Am I not to speak of what is plain to see?"

Plato was seething, and Calvin knew why. It had nothing to do with Calvin's speaking freely about Goody Lamb's musculature, and everything to do with the fact that Plato thought his wife was too enamored with Calvin by far.

As she should be, thought Calvin. I'm giving her what she wants.

"It won't bring Nat back to us," said Plato.

"I just want to see if he's still alive, and maybe where he is."

"And if you see a vision of him dead at the bottom of the sea?"

Goody Lamb gasped and turned away from him. Several of the watching men said things like, "That was harsh, Plato," and "Have pity on the lady," and "Have some manners, man."

Goody Lamb turned back around to face him. "If that's what I see, then I'll know."

Calvin felt obliged to intervene. "Even if you see just what your husband said, it doesn't mean that it's true. It might be a sign of something that *might* happen. Sometimes visions in the crystal don't have any meaning we can guess at."

"Then why are we doing this?" demanded Plato.

Mildly, Calvin said, "Sir, this is what your wife asked for. Have I promised her a clear vision of something true? By word or hint?"

"No," said Plato.

"We're here because your wife wanted a *chance* to learn something about what your son is doing now. I told her that the quest might be fruitless, didn't I?"

"You did," said Goody Lamb, defending him.

The onlookers nodded and murmured their agreement.

"He promises nothing, and yet fools like us keep coming to him hoping for . . . *something*."

"Hope isn't foolish, so you're not fools. Nor am I. I didn't ask to be a seventh son like my brother. Nor have I sought to have the same powers as him, only whatever I'm granted by birth. I try to help when people ask, but if nobody wants what it's in my power to give, I won't force anybody to take it as a gift. Nor do I ask for payment of any kind, any more than Alvin does. How can I deal with you more honorably than I have?"

Of course, he knew exactly which of his statements were lies, and the whole gist of this little speech was dishonest. Of course he would have his payment. Of course he knew that by using Goody Lamb's blood to make a crystal cube out of muddy river water, more people would to come to him, asking for this or that miracle.

"I'll carry it for you," Plato said to his wife.

"I wish you could," said Calvin, "but it's her blood in the crystal, and only she can carry it, if there's to be any hope of vision in it."

Plato looked at the crystal in consternation.

Goody Lamb reached out again to take the cube.

"Wait," said Plato. "Her wrist is wounded. What if it weakens her hand and she drops it?"

"Then we'll find out if the crystal is too fragile to be dropped," said Calvin. "No one will take sick, no boat will sink, no bridge will collapse, no farm will get a blight—so, what *if* she drops it?"

While Calvin was talking, he watched Plato Lamb examine his wife's wrist, turning it over again and again. "You gave me the wrong wrist," said Plato.

"That's the one," she said.

"Give me your other wrist."

She rolled her eyes at Calvin—she's on my side now! he gloated—and held out her other wrist to her husband. He examined that one, too.

"Blood came out of the wound," said Plato.

"I think we all saw that," said Calvin.

"Where did the pin go in? Where did the blood come out?"

Calvin handed the cube to Goody Lamb, who held it easily. Then he bent down and picked up the pin from the grass. "I see no blood on this pin," he said. He handed it to Plato. "Can you see any sign that this pin ever made anyone to bleed?"

Not for the first time, Calvin wished he had paid more attention when Alvin tried to teach him how to heal deep. He could close up the superficial wound and block up the blood from coming out anymore, but injuries deeper in along the pin's trajectory through her wrist, he had no idea what to do about those things. So blood would continue seeping out within her wrist, and the bruise would be vivid and sensitive, and Calvin knew that Alvin could have made it like new. But making it *look* healed was enough for these trusting folk. And it *should* be enough. Alvin put himself to a lot of trouble that nobody would ever understand but Calvin, and he thought it was all wasted effort. What mattered was that they were content, they believed she had been healed.

Calvin didn't bother claiming that he had done it. Who else could it have been?

"It isn't heavy, Plato," said Goody Lamb, "and it doesn't slide in my grip, so I'll carry it."

"Where to?" asked Calvin.

"Why . . ." It was clear she had given this no thought. "Home?" she asked.

"It's *your* crystal cube," said Calvin.

"But you don't think I should take it home."

Calvin shrugged. "What do I know? Alvin probably could answer you. He's older and more experienced and more powerful, so all I can say is, there's a reason Alvin puts the crystals all together to make walls and towers. I think the crystals give each other clarity and strength. I think that in isolation, you may see far less than your blood has earned you the right to see."

The whole assemblage followed Goody Lamb and her husband up the hill to the main hall of the Crystal Palace, as many called it. Crystal *fortress*, that's what it looked like to Calvin. In the first hall, Goody Lamb stopped. "Where should I put it?" she asked.

"I think you shouldn't remove any blocks that are already there. Though your crystal has as much right to be in the wall anywhere you see fit."

Then Calvin turned to the onlookers. "You've seen all there is to see. None of you should know where Goody Lamb chooses to put her crystal. Not even you, Plato, my friend. It's hers to gaze into, not for anyone else. Her blood may have opened vistas into memories and histories that no one but her has a right to know."

Heeding his words, Goody Lamb simply stood there, waiting for the others to take the hint. One by one, and then in bigger clumps, they broke away and left the building. Plato was last to go. "I want to know where you put it," he said.

"Why?" she asked. "It's not yours to look at."

"What if you need help putting it into place?"

"I'll choose a place where I can put it without any help," said Goody Lamb.

Calvin thought: When I'm out of sight, she will remove one of Alvin's crystals and replace it with this one of mine. They always did.

"I'm going," said Calvin. "This is a matter for Goody Lamb and the walls and no one else."

Calvin walked down a hall, *not* toward the door they had come in through.

When he was far enough away, he sat down with his back against a wall and perused the blocks opposite him. The light was still good and he could see little scenes playing out. The people couldn't be real—they were too small—so this was only a vision, or several visions, Calvin couldn't be sure if the scenes all worked together somehow. He saw boats sailing on a choppy sea. They were small, and many of them shouldn't be on a rough lake, let alone on the open ocean, yet he could see that that was where they were.

Then he saw that Alvin was standing in the lead boat—standing! Had he never been in a small boat before?

He didn't have to stay here and watch Alvin do some amazing thing. He stood up and walked by another way to where he sensed Goody Lamb would be.

She wasn't there. He kept looking, and soon found her. She was sitting, sprawling really, with her head leaning against the wall. She was weeping.

Calvin knelt beside her, rested a hand on her shoulder. It was a gentle touch, but he made sure that it felt electric to her, not a shock but a trembling that went right through her. It was, by his power, as intimate a touch as was possible while she was wearing clothing.

She calmed and stopped crying. "Calvin," she said. "I can't see him."

"Crystals don't always begin to work until they've had a chance to clarify," he said. A lie—Alvin's crystals worked the moment they were set in place. "May I see?"

Goody Lamb placed her palm flat on a block that was, of course, a perfect cube. She had to have removed a block of Alvin's in order to put it where it was.

"The crystal that was here before," Calvin said.

"I pushed it back so this one could take its place."

"But none of these blocks are cubes," he said.

"When the other one was gone, the adjacent blocks stretched to fill the gap," she said.

"Well, then, of course it will take some time for the crystal to get used to its new place, and for the adjacent blocks to welcome it."

"So it might still work?" she pleaded.

"I don't know," said Calvin. He moved his hand across her shoulder to her other side, then drew her closer to him, folding her shoulders into his embrace, and turning her to rest her face against his chest. Again, he sent a trembling through her body, the kind of trembling that he knew women liked to feel.

"Is there anything I can do to help it now?" she asked.

Calvin held his silence, wanting it to unfold gradually. Wanting it to come from her.

"It's my blood in the cube, isn't it? Can't I . . . do something to call forth visions? To call my son to show himself?"

"Your son has no control here. If it shows him, he won't know you're seeing him. As I told you."

"I know, but . . . *he* is my blood, and the crystal has my blood."

"And my power," Calvin reminded her.

"Yes," she said. "Your power and my blood."

Almost there, thought Calvin.

"Can we . . . join together somehow, to make it come to life?"

"I don't know," said Calvin. "It isn't magic, and I don't know the science behind it."

She rested a hand on his chest, then his neck, then his cheek. "What if we drew closer together? Combining, the way the blood and water are joined in the crystal?"

"I have no idea," said Calvin, once again giving her a thrill of pleasure. Encouraging her to speak boldly.

"I'm a good woman, Calvin," she said.

"I know you are," said Calvin. "A mother who longs for her son, who will do anything that might bring you word or sight or sound of him." Too obvious? thought Calvin.

Her hand stroked his cheek, then moved up into his hair. "You have shown me such kindness," she said. "You understand me so well."

"I think I do know the longings of your heart," he said. Another thrill through her body.

She leaned up and put her lips on his. A sweet kiss. And then another. And then a hungrier kiss. Of course Calvin cooperated.

"I do feel closer to you," he whispered.

"And I to you," she said. And then, "Would you . . . would you be willing to call me Jane?"

That was not her name, he knew. "Why that name?" he asked.

"My name before I married Plato, it wasn't Lamb, it was Grey. And my mother always called me Lady Jane Grey. The Nine Days Queen. I . . . want to be your queen for a little time, Calvin."

In reply he reached up, loosened his tie, took off his collar. Then he knelt up and shrugged off his coat.

She was already halfway down her bodice, unbuttoning as she went. "Oh, Calvin, there are so many clothes."

"And inside them," said Calvin softly, "our truest selves, waiting to be joined together in power and love . . . for your son, for Nat."

And as he kissed her again, and then took off his shirt, he sent his doodlebug to close off both ends of this corridor by shutting some doors and opening others. No one would disturb them.

15

THIS WAS THE tedious kind of job that wore Alvin out. Every board in every ship and boat had to be joined to the boards next to it, with an unbreakable bond, as if the boards had grown together in the same tree. It would not guarantee that the hull would not be shattered by some outside force—two boats ramming each other, or being attacked by a whale or shark in arctic waters—but the hulls would be all of one piece, so that the normal flexion of the wood in shifting water would not cause friction between them or spring leaks in the hull.

Or so he reasoned. He had carefully done something like this with the hull of the ship that brought him and John and Measure over to Ireland, and the main result was that he heard the captain and first mate of the ship talking about how strange it was that they couldn't pump out the bilge, because there was no water in it. Apparently, larger ships were equipped with pumps, because hulls *always* leaked. And Alvin's version of their hull didn't.

That had been one ship, bigger than any in Alvin's little fleet, and it had exhausted him the first two days of the voyage. He had been working at a greater distance from the wood that time, because he didn't think the crew would look kindly on a passenger wandering around in the bowels of the ship. Here, he could see the boards he was joining. He wished now that he had brought Verily Cooper along to help, to do half the boats, at least. But Verily was needed back in Crystal City, to help fend off any legal challenges to the Crystal City charter that gave the city virtual independence from the Noisy River state government.

This boat was done. Ship. One of the seafaring folk had called it that. He didn't ask what the difference was, because they called some larger vessels boats, so it wasn't just a matter of size. Every board in the hull was part of a single, well-shaped board. How strange the tree would have looked, that could have this hull-shaped board cut out of it.

He lay down in the bottom of the . . . ship. Under the deck. Was it having decks that made a boat into a ship? He closed his eyes, just for a moment.

And opened them almost immediately, because of some called-out commands and the sounds of heavy feet on the deck above him. Apparently they were loading this ship and reinstalling some of the fittings that he'd had them pull out while he was working on the hull. The fittings all had to be removable during the voyage, without harming the integrity of the hull. It wouldn't do to have a bulkhead that was not movable because Alvin had accidentally fused it to the hull.

Alvin sat up, feeling strangely refreshed, stooped under the rafters, or whatever they were called on a ship, everything had different names on the sea. He made it to the ladderway up to the lower deck, and then the next ladderway up to the top deck, the one that got sunlight in good weather and rain the rest of the time. Which in Irish waters meant nearly every day, or so it seemed.

Sunny today.

Sunny *this morning.* The sun was a hand above the horizon on the east side of the ship. Alvin had not taken a quick nap, he had slept through the night.

Jedediah was supervising the loading of stores aboard the ship. He was having various crates and barrels arranged on the deck, to balance the load before it was hauled below deck.

"Leave some room for the passengers," said Alvin cheerfully.

"Still alive," said Jedediah. "Had us worried."

"Why didn't you wake me?"

"You don't think we tried?" said Jedediah. "I never heard there was a knack for sleeping like the dead, but if there is, you've got it strong, boy-o."

"I never sleep that sound," Alvin began.

"We didn't say you was noisy!" said Lovey Maloney, who was loading candles into the cabin under the poop deck. "You slept silent, sir. But Sheen even tried tickling your nose with a feather, and you never even changed your breathing, you like to sucked in the whole feather, but Sheenie didn't let go of it, no sir. That's why you don't have a feather in your chest."

Alvin could picture Rosheen doing that—she was respectful, but she would also do what it took to make sure whether Alvin was breathing or not.

"I'm glad she held on tight," said Alvin.

"She always does," said Lovey. "But it isn't her knack, if that's what you're thinking. She's just careful, and I've felt her grip before, sir. It's no knack, it's just brute force, about as strong as Da."

Since Alvin had never met Rosheen's and Lovey's father, he couldn't size him up in his mind. Maybe Lovey was exaggerating. Or maybe Da gripped with only a part of his strength, while Rosheen would clamp down with all her force on her sister's arm. And anyway, gripping a feather had more to do with the strength of her fingers. "Where's your sister now, Lovey?"

"Bandaging some injuries. That's what she mostly does, cause people keep getting bashed and sliced and broken."

Jedediah spoke up again, having placed the last of the casks and ascertained that the ship was level in the water. "A lot of landlubbers who can't get used to walking and working on a deck with a bit of movement to it. I think during the voyage we're going to need to keep everybody tied to a rope so they aren't always falling overboard."

"Sliced and broken?" asked Alvin.

"And bashed," said Lovey.

"Looks like you've done a fine job here, Jedediah," said Alvin.

"A perfect job, cause nothing less will do at sea," he said. "Now if we can just stow it below exactly as it is right now on deck."

"I'm curious how you knew to plan out the lading on deck like this."

"My da was a first mate on a warship when it captured an enemy ship worth thousands of pounds. My da's share wasn't enough to buy a farm in England, where he grew up, least not a farm big enough to sustain a family. So he bought him some land in the north of Ireland and that's where I grew up. But he told me stories, and about foolish first mates who thought they could balance a load by eyeballing and guessing."

"You don't hold with guessing."

"What can't be known, you guess at," said Jedediah. "What can be known, you figure out. My da's words."

"Have at it," said Alvin. "I'll stay out of your way."

Jedediah started ordering his crew to carry things below in a certain order. "No, no, we can't get that down by carrying it. We'll sway it down in a minute or two."

Alvin reached for Lovey's hand, and she gave it to him readily. "Take me to Rosheen, would you, Lovey?"

"I can fetch her for you, if you like!" said Lovey eagerly.

"Thanks, I know you would, but I want to go see her at her work."

Getting down the gangplank took some concentration, particularly since he was holding on to Lovey behind him and half-dragging her. She was terrified of the harbor water, of falling in. And Alvin didn't blame her—it wasn't the cleanest water in the world, with all kinds of detritus floating and soaking or dissolved in the water.

Soon enough, though, they were on firm land, and Lovey let go of his hand and bounded on ahead, her pigtails dancing. "Wait for me!" called Alvin. "I can't keep up when you run!"

She slowed down and then stopped, waiting for him to catch up. Of course he could outrun her any day of the week and twice on Sunday, but walking was safer than running into people. The Quay was busy today, as every day, with all the people doing their jobs. No slackers among them, Alvin was happy to see. And many had found ways to use their knacks to help. But there was no job that able-bodied people didn't do, right willingly, whether they were trained for it or practiced in it or even fully understood what the job was. They knew their lives depended on it. Being sentenced to transportation to the New World by the Catholic Inquisition only marked them more surely for death as long as they were on Irish soil—nobody believed that the Church of Ireland wasn't aware of who they were, where they were, and what they were doing.

Rosheen was not indoors on this clear sunny day. Near her in a couple of rows were men lying on the ground, with scarce a blanket to smooth and soften under them. But as Alvin stood and studied Rosheen's patients, he realized what her knack really was. Because every broken bone—and there were six of them, divided among four unlucky (or clumsy) men—had been expertly set and was already half healed. Only Alvin himself could have done better.

So he didn't interfere by completing their healing. Rosheen's knack was sufficient and Alvin would leave it to her. Someone had once accused him of having no respect for anyone's knack except his own, and he made it a point to let others do what they knew how to do.

The gashes were bandaged, but Alvin could tell that when the bandages came off, there'd be little sign of a healing wound, perhaps not even a scar. Skin and muscle healed up faster than bone.

Lovey went up to Rosheen and whispered in her ear. Rosheen didn't lose concentration on the man whose crushed hand she was working on. Alvin walked over to her and stood behind her, using his doodlebug to see what she was dealing with. It was a mess, and no regular surgeon would have had any idea but to cut off the whole hand before a bad infection set in. And there *was* an infection taking hold within the bloody mass. Had the man caught his hand between ship and dock? He couldn't think what else could have done this.

Rosheen seemed to have no knack with infection. Why would she? She could knit together bones and flesh, but something as small as the animalcules that caused infection would be beyond her ken. It had taken Alvin a good while before he even discovered what infection *was.* So he took a while, standing there, to purge the man's mangled hand of the gangrenous humors that he found there.

If Rosheen noticed what he had done, she gave no sign. Her concentration was obviously devoted to putting bones back together, encasing them with the cartilage that held it all together.

"So now I know your knack," murmured Alvin.

"Didn't know myself," said Rosheen. "But now I see why people came to me back home, when they had cuts and breaks."

"And bashes," said Lovey.

"Bashes are the hardest," said Rosheen.

"You've fixed this one up pretty good," said Alvin.

Rosheen shook her head. "Pretty good is less than good, and less than good is not acceptable."

"I correct myself," said Alvin. "Your work here is far better than acceptable. It's superb."

"I thank you sir."

Her patient held up the bloody hand and flexed and stretched all the fingers. "Lord Almighty, girl," he said, "it's like Jaysus himself come and had at me."

"I think Jesus had the same knack, most likely," said Alvin. "Among others."

"He had the power of God," said Rosheen. "Him *being* God and all."

"Are you so sure *your* knack doesn't also come from God?"

Rosheen shook her head. "I always thought my knack was to bring peace to our home. To unify us. Harmonize us."

"So it was a peaceful home?" asked Alvin.

"You were there, inside it."

"But your father was away."

Rosheen nodded. "That he was. But he wasn't one of those drunken louts who come home and beat up their wife and children."

"Ah. So your house was in harmony all the time."

"Liquor isn't the only thing that causes quarreling," said Rosheen. "Mam didn't drink, neither, but she could lay into my da . . ."

"It was your mother who started the hitting?"

"Beating, I have to say. She already knew her fists couldn't do anything to bother him. She broke more than one broomstick over his back. Got so she'd find a stout limb of a tree, wheedle off the twigs, and use that branch to beat him with. Left him some bloody scrapes."

"Did those scrapes heal remarkable fast?" asked Alvin.

Rosheen rolled her eyes. "He hit her back, of course. Only time he hit her was to defend himself. Grab the broomstick or the branch, pull it out of her hands, throw it out the door."

"And what did *you* do?" asked Alvin.

"I calmed her down, reminded her how hard Da worked, how he didn't waste a penny in the public house, how he cared for us children, how he played with us. I'd say, 'He's a good da,' and she'd say, 'So I'm a bad mam?' And I'd say, 'It's a good mam gave us a da like that, and a good da gave us a mam like you.'"

"And that worked?" asked Alvin. Having known his share of angry married couples—*not* his own parents—he had found that calming down a raging parent or spouse was harder than calming down a charging boar.

"They didn't want to fight," said Rosheen. "They didn't want to hit each other or hurt each other. Talking made the anger cool, too, I think. When I was done, they were reconciled. So much, sir, that my da would even bring the broomstick back into the house. Though not the branch. If she wanted *that*, she'd send one of the children out to fetch it."

"And you did that?"

Rosheen chuckled. "I never heard her ask me to do that. I can be remarkably hard of hearing sometimes."

"I bet you can," said Alvin, chuckling.

"I couldn't think how to use my knack to help, till I realized that sometimes when I bandaged people up, just being helpful, you know, the wound was already healed before I finished, and after a while I learned to feel when I was doing it, and work on that so I could *make* it happen."

"Like everybody with their knacks."

"Is it likely I have *both* knacks?"

"Could be. Or could be that your peacemaking skills were no knack, just love and wisdom and patience—"

"Can't accuse me of patience, just ask Lovey."

"She worships you," said Alvin. "If you had no patience with her, she'd fear you or resent you, but she adores you."

Rosheen appeared doubtful.

"I'm a seventh son in a family that had girls, too," said Alvin. "I know when sisters don't get along, and I know when the love beats strong as a tempest in all their hearts. Your sister has a tornado of love for you, as you do for her."

"Never thought of love as a tornado," said Rosheen. "Tearing trees out of the ground and roofs off houses. I read about them."

"I've seen them. Been inside one once, with a Red Prophet keeping me safe."

"Red? A native?"

"A fine man, and still a friend."

"You actually *know* Red people?"

"Can't help but know them," said Alvin, "at least if you leave your house now and then."

"Is it true they're all drunks who scalp people?"

"They're all different kinds," said Alvin, "just like White folks. My friend drank some for a while, and then he stopped."

Rosheen brightened up. "Mam told me that Da used to drink up a storm. Drunk whenever he had a tuppence. A nasty drunk, too, Mam said. She had to fight him off many a time."

"I take it something changed him?"

"I didn't believe her, when she told me that," said Rosheen. "Because I never saw it. But she said it was so, and here's what changed him. He nearly killed a man. She was there and saw it—I was a babe in her arms at the time, so I saw it too, but I didn't remember. Da got in a fight outside the pub—well, it began inside, but *moved* outside the pub, and Mam said Da was a powerful fighter and he beat that man down to the ground and he was too drunk to know that he already won so he kept pounding, even though his own hand was most as broken up as the other man's head.

"Well, that's what Mam said," Rosheen went on. "And then she said that when Da was finally pulled off the fellow, some men thought he must be dead, he lay there so still and quiet. But then he sat up, holding his head, complaining of a headache. Mam says he shook his head and said it was all better. His jaw wasn't even out of joint, which, the way my da beat him, his jaw should have been lying in the road with all the teeth knocked out of it."

Alvin chuckled.

"Mam said," Rosheen insisted. "She's no liar, sir."

"Oh, I believe every word of the tale. I'm just surprised you didn't see what was really going on."

"I wasn't two years old, sir. Whatever I saw, I don't remember now."

"I'm saying that given your knack for healing, I bet you were healing that fellow even while your dad was pounding him into the cobblestones."

"No cobbles in that village," said Rosheen. "And I don't know how I could have been healing anybody at that age. I couldn't even concentrate on burping without getting whupped on my back by Mam's hand."

"You had nothing else to concentrate on. I think the man's pain spoke to you. Or maybe it was the breaking and the tearing. But Rosheen, you already had your knack, even as a wee baby."

"Maybe," said Rosheen. "Can't say."

The man held up his naked, pristine arm. "Sure got it now, girl," he said.

"If you're healed," said Alvin, "don't you got some work to do?"

The man sprang to his feet. "Thanks for saying that, I still have a lot of hauling to do."

"Just keep your hand out from between boats and docks," said Alvin.

"How did you—" He left his sentence unfinished. Then he got up, thanked Rosheen, and went on his way.

"Now *there's* a man whose heart you stole," said Alvin.

"Nothing of the kind. I'm not old enough to steal no hearts," she said.

"Well, be prepared. That time will come."

"Not for me. Not pretty enough."

"Where'd you get that silly idea?"

"I was an ugly baby," she said, "Mam said the angels got mad at me and uglied me up before I was born."

"Which means that your mam knew you were remarkable pretty and called you ugly to keep you from becoming vain."

Rosheen looked skeptical.

Alvin patted her shoulder. "You've got work to do," he said.

"You can stay and help. I have a feeling you're a better healer than I am."

It was true, but mostly because he'd had a lot more experience. "I've met no better healer than you, Rosheen." After all, a man can never say what day he met *himself.*

"I'm sad to hear that," she said, "since I work so slow."

"Rosheen," Alvin said, "I can't help but wonder. Do you have to be right close to help a body heal?"

"I don't know, it just makes sense to be close."

"I wonder if you could try being a little farther off, and then a little more the next time."

"Wouldn't that slow me down even more?"

"Might," said Alvin. "But I'm thinking, what if you're in one boat and a man with a broken arm is in another boat, but close by, close enough to see him."

Rosheen's eyes went wide. "You're thinking about the voyage west."

"I don't know how to get you safely from boat to boat, especially in seas rough enough for a man to break a bone, but if your knack has some reach to it, maybe the whole expedition can benefit from your healing gifts."

Rosheen thought for a moment. "Who knows, until I try?" she said. "I'll experiment with trying to heal from afar. Like on that man." She pointed at a fellow lying on the ground.

"Rosheen, you healed that fellow's sprained ankle before he finished laying himself down."

"I did?"

"Somebody did," said Alvin. "Right now he's just idling because he's so tired. I've learned in my life that you can't heal weariness, it has to be healed by rest and sleep."

"Well, let him sleep, then," said Rosheen.

"Oh, he's awake now, and listening, and I reckon he's so ashamed of slacking when *you* work hard that he's about to bound to his feet and run back to work on his perfectly good ankles."

The man stood up and bowed sheepishly to Alvin and Rosheen. Then he did indeed run off, loping without a sign of a limp. He *did* have work to do. Rosheen laughed as he sped away.

16

"It's kind of my sister-in-law to take time away from running this whole shebang in order to talk to me, a young man of no office or function in Crystal City."

"One might wish that it were so, but office or not, you definitely *function*. Not a bad word for it. Functioning."

"I don't know what you mean," said Calvin. "Would the fine lady like to sit down on my third-hand furniture?"

"Are you indicating the chair *least* likely or *most* likely to collapse under my weight?" Margaret smiled, and her amusement seemed genuine.

"Even if I had such a prank in mind," said Calvin, "and even if you laughed when it was done, and were not injured at all, I think I'd have a heavy price to pay when he gets back from Ireland."

"So you think ahead before you do mischief, is that it?"

Calvin spread his hands in a shrug.

"Have you thought ahead to what happens when at least fourteen babies are born in Crystal City that bear a much stronger resemblance to you than to their putative fathers?"

"Putative," said Calvin. "You lost me, Mistress Larner."

"You've been providing your favorite function to many ladies of mature enough years to be married to men who aren't you," said Margaret.

"Putative," said Calvin. "Does that mean *not*, but people think it *is*?"

"Your recreational activities are known to few, but word *is* spreading," said Margaret. "This will be damaging to the social fabric of this community. Most recently Goody Lamb, a woman worth ten of you."

"She asked me to call her—"

"Jane Grey, the name her mother called her," said Margaret.

"So you've been watching," he said, nodding wisely.

"I still see it in your heart. How little it meant to you, considering how much it will cost her."

"Meaning there'll be some screaming and hitting?" asked Calvin. "I don't think so. In fact, I daresay that not one husband will speak to his wife in such a way as to imply he suspects her of being untrue to him."

"Mayhap you're right. Mayhap there'll be no open arguments at all."

"Count on it," said Calvin. "Though what this has to do with—"

"Spare me. Spare us both. Every lie makes you look more like a . . . like a liar to me."

"Since you can see into my heartfire, Mistress Larner, can you tell me where this ruinous path will lead me in my life?"

"You already know," said Margaret.

"I don't know with the clarity *you* have."

"Alvin will come home and find your crystals in his walls."

"Did he forbid me to create new blocks for Crystal City?" asked Calvin. "I have no memory of that."

"Nobody ever sees anything in your—"

"Nobody sees anything they *understand*," said Calvin. "But that's true of most of the visions in *Alvin's* crystals, too. It's a tricky thing, understanding what you do and don't see. I reckon heartfires is more sure-sighted."

"Alvin *will* come home," said Margaret.

"I'm glad to have your assurance of his safety during his ocean crossing."

"And even if the husbands and wives you've poisoned don't quarrel openly, you're sowing distrust in marriages and—"

"But am I? The distrust is surely warranted and completely rational, wouldn't you say, considering that so many of these women have alien babies in their wombs."

"Calvin, I know what you—"

"If you really do," said Calvin, "then you can look into my heartfire and discover that I did *nothing* to compel my paramours. I always waited for them to make the first overt move or say the first clear words. It was by their free choice."

"It was by your choice that they felt an intimate thrill with each touch of your hand."

"Oh, have you felt those intimate thrills yourself, Mistress Larner?" And as he said it, he gave her one of those exact thrills, a strong one, trembling her right to the bone.

Instead of sitting there in bliss, however, she leapt to her feet and with one foot pushed his chair over backward. "Some of these aren't so sturdy after all, I see," she said—softly and grimly, like a shy madwoman. She loomed over him, standing between his legs as he lay sprawled on the dirt floor of his miserable little house. She raised a foot as if to stomp his genitals, and he forced himself to hold still and not shy away.

"And some parts of me aren't sturdy either," said Calvin. "Isn't it wise of me to exercise those parts to make them stronger? And what if some enemy were to step on those parts and drive them permanently out of service? Wouldn't it show forethought on my part, if there were already fourteen of my offspring to carry my blood, unknowingly, into a hundred generations to come?"

"Fourteen," she said. "So you know the count."

"On the contrary. A gentleman would never keep a count, as if one liaison were the equivalent of every other. I took the number fourteen from what *you* said."

"So the number could be higher," said Margaret.

"I'm quite sure that it is, or will be, before Alvin gets here." Then Calvin grinned wickedly. "We could make it fifteen in the next ten minutes—or the next hour, if you'd like to linger with me."

Her foot did come crashing down than, but she apparently didn't know enough about male anatomy. She didn't even touch his stones, just bruise the skin over his pubic bone. It was painful, but not agonizing, and there'd be no interference with his procreative competence.

She must have seen the smugness in his face, or seen her ineffectiveness in his heartfire, because this time she swung her foot forward, just above the floor, and the point of her boot drove hard into his scrotum. He cried out before he was able to reach inside himself with his doodlebug and heal the damage and subdue the pain.

"Is this why you came to my cabin, Mistress Larner, to assault me in my own home?" he asked.

"I came to find out what kind of man you are. A Don Juan? A Lothario?"

"And which am I?"

"Neither. They were in it for pleasure."

"I believe they were both fictional," said Calvin.

"You, however, there's not much pleasure for you in the coition. The pleasure is in the damage you might do to Alvin's city."

"I don't think I've done any damage at all."

"In your own small, meanspirited way, you've done all the damage you *could*."

"Why, I think I'll take that as a challenge, Mistress Larner, to see if I can think of something that will *really* consternate my big brother."

"The biggest pain you can cause him, Calvin, is the pain of seeing the kind of man you've become. He loves you, and when he learns of this it'll break his heart."

"Then if you value his happiness," said Calvin, "you'll hold your tongue."

"Do you think I need to *tell* him what you've done?" She spat on the ground and turned in a swish of skirts toward the door, which in that tiny cottage was only one step away, and still standing open.

"You need practice with your spitting," said Calvin.

She paused in the doorway, her back to him.

"Some of your spittle trailed onto your own skirt," he said. "You need to build up a good wad of phlegm before you spit, to glue it all together and give it more range."

"I imagine you've been spat on by more perilous foes than myself."

"I'd be sorry to consider you a foe, Mistress Larner, when I've tried so hard to accommodate your needs and provide you with such comforts as philosophy allows."

Margaret sighed. "Not all philosophy is stoicism, Master Calvin, which you would know if you opened a book as often as you open women's bodies."

"They open their own bodies, and beg me to come in."

Margaret turned toward him and took a step, with that dangerous foot coming near again.

"Is there no limit to the pain you choose to cause me?" asked Calvin.

Margaret stopped, then turned around and walked, the image of stately posture, to and through Calvin's door. She didn't bother to close it, another sign of her disdain. Calvin struggled to his feet, subduing the pain still further, and staggered to the door and pushed it closed.

So Margaret knows all, and tells nothing. Calvin could live with that . . . until Alvin came home, at least. Then it would be interesting indeed, to see how he reacted once he understood all that Calvin had done, all he was doing, all that he had yet to do.

17

THE BOATS AND ships were being taken out two or three or four at a time, and Alvin was pleased to see that there were no leaks. Not as pleased, however, at how clumsily the Irish crews handled the boats. There were a few more-or-less gentle collisions. But most of the crews were learning, and the ones who did it best were helping the others to learn, so Alvin believed the expedition was going to be possible. He couldn't go so far as to say that its success would be probable. But at least they should be able to start off decently.

A carriage with two brisk horses rattled over the rutty track leading into the camp at the Quay. A carriage was a reason to worry—that was how church officials and government officials and other English overlords traveled. Never by the new railroad that had just connected this town with Dublin. That would be faster, but the so-called Anglo-Irish did not like sharing transportation with the hoi polloi. Or, as some jokingly said, the Hoi Malloy.

The carriage door opened and one lone man got out, nicely but not brilliantly dressed, looking like a lawyer or a professor. Except that he was remarkable young. But confident. The young man scanned the crowd of hard-working or fast-walking people and picked Alvin right out of the crowd.

"Like he was looking for you," said Measure, not five feet off.

"I daresay he was," said Alvin. "You're so tall nobody has to *look* for you."

"But when they spot you, they stop looking."

Alvin and Measure grinned at each other. Measure liked to tease him about being famous, and Alvin knew perfectly well that there was not a speck of envy in it, because Measure would run and hide if any newspaper people came looking for *him*.

Alvin strode to meet the young man from the carriage, extending his hand for a handshake—or a nice quick wrestle to the ground, if that seemed indicated. Fortunately, the young man extended his hand, too, and they shook.

"Alvin Smith, at your service," said Alvin.

"Alvin Miller, Alvin Maker, I take it," said the young man.

"Now that we're sure of my identity, perhaps a hint at yours?" Meanwhile Alvin was scanning the fellow's body on the inside, and quickly found that his heart was sick and weak. Yet he did not look like a man nursing a bad heart.

"Gladly. I'm Elisha Kent Kane, from Philadelphia, where my father is a judge, and most recently from Yale University, where I got a medical degree."

"You know those fellows there got no idea how the human body works."

Elisha grinned. "Let's say that anatomy and physiology are knacks sorely lacking in the medical school. But they're not all fools, and I learned all I could."

"I hoped you were American," said Alvin. "No honest Irishman would look so well-fed, and we're not happy when stout Englishmen show up around here."

"American, through and through, tried and true. Well, not really *tried* yet, but true."

"What puzzles me is why you hired a carriage from the railroad station just to come here. Most people walk."

"When a stranger says, 'It's a far piece down that road till you see the bay,' I don't estimate the 'far piece' as near enough to walk in less than half a day."

"It really isn't that far, but . . . you paid for passage to this island—"

"But not from America. I was testing my German in Hamburg."

"How did you do?"

"My German is wretched, so embarrassing that even the Germans didn't laugh at me, out of pity."

"But you made yourself understood?" asked Alvin.

"Do you have need of someone who speaks German?" asked Elisha.

"I have need of someone who'll talk to me long enough for me to get his measure."

"I'll talk all you want, though I talk better with my pen, I think."

"I listen best with my ears. Do you have an errand here?"

"Half accomplished, because I met you."

"And the other half?"

"Word is that an expedition is underway to cross the Atlantic in ridiculous small boats," said Elisha.

"There's word of many things going around," said Alvin. "But such word is sometimes true, often mistaken, and sometimes just outright lies."

"Not from me, sir," said Elisha.

"But what if you've been lied to, and came here in good faith, and find you were misled?"

"You're here, and there are boats being piloted clumsily out in the bay, and wagons bringing in loads of stores."

Alvin nodded. "I reckon we're past the rumor stage. You know that the people making this voyage are mostly of a kind the Church of Ireland—and the Church of England—call witches."

"Folks with knacks," said Elisha. "I've been intrigued by such people my whole life. My father, even before he was appointed judge, said that locking up or killing people just because they're very good at doing something makes the law into the criminal. Which is why I don't think he's planning on moving to New England."

"How's your father on slavery?" asked Alvin.

"We never owned any slaves and never would. My pa says, 'If it isn't a free country for all, it isn't a free country for any.'"

"I like your father," said Alvin.

"So do I," said Elisha.

"Will I like you, too?" asked Alvin.

"My father's opinions on such things run pretty concurrent with my own. I like to tell him I taught him everything he knows."

"You have a degree in medicine."

"Also at Yale I studied geology and geography," said Elisha.

"Wouldn't happen to know any navigation?"

"Not from college, but yes. My family isn't rich—my father is an *honest* judge, which is suitably punished by modesty of means—but I had friends whose families owned boats, and on holidays the yachts would come and pick them up. They'd show me how to navigate until I could do it myself. Never missed the port yet."

"What about in the open ocean? Can you find your path?"

"I've been all up and down the American coast, Crown Colonies and all, but none of that was open ocean. And on the way here, my curiosity kept annoying the chief engineer—it was a steam crossing, I made sure of that—but you've got no steamboats here, so that was probably wasted effort. Still, I got the use of compass and sextant and clock and I pretty much have an idea of what I'm doing."

"Good," said Alvin. "You'll be sailing with me."

"The flagship!"

"I got no flag," said Alvin.

"Sir, you *are* the flag. Wherever you sail, that's the flagship."

"I'm a man, not a flag," said Alvin mildly.

"Sir," said Elisha. "Have you a place where I can rent a room?"

"All the rooms in the Quay were let months ago. But I've got a cot in my tent that isn't being used," said Alvin.

"I snore, sir."

"So do I."

"I've been told that my snoring has caused earthquakes in Chile," said Elisha.

"And mine has caused the moon to change its phase," said Alvin. "But the people who told us all that nonsense were just trying to make us feel bad."

Alvin helped Elisha carry his bags to the tent. The man was not a dandy, with a dozen changes of clothes. But he *was* a physician, with a bag of instruments as well as his bag of clothing. Elisha also slung over his shoulder a coat so thick and furry that from behind, it made him look like a bear. "That's a mighty hefty coat, even in Ireland," said Alvin.

"Crossing the Atlantic in winter, everyone will wish for a coat like this," said Elisha. "We can't ride the Gulf Stream, it flows in the wrong direction. We'll have to sail farther north, skirting Iceland and Greenland before we reach the Labrador coast, or Nova Scotia."

Alvin quickened his pace till he was walking beside the young man. "You really did study geography."

"That much I'd have known from looking at a good map."

"Good maps are things I don't own," said Alvin. "Nor anyone else with us."

"I didn't think I could handle the weight, nor that they'd fit inside my bag, so I left my atlases at home."

"Do you know where we could acquire some?" asked Alvin.

"Why would we need them?" asked Elisha. "I already told you everything they could tell us. Iceland, Greenland, Newfoundland, Nova Scotia, take a wide path around New England, and then make landfall on Long Island or New Jersey or up the Delaware to Philadelphia."

"I have heard the names of all those places, but I'm not sure I could pick them out on the map."

"Sir, it's not my knack, but it has been my study, and I think that at any landfall, I can figure out where we are fairly quick, weather permitting."

"Then I think you must share my cabin on whatever ship I sail in."

"Are any of your vessels large enough to have a captain's cabin?"

"Not yet," said Alvin, "but I have hopes of bigger ships to come."

"You're not planning to turn pirate, are you, sir? Because near as I could tell, you don't have a decent-size cannon aboard any of your boats."

"No piracy, but perhaps . . . well, if you don't want to skirt the edges of the law, what in the world are you doing here, where almost every man and woman stands condemned already by canon law, and civil law as well, along with being Irish, which also seems to be a crime in Ireland."

"Taking a ship without a skilled crew is madness. You'll be overtaken and boarded within the day."

"You do think ahead, don't you," said Alvin.

"My father required that of us at all times. 'What was your plan here, son?' he'd say, and if I had no ready answer, *then* I'd be punished instead of consoled for any hurt I caused myself."

"I hope to meet your father," said Alvin.

"I hope you don't, sir," said Elisha. "Because the surest way to meet him would be getting haled into court in his part of Pennsylvania."

"But I'm innocent," said Alvin.

"Not if you steal a ship and sail it to America," said Elisha, "and even if I'm a passenger on it, my father would uphold the law."

"My plan is not to steal anything, my young friend, but to make use of what others have discarded. Could you pilot me around this green island to the port of Belfast?"

"Not with pinpoint accuracy, and not with any knowledge of shoals, reefs, or rocks, but if we stand far enough out to sea, and then came back to the coast from time to time, I think I could get us to Belfast. But why would you go there? It's the least Catholic part of Ireland, where the English are most supported by the populace."

"We're Americans," said Alvin. "And not Catholic, if I guess correctly."

"Foreign," said Elisha, "and not invisible."

"We don't have to walk far on land. We only have to check on the location of the prison hulks."

Elisha thought about that in silence, and then they were at the tent. Alvin was pleased to see that, despite carrying the heavier load, Elisha was not at all winded from their walk. After his bags were placed and the cot made up into a bed—the women of the encampment made sure that Alvin's linens were always clean and pressed, and his blankets beaten—the two of them lay back on their cots, Alvin's being no whit better than Elisha's, and discussed how many men they'd need to man the hulks, if they were made seaworthy and liberated.

"If we can sail them at all, we'll have to go north, around Ulster, because to the south lies Dublin and far too many English ships to slip past unnoticed."

"You are my guide in this," said Alvin.

"And what about the prisoners?" asked Elisha.

"Father Lukasz has heard that the hulks are populated mostly by Irish folk imprisoned for being too Irish, by which he means too Catholic," said Alvin. "Only one hulk carries violent prisoners convicted of actual crimes against persons or property."

"'Persons or property,'" echoed Elisha. "Now you sound like my father."

"I've spent a good deal of time around lawyers. Do that, and you pick up a bit of the language. Nary a bit of the law, mind you, just some language."

"Same thing with sailors," said Elisha. "I've used my time on several voyages to try to learn about the running of a ship, and along the way I've learned words I never thought would have any reason to exist."

"If you can think of it, there'll be a word for it," said Alvin.

"Just my point," said Elisha. "I would never, *could* never have thought of the things that sailors have words for."

"I hope our people don't pick up any bad habits at sea."

"Unless you plan to bring real sailors with us—"

"I plan to offer every prisoner in the hulks we borrow a chance to sail west with us."

"Being a prisoner on a prison ship doesn't prepare you to be a sailor."

"But it does prepare you to live aboard a ship."

And then Lovey came to the door of the tent—she most always volunteered to carry messages to Alvin, partly because she kept track of where he was—and in her piping voice said, "You are called to supper, Alvin, and your guest, too."

"Does food sound good to you?" asked Alvin.

"With this blight on the land, how do you find enough food for such a company as you have here?"

"My brother forages and buys, barters and begs. There are still surpluses in Ireland, which won't be true in a year."

"I asked in England if Parliament had any plan to bring food to Ireland during the famine to come, and people looked at me as if I had suggested bringing Irish families in to live with them."

"A genuine solution, if no other can be found," said Alvin.

"England may rule over Ireland," said Elisha, "but I get no sense that the general population of Englishmen feel the slightest responsibility to provide good government or any kind of aid. The Irish are universally despised and yet also resented in England, as if the Irish deserved the treatment they've received."

"Yes," said Alvin. "The Irish have committed the unforgivable sin of wishing the English to go away."

"So many places around the world share that hearty wish."

"Despite the fact that it is the yearning of the English to bring the blessings of civilization to benighted people everywhere."

Elisha chuckled. "So what's on the menu for tonight?"

"I don't know what Measure's been bringing in, so it's always a surprise to me. Stewed clams a couple of times, and crabs—I never lived near the sea and I never acquired a taste for such strange creatures. Clams—all mouth. Looking at them you'd never know they had flesh inside that bony exterior."

"Sometimes you talk like a Westerner, Mr. Smith, and sometimes you use words like 'exterior.' I don't know what to make of you."

"I had a fine teacher, but I didn't pay attention as well as I should," said Alvin. "So she married me to continue my education at her leisure."

"Margaret Larner," said Elisha. "The one they call the Seeress."

Alvin was taken aback. "I did not know her name was familiar to strangers."

"Not like yours, sir. Witch-haters know *your* name like they know the names of Lucifer. But your wife is spoken of with awe, mostly, and I only heard of her when I worked with Professor William Barton Rogers, exploring the rocks of the Appalachees."

"People from the mountains do make the trek to Crystal City sometimes, to counsel with my wife."

"I've heard the mountainfolk disparaged as superstitious possum-heads, but I reckon their superstitions are more likely to be knacks they know of and miracles they've seen."

"That's possible," said Alvin. "I can smell supper now, and it's stew. No shellfish, just mutton or lamb or goat, or all three."

"Beef?"

"Beef belongs to the English Army and the English Fleet," said Alvin. "By law. If you own a cow, and it meets with an accident and dies, you're forbidden to eat its meat, but you must notify the authorities, who come and seize it and salt it down to pack in barrels for the ships at sea."

"Speaking of which," said Elisha, "when we're in Belfast I wonder if you would have the funds to buy a supply of limes."

"Limes don't grow in this climate."

"I'm not asking you to grow them, just to buy them. I've heard that it prevents the scurvy."

"I hope there's something else that'll do that job, then. Nobody brings a great number of limes into Ireland."

"Not a *great* number," said Elisha. "Just one per person per week of the voyage."

"That could be half the limes of Spain," said Alvin. "We can't guess how long we'll be at sea."

"Cabbages and carrots also work, but they can't be stored as long on board ship," said Elisha. "The secret is to not cut them and not wash them. Keep them in a dark damp place—"

"Which is *every* place below decks on a ship," said Alvin.

"And keep them as cold as possible."

"And how can we do that?"

"Store them in a ship going past Iceland, Greenland, Newfoundland, Nova Scotia . . ."

Alvin smiled and nodded.

"Starbug is what the Danes call the disease. Scurvy in English. I like starbug better. It can kill off a whole ship's company in a few weeks. Physicians have pronounced a hundred different things the cause, all of them nonsense. An imbalance of humors? *Which* humors? There are only four.

But we don't know anything about these humors, and after centuries of bleeding our patients we have no idea if it accomplishes anything at all. So much ignorance—"

"Plenty of that to go around," said Alvin.

"Cabbages are cheap. Well, they *were* cheap, till potatoes got so dear," said Elisha. "Cabbages and carrots. Haul them here and make sure everybody is getting at least a carrot a day. Don't peel them. Don't cut them up. If you cut up a cabbage, share it and eat every bit of it within a day. But until it's cut, if you wrap it in oilcloth in a cold place, it can keep for a couple of months, sometimes three. Eating these things—or limes or lemons or oranges—will keep the starbug away. You won't lose a soul."

"Babies with no teeth—"

"Have the mothers eat two carrots, and the baby will thrive."

"Why do you know this and the Navy doesn't know it?"

"They've been told," said Elisha. "Repeatedly. All the scientific investigation has shown that scurvy is completely cured because of something in certain vegetables and fruits. If we can't get citrus, we can get cabbages and carrots."

"Cook them?" asked Alvin.

"Less effective, but they still help. Pickle them, that can preserve them in vinegar and brine. Store the carrots in water, with a lid on the pot."

"Why do you know this?"

Elisha smiled. "I looked up what kills the most sailors. It isn't sea battles, it isn't pirates, it isn't sharks, it isn't plague or smallpox or mutiny or getting lost at sea, it isn't running out of water or food."

"Scurvy," said Alvin. "Starbug."

"At sea you're eating salt beef or salt pork, fish you might catch on the way, hardtack and the worms that live in it, but no lemons or carrots, limes or cabbages, because you can only get those if you make landfall where such foods are available to buy."

"That was in the books."

"Newish books, but some of this has been known for centuries. The Norwegians have cloudberries. They make it into a jam and seal it under butter, so it doesn't go bad. They tried to grow cloudberries in Denmark but no, it's only Norway."

"And even though this knowledge is available . . ."

"My friend Mr. Smith," said Elijah, "the Navy and the Army prefer to do things as they've always done them."

"Including the deaths of hundreds of sailors a year from scurvy—"

"Thousands, most years," said Elisha. "They consider it a sign of a robust military to weed out those who are susceptible to scurvy by letting them die of it."

"Who *isn't* susceptible?"

"Everybody can and will die of scurvy. Cabbages and carrots, unwashed, stems cut off the carrots, don't skin them, keep them cool and dark, we should reach America without a single death from Starbug."

Others had gathered around the table where Elisha and Alvin ate to listen to their conversation. Some seemed to be annoyed by the things this stranger from America was saying, but others seemed to feel enlightened.

"In ten years," said Elisha, "everybody will know. The British fleet will buy all the limes of Portugal and Spain, mark my words. The American navy will send their ships out with fruits and carrots and cabbages. When nobody dies of scurvy, they'll know it wasn't this humor or that. It was the lack of certain fruits and vegetables. Partial starvation. Mr. Smith, please tell me what this is that I'm eating?"

"First call me Alvin. This Mr. Smith nonsense is already annoying."

"Alvin," said Elisha. "What am I eating?"

"I have no idea." Alvin turned to the people gathered around. "What is this a stew of?"

"An ox that was very old and couldn't pull its weight anymore," said a man.

"How do you know this?"

"It was my ox."

"How long stewing?"

"Seething and simmering since dusk yesterday," said the ox-owner. "That's why the meat is so tender. And why the gravy is so rich."

Elisha held up a forkful. "With food like this on shore, who's going to want to go to sea?" he asked.

Several in the crowd answered, "People expecting to be hanged or burned or pressed or drowned for witches."

The crews of the ragtag little fleet were getting pretty competent in the relatively calm waters of the bay. There were no more collisions. The sailors responded right smartly to changes in the wind. Alvin knew that the open ocean would be different, especially if there was a storm, but they had two in the community who had weather knacks, and they were hard at work trying to raise a wind or calm a wind, both of which might be needed in the same day at sea.

While they worked on, Measure and his team bringing in supplies, the cooks cooking, the loaders lading, the crews practicing, the ropers making miles of sturdy rope because Alvin once asked, "What if we needed to tie all the ships together in a line?" While they all did their work, Alvin and Elisha and a crew of the better seamen sailed out of the bay and north around the island. It was a long voyage, considering that they were never all that far from land. But first they sailed north, then east, then south, and the wind didn't change direction on command.

But when they got to a certain eastward point, Alvin said, "Let's go south." Elisha looked at him, puzzled. "Don't we need to get to Belfast?"

"Better if we walk into Belfast and don't show that we have this ship."

"Who will stay with the ship?" asked Elisha.

"Everybody who isn't you and me."

"Ireland is bigger than you think. It's going to be a long walk across Antrim."

Alvin nodded. "We both have been blessed with sturdy legs."

Elisha still looked like he had misgivings, no doubt because he knew his heart was weak. But Alvin had been working on him day by day, fixing tiny things that were weak or broken in and around his heart. Elisha might not know it yet, but he was well on the way to having a heart undamaged by his youthful bout with rheumatic fever. If it was up to Alvin—and so far, it was—however Elisha eventually died, it wouldn't be from this weakness of the heart.

The men were not happy about being left aboard, but Elisha designated a couple of reliable men to get fresh victuals from town, and Alvin gave them money to do it.

As Alvin and Elisha walked through Ballycastle and onto the road to Belfast, Elisha asked him, "How do you have so much money?"

"I don't have that much," said Alvin.

"But you keep having just enough."

"Do I?"

"When you need cabbages, when you need to victual the ship, when you need warm fur coats for as many women and men as possible, you have the money to pay."

Alvin said nothing.

"Story is that your knack can turn iron into gold."

"That's an old story."

"About a golden plow."

"People believe so many things," said Alvin.

"Sometimes true things," said Elisha.

"I haven't transmuted any metal into any other since I was a lad," said Alvin. "And I can't turn rags into furs."

"So what *have* you transmuted into gold? Grass? Ireland's not running out of *that*."

Alvin chuckled. Then he said, "The bishop of the Church of Ireland puts you under oath and says, 'Do you know if Alvin Smith turns anything into gold?' what will you tell them?"

Elisha nodded. "I'll say, 'Not that I know of, not that I've seen, not that he's ever said.' "

"And you won't have to think, Except that time walking from Ballycastle to Belfast, when he told me he could turn pebbles in the road into silver or gold, and then shape them into perfect replicas of English money."

"But would I be wrong if I figured you just now told me exactly how you lay your hands on all the money you need?"

Alvin shook his head. "You asked me, and I sighed—here, listen to this." Alvin gave a sigh that began deep in his belly and ended with a long whistling whine. "I sighed and said, 'If I could make pebbles into gold, why wouldn't I just buy the ships we need?' "

"Something I've been wondering," said Elisha.

"A ship is a big, expensive thing. When somebody buys one, it attracts the attention of the Fleet. Is this a fellow planning to smuggle things into Ireland or England to avoid paying duties and taxes? Or is he bringing weapons into Ireland? What need has a man who is no merchant for a ship, and how did he pay for it in cash?"

"Those are not comfortable questions," said Elisha.

"I can't afford to buy a ship," said Alvin. "Nor can I steal a ship, without setting off a hue and cry from north to south along this coast. Yet ships I must have, and not tiny ones—I have enough of those."

"I'm with you, Alvin," said Elisha. "I'll do your bidding because I know you always have a plan."

"I do, truly," said Alvin. "But I'm never sure that it's a *good* plan."

The plan was good enough, as long as everybody acted as Alvin expected them to act. In Belfast they first found lodging. Then Elisha walked alone to the docks and saw ships being loaded and unloaded and wondered, would any of these sailors come if I offered to hire them for a highly illegal voyage of witches to America?

He did ask a passing gentleman—which he could do, since he himself was dressed like a young gentleman—"What are those ships so far from this dock and the warehouses?"

"Hulks," the man said.

Elisha fell into step beside him. "Hulks?"

"From your speech I'd say you're not from Ireland *or* England."

"Maybe every gentleman in Ireland knows what a hulk is—"

"Prison ships. No longer seaworthy, so they're anchored and tied up and prisoners are kept aboard."

"How many prisoners?"

"That's not a thing the authorities divulge to us," said the gentleman. "Irish riffraff, criminals and rebels, traitors and seditionists."

"A bad lot, then."

The man stopped, and put a hand on Elisha's shoulder. "Don't go asking anybody about the hulks, young fellow. The authorities are particularly sensitive about the hulks, and anybody asking about them is going to find himself getting asked a lot of questions in return."

"Sir, your advice is both wise and kind. Thank you."

Elisha turned and walked the opposite direction from the gentleman. Would this man report Elisha for asking such questions? There was no reason he shouldn't. What if an English agent saw them talking together, walking together? What would the gentleman tell them about their conversation?

Yet Elisha did not yet know all he needed to know. So he went along the shoreline, outside the city, to long stretches of shore where there were only reeds and grasses and a fishing boat now and then. At last he came to the somewhat fortified area around the docks where the hulks were anchored.

"It's my sister, sir," said Elisha to a constable, avoiding the men who looked like soldiers or marines. "She thinks her friend's husband is aboard one of the hulks, but she—"

"If he is, then he's a bad'un," said the constable, "and if your sister knows his wife, then she ought to keep her distance, because the wife is probably a bad'un, too."

"That's what I'm afraid of, but she insisted that I—"

"Tell her to stop insisting or she'll end up putting your head through a noose."

Elisha wanted to say, For asking? But instead he said, "There are four of these hulks," Elisha said. "Her husband was arrested for stealing bread. That puts him in one hulk, and not in any of the others."

"If she or you think you can get a man freed from his lawful imprisonment—"

"Sir, we think no such thing. The man used to beat her."

"Of course he did. That's what drunken Irishmen do."

"Are the convicts all mixed up together?"

The constable pointed at the nearest hulk. "That's where the criminals go, the thieves and footpads and burglars and swindlers."

"She'll be glad when I tell her that it doesn't look as though he could escape and swim to shore."

"It's been tried, more than once. We have sharpshooters on every hulk. The divers and swimmers always reach shore—when we pull their dead bodies in with a boathook." The constable seemed to take pleasure and pride in the killing of men trying for freedom.

"I'll tell my sister enough to be sure he won't be coming home to beat her again, no time soon," said Elisha.

"To beat your sister? I thought he was husband of your sister's friend."

"That's what I said," Elisha answered, annoyed at himself. "He won't be coming home to beat her—her being my sister's friend. What did you think I meant?"

"Be careful, my American friend," said the constable. "I can easily point you out to the authorities."

"Yes, you could," said Elisha. "And then my father, a judge in America, will get the Governor-General of Ireland to investigate a constable who likes to make idle threats to passersby who ask harmless questions."

"Your father has no authority here."

"You know that. I know that. He knows that. But what my father does have is more money than the Pope. And money can purchase a lot of authority in out-of-the-way places."

The constable stiffened. "Are you trying to bribe me?"

"The farthest thought from my mind," said Elisha. "And if I tried, I'm sure you'd refuse any such corruption."

"That I would."

"But it's no bribe to take a friendly fellow to dinner and a few drinks at that tavern yonder, is it?"

"I'm on duty."

"Forever? Or do they let you go home to the little woman—"

"There's no woman. What woman of quality would marry a man as poor as me?"

"A woman who values honor above money."

"As if there *were* any such woman on God's green Earth."

"Many such," said Elisha. "And I pray you find one, and soon, too." Though he knew that the only woman this constable would find would let him do her standing up against an alley wall for two shillings.

"Here's an earnest. When your shift ends, these two shillings will buy you a couple of pints till I show up, unless I'm already there when you come off your shift."

The constable took the shillings. "Just a couple of drinks, not any kind of *real* money, not a bribe."

"Of course not," said Elisha.

He sauntered away, back toward the main commercial docks. He had all he needed—which of the hulks held the real criminals, though for all he knew they were all imprisoned because they had stolen food for their families in this time of spreading famine.

Back in their room above a tavern in Belfast, well back from the docks, Elisha found Alvin asleep with his boots on. Since there was only the one bed, Elisha didn't like to have boots dirtying things up where *he* would sleep.

"If I don't want my boots to leave dirt on the bed," said Alvin softly, "there'll be no dirt on the bed. Just as there are no fleas, no bedbugs, no mosquitos, no roaches, no potato bugs, no silverfish, no moths or flies or baby dragons. Have you ever stayed in a cleaner hotel than this room?"

Elisha chuckled. "You're a fine traveling companion." Then he described to Alvin which was the hulk with all the actual criminals. "Including my sister's friend's husband, who's in for stealing bread."

Alvin cocked an eyebrow. "Are you such a practiced liar that nobody doubted your story?"

"I believe he assumed that I was lying, and because I *was*, I wasn't, don't you see?"

"He thinks you're a liar, you pretend that you're not, but in fact you are, so his belief is justified, but he doesn't know that."

"I don't think you made it any clearer," said Elisha. "You just tangled it up more."

"Explanations aren't among my knacks," said Alvin.

"When do you start?"

"We already started. You found out which hulk we don't want to take, *and* you alerted a constable that somebody is interested in what happens to that ship."

"So we can't go near it now."

"We don't have to be close. Just for the pleasure of it, we should be close enough to watch. From that hill." He pointed out the window in the right direction.

"Tonight?" said Elisha.

"Hungry?"

"I could eat."

"Bread and cheese in that bag," said Alvin. "I only licked your cheese a little."

"Thereby improving the flavor considerable, I'd wager."

"Maker spit isn't a seasoning, Elisha, it's a toxin. But I'm weary, so you're safe enough."

Elisha clutching the bag with food inside, they left the hotel and wandered off into the hinterland, finally reaching the knoll at sundown. Since the shore here faced east, the waning sun was at their back, and if anyone saw them, they'd just be two silhouettes against the setting sun.

"What do we do?" asked Elisha.

"You sit, enjoy the scenery, sleep if you want."

"While you?"

"Put that hulk out of business for a while." Alvin sent out his doodlebug and ran it through the ship's timbers, its well-tarred hull. As Alvin worked, a layer of tar and then another slid down into the lowest bilge, leaving the timbers of a few yards of the hull unpitched.

Then Alvin made a gap between the boards right in that area, and water started spraying in. He widened the gaps and the water became a flood.

Before long, the ship lurched downward where the water had pooled in the bilge. And even at this distance, Alvin could hear the ship's bell ringing, not to tell time, but to rouse the crew. Lanterns were rushed down below deck, out of sight—but Alvin still knew where they were. Looking down into the bilge and seeing the gushing water.

Then the lanterns all came back on deck, and a couple of them hurried down the gangplank onto shore, and then more lanterns appeared in the mini-fortress and hurried to the ship. It lurched again, and one of the lanterns fell overboard—and judging from the shouting, there had been a man attached. They'd pull him out of the water. Alvin took a minute to make sure the fallen man's body had not been infected with anything nasty from the filthy water around the hulks, since all the sewage from all the guards and prisoners was sluiced down into the bay to feed the krill and a lot of nasty little germs.

It took a while, but soon the prisoners, chained together, were being paraded across the deck and down the gangplank. If these prisoners had been under sentence of death, they'd already be dead. Therefore they had to be kept alive, saved from the sinking hulk, whose boards had finally given way.

Elisha chuckled. "I find myself trying to guess which prisoner is my sister's friend's husband."

"The best liars are the ones who believe their own lies," said Alvin.

"Not a skill I knew I had," said Elisha. "Maybe I should go on the stage."

"Making things up and saying them is very different from memorizing speeches written by someone else and saying them so an audience will believe them."

"You're a pessimist," said Elisha. "Why do you think I wouldn't be a good actor."

"You're a superb actor," said Alvin. "But there's still no sister's friend's husband down there."

The prisoners were herded into a holding area surrounded by lanterns. More and more came down the gangplank. Where were they going to put all these prisoners?

"Well," said Alvin, standing up. "Time for us to get busy."

"Doing what?"

"Wading through the water behind those hulks. To get to where the hawsers are moored."

"Wading? Like—my pants and shirt in the water?"

"I'll get you dry. I'll even keep you warm."

"With all the things that you can do," said Elisha, "why do you need me?"

"I needed you to find the criminals' ship. I needed you to make the constable suspicious."

"I was trying *not* to do that."

"And I need you now, as we commandeer the other hulks."

"But they still have all their prisoners aboard," said Elisha.

"Don't think of them as prisoners, my friend. Think of them as crew."

They made their way down the slope, not directly toward the hulks, but around the walled-off fortress area and into the water, well back from the emptying (and sinking) hulk. Elisha was surprised that the water barely topped his belly.

"Stay right behind me. I know where the deep spots are."

Elisha needed no more explanation than that.

They walked out between two of the other mooring posts, in a spot where no light fell. Alvin just stood there, and Elisha waited patiently. Alvin's doodlebug went into one ship, then another, then the last, sealing the hulls together as he had done with the ships of his pathetic fleet back at the Quay.

When the ships were all sealed up tight, Alvin loosened the hawsers connecting them to shore, and shortened the chains that held the anchors, so that they were aweigh and the ships could move. There wasn't much current in the water, and no sails open to catch the breeze, but the ships were drifting.

"How are you at climbing up a thick rope?" asked Alvin.

"In the dark? As thick as a hawser? A rope designed for rats to get on and off the ship?"

"That's the rope I meant."

"Let's see if I can do it," said Elisha.

Soon enough they knew that he could. And by the time he was on the deck, his clothes were bone dry and he was not chilled at all.

Neither of them held a weapon. But then, neither of them could possibly have gotten aboard, so no one was watching for them. The guards were running around, debating about whether to do the obvious thing, firing muskets or firing off the tiny cannons at bow and stern. Because clearly no one on shore could see that all three of these fully-occupied hulks were drifting farther and farther into the harbor. Very slowly, but without a pause.

Alvin strode onto the main deck among them. "Gentlemen," he said, "perhaps you've noticed that your ship is adrift. It will be going to America very soon, full of people the priests have taught you to call witches, though they are nothing of the kind. If you want to make that voyage, stay aboard and help us crew this vessel. Or you can jump into the harbor—the water is soon shallow and you can wade to shore with only the occasional ducking. You have about three seconds to decide."

"You can't make us do anything," said one of the men. "We have all the guns."

"Time's up," said Alvin. Instantly all the guards lost their footing and fell heavily on the deck. Not one of them could get up—their hands and shoes kept slipping as if the deck were made of soap.

"Have you made up your minds?" asked Alvin.

The guard who had mentioned guns before tried to pick his up. It went soft as a wet noodle and was completely unusable.

"You're one of *them*," said a guard.

"He is," said Alvin, pointing at Elisha, who had the presence of mind to keep silent with a stern face.

"They'll come after us and set us free."

"Oh, you're free now," said Alvin.

The ship tilted on the starboard side, the side closer to shore. The guards, prone and supine and waving their arms and legs, slipped very quickly toward the side of the ship and then fell through wide new gaps in the gunwale. There was much splashing in the water below.

Three of them were still clinging to the ship—one to the mainmast and two to stanchions on the deck.

"Are you trying to communicate to me that you want to stay with the ship and sail to America?" asked Alvin.

One of them—the one at the mast—said yes. The other two said nothing, but the terror on their faces said that they were afraid of the water. "Just splash your way toward the land. As soon as you reach shallow water, stand up and walk," said Alvin, and the two stanchions became slippery and the men slid off the deck.

The man at the mast still clung to it as the ship righted itself. "Do you give me your solemn oath before God that you will obey my orders and the orders of any man I place over you?"

"I will," said the man. "These are good men on this ship, not criminals. Are you going to set them free?"

"They don't know it, but I already have," said Alvin. "Elisha, will you stay in command of this vessel while I go liberate the prisoners on the other two hulks?"

"This ship isn't seaworthy," said the former guard.

"It wasn't," said Elisha, "but now it is."

Alvin walked to the gunnel, swung over, and splashed into the water. The ship had drifted a few yards on, so the sputtering guards were wading to shore. "You'll pay for this!" yelled one of the guards.

"Be sure to testify at my trial," Alvin called back. "Tell how you slid off the deck and waded to shore without firing a shot."

The waders said or shouted nothing more, and Alvin swam rather quickly to the next hawser. Alvin climbed up onto the deck. Within a few moments another coterie of guards was splashing to shore, this time through somewhat deeper water. Alvin made sure they were in no danger of drowning. Two men this time had volunteered to stay for the voyage to America. Alvin left them in command of the ship, suggesting that the prisoners ought to be brought up on deck and informed of their destination. They were also to resign as guards, ask the men to forgive them for any wrongs that were done to them, and ask their cooperation to get the ship fitted out for voyaging.

The third ship was crewed by guards who had seen the men from the other ships getting to shore. Alvin knew that any who volunteered to stay now could not be trusted until they proved themselves, but Alvin would be on this ship—his flagship, as Elisha would say—and he knew how to deal with any mutineers.

Meanwhile, someone on shore had finally realized what was afoot—or asea—and the arriving waders raised the alarm and Alvin figured it would not be long till a few military ships were in pursuit. He helped the men on all three hulks, who were going aloft to unfurl the rotting sails. The canvas needed mending—a stiff gale would tear them into tatters—but they would do for now. The breeze was out of the southwest, perfect for their purposes, and soon all three ships had men at the helm who were steering the ships northward, to rendezvous with the ship Elisha and Alvin had come in.

As they passed the first hulk, Alvin carefully knitted back together all the boards he had parted in the hull, and slipped the tar back up the inner surface until it was indistinguishable from the rest of the tarring. Then Alvin drained the water from the bilge. No sign remained of why the ship had been abandoned. Alvin felt a spirit of mean delight, imagining the trouble those men would face, having such an unbelievable story to tell.

After a while, Alvin could see a couple of military ships, probably with no more than a dozen cannon between them, set sail in pursuit. Alvin was no longer interested in subtlety. Their hulls dissolved into sawdust in the water, their upper decks crashed down, the cannon toppled into the harbor, and the men scrambled to launch a small boat to carry away the crew and rescue the men in the water. The danger of pursuit was over. And if the Bishop of Dublin had any kind of memory, he would know exactly who could make wooden floors give way without touching them. By the time Alvin's new flotilla got to the Quay, there would be little time to get everyone loaded aboard one ship or another and set out into the Atlantic, where he was quite sure whatever ships the English overlords sent after them, they would not see a sign of them.

I hope you have all the carrots and cabbages we're going to need, Measure, since we just doubled our number with these prisoners, who might none of them have a single useful knack, but who still need to be fed.

As they rounded Ireland and headed south on the west side of the island, Alvin watched Elisha's ship struggle to demonstrate tacking into the wind. It took a long ragged time, but the other ships began to pick up the procedure. Tacking wasn't something you should have to learn with a completely untrained crew under emergency conditions. But then, for all Alvin knew there were experienced seamen on the other ships. He even found a few on his.

They came into port, tied up at the Quay, and dropped anchor. The former prisoners rushed down the gangplank, but Alvin bade them gather around him, and they did. He explained the voyage they were going to take, that there were hundreds of people with knacks contributing to make it a safe, successful voyage, and the liberated prisoners could come to America with them, or remain in Ireland, trying to elude the English on their own. "We'd like you to come with us to Crystal City on the banks of the Mizzippy River, but no one will be brought across the Atlantic unwillingly."

"We'll be dropped in the icy waters to die!" shouted one of the former guards from Alvin's ship.

Measure and a couple of rather large men escorted the man quickly from the crowd. "Don't worry," said Alvin. "He'll only be kept in gaol till the English come and liberate him. And *he* was a guard, not a prisoner. He will bother you no more."

A cheer—not a loud one, but clearly a shout or murmur of approval.

The men staying in Ireland were given provisions to help them on the road back home. They were also given clean clothes by the women, so they wouldn't be easy to identify as escapees on the road. And Alvin gave the men who were heading home a couple of shillings each. "Go to your families, they need you with this potato blight. Work hard to keep them alive," said Alvin. "And I'll work hard to keep my fellow voyagers alive."

The next morning, they loaded passengers and their meager belongings onto the well-stocked ships—the former hulks first, since they held the most, were best provisioned, and had a crew with some small experience during the voyage from Belfast and Ballycastle. The tide, said Elisha, would favor a departure about noon, and so it went, the hulks leading the way, the little craft bobbing after them, with the smallest vessels swayed up onto the decks of the hulks, to be used as ship's boats if they were wanted, for passing between vessels during the voyage, or taking small parties of men ashore on some errand. No reason to put the least seaworthy boats into passenger service until and unless they were sorely needed.

Many gathered on the decks to watch their former town on the Quay fall behind them, their tents and hovels and houses intact, as they left their homeland behind. The cold Atlantic awaited them, and the perils of a voyage that had killed many over the centuries, yet had brought far more safely to the American shore.

18

PHILADELPHIA THROWER DID not think of himself anymore as a Christian minister. Other men were doing that work—a good work, indeed. But it was too small for Philadelphia Thrower. He had been chosen to do a greater work. Surrounding the good Christians in the British Isles and in America was an infestation of witches, people using magical powers to change the world to their liking, without even asking the Lord's permission.

Naturally, the scientific part of Thrower's mind did not believe there was any such thing as witchcraft. For one thing, it affected men as much as women. For another, there was not a whit of evidence, even under torture, that there was any communing with Lucifer. It seems that the afflicted ones first discovered their arcane powers in their youth, some as early as four or five years old. The powers corrupted them immediately, of course, teaching them to rely on their own hands rather than turning to and depending on Jesus Christ and the Holy Spirit.

Most of them, Thrower had learned, after long years of chasing down the miscreants, were harmless by intention. They had no desire to use their powers to hurt or control others. Not like the worst of them—Alvin Miller and his brother Measure, Verily Cooper, John Binder—he had a catalogue of powerful men who hovered in Alvin's shadow.

God had sent an angel to Philadelphia Thrower when he was a young minister in a new church in the frontier settlement of Vigor Church. It was there that Alvin Miller, Junior, was reaching an age to become truly dangerous. The commandment was given to Thrower: Destroy this child. Kill him and let Lucifer deal with him. The angel did not give his own name.

But he named Alvin Miller, Junior, and Thrower was entrusted with the responsibility of cleansing the nation, the world, of this most abominable pollution.

In the end, he had stayed his hand, and disappointed—no, enraged—the angel, who took the form of a flaming salamander that ran around the meetinghouse *on the walls*. Thrower had been terrified, not knowing what God would do to him for having been such a coward, for having shown pity where it was not owed.

But the grace of Christ touched Thrower, and he began his ministry. He did not try to confront Alvin Miller anymore—the angel said that the boy was too powerful, and it wasn't Thrower's fault. Lately, Thrower had moved in the orbit of the lands round about Crystal City, preaching against the abomination of the place, an artifact of Satan constructed of water and blood in a perverse mockery of the blood of the Savior in the Eucharist.

"Whatever you see in the walls of Crystal City," he told the people who came to hear him, "the visions are not from God. They are of Lucifer's sending, in order to tempt you to enter onto paths of self-destruction. How can God protect you from the devil, if you seek visions at the hands of the greatest enemy of Jesus Christ in history?"

His mission had taken Thrower to Ireland when Alvin went there. He warned the Bishop of Dublin about the menace abroad in the island. But the bishop did not take Thrower seriously until after Alvin had demonstrated his irresistible power, dropping the floor out from under the poor man. You should have heeded me and slain him without ever speaking to him, he wanted to say. But he understood the bishop's reluctance to sentence a man to death in absentia, untried, on the word of only one witness. "If you're so sure that's the will of God," said the bishop, "then raise your own hand and strike him down. I will see that you are not prosecuted for the killing. Do it, and show me how to be truly ruthless."

But Thrower knew he did not have the power to raise a hand against Alvin Miller, Junior. So Thrower spent several months building up a small cavalry force and training them with saber work from the saddle. "You will not dismount, you will not converse. Every being you encounter in that hideous camp of iniquity, man, woman or child, you will slay, preferably by removal of everything above the neck."

Thrower had nearly hesitated at issuing the order, but he could see that to do anything less would defeat his righteous purpose. If his posse tried instead to herd Alvin's followers into one area for holding, it would give the children and the young women a chance to work on the hearts and natural compassion of Thrower's men, who might then allow some of the witches and witchlings to run away, or others to get the materials they needed to exercise their violent "knacks."

No, William Henry Harrison had the right idea at Tippy-Canoe. Trap your enemies—men, women, and children—and then slaughter them from every side. No parlay, no compromise, just a rain of death. And even though the massacre was stopped prematurely, the effect was total—the Red Prophet withdrew all his surviving people, along with many other tribes, west of the Mizzippy. White men could not go there, but everybody knew it was just desert and grass on that side of the river, and millions of bison. Who on Earth wanted to go?

And if we ever decide we *do* want to go, will God let Christians be stopped by devilish magic?

So far, the answer to that was apparently yes, so Thrower didn't dwell on *that* idea for long.

Thrower led his men slowly across Ireland from Dublin to the west coast. He wanted news of their approach to precede them. More than once he wished he had just sent a letter alerting Alvin that his days were numbered, and then ridden the train. Hang the horses. He knew a cavalry charge would be intimidating, but he also began to doubt that his men, despite their training, would be as ruthless as he needed them to be. And Thrower himself, though reasonably strong, wasn't entirely certain he could take off a man's head in a single blow from horseback.

A local farmer accepted a loaf of bread as payment for walking ahead of them, leading them to the Knacky Camp, as some locals called it. "No worse than having gypsies around," he said, "and better, because these folks don't steal."

Thrower restrained himself and made no reply. It didn't speak well of gypsies that these devils were rated better.

The man wasn't a fast walker, but Thrower *and* the horses were content to climb the last hill quite slowly. With a sense of gathering triumph, Thrower allowed himself to imagine the looks of consternation and then fear, when they realized what was about to come riding down on top of them.

And there before him stretched the camp, right down to the Quay at the water's edge. Apparently nobody had seen them top the ridge, because no alarm was being sounded and no one was scurrying around in a panic.

"Nobody here, Rev," said the youngest of his posse.

Thrower turned to the farmer. "Give back the bread, sir. You led us to the wrong place."

"They were here yesterday," said the farmer, holding the bag with the bread in it behind his back. "I led you fairly to the place of their encampment."

Thrower held out his hand to his first leftenant. The man immediately understood, pulled out his telescope, and handed it to Thrower.

"They were at least three hundred and probably more," said the farmer.

"They didn't just disappear," said the leftenant. "Were they moles? Did they go underground? Or bats, who only fly out of their cave in the dark?"

But Thrower held up a hand to end the conversation. "I see a flotilla of ships moving out of the sheltered water. The prison hulks they stole, I imagine."

The leftenant reached for the telescope and took his turn looking through it. "How can those be the prison hulks? Everybody knows they're covered in barnacles and the wood's weathered and starting to rot all over."

"Water isn't kind to wooden boats," observed Thrower.

"Wherever the witches got them, those are three fine-looking ships."

"And a bunch of barely seaworthy washtubs following like baby ducks," said Thrower.

The farmer dared to speak again. "They said around these parts that if Alvin Smith wanted them to float, they would damned well float."

"They are damned indeed," said Thrower. "Now we'll see if the Atlantic lets them cross."

"How will we see that?" asked the leftenant. "My telescope isn't as powerful as *that*."

"I forget your name, son," said Thrower.

"Everybody does, including me."

"If you went by your birth name, maybe we'd all remember," said Thrower. Several of the men chuckled.

The leftenant touched his hand to the brim of his hat. "Reverent Thrower, sir, you have me caught out. I call myself Sahara Desert, but my dear mother named me Alexander, and then eke-named me Sandy, which is what I hear the Sahara is like. And my mam's last name was Grass, God rest her soul."

"I assure you, God is indeed resting her soul, in peace and joy," said Thrower. "Sandy Grass. Yes, in choosing a false name, for some godly purpose I am sure, Sahara Desert was not far from Sandy Grass. Not even a complete lie, that name."

"I think so, sir. Especially cause Sandy Grass has two warrants and a sentence of death hanging over him."

Thrower almost laughed, but stopped himself. "How did you acquire those?"

"Not by asking, that's for sure. I believe that after some disturbances in Killarney, that name got bandied about until the English thought it might be worth having a chat with him. Clearly the name Alexander Grass, eke-name Sandy, is a fairly common one in Ireland, but you know the English don't much care about making sure they hang the *right* Irishman."

"Troublous times," said Thrower, convinced that Leftenant Desert was in fact the very rebel the English soldiers were looking for. In Dublin there was such poverty that for a reward—for a meal—many a person would put the finger on a wanted man. But everywhere else in the country, the English found that the Irish were the least neighborly people on Earth. None of them knew the names of any of their neighbors, or anything about their business, their families, their livelihood.

"Leftenant Sahara Desert, I'm going to dismiss all these other men. Not yet!" Thrower barked at the others already moving to disperse. He turned back to the leftenant. "I wonder if you're knowledgeable about the sea."

"I've been in boats, sir," said Sandy Grass.

"On open water?" asked Thrower.

"Aye, sir," said Grass.

"Have you raised and lowered the sail on a one-masted boat?"

"I've watched it done. I even know why you raise and lower it. I take it you have your eye on that sloop by the Quay?"

"I can't think why Alvin would have let it behind. As a trap for us? To mock us?"

"It's smaller and less masted than some he took," said Grass.

Thrower turned to the others. "Men, you may return to your homes. Remember that these horses you ride belong to the bishop. Take care of them, keep them fed on grass that your family can't eat anyway."

"Can we plow with them, too?" asked one.

"Use them in your labors. Just don't beat them. They're proud animals, and humiliation leaves them broken, spavined, hoof-cleft. The bishop and his men will know that the horse has been misused."

"Won't they claim the horses back?" asked another man.

"They're the bishop's horses. Generously, he allows you to use them on your farms until he wants them again."

The men looked to each other, several nodding their assent.

"I'm grateful for his generosity and liberality," said one. The others all echoed those sentiments, until another piped up.

"So we don't have to cut off any heads today?"

The easy way the fellow spoke it filled Thrower with a sudden rage, he wasn't sure why. Was it because he'd assumed the men were like him, only willing to kill for a just cause, but in fact they were happy to shed blood for any reason at all? Or was it because the success of their attack had never really been possible, and everyone had known it but him? Either thought made Thrower feel like a fool, which was its own injustice. He drew in his breath a bit sharply.

"I hope you never have that solemn duty," said Thrower, calming himself with his well-practiced preacher's intonation. "But Jesus honors you for being willing to do such an unpleasant thing in his name and in his service."

The posse left, then, their horses at a walk, some going north, most south and east. Only Grass remained. "No one asked for money or food to take with them," Thrower said.

"They didn't fight the battle, so they didn't expect to be paid," said Grass. "And they know exactly how much food is in our saddlebags. I'm sure they all have a little tucked away. Ireland is not so vast that they'll starve to death before coming home."

"No, only after they come back will they find that Famine has set up his throne in their house."

"Something will come and save them," said Grass.

"Said the people drowning in Noah's flood."

"Is that what this potato blight is? Our flood?" Grass had another thought. "Are those boats that just sailed away, are they the ark provided for us, and we came too late?"

"The Lord promised no more floods. He didn't say he had no plan to destroy the human race again."

Grass absorbed that. "Shall we go see what they left behind?"

Their horses led them to a particularly large tent, and they dismounted to explore. It was in a modest, out-of-the-way tent that they found Alvin's dwelling place. There was a wheel of cheese sitting on a table—not a large one, but enough for a man to eat half and be right full.

There was a note painted on the outside of the wheel.

philadel have supper on us
sorry had to go, would
of took you with

"You think he meant it?" said Grass. "That he would've took us with?"

"Not if we came in beheading everybody in our way," said Thrower.

"Mmm, I don't know," said Grass. "What I heard of his power, I think that might have made him *more* determined to take you with."

"I will never put myself in his power," said Thrower.

"From what I hear, you're in his power right now, if he feels like it."

"Leftenant Sahara Desert, if we're to cross the Atlantic in each other's company, I don't want another word from you on what you *heard* about Alvin Miller, Junior."

They left the camp and went to look at the sloop, going around to the Quay and tying up the horses at a hitching bar in front of a closed-up tavern. A window opened and the tavernkeeper stuck his head out. "Closed this morning, gents," he said. "But we have rooms aplenty and supper is cooking away in the kitchen. Come back then!" The shutter closed.

"I guess that with all their customers out at sea," said Grass, "there was no reason to keep the tavern open on the same schedule."

"If they had known you were coming, Sandy . . ."

"I never touch alcohol, sir. My ma says, God means man to be wise, so it's an affront to God to make ourselves stupid with drink."

"If a man can't have the Holy Ghost as his guide, Brother Grass, then the advice of a good and loving ma might do almost as well."

"So far it's been effective enough," said Grass.

Reverend Thrower stood on the Quay, not interested in stepping onto the slightly-bobbing boat. Grass, however, swung right down onto the deck, and then below. He moved like a habituated sailor. A deserter from the Navy, thought Thrower. Didn't want to let anybody know about a former sailor named Sandy Grass. Well, God is with me still, providing me with a sailor when I most needed one.

"Is it solid enough to take us to sea?"

Grass didn't answer for a few minutes, until he came back up to the deck. "By the light from the hatch I could see one area of the hull, and I'll be jiggered if it isn't a single solid hull-shaped piece of lumber."

"What do you mean? Like a hollowed-out canoe?" Thrower had seen a couple of dugouts on the Hio, the Wobbish, and the Hatrack. Reds didn't seem to realize that they were ungainly craft, impossible for one man to manage. They just paddled them wherever they wanted, without a care.

"Like the tree grew in this shape, they cut it down, and set it in the water like it is today," said Grass. "I'd say Alvin's got him a nice set of knacks, if a miller, smith, and stonemason can also do that kind of perfect work below decks on an old sloop."

Thrower didn't want Grass admiring Alvin, but how could he stop the man, considering that Thrower himself was in awe of what Alvin could do.

From the remnants in the tents and cabins, plus everything they could buy from the tavernkeeper, Thrower figured they had supplies enough to cross the Atlantic. Maybe.

Then Grass said, "I hope you have some more of those coins, because in all our provisioning, what we don't have is drinking water."

Thrower blushed with embarrassment. "I suppose we would have noticed that mistake when we were somewhere near an iceberg and we could chip off a few blocks of ice to melt and drink. How do we buy the water?"

"Small kegs, filled up from the tavern's spring."

Thrower nodded. "Let's go see what he has in the way of casks."

"And ropes to tie everything down," said Grass. "A couple of big waves, and all our stores and water will be in the Atlantic, bobbing along behind us."

"A lot of things can go wrong," said Thrower.

"Rule of seafaring: If it *can* go wrong, it will, so be ready."

"I chose the right traveling companion," said Thrower.

"No sir," said Grass. "Once we board this ship, I'm the only one of us who has any idea what he's doing. That makes me captain, and you a most obedient and humble seaman."

Thrower looked at Grass and smiled. "That is *not* mutiny, it is wisdom, because there's something you don't know."

"You have dysentery?" asked Grass, wincing.

"I vomited about every six hours on my way across the ocean to America the first time. In a *big* ship, with a regular bed and good food provided."

"We won't have fine victuals, but we do have enough buckets that we can designate one as your particular companion."

"When I ask you to kill me," said Thrower, "I assure you that I *will* mean it, but don't you do it, because God still has work for me in this world."

"When I have to throw you overboard, Mr. Thrower, I hope the Lord sends a big fish to swallow you and puke you up on shore."

"Already arranged it," said Thrower. "Don't you worry."

19

Lovey came to Alvin again when he was sleeping. Since he didn't respond to her voice, she began poking him.

He opened his eyes.

"Elisha Kent Kane told me that in America they grow their cheese on bushes."

"Did he think that was good or bad?"

"He said the cheese in wheels and under wax is better, but the English don't let them bring Dutch cheeses into the United States."

"Does he have any cheese-bush seeds?" asked Alvin.

"He said they grow from starts."

"So you already asked about the seeds?"

"I know how to farm, cept when there's blights."

"Well, you find a cheese bush in America, we can take a few starts from it and I'll try to get it planted and strongly going, unless you find it in winter."

"So you never saw one?" asked Lovey.

"Never even heard of one, and truth to tell, I've been in every part of the United States, a couple of places in New England, and even spent some serious time in the Crown Colonies and Nueva Barcelona."

"And none of them places had cheese bushes?" asked Lovey.

"If they did, nobody told me a thing about them," said Alvin.

"Are you lying to me?" asked Lovey.

"About what?"

"About cheese bushes."

"I didn't tell you a blamed thing about them," said Alvin. "Because I never heard of them."

"But you're from America!"

"True," said Alvin, closing his eyes again.

"Elisha Kent Kane said they grew in every state and Crown Colony and even in New England. Everywhere."

"Then don't you think it's Brother Kane's job to lead you to one of these cheese bushes?"

"He said he won't have time."

"That's a crying shame. Because I don't even know where to begin looking."

Alvin could tell from her breathing that Lovey was still there.

She poked him.

"I'm already awake," said Alvin, allowing himself to sound a little irked, since poking sleepers wasn't the smartest habit to let her develop.

"I been thinking, while you was lying there pretending to sleep. First thing is, you're older than Elisha."

"I imagine that's so, though we haven't traded birthdays yet."

"And you been everywhere in America, right?"

"Everywhere a White man is allowed to go, and even a few where he isn't."

"And you *never* heard of cheese bushes even though they're supposed to be everywhere."

"Never heard of them."

"That's three things. You're older so you've experienced more than Elisha Kent Kane. Second, you've been all over America, at least way more than Elisha Kent Kane."

"Way more than most anybody," said Alvin, but he thought of his old friend Taleswapper and was pretty sure Taleswapper would mock him for making such a claim.

"Third, you never heard of cheese bushes."

"Not yet, except from you."

"And you aren't lying to me now because I'm a child?"

Alvin sighed. "You have the impression that adults lie to children?"

"A lot."

"Wow," said Alvin.

"All the time," said Lovey.

"So why did you believe that yarn about cheese bushes?"

"Because Elisha Kent Kane has been to Yale!"

"Do you even know what Yale is?" asked Alvin.

"It's where you learn *everything*, and he's been there."

"Then I'll expect you and him to lead me to a cheese bush as soon as we get well ashore."

"When will that be?" asked Lovey.

"I wish I knew. We've been caught in this strange patch of still waters, which I never heard of happening this far north, so I don't think we're making much progress."

"Are we going to starve to death?" asked Lovey.

"I don't plan to. Is that something you wanted to do? Because you could have stayed in Ireland for that."

"Sheen says that Elisha Kent Kane never been to Yale," said Lovey.

"I wonder how she came to know that," said Alvin.

"Because she says that if he went to university, he'd be smarter than anybody who hadn't."

"I wonder if that's true," said Alvin.

"Sheen doesn't lie, not to me."

"Who does she lie to?"

Alvin could hear Lovey catch her breath. "Never known her to tell a lie."

"That's what I might have said of you, till you laid that whopper on me just this minute."

"What whopper!"

"That you never knew Sheen to tell a lie. You've heard her lie all the time. So have I."

"Not *bad* lies."

"Does that mean there are good lies?"

"If somebody is hiding and if you tell about them, they'll be arrested and maybe kilt, so you say you don't know where they be, and the bad men ride away."

"That's a good lie, you think," said Alvin.

"And when you tell a child everything's going to be all right when you know that it isn't true, but if you tell her the truth it won't make her any happier, so why not tell the lie that keeps her happy?"

"Good lies, happy lies."

"Why would Brother Elisha tell me all about cheese bushes if there's no such thing?"

Alvin chuckled. "Because you believed it. And it was fun for him to make up all kinds of facts about those bushes, because he *did* go to Yale, so he knows how to talk pretty scientific about a lot of things in the natural world."

"He went to Yale so he could tell better *lies*?"

"What do you think, Lovey?"

"I think I'm never going to believe him again."

"Well, I hope he's never the one they send to call you to supper."

Lovey stood there beside Alvin's hammock a little longer.

"Still got a question?" Alvin asked.

"In all our talking about cheese bushes, you never once called Mr. Elisha Kent Kane a liar."

"Of coursc not, bccausc hc's not a liar."

"He lied to me all morning."

"Did he?"

"*Are* there cheese bushes?" demanded Lovey.

"As far as I know, there's—"

"Don't lie. 'As far as I know' is a lie. Don't say it. Say what you know."

"What I know is that cows, goats, and sheep all give milk, and if you put it in cheesecloth and tie up the top and hang it in a springhouse or some other cool place, some of the milkwater seeps out of it and when you open it, there's cheese."

"No bushes," said Lovey.

"You said for me to tell you what I know. I helped my parents and my sisters make so many pounds of cheese—good cheese, too, which we sold to our neighbors around Christmas and they called it the best cheese in the county."

"Your sisters. Why not your brothers? I know you've got at least the one."

"I was laid up with a bad leg, so I couldn't go out and earn money by working like my brothers could. So I stayed home and learned women's work from my ma and my sisters."

"Women's work?" asked Lovey.

"Not when *I* was doing it. Then it was lame boy's work."

"So a lame boy is as strong as a regular woman?" asked Lovey.

"Lovey, when a woman comes out in the field to split rails or lay fences or dig ditches, she's slow and clumsy because that's not the work she's used to doing. She doesn't have the muscles for it. If I handed her my hammer and tongs at the forge, she wouldn't even know how to begin doing my work, because I prenticed with a blacksmith and I learned everything he knew, plus a few things he never dreamed of."

"So women are bad at men's work."

"Everybody's bad at work they don't know how to do. Did your ma teach you how to sew a seam?"

"As straight a seam as you ever saw," said Lovey

"I can't do that," said Alvin. "I've tried, but it keeps wiggling away and tries to get off the seam."

"That can't happen if you're *watching*."

"What about if I'm watching, but my fingers don't push the needle up through the cloth from the right place on the underside?"

"You said you *did* women's work, so you should know."

"I didn't say I did it well," said Alvin.

The boat moved. Or the ship, rather. It had masts and sails for a breeze to catch.

"Either a huge shark just bumped into us from below," said Alvin.

"Or a whale," said Lovey. "They're nice."

"Not all, but mostly, yes. Either it was some big swimmy thing that made us move, or . . ."

"Wind." said Lovey.

"How can we be sure? Whale or wind?"

"We could go outside and look," said Lovey.

"That feels a bit like cheating to me, but we're not in school, so if you want to get all empirical about it, by all means go and see."

Lovey burst back into Alvin's cabin only a few seconds later. "Not a whale," she cried. "Not a shark! Not a dolphin, not a conspiracy of seagulls, not a thousand flying fish circling over the boat—"

"Wind?" asked Alvin softly.

"Yes."

"Waves?" asked Alvin.

"A little bit of chop, but no, it's the wind driving us, the sail is full."

Alvin smiled, lying there in his hammock.

"You smiling because we're moving again?"

"That, and also smiling about *why* we're catching this breeze."

"So tell me why?"

"The calm water we were caught in, that wasn't natural."

She thought a moment. "Somebody's knack?"

"Not exactly, but close. The water was flat and I couldn't do a thing about it. Neither could any of our knacky folk, even the ones who had a tolerable good relationship with the wind or with water."

"Who was doing it? Making the water still?"

"I've heard you children calling boat to boat, talking about the follower."

"Little ship, two-man crew, never gets close enough to hale or far enough to lose sight of us," said Lovey.

"Starting to talk like a sailor."

"Sheen says she'll feed me soap if I ever talk like a sailor!"

"Oh, there's no bad-talking sailor in our flotilla right now. I just meant that you know something about the sea, about the ships and sails. And you see well afar off."

"Thank you," said Lovey, "but that's not my knack."

"How do you know?"

"Because it would be so dull if I didn't have a really useful knack. So I'm still waiting to find it."

Good luck, thought Alvin. Them as don't have a knack wish for a really extravagant one—walking on water, raising the dead, turning foul water into pure, getting dolphins to bring us fish. But us as has that kind of flamboyant knack, or several, or a lot of them, we'uns wish we could just eat and drink and plow and plant like everybody else. Just wield a hammer at an anvil beside a forge, a man's work to make a man's living. I didn't ask to be the seventh of seven. And why not the seventh *child*? Why weren't girls in the count? That would be his sister Matilda, still living in Vigor Church because she said, "I don't like to leave the old homeplace."

Matilda was the seventh *child* of our parents. She had knacks, some good ones. Nobody made tighter baskets than Matilda. Folks said, you get you one of Matilda's baskets, you'll never want for a bucket, cause her baskets hold water better.

Matilda laughed at such praise. "I try to weave a tight basket, but you go carrying water in baskets, the handle will break or the reeds will get too soft and spring leaks. Just isn't practical. What I ask of my basket is that no berries fall through, and no snake get in."

Alvin realized now, for the first time, that Matilda might have been claiming her real knack. Berries falling through, that was about the weave. But no snakes inside? A basket with an open top would be no barrier to any self-respecting snake. But snakes never got in her baskets, and Alvin believed it. It's a knack right enough. He just wondered if the barrier was only against snakes or if it kept other bad things out, too.

Can't ask her now, too far away, though maybe I'll pass through Vigor Church as I lead this company to Crystal City.

Not exactly on the way, but they weren't in a race, now, were they. No reason they couldn't stray from the road for Alvin to take a visit home.

Alvin swung his legs out of the hammock, which pushed it back against the wall, so he was immediately balancing on his feet. Hammocks are the most ridiculously unmanageable bed you could imagine, except that there was nothing better in a ship at sea. Wooden beds would keep sliding all over, or be hinged to a bulkhead, and no matter what you did, they were still made of wood. The hammock swayed with the motion of the ship, but it never jolted unless something was wrong that made it necessary to stand up and go somewhere.

He stood up from the hammock and saw that Lovey was already gone, the door to the cabin open. Didn't matter. Nobody came in without knocking either way. Alvin strode out onto the deck and saw that everybody was securing the sails. Alvin imagined they might have slacked off in their duties, during so long a time without wind or current.

Alvin looked back at the followers. He knew one. It was Reverend Philadelphia Thrower, Scottish Rite preacher, graduate of a seminary, who came out to the American West to convert the Reds. A man who had truck with the Unmaker and thought it was an angel. If Thrower had a useful knack, Alvin had never seen a sign of it. Certainly calming the sea and stilling the wind were not in his toolkit.

So Thrower had gotten the Unmaker to do it. The Unmaker worked powerful strong on water. Alvin knew *that* all too well. So many times he came near to death from water, and yet always something saved him at the last moment. *Now* he knew it had always been Margaret, who pulled a caul from his face when he was first born, so he could draw breath. She kept that caul, because it had been part of him in the womb, and when it dried, she would pinch off just enough of it to give her part of Alvin's power. She used bits of his power to save baby Alvin's life from whatever danger had caught him. She was just a child herself, but she took on the responsibility of keeping him alive, because she had seen in his heartfire and he knew she had seen him dying a hundred times in a hundred ways, and it was her job, she had decided, to keep him alive.

That wasn't why he married her—gratitude. Margaret didn't need someone to marry her for any reason but her own beauty, her grace, and her marvelous knack of always knowing what was in the other person's heart.

"You're thinking about her," said Elisha, standing beside him now.

"I was looking at the followers."

"Oh, I know, I saw you. But then that look came over your face, the look you always get when you think of Margaret."

"Do I?"

"I hope someday I'll love a woman the way you love her."

"I hope that for you, too. But there's no other such, so I'm afraid you'll just have to make do."

"What do you see in the followers' ship?"

"I know one of the men, knew him immediately. Reverend Philadelphia Thrower, a preacher in my family's church when I was a child."

"Why doesn't he come forward and give us good-day?"

"Because the highest ambition in his heart is to murder me, in the service of his god, the Unmaker."

Elisha looked shocked. "Wants to kill you?"

"Oh, he's tried. Never can bring it off."

"How do you stop him?"

"He stops himself. Whatever else is true of him, he's not a killer in his heart. Not even when he's convinced that his victim is the most evil human being ever born, worse than Judas Iscariot, worse than Pharaoh, worse than all the priests of Baal put together."

"So why did he follow us?"

"I connected this calm we were in to the Unmaker, which was why my knack couldn't do anything against it, not out here surrounded by water. But for all that the Unmaker was able to do, he couldn't make us sink, he couldn't pry apart the boards of the hulls of these ships. Even *his* little ship is one I fused together to have a perfect seal."

"So did the . . . the Unmaker change his—its—mind?"

"Not even sure if it has a mind," said Alvin. "But no. You can see the sea is still flat, except for the tracks our moving vessels leave behind them in the water."

"So it's wind alone moving us now."

"I toyed with asking whales to give us a push, but so many ships go out to kill whales for lamp oil and ladies' corsets that I didn't want to give any whale a reason to trust men in boats."

Elisha swallowed. "You can talk to whales?"

Alvin chuckled. "Margaret Larner had me read Shakespeare and memorize some lines. My favorite has always been, this Welsh military man brags, 'I can call spirits from the vasty deep!' and Hotspur answers him, 'Aye, so can I, and so can any man. But do they come when you do call for them?' "

Elisha laughed. "Henry the Fourth, right?"

"One of the Henrys. Miz Larner never insisted that I know the play, the act, the scene. She knew I wasn't headed for a life on the stage."

"You still haven't told me where the wind came from."

"Not sure that I should. Where the Unmaker can hear."

"It has ears? It can hear?"

"Reckon so, but as I said, not all that sure of how smart it is. Thrower's companion and crewman on that ship, he came with Thrower intending to do slaughter at his command. But he also had a plan of his own. Because he's one of us—he has a knack."

"A knack for wind," whispered Elisha.

"I didn't know, but I hoped. I suspect he and Thrower are running low on food and water, and he thought we must be the same, so out of mercy he ended our captivity and freed himself and Thrower from their vigil."

Elisha said, "Won't they still come after us and do it again?"

"Do you see any wind in their sail?"

"Oh," said Elisha. "It's slack against the pole."

"No, blowing in the opposite direction from ours," said Alvin. "That's some powerful knack."

"You don't think Thrower will notice?"

"Oh, I'm sure he already has. He knows that his servant has risen up against him and is helping his enemy—that would be me. You know how I said that Thrower wasn't a killer."

"Of you, he's not a killer of you."

"Not really of any man. Or animal. Don't expect him to slaughter a pig. He's fine with swatting flies, though."

"So his companion the windmage is safe?"

"Oh, no. Thrower is probably planning to give him a push into the water. He just doesn't know how strong a swimmer the fellow is, I bet."

"Do you see all this in his heartfire?"

"Not seeing, exactly. I know things from his heartfire. A few paths open to him. Nothing like what Margaret sees. I can see a drop of water; she can see the river that's inside of everyone."

"And there's your face, doing what it does when you talk of her."

Alvin smiled. "Glad to know that such a thing is true."

"If he's going to find a way to kill the good man who used his knack to save us—"

"I have a plan," said Alvin.

"A good plan?"

"Good enough."

"Can I help?" asked Elisha.

"Do you know what your knack is yet?"

"Pretty sure it's either handwriting or peeing standing up."

"Not a rare knack, that one."

"But when I think of the activities I do best," said Elisha, "that comes up."

"High on the list, is it?"

"Not really 'high.' It's that everything else I try to do ends up pretty low on my list of talents. Below 'pissing against the wall,' to use the biblical phrasing."

"'And there shall not be left one that pisseth against the wall.' Isaiah, I think, but for all I know it's Obadiah."

"Pretty convoluted way of saying, 'There won't be one man left alive.'"

"But poetic, as long as the word for micturation doesn't give offense."

Elijah stared at him. "Micturation? Did Margaret Larner teach you that?"

"She did indeed," said Alvin. "To give me a better word than 'piss.'"

"I barely learned that. From a foul-mouthed sophomore who was making fun of me for avoiding coarse language. 'He can't even say urinate. He says "micturate."' Nobody laughed because none of his friends knew the word either. And I remembered it and looked it up, and now, for the first time, I've heard someone say it in a sentence."

"I didn't know how to sing it in a song," said Alvin.

"What's your plan for this beknackèd person?"

"You said you want to help?"

"Yes," said Elisha.

"Can you carry yon jar of fine whisky with you on a little walk?"

"Reckon so. I thought you'd want me to do something hard."

"It'll get harder, the farther we go."

Elisha chuckled. "A body might think you plan to walk on the water."

"I don't do it often, because I don't mind getting wet and I'm a good swimmer, with these blacksmith arms. But my friend Lolla-Wossiky once took me out on a lake and wrapped us both inside a waterspout and showed me things I never imagined."

"Lolla-what?"

"He goes by Tenskwa-Tawa now, and his power befogs the Mizzippy."

"The Red Prophet," said Elisha. "You know him?"

"Better than most, but not as well as I'd like to."

"And he taught you to walk on water."

"I saw what he did, though I use a White man's knack, not the Red man's harmony with nature."

With that, Alvin lowered himself over the side of the ship and dropped down into the—no, *onto* the water. He hung on to the ship so he stayed with it as it scooted through the mostly smooth water. "Jump," he said softly to Elisha.

"Not holding this," said Elisha. He reached down and handed the jar of whiskey to Alvin. Now Elisha could use both his hands. But he still stood behind the gunwale, gripping it tightly.

"You done harder jumps than this a dozen times since we met."

"Never on top of water that looks wet but is really solid."

"True, that doesn't come up much."

Elisha rocked his head to one side. "I'm afraid."

"Very sensible. Glad to know you're not such a fool as to pretend you're never scared." Alvin slapped on the side of the ship. "Lower yourself first, like I did, so you don't have so far a drop."

Elisha took a breath and then did as Alvin instructed, clambering over the gunwale, hanging by his arms, then letting go. He, too, landed on the water and it held him like a marble floor. "How can I be doing this?"

"You learned how to stand on a solid floor as a toddler," said Alvin. "And that's *all* you're doing. Standing. Except it's time for us both to be walking." Alvin handed him the jar of whiskey. "I got other things to think about than trying to keep a jar of hooch from spilling."

Elisha took the jar, then looked around, not knowing where on the water it was safe to step. Alvin finally had to take Elisha's arm and guide him along. But soon they were both striding with ease.

"Could a shark eat us now?" said Elisha.

"I don't think we look delicious, seen from under our feet," said Alvin, "but I guess if a shark was hungry enough. . . ."

"This is a long walk," said Elisha.

"Their ship was closer before the wind started blowing."

"Why am I holding this jar of whisky?"

"Many times you don't know the use of something till you're glad you happened to have it."

Walking steady caught them up with Thrower's boat, even though Thrower and his friend had managed to turn it around so it could catch the wind that would take them back to Ireland.

But suddenly their sail went slack, and the ship shuddered to a stop.

"I thought you had no knack for wind," said Elisha.

"Not for a dependable wind you can sail with,' said Alvin. "But in this case, what I used was my knack for making tiny invisible perforations in sailcloth."

With the ship stopped, Reverend Thrower was out on deck in a moment. He seemed unfazed by the sight of two men standing on the water.

"I thought you didn't like water," said Thrower.

"We're on friendlier terms now," said Alvin. "Would you mind giving my friend Elisha a hand up? Elisha studied at Yale."

"It doesn't have a bad reputation," said Thrower. "But it's in New England, where your kind aren't tolerated."

"My kind?" asked Elisha. "Oh, I see. You think I'm standing on water through some knack of my own. It's all Alvin, as you should have guessed. So far as I know, I've got no knack at all."

"We get along fine with folk who aren't just like us," said Alvin, "unless they're trying to kill us. May we come aboard? Will you give Elisha a hand?"

Thrower reached down with his hand, and Elisha took it willingly. "I don't know if I'm strong enough," said Thrower.

"I am," said Elisha. He pulled on Thrower's hand, cramming him hard against the gunwale, but it was all Elisha needed to leap high enough to grab the top of the gunwale and hoist himself in.

"You had a one-man crew with you," said Alvin. "I'm surprised he didn't come out on deck to greet us."

"He's ill," said Thrower. "I'm sure *you* never get sick."

"You've seen me with a powerful sickness, Reverend Thrower. I was like to be somewhere between lame and one-legged, as things were going."

Thrower didn't care for the reminder of his earlier failure. "Ordinary folk get ill from time to time."

"But I am afraid, sir, that your crew, a Mr. Grass, I believe, Sandy Grass, I'm afraid that he isn't so much sick as unconscious, with a strong possibility of dying from a lot of loose blood in his brain. Would you mind if I took a look at him?"

"Ridiculous," said Thrower.

"Since Mr. Grass can't offer me a hand up into the boat, it's only proper that you should do it."

Alvin reached up. Bracing himself for another pull like Elisha's, Thrower reached down. Without pulling on Thrower's hand at all, just holding it like a handshake, Alvin jumped up and with his other hand caught the gunwale and pulled himself up by one arm. It had been no strain on Thrower at all. Alvin thought, Thrower thinks he saw me using a knack, but I'm tall and I jumped and I pulled myself up with one blacksmith's arm. No knacks at all.

Alvin headed for the cabin.

Grass was not lying on the bed or in a hammock. He was on the floor, bleeding from a serious head wound. Alvin glanced around for the weapon.

"I threw it overboard," said Thrower. "I wasn't trying to kill him."

"I know," said Alvin.

"I was just so . . . angry and disgusted to know that I had been traveling with a witch. A windwitch, no less, who betrayed me by setting you in motion."

"And here I thought you had brought him just for that reason, to let us get going again."

"You're such a liar," said Thrower.

"That wasn't a lie," said Elisha. "That was sarcasm. Don't they teach irony in your seminary, Reverend?"

"A lie's a lie, even if you think it's amusing," said Thrower.

Alvin was kneeling by Grass and resting a hand on his head.

"How is he?" asked Elisha.

"Better than I feared," said Alvin. "I can't do much if a man's already dead."

"Oh," said Thrower, "I thought that after walking on water, raising the dead would be your next deceptive miracle."

"I don't do miracles. I just make use of the tools God put into my hands at my birth."

Thrower said nothing, because Grass's eyelids were fluttering. Then he saw Thrower.

Grass shied away, put up his arms to cover his head.

"Don't worry," said Alvin. "Do you think I'd let a man like *that* harm our friend, who freed us with a kindly breeze?"

"But I. Didn't . . ."

"Mr. Grass, you don't need to hide your powerful knack around *me*. Elisha and I came here to invite you to join us on our voyage to America."

Clutching at Alvin's knee, Grass sat up. Alvin and Elisha both helped him by pulling at his shoulders.

"Thrower knows what I can do, what I have done. He can denounce me to the Bishop of Dublin—"

"I promise I won't," said Thrower.

"He's already planning how to do it without your knowing it was him who did it," said Alvin.

"And I didn't need a knack to tell me *that*," said Elisha. "The slime of a betrayer is in your eyes and on your lips."

Thrower licked his lips as if to see if there *was* something on them. "I keep my word."

"Doesn't matter, long as you come with us, Mr. Grass. Thrower will never come near you again, as long as I'm alive."

"Be sure of it," said Thrower.

"He tried to kill me," said Grass.

"He came within a couple of minutes of succeeding," said Alvin. "But you're good as new now."

"Because you're—you're the Maker himself, aren't you."

"Some have called me that," said Alvin. "But there's strict rules about makering. The hardest one is, the Maker is the one who is part of what he makes.'"

"I don't know what that means," said Grass. "I'm not part of the wind."

"Well, actually, you are, but it doesn't matter whether you understand what you're doing, as long as I do." Alvin grinned.

"You got a nice grin," said Elisha.

"I knew a man with a grin that could draw a bear down out of a tree. He ended up in Congress."

"The man with the grin?"

"No, the bear won the election. The grinner went with him to Congress to interpret for him. They never missed a vote, not even during hibernation season."

"If you believe that," said Thrower.

"His name was Davy Crockett," said Alvin. "One of the best rough men I've known. Congress was the wrong place for him, too many liars and lawyers and larcenizers. But the bear liked it there, so Davy stayed with him till he died of something he ate, probably. They offered Davy the bear's seat in Congress, but Davy only laughed. 'I'm not as patient as a bear,' says he."

"You weren't even there," said Thrower.

"I have a friend who writes down the stories he hears that he actually believes, and he told me that tale. Knowing Davy, I reckon it was true to his character."

Grass rose carefully to his feet. "I'm a little wobbly on my feet."

"Probably will be, for the next few days."

"How did you get to our ship?" asked Grass.

Elisha laughed, and Alvin looked to Thrower. "They walked," said Thrower, hating the words as he said them.

"I reckon that would have been a sight," said Grass.

"You're going to see it," said Alvin, "and you're going to do it."

Before long they were standing on the water beside Thrower's ship. Thrower himself wasn't on the deck to see them off, of course, but Alvin knew he could hear every word they said.

"The water is surprisingly firm under my feet," said Grass.

"Don't try stomping your feet, because once the water starts splashing, it gets the wrong idea about what it's supposed to do."

Elisha now seemed to take on the role of a seasoned old adventurer. "Alvin's firm water doesn't weaken," said Elisha, "but nor does it extend on forever. Stay close by me, and we'll stride boldly to catch up with our own ship."

Grass turned to Alvin. "Would you like me to slow the speed at which the wind is carrying them away from us?"

"That would make catching them up a bit easier," said Alvin. "Or I could run on ahead and ask them to furl sails."

"I'd rather you . . . I'd rather you stay with us," said Grass. "I trust in your knack, I truly do, but seeing is not necessarily believing."

"A wise man. Now, if Reverend Thrower were here on deck, I'd tell him that the jar of whisky is actually *Scotch* whisky, not Irish at all. I believe Mr. Thrower has a taste for that whisky and will find much consolation in that jar, while the wind carries him home."

"Whether the sea stays smooth or turns rough again," said Grass, "I can promise that the wind will be always at his back."

"He may want to take the helm near the coast," said Alvin, "because the wind doesn't know about the difference between heading straight for a cliff and passing into a bay."

Alvin started walking away. Immediately Grass clutched at Elisha's arm. "Don't worry," said Elisha. "I've got you. And . . . he's got *me*."

When they were a few steps away from Thrower's ship, Alvin healed the openings in the sail until it bellied once again with the steady breeze from the west. They heard the sound of breaking glass.

"Do you think the jar fell, when the ship moved?" asked Elisha.

"I think he threw it to the floor, not wanting to take any gift from you," said Grass. "You should hear how he curses you and the vile things he—well, no, you *shouldn't* hear any of that."

"He says it to my face, so I've heard it often in my life, from childhood on," said Alvin. "Mr. Grass, is your injury healed enough that you can stride a little bolder?"

Grass touched his hand to his forehead. "I don't feel any pain at all," he said.

"Dizziness? A sense of falling?"

"Mostly what I feel is hungry and thirsty."

"If our voyage succeeds, Mr. Grass, we will owe it to the good you did for us, unasked."

"I couldn't let you stay and starve, like he planned."

"And you were running out of food, too."

"Ran out two days ago. Still had water, though. He was talking about catching a rat, but I figured we was neither of us quick enough."

"Would you have eaten rat, if you caught one?" asked Elisha.

"Hunger adds a fine flavor to everything edible," said Grass, "and if you would eat squirrel or beaver, then rat will be fine for you, since they're all rodents together."

"You know your rodents," said Alvin.

"I know what I happen to have heard, and I have a good memory."

"Then do you remember which ship is mine? Because I've never seen it from the stern."

"*I* remember," said Elisha, "even if his bruised brain can't recall."

20

REVEREND PHILADELPHIA THROWER stood before the large table that served as a replacement for the earlier one, which had dropped suddenly down into the cellar. "How are you, Your Grace," said Thrower.

"I'm not superannuated yet," said the bishop, "but so many younger men are eagerly interested in how long I'm going to occupy this see."

"Not I," said Thrower. "I'm Scottish Rite."

"They have bishops in Scotland," said the bishop.

"And they have parrots in Guatemala," said Thrower. "But I can't be a parrot, because I'm not in Guatemala."

"A stupid comparison," said the bishop, "but at least you're awake."

"The witch village had already been evacuated when we arrived."

"I heard it took you two weeks to get there."

"I didn't want to push the horses—we would need their strength for the charge when we arrived."

"Might your slowness have given them plenty of time to get away?" asked the bishop.

"I had hoped that the village might panic and disperse themselves."

"Which is what happened, except they dispersed aboard three former hulks in the prison fleet."

"They had many smaller craft as well," said Thrower.

"So now they belong either to the Atlantic or to America."

"Given what I saw of the Maker's mastery over—"

"He is not a Maker. There is only one Maker, and he dwells in heaven."

"Quite so, Your Grace. I spoke sarcastically, ironically, because his people call him a Maker."

"Irony is a double-edged sword. Use it too often, and you'll cut yourself."

"I will remember that, Your Grace"

"No you won't," said the bishop. "The men you took with you?"

"I sent them to their homes, each with the horse he had ridden. The two horses Mr. Grass and I rode, we sent back by the local tavern keeper."

"He fulfilled his office perfectly. The horses arrived promptly and in perfect condition."

"The men of our nonce raiding party were, I think, relieved not to have to kill anybody, there being no one there to kill."

"Do you think they have it in them, at some future date, to kill in the service of Christ?"

"If Your Grace had blessed them before they—"

"I will have no direct personal connection to any such raid."

"May I bless them?"

"Not in my name."

"I was thinking of . . . blessing them like Knights Templar . . . in the name of Jesus?"

"And have them called my 'Jesuit army'? No thank you."

Thrower stood patiently.

"Why are you still here?"

"I offer myself if you have further need of me for any task now or in the next few days."

"You know what your task is! Your only task, a duty from which you have not been excused."

Thrower still stood there. The bishop slapped the table and things bounced.

"Your Grace," said Thrower, "I think you are speaking of my duty to purge this world of a particularly diabolical presence."

"I was carefully *not* mentioning that duty, but yes. We understand each other."

"He has gone to America, Your Grace."

"And you have been in America. Indeed, you have citizenship in the United States."

"I was present in a state when it joined the Union, making me a citizen auto—"

"Have you never in your life managed to speak with *less* blather, or is this what I should expect from your forever?"

"Your Grace, I am an inveterate blatherer, as my professors in the seminary said, 'Only death or a sudden onset of wisdom would silence this blatherskite.' "

"And which did you choose?" asked the bishop.

"I practice self-control daily, Your Grace, and I say less than one in ten of the ideas that come into my mind."

"I will count myself blessed on that score," said the bishop.

They waited.

"Reverend Thrower," said the bishop. "You are still here."

"How will I be able to let you know that I have achieved my purpose?"

"How did you imagine? A letter carried by a packet boat? A proclamation by heralds with horns?"

"I didn't think—"

"No, you didn't, you never do. Why did God waste a perfectly good head by putting it between your shoulders? I know, I know, every idiot comes with a head, whether they ever use it or not. Speaking of heads, I will look forward to seeing one particular head in a box."

Thrower felt a thrill of fear run through him. "Through the international post?"

"A valise will do. Bring it to me in a valise."

"In person, another Atlantic crossing."

"By balloon this time. In Paris they're talking about having a man ride across the ocean in a basket under a balloon, carried by wind and having no fear of collision or potholes or weather, since they say they fly above the clouds."

"I don't think I—I don't know if I could—"

"Calm yourself, my friend. A newspaper clipping, hand delivered to my secretary should be sufficient. The man *is* famous enough to warrant an obituary, isn't he?"

"So you wish it to be a public death, rather than a stealthy one, where no one ever knows what became of—"

"Why must you speak of death? It comes to all of us, and always too soon. Why should this young American blacksmith be any different?"

Thrower bowed his head and strode from the bishop's office. Immediately someone else was ushered in, and Thrower wondered, not for the first time, how much of what was said within those walls was overheard.

All of it, thought Thrower. The bishop is vain, and he will want all his words recorded for posterity. There are scriveners hiding in the walls, taking down every word. Words of *mine*, that can be used against me. The bishop wasn't the "servant of all" that was extolled by Christ. In his own pious way, he was the enemy of all.

Thrower was halfway to his assigned room in a former monastery that now was a dormitory for visiting church dignitaries before it dawned on him. The bishop serves only himself, certainly not God, but he is *not* the enemy of all. Thrower knew who was, knew him well. Into his mind flashed the image of the charming, beautiful face of the angel who had first given him the mission of killing Alvin Miller, Junior, as a child.

Why would that face come into his mind when he was thinking of the enemy of all? That was Alvin Miller, Alvin Smith, Alvin "Maker," a blasphemous title. But when he thought of his worst enemy, he did not imagine the face of the bishop, nor did he think of any of Alvin's cohorts that he had been tracking for years. Nor of Alvin himself. Instead he saw the kindly, loving face of his spiritual friend, his Visitor. Was God whispering something to him?

Of course not.

He prayed for two hours before going to bed. But still his angel did not appear.

Maybe the bishop was supposed to be his angel now, the representative of God who would give him his missions. That was it. He did not *need* the angel anymore.

He closed his eyes to sleep.

Sometime in the darkness he woke up weeping. O my angel, my angel! How I need thee! I need thee now!

21

Eliza Nutbutter rose from the bed in darkness. It was not her bed and she was not in the cabin she rented behind the tavern—a no-alcohol tavern, such an absurd thing, but people did come most nights to sing and dance and drink either Adam's Ale or a concoction supposedly invented by Alvin Smith himself. It had tickly bubbles in it. It made her need to either belch or break wind, both potential obstacles to her work.

Adam's Ale it was—and it was the purest, clearest, most refreshing water she had drunk in her life. Not that she was a connoisseur of water. She usually drank liquids with at least a little alcohol in them. Or enough of something else to take away the taste. Rum was the foulest of the hard liquors, and so she was fascinated with it, could not leave it alone, always experimenting to find some way to mask the vile taste while preserving the proportion of alcohol.

Calvin was still in bed—he liked to sleep long and hard, especially if he had worked long and hard the night before. But to her surprise he was awake, watching her dress.

"So many layers of cloth between the living body and the eyes of the world," said Calvin.

"Our clothing makes us beautiful," said Eliza.

"Your clothing hides everything that makes you beautiful except your face, your hair, and your stature."

"And my graceful hands and arms, and my shoes that peek out from under my skirts when I walk, and my lower legs, which you glimpse when

I spin around in a dance. Oh, there is so much of my body on display. It's a shame that wide, deep necklines are not fashionable in Crystal City."

"They're fashionable in my bedroom," said Calvin.

"No matter what I wore, you'd have it off me in fifteen seconds after we got into this room."

"When has it ever taken that long?" asked Calvin, acting hurt.

He *was* a charming boy, and he might prove very useful later. But right now, Eliza Nutbutter had an errand to run.

"Did anyone see you come here?"

"No one ever sees me when I want not to be seen," said Eliza. "You know that's my knack."

"I thought your knack was escaping from anything and anyone, anywhere."

"When I come to you, my darling boy, I'm escaping from all the prying eyes of Crystal City. Still well within my knack."

"Just so you don't escape from me," said Calvin.

"My darling, darling boy—"

"What does that even mean, 'darling.' I've never darled, have you? Darled?"

"You're the clever one, you tell me."

"We use 'ling' endings to express affection for things we own. A piglet suddenly becomes a darling pigling when it's time for the slaughter."

"I wouldn't know," said Eliza. "I've never been present at the slaughter of a pig."

"Nor should you ever be," said Calvin. "No blood should ever be spattered on those fine—"

She looked banefully at him.

"Clothes. Your gownling, your corsetling—"

"I know what you were going to say, and I approve of the sentiment, just not the saying of it. Calvin, I don't need to escape from you. I'm not your prisoner, I'm not held against my will, and I tell you everything."

"Or so you say."

"*Everything.* Every bit of nice or nasty gossip that I hear, everybody who is losing money or making money, all the people committing adultery on the sly."

"But you never hear about *me*, do you?"

"A few scattered rumors, weeks apart, and usually about something audacious you said or did back in your childhood. Which you're barely out of, my duckling."

Calvin chuckled. "So now it's duckling instead of darling."

"Darling starts with dar, which used to mean dear, as in something of great cost or value. So dear, add on the affectionate ling, and . . . darling."

"If you knew—"

"Silly," said Eliza. "I didn't know at all, till you started explaining it, and then I understood at once what you were going to say. Is that a knack I have? Or have I already heard everything that any man has to say, so it just comes back to me when I need it?"

"Someone explained to you the origin of the word 'darling'?"

"I don't remember, darling. Or if you were a bear, should I call you 'barling'?"

"I like that. As long as you never call anyone else by that name. I'll know if you do, by the way."

"My all-knowing, all-seeing barling, the junior Maker."

His eyes darkened and he rolled under the covers, turning his back to her.

"Don't pout, my duckling," said Eliza. "I need to run a little errand and I don't want you to worry when you don't see me for a couple of weeks."

"Weeks? An 'errand'?"

"There's something I need to do in Irrakwa."

"Didn't Alvin rescue you from Irrakwa?"

"He gave me safe passage. What he rescued me from was unimaginable wealth."

"You have no idea how much wealth I can imagine," said Calvin. "How *do* you make your money, Eliza? You never ask *me* for any."

"You don't have any."

"I'm a Maker. If I need money, I can make it."

"So you say. Never saw you do it, but why should I doubt?"

"Who pays you?"

"Nobody *pays* me. Nobody hires me. They give me gifts, lovely gifts, mostly the clinky coiny kind of gift. Which I carry between my breasts like any sensible woman, because, while men are constantly trying to get an angle to peer down between them, it is very dark, my bag of coins is fuliginous, and therefore they are deceived into thinking that they have seen nothing but an unfathomable deep bay of black."

"You could have said 'sea of black' or 'ocean of black.'"

"There isn't room here for more than a bay, a little inlet." Her corset in place, the stays doing their noble, uplifting labor, Eliza settled the fuligin purse into place. Calvin had never seen anything so black. It wasn't a purse, it was a hole in her chest leading, not to the back of her body, but into the starless dark of space, infinitely deep.

"You can't take your eyes off my coins, is that it?"

"I have never seen such complete and perfect black. Black itself would look pale compared to it."

"Fuligin. I had never heard of it either. But an Italian woman in Philadelphia told me that her knack—we were being quite open with each other—her knack was to take soot and lampblack and make a dye that could turn the whitest cloth into the color fuligin, which she promised me was blacker than black. And it *is* true, don't you think?"

"Where is she now?"

"Philadelphia, for all I know."

"How did you pay her?"

"It's so complicated," said Eliza.

"And yet, if you tell me the truth, it will be so simple."

"Are you going to make me walk home in the light of dawn?"

"You helped her escape, since that's your knack."

"Well. Yes. That wasn't my plan. I was arrested for walking on a public street an hour after dark. The Quakers can out-puritan the Puritans sometimes. The law assumes that an unaccompanied woman on the street at night must be in a much-wanted but apparently never-available trade."

"So they threw you in jail."

"They gently led me to jail. I was dressed like a lady, I spoke like a lady, and so the constables were a little bit in awe of me. They didn't put me in a crowded cell, but in a smaller one with only one other occupant."

"Your Italian blackmaker."

"Fuligin. Yes. I happened to mention that I had a knack for escaping and probably wouldn't be there by morning. And she said, 'Ma'am, I have two babies at home to feed. Would you take me with you?'

"'With *your* enormous powers, you need my help?' says I to her. 'My powers!' she says. And I say, 'Somehow, before this night is over, you're going to conceive, carry, and bear two babies and somehow smuggle them out of here and into your home, so that you can fulfill your word and have two babies at home to feed.'"

"So you called her a liar, and she made you a purse, and you took her with you."

"Not in that order, of course. She didn't have the makings of my fuligin purse, but her gratitude was the rare kind that lasts for more than an hour."

"What if I came with you on this errand?"

"Then I wouldn't go."

"Because your errand is secret."

"My errand is private," said Eliza. "What if there were a doctor in Philadelphia who I trust not to poison me with his remedies."

"Which are probably rum and lots of strained lemon juice and—"

"I know that you can tell all the ingredients that any medicine show's elixirs contain."

"Some very harmful."

"I don't have a doctor, so no one gives me potions. I said what *if* there *were* a doctor I trust. There is no such doctor. There's almost nobody I trust."

"Am I one you trust?"

"Implicitly, my duckling, my barling."

"Well, that's foolish of you."

"I trust you implicitly to always do whatever you believe is in your best interest."

"Not foolish, then."

"Like everyone else on God's green Earth, Calvin. Everybody acts in what they *think* will be in their best interest. Most people are so stupid or powerless that they can't figure out what their best interest is, and if they *do* find it out, they are unable to achieve it."

"Even my altruistic brother?"

"Which one is that?" asked Eliza.

"Well, you really are cynical."

"Is that a nice thing? Is it beautiful?"

"You know the word perfectly well. I can't persuade you to stay another fifteen minutes, could I?"

"You can't," said Eliza. "And it never goes so quickly as fifteen minutes."

"Twenty minutes."

"Not one more minute." Eliza flounced out of Calvin's modest house, through the back door, where she knew nobody would be watching, because she thought of herself as escaping, getting away from Calvin's possessive devotion. So naturally, nobody would be able to tell him, if he asked, which way she went, because nobody knew she was there last night, and they never noticed her this morning. So she walked rather openly, not furtively, along the dirt road, and when she got to the paved part, she walked in the grass beside the road, because cobbled streets were almost impossible to walk on without turning an ankle. "Why do they use cobblestones?" she demanded that Calvin tell her.

"They last longer than brick, and they don't get muddy like dirt."

"Yes they do, and the mud makes them slick and even harder to walk on. Dirt roads are best—they can be repaired with a bucket of dirt and a rake, they aren't always trying to break your ankle. Or hip."

To which Calvin had only responded with a kiss. "I wish I could make all roads smooth and safe for you," he said, which was sweet, but also stupid, because if he had half the power he claimed to have, he could do *exactly* that instead of wishing. But it was a helpful thought, and maybe when he figured out what he wanted to do with his life, he'd figure out how to smooth roads ahead of her wherever she walked.

In her own little house, she changed into traveling clothes, which covered her more thoroughly than usual. She had a few other things hidden on her person, but within easy reach even if somebody was watching her. No point in hiding them in her bags, which could be snatched out of her womanly hands by any ruffian. The clothes she was taking with her weren't so elegant that she couldn't replace them by purchase if they were stolen.

There was coach service—three a day—from Crystal City to Carthage, the biggest city on the Hio River. It was the first stop on your journey, if you didn't want to ride on the railroad. On the train, you couldn't call to the driver to stop. Coachmen were trained to assume that if a lady of quality asked them to stop, she knew what she was doing, so he should stop and stay in his high seat and not watch where she went or what she did. She knew what they assumed, but mostly she did it because she was getting stiff from sitting too long, or she needed a nip of something that had a touch of spirits in it, or she wanted to flounce provocatively in front of another passenger who would feel very well paid for the effort of looking out the window.

What will I ever do if I get fat? Some men won't be put off by that, but others will, and my world will shrink. But just as awful to turn into a rail-thin old biddy with veins and creases in her neck crying out, Look how old she is!

Her only consolation at such thoughts was to remember one of her best sayings: I'll be dead before any of that happens. She had already been shot at several times—not when she was escaping from something—and stabbed once, but not deeply enough to score a vital organ. Dying was never all that very far away, and she rarely minded thinking about it. I'd rather die when I still look good enough in my coffin that people will say, What a shame,

I would have liked to get to know her well. Because men were not above thinking such thoughts about an attractive corpse.

Not dead yet, she always said to herself, even when she was thinking about being an enchanted dead but never-fading princess, and Alvin Maker would come and kiss breath back into her lungs, and raise her up out of her bed and laugh when she said, "But what about Margaret?"

He would say, "I should have turned *her* to tin and sent her away instead of the gold," and as she thought these things she knew she was a truly wicked woman, to covet another woman's husband, and imagine the wife tidily disposed of so Eliza could take her place.

Never mind that she had a knack that would be useless to an honorable woman married to the founder of Crystal City.

The train was much faster, but she knew she had time. She had seen in a block of water in a vision wall. Alvin was on a ship in the midst of a flotilla of ships on a very still sea, not moving at all. She couldn't guess whether that was past, present, or future, but if it had happened, Alvin's return to America would still be a few weeks off. Time enough to make a leisurely trip in the coach, wishing Calvin would keep his promise and smooth all her roads, even when she wasn't walking.

It took her two weeks to reach Philadelphia. The train would have taken only two days, with one change in Erie. But she had done that before, and it held no allure for her. Speed was good when you needed it. But in the coach, she had been able to receive some lovely gifts from two of the men who rode with her when they reached a roadhouse to spend the night.

She wouldn't have made a bit of money on the train. There was no privacy in those hot miserable cars. She was a lady, not a street woman who would please a man with her back against a wall and her own skirts in her face. Not that she had never done it, but, like the train, it was an experience she preferred to never have again, unless there was no other way.

A hansom cab took her to her favorite hotel in Philadelphia—the kind of place with a few luxuries she appreciated, where they always remembered her by name, and where nobody asked about any man who told them he had to see her on business. It was usually true, though once it had been one of the men who shot at her.

She went to the docks every day around noon, to see if any ships had arrived—or a flotilla of three big ships and a lot of smaller ones, down to the size of rowboats. Day after day, no such boats and no word of them. She began to wonder if Alvin wouldn't bring them to the largest port in the

United States, the capital, for heaven's sake. With a bunch of knacky Irishmen, he would definitely need to get them legally admitted into the country, which could only be done in the capital, at least with enough authority to make it stick.

She even bought a map of the whole English-speaking coast from Georgia to Acadia. What would stop him from entering the continent at Halifax? Or Boston? Well, he wasn't *that* stupid. He could only bring them, really, into the United States, and Philadelphia was the best port of entry.

Eliza walked up and down the higher boardwalk, where she had a view of the whole riverside. It smelled better up and away from the cargoes and the stevedores. And the passengers and the ferries and the fishermen. Since it wasn't winter but spring, the fishing boats couldn't be half filled with ice, to keep the fish smelling fresh, though they often tried to keep the fish alive in their iceless holds by letting the bilge get high enough to keep them in water. Eliza heard from one scientist she talked with that of course the fish couldn't live in the hold. "So many fish piled on top of each other, none of them can breathe."

"Fish breathe?"

"Oxygen, just like us, but their gills only work when they're moving, and when there's free oxygen in the water. Fishermen know that, too, so I think they only do that business with the water to assure their customers that *their* fish are fresher than anybody else's."

It was one of her most pleasant mornings, and the professor of Ichthyology—she made him teach her how to spell it *and* say it—gave her such a nice gift that she thought, first, how much do they *pay* these scientists? And second, didn't he know I would regard his conversation as enough of a gift to satisfy her covetous heart? But, third, it was a very substantial gift. Enough to buy and keep a carriage of her own, if she had had any use for such a thing. And a carriage was no use without at least one horse, so that would be a waste of her money. If she wanted to be responsible for another living thing, she'd have a baby.

Alvin's baby.

Knowing his power, it was probable that no woman would conceive his child unless he wanted her to.

But who knew how far knacks went in any direction? Being a Maker didn't make him God, who was all powerful. At best, Alvin Maker was *much* powerful, but not *all* powerful.

There on the upper boardwalk, there stood a man looking out over the river, downstream like her. He was getting on in years, and though he looked lean and healthy, he did not look rich. He was a gentleman, certainly, but beyond that, he was hard to read.

He noticed her looking at him and beckoned to her mildly, not smiling, not *ingratiating*, so he didn't want what most men wanted from her. When she got near him—holding her bags, which were getting heavy—he reached out and took the heavier bag from her. She knew he was not a thief, and when his expression asked her for permission, she said, "You are kind, sir. Even lightly packed bags can become heavy in the gathering heat of the day."

"You're waiting here for someone?"

"I don't know when he'll arrive. There was certainly no *schedule*, so I merely come each day to see, hoping that he'll come."

"Hoping *he* will come."

"Just a friend. We once traveled in the same company on forest roads until we came to . . ." And there she stopped, because saying she was from Crystal City might make her a target of punishers from New England.

"Crystal City," the man said.

That set her back on her heels. How could he know?

"I only made that guess because the man *I'm* waiting for is closely tied with that city."

"You're his friend?"

"I try to be, though he's probably the most self-sufficient man in the world."

"So you're waiting for the . . . for the blacksmith?"

"And smith of other metals, I've been told," said the man.

"I would wager—and I never wager, sir—that you're a man of the cloth."

"What gave me away?" asked the man.

"You have no luggage."

"But I didn't just arrive, as you did. You came here even before getting a room."

"They didn't want to rent me a room till midafternoon, after the maids had cleaned all the rooms."

"And they wouldn't hold your bags for you?"

"Everything I have in the world is in those bags," she said simply.

She saw at once that he knew she was lying. He gave a little smile. "Then you must have judged me *very* trustworthy, to let me hold your whole estate!"

"You have a foreign accent. English, I think, but don't I hear something else?"

"I have lived in several places and learned the local language. I doubt you speak any of them."

"Oh, sir, I speak only two languages. American and money."

"Two very powerful languages. Many people speak the language of money, but most of them only enough to be able to bid the coins farewell as they run away."

"I'm frugal," she said. "Which is why I won't buy you dinner."

"I'm well provided-for," he said.

"Catholic," she said.

"It happens that I am."

"You didn't look like a German or a Viking."

"I never thought I looked like anything. But until last year, I had lived quite comfortably in Portugal, a lovely country with fine harbors."

"And last year, what happened to move you out of Portugal?"

"I received an urgent request to go and help purify the Church of Ireland."

"Aren't the Irish Catholics?"

"Tried and true," said the man. "But the established Church of Ireland is really run by the church of the conquerors of Ireland, and it is most definitely *not* Catholic."

"Church of England—like New England. Were you going to get rid of the people with knacks?"

The man laughed. "In a way," he said. "But my role was to convict them all of crimes that would allow me to sentence them to be transported."

"To where?"

"Here. Where I plan to help them board the trains that can take them west to Crystal City."

"You *are* generous, sir."

"My patron is generous."

"And who is your patron?" she asked.

"Our Savior, Jesus Christ," he said, and crossed himself.

"Well, now *everybody* knows you're Catholic."

The man laughed.

"Do you have a name?"

He seemed about to answer, but at that moment a racket that had started upriver was now coming near enough to make it hard to talk. They watched four noisy steamboats paddling downriver.

"Don't you wonder what their errand is?"

"No," said the man. "Because I paid for their errand."

"But they're not stopping here!"

"They were notified by telegraph that there was a flotilla arriving at the mouth of the Delaware River, with sailors so little skilled that it would be a miracle if they could sail upriver against the current. So, as arranged, they're heading down to greet those ships and attach hawsers to them and tow them upriver to here."

"Why would a man of the Catholic Church—"

"I am, or was, the Lord Inquisitor of Ireland, my lady. It was I who sentenced all of Alvin's companions to exile in America, where they could use their knacks without fear. As you use *your* knack."

"I don't like how you know things you couldn't know."

"Alvin told me about you," said the man.

Eliza hoped that she was poised enough not to blanch. "What did he say?"

"He met you in a forest glade, and you were accompanied by men who were unaccountably carrying a wagonload of tin through the edges of Irrakwa country."

"Alvin the blacksmith guided us all the way to Crystal City," said Eliza.

"And you the only woman in that company of men."

"One must be vigilant, but one must also trust sometimes."

"Oh, no. Alvin was quite sure you were the ringleader and thought up the whole thing."

"Why would he think that?"

"Because he couldn't conceive of you following anybody on such a madcap adventure. So you were the one *they* were following."

"People leap to a lot of conclusions around here."

The man held out his hand. "You asked my name just before the riverboats came by. My name is Lukasz, Father Lukasz, but between me, a priest, and you, a dedicated and determined sinner, let's not stand on ceremony. Just call me Lukasz. And I believe your name is Eliza?"

Eliza was actually flattered that Alvin had remembered her name, and then talked about her enough that Lukasz remembered it, too. "I *am* a sinner, or so most religions would judge me to be."

"Like the woman at the well, you have had a number of husbands—"

"Well, not exactly hus—"

"And the one you have now is not your own," said Lukasz.

"I don't have a husband now or ever, Father Lukasz."

"I'm sorry if I misjudged you," said Lukasz. "Since you are not going to buy me dinner while we wait, will you let me pay for yours?"

"Isn't your money . . . what, consecrated?"

"Money can never be consecrated. It can be used in a consecrated cause. But also for simple things like feeding the body to keep up our strength. I've eaten at the fish shop just down there." He pointed. "I found it tasty and healthy. And because the owners are neither Quakers, Puritans, nor Baptists, this charming dockside vittler serves a very good ale of his own making. Since you're expecting to meet Alvin and make one more attempt to seduce him, I'm sure you don't want any of the stronger spirits."

Eliza, by reflex, went into mortally-offended mode, but Lukasz just chuckled. She stopped protesting, then stood at the rail looking out across the Delaware.

"Please don't pout, my daughter. Alvin knew what you were doing, and when his Margaret met you, she knew you down to the bone. We hope that your heart will soften and that you will join Crystal City as your village, as your home."

They had discussed her, knew her motives and plans, and still wanted her to stay in their city. "Why would they want a woman like me?"

"There are no women like you, my daughter, my child. I wish you had any inkling of who you really are. Precious in the sight of God. One of his dear children, for whom he has such high hopes."

"How would you know *that*?"

"Do you think priests are utterly without knacks?"

"What, you hear people's confessions before you even meet them?"

"You dread my judgment of your sins, but you doubt my knowledge of the Savior's love for you."

And with that, Eliza burst into tears.

Any other man, *any*, would have put an arm across her shoulders to comfort her. But Lukasz was a priest, a man of God, and he did not choose to touch her.

She calmed herself. Dabbed at her eyes with the kerchief from her left sleeve.

"What a beautiful, finely crafted handkerchief," said Lukasz.

"It is not," said Eliza. "I hemmed the thing myself, with not very straight seams, and there's not a speck of lace or embroidery on it."

Lukasz merely smiled at her, and then said, "If we go down into my favorite fish house in Philadelphia, we will still be able to order a fine dinner."

"They'll be out of all the good fish by now," said Eliza.

"I waved at the owner when I arrived, and he waved back. He knows I'm here, and since I rarely dine alone, there'll be plenty of his best for both of us."

"What's his best?"

"Sometimes cod, sometimes tuna, sometimes haddock. Black sea bass, striped bass. Walleye, perch. Flounder and bluefish—they're just coming into season, they're the best catch from the middle of the bay at the river's mouth."

"You're telling me that his best is . . . fish."

"Whatever fish he thinks is best will be prepared for us with a skill that I suspect is a knack, and we will dine. And when we're done, we'll hear the steamers coming up from downriver."

"I'll pay for my own dinner," she said.

"As you wish, daughter. But if your means are tight, I'll share what I have."

Eliza knew when she was seeing a performance. He was acting the role of man of God, and he had very good lines to say and he delivered them well. And yet, despite her cynicism, his offer to share what he had resonated with something deep within her, something she had known was there, but hadn't touched in years.

22

ALVIN STOOD IN the bow of the riverboat, marveling at the sheer power that could draw a retired but full-size man-o'-war and five other ships upstream on the Delaware. He could feel the vibration of the steam engine, could even feel when coalmen tossed another shovelful of fuel into the burner. He felt how the ship grew just a bit lighter as the coal burned, yet there was no loss of strength.

There was the dock of Philadelphia, the little-used lower dock because it was too low for steam traffic, and any sailing ships that came this far upstream were piloted by men who knew these docks and brought their ships right close to the warehouses. Father Luke had given good, clear instructions to these men.

When Luke had left their Quayside community, Alvin asked if he was going back to—Rome? Portugal? And Luke said, "My work in Ireland has barely begun."

"When *will* it be done? When you're executed for helping witches? Or simply for being a priest."

"I will plead guilty to both, if it comes to that. I wouldn't want my executioners to have any doubt of my guilt preying on their consciences."

"Forgive them, for they know not what they do?"

"He showed us all the way."

"So much wickedness is done in his name," said Alvin that day.

"I will sail to America, and I imagine my ship will get there much more quickly than any of yours."

"Why will you go there? The Irish are here!"

"I go to prepare a place for you. Where would you most like to disembark from your fleet?"

"Philadelphia, I think. There are more trains out of Philadelphia than anywhere else, and a lot of them go west."

"And a sudden influx of starving Irishmen won't be so hard for the city to absorb."

"They won't be starving," said Alvin.

"You can't carry enough provisions in those boats for the people you'll be carrying. Unless you can do that business with the loaves and fishes."

"No loaves, but in the ocean there are plenty of fishes. Not to mention air-breathing mammals like dolphins and seals."

"Mammals?" asked Luke. "I thought dolphins were fish."

"There is a type of dolphin that *is* a fish, but the rest are mammals. We won't eat them, we'll ask them to bring us all the fish we need, if we get low on provisions."

"You've been to sea before."

"I met some very clever dolphins who wished me well and offered help if I ever needed it."

"Expect me to be waiting for you in Philadelphia, with as much help as my wit and someone else's money can organize."

Lukasz was a good man, for a Catholic, and Alvin figured he wouldn't've burnt Joan of Arc as a witch if *he* had inquisitioned her.

Now here he was, as good as his word. Better than his word, because Alvin had been in despair, trying to think of how to get the whole flotilla upriver. Sandy said he was good with wind, but with the boats all spread out along the curves of the river, there wasn't one wind direction that would serve all of the ships at once. "They'll run aground, and not close to Philadelphia, either," Sandy told him. "Though the wind *is* mostly out of the south or southwest, this time of year. If we had expert pilots . . ."

Alvin had no response to that. He could imagine strolling along the waterfront, searching for a pilot willing to steer a bunch of witches up to Philadelphia. There would be no pilots.

Until four steamboats chugged their way out into the middle of the Delaware Bay. It was a bit of a mess, as the pilots of the riverboats assessed which of their vessels could tow each of Alvin's. After they did all their figuring, they concluded that between them they could pull them all—if these landlubbers could manage to tie boats together.

This was when John Binder proved the worth of his knack, because he and Alvin both knew that a rope gathered and assured by John Binder would not break from pulling it or from bending it, or even cutting at it with any blade except John Binder's own, held in his own hand. Nor were the ropes stiff—you could make a knot, as small and tight as you needed, and the knot wouldn't slip unless you wanted it to.

John Binder's work was done at the wide mouth of the Delaware. The steamboats dragged their trailers upriver against the current. Alvin stayed on the deck of the lead steamboat, looking back and adjusting the currents so that none of the flotilla of Irish boats capsized or grounded. The river looked like one smooth current to the sea, but going upstream they learned that it was a hundred currents, all competing with each other, and the boats were in greater danger in the river than they had been in out on the open Atlantic.

But the greater danger happened when the lead steamboat pulled up parallel with the low docks they were going to have to use. The steamboats themselves used the higher docks, as did the large ocean-going sailing ships. But the old, lower docks were still there, and those were the only ones capable of disembarking Alvin's people from the little boats.

But the lead steamboat didn't even slow down. It pulled Alvin's flotilla upstream and out of reach of the docks.

It took Alvin only a moment to realize that this was an extortion attempt. We were paid to bring you upriver, the steamboat pilots would say, all the way to Philadelphia. We did that. Now if you want us to manage the docking and unloading of all these miserable little boats, that's going to cost you just as much again.

John Binder stood there on the deck with Alvin, and they looked at each other. John rolled his eyes. Alvin said, "John, I know your knack is binding things together. Have you worked much on disconnecting things without having to lay hands on them?"

"Never spent much time on it. But when I need things to come apart, they usually do. You want me to undo all my knots and turn our Irish boats loose on the current?"

"No, I think that might well drown all our people. Here's my problem. If the steamboats turn around, they'll be towing the little boats *with* the downstream current. As the steamboats slow down at the docks, the current will carry *our* little boats right past the docks."

"Sounds about right," said Binder.

"How can we handle this, without giving in to their extortion?" asked Alvin. "How will *they* get our boats back downstream to Philadelphia?"

"Near as I can figure, they'll slow down their paddlewheels enough to let the current carry the trailing boats back down to the docks, but with the steamboat pouring on just enough power to keep them in place while we get the boats up to the docks, tie them up, and disembark."

"I see," said Alvin, picturing it in his mind. "And if we pay them enough, they'll slow down their steamboats and get us lined up just right. Almost effortless for them."

"Sounds right."

"Why haven't they come to make the demand yet?" asked Alvin.

"I think they expect us to go running up to the pilot house and demand what's going on," said Binder.

Alvin nodded.

"So what do you want me to disconnect?" asked Binder.

"The steam engines make those pistons go, and then *they* make the paddlewheels turn, right?"

"You want that connection to be broken," said Binder.

"I want it to slip and jam and otherwise misbehave. So the wheel stops turning and the current starts pushing the steamboat downriver. But nothing should be broken. Just . . . faulty connections, which you can fix without touching anything."

"Because you don't want them to be able to prove sorcerers were interfering with their boats," said Binder.

"So let's make all their steam engines lose a reliable connection with their paddlewheels."

"When?" asked Binder.

"Now," said Alvin. "All of them, all at once."

It took Binder a couple of minutes to locate everything he needed to do, and then use his doodlebug to make gears slip and pistons jam. On all the steamboats at once. The last one hadn't reached the low docks yet, but the other three were all upstream of them when they stopped moving forward and started slipping backward.

The steamboats were getting carried downstream a little faster than the boats they had been towing. They were going to get tangled up in those boats pretty quick.

Alvin put his hand on Binder's shoulder and said, "Let's go ask the pilot what's going on."

The pilot was already out of the pilot house, and they ran into him on the starboard upper deck. Alvin sounded pretty peeved when he said, "I thought you ran a tight ship, sir."

Binder poured on the outrage. "Don't you know you're moving downstream faster than the boats tied up behind you? They can't get out of the way!"

"Untie the lines and cast them off!" shouted the pilot.

"How are we going to do that?" asked Binder. "Show me how to do it."

The pilot ran to where the lines were tied. There was no undoing a knot John Binder had worked on—plus, the ropes were wet.

"Do something!" the pilot shouted at Alvin.

"Isn't this the part where you tell me I have to pay double before you'll let my boats get tied up to the lower docks?" asked Alvin.

"You think I'm doing this on purpose?" yelled the pilot.

"I think you steamed right past the Philadelphia harbor on purpose," said Alvin.

"Only I guess you forgot to tell your steam engine about your extortion scheme, so the engine didn't know how to act."

"I know you two did it, somehow!"

"Don't hear you denying the extortion plot," said Binder.

"We weren't going to ask for much!" said the pilot.

Alvin grinned. "We'll see what we can do. And if we get your engine running and your wheels turning, we won't ask for much."

"I know you ensorceled them," said the fuming pilot.

"You know more than I do," said Binder. "Can you *un*ensorcel them?"

"Of course not," said the pilot.

"I better get a look at the engine on this boat first," said Binder.

The pilot led them down to the engine room. Binder immediately saw a few connectors on the deck, where they'd landed when Binder popped them off the pistons.

In order for the pistons to be still while Binder reattached them manually, the engine had to be disengaged completely. Then it took Binder a long time, what with having no tools, to get the pistons connected and a few other things repaired. "Of course it got all gummed up," said Binder. "You aren't washing the gears every day."

"Nobody washes the gears," said the pilot. "You lubricate them."

At the time their steam engine was working again, all the other steamboats also kind of self-repaired—Binder was almost as skilled as Alvin about using his knacks without being caught at it.

By then, of course, most of the Irish boats were running aground or taking on water. There was a lot of screaming and yelling. But as the wheel started turning fast enough to resume upstream motion, the tangle of boats sorted themselves out until they were all dancing at the end of their lines.

This time when the steamboat had the towed boats parallel with the lower docks, the crews had them moored to the dock in a moment. Then it was Binder's turn to let loose the knots he didn't like.

When all the boats were separated from the steamboats, they loaded up several carts and everyone got cheerful as they hauled the carts to the warehouse Father Luke had bargained for. They made sure everything was in the right trunks. "Tomorrow we get these all aboard the railroad train taking us west," said Alvin.

On shore, Father Luke told Alvin that the last boat was unloaded, so he was going to go pay the steamboat captains.

"Just a couple of things, Father Lukasz," said Alvin. "When they try to tack on more charges for anything at all, tell them that you are deducting a portion from *each* steamboat's fee because John Binder and I had to fix their engines, which we did."

Father Luke grinned at Alvin. "They were trying to cheat you, right?"

"Yes," said John Binder.

"They have a reputation for that kind of chicanery," said Luke.

"Then why did you hire their boats?" asked Alvin, exasperated.

"Their bad reputations had left them desperate for customers, so all four steamboats were available for a reasonable fee." Luke grinned at Alvin. "And I figured you'd soon have the situation well in hand."

When the pilots all demanded that the local police force Father Luke to pay the full fee, Alvin intervened. "Why don't these good policemen lead us down to the station where we can hammer it all out?"

By the time the police had conveyed Alvin and Binder to the station, the pilots had slipped off to disappear in the city. They may not have been paid everything they hoped for, but they got most of their original fee, which was, as Binder said, "more than they deserved."

Still, Alvin and John got to the police station, and the police didn't take long to make it clear that they would never have listened to those shady riverboat pilots. However, what concerned the police was a sudden influx of Irishmen—and their wives and children and *grandparents*, in some cases—and nobody wanted them there.

"On account of they're Irish?" asked Alvin.

"On account of they're witches," answered one of the cops.

"No such thing as witches," said Alvin, and he and Binder headed for the door.

23

"DON'T TAKE ANOTHER step toward that door, sir," said the desk policeman. At the sound of his voice, a couple of other constables stepped out of the back. They said the Irrakwa had invented a reliable breech-loading pistol with five chambers for bullets. Just what these fellows needed. What they had were ancient flintlock one-shots where the ball would sometimes roll out of the barrel and bounce on the ground if you tipped it down and it got jolted.

"Gentlemen," said Alvin. "Those pistols couldn't shoot a cockroach iffen you stuffed the cockroach down the barrel."

"Better than the bullets you got," said the man who seemed senior. "Are you with that Irish group?"

"Not Irish myself. Born in Hatrack River, near the Hio. But now I live in Crystal City."

Alvin saw the men putting their pistols back in their copious pockets.

"That's not a very secure way to carry those cannons," said Alvin. "They could go off and shoot your leg. Or something."

"You have a name?" asked the senior constable.

Alvin stuck out his hand. "Alvin Miller, Junior, at your service. But I'm a journeyman smith, so I suppose I should call myself Smith instead of my dad's trade."

Now all the guns were put away.

"I heard you had something to do with these ships of Irishmen as landed just this forenoon."

"I sailed with them. All the way from Ireland to Philadelphia, so I'm afraid I look a bit bedraggled."

The men were all looking at him quizzically. Except one man who was outright hostile-looking. Alvin walked up to the hostile man and said, "Looks like you got an opinion that's busting to get out of you."

"Got lots of opinions." The man tried to pull his hand away, but with Alvin's strong hand gripping his wrist, that wasn't going to happen.

"I'll wager you got a poor opinion of Irish folk."

"Catholics," said one of the other constables.

"Legal in the United States. New England don't have a say in United States law, right?"

"Nor the King down in Camelot," said the desk constable.

"I like living in a free country," said Alvin. "So I get concerned when I see a sign that the constabulary here at the port of Philadelphia includes someone who doesn't like people with knacks."

The hostile man stopped trying to pull his hand back. "Having a right strong grip don't count as a knack," he said.

"Right you are," said Alvin. "What worries me is, you might try to find some New Englanders who happen to be sojourning here in Philadelphia, and tell them about a whole bunch of witches who just came ashore, and then you might lead that mob right to where we're all lodging for the night. There's women and children and I wouldn't like anything waking them up and scaring them. You can understand that, can't you?"

The hostile constable nodded.

"But I think you're all the more determined to duck out of here and cause a riot, because I held your hand. Could've thrown you to the ground, I'm a pretty good wrestler."

The senior constable said, "I hope you're not threatening violence against an officer of the law."

"Violence? Out west, two men can't hardly be said to know each other if they hadn't had a few rounds of stick-pulling or just riverman wrestling."

"You must know that that ear-biting, eye-gouging style of wrestling is illegal here in the City of Brotherly Love."

"Nobody loses eyes or ears if they don't try taking the other fellow's."

"Your rules?" asked the senior constable.

"Back in Crystal City, yes sir," said Alvin. "But I haven't blinded anybody or taken no ears nor noses in, must be, say, fifteen years. Mike Fink taught me how to make a fellow think I'm taking some precious body part, but cause no permanent damage. The world's already got plenty of folks as can't see or hear straight."

"Don't think I can't hear straight enough, witch, how you hide curses inside every word that slips from your mouth," said the hostile constable.

Alvin looked at the senior constable. "I'm not likely to sleep well tonight, knowing he's walking around with authority and resentment."

The senior constable walked over and put an arm across the witch-hater's shoulder. "Vaughan," he said. "You know I can't let you do any patrolling tonight."

"Taking orders from the devil's children now?" asked Vaughan.

"Only person taking orders from anybody tonight is you, taking them from me. You'll work your whole shift till midnight, and then you'll stay here in a locked office till dawn."

Vaughan was outraged. "Are you arresting me?"

"Maybe it's protective custody," said Alvin. "See, I feel responsible for all these knack-users I helped escape from witch-killers in Ireland. Now that I'm here in the land of tolerance and freedom, I think if somebody should attack my people—a mob of angry New Englanders, or knack-hating Philadelphians, for instance—I'd be worried about folks getting beaten and maybe killed dead, and I can't allow that."

"Wouldn't kill anybody."

"Oh, you didn't understand me, Vaughan," said Alvin. "I wasn't worrying about *my* people getting beaten or killed. You don't have any idea what a lot of angry, frightened people with knacks might do to somebody threatening them or their children."

"I told you they were dangerous," said Vaughan to his boss.

"Sounds to me like they'd only be dangerous to people as tried to harm them, and despite the Quaker heritage of this city, a man has a right to stand up against the threat of violence."

Vaughan only looked angrier than ever. So Alvin did what was within easy reach for him. He got all the balls to drop out of the barrels of their pistols at once. He made sure the ones in pockets found a hole and hit the floor only a moment or two later. None of them now had a loaded gun.

"See?" asked Vaughan, his voice trembling. "How can we keep the peace when this witch can—"

"Wizard," said the desk constable. "The men are called wizards. Or incubuses. Incubi."

"You're getting your wicked spirits all mixed up," said the senior constable.

Vaughan got down on his knees, picking up pistol balls.

"Stop that, Vaughan," said the constable. "You know we got casks of those in back. These don't have to be picked up now."

When Vaughan reluctantly got back to his feet, every button on his uniform stayed behind him on the floor. His pants fell down.

"I recommend suspenders," said Alvin. "Or a better tailor."

Humiliation worked where intimidation hadn't. Vaughan fled the room, holding up his pants, of course.

Alvin shook hands with the senior constable again. "You know I don't want to harm him," he said.

"I don't know what you *could* have done to him, but I bet it's a lot worse than dropping his pants and unloading his pistol."

"I really try not to do things more harmful than that."

"How soon are you going to be getting your Irish boatloads out of the city?"

"Already got them in some inns and roadhouses near the railroad station."

"Which one? Philadelphia's got four."

"But we're heading west, so . . ."

"Not Manhattan, not Baltimore, not up the Hudson."

"All the way to the Foggy River."

"The Mizzippy."

"So," said Alvin, "unless Vaughan can get his mob to chase the train all the way west to the river, I think from tomorrow on, we won't be butting heads."

"Fanatics," mumbled the senior officer. "Nobody believes in letting people alone nowadays."

"I do," said Alvin. "Which is why Vaughan got no worse than embarrassed."

The desk clerk chimed in. "If he's *that* Alvin Miller, he can break a man's bones from a hundred yards away. Or just stop his heart. Or constipate him till he chokes on his own—"

Alvin shook the desk constable's hand, *not* taking possession of it. "Young man, if you find your assignment here tedious and unrewarding, and if you have a knack you've been hiding from everybody here, just come on with us. Crystal City needs honest young men."

"I got no knack at all, sir," said the desk constable.

"He farts violets and roses," said another constable. "He thinks we don't notice, but he dribbles petals everywhere."

The desk constable rolled his eyes.

"Peter Young," said Alvin, "I still think you're an honest young man. Come with us if you want. Preferably without your pants full of flower petals."

Alvin touched his forehead in a little salute, and left the Constabulary Post.

John Binder, who had been watching from the open door, walked beside him now, and said, "What's your plan here?"

"I had to see how many of them hated knacks, and how much."

"You think that one loudmouth is the only one?"

"I know who all the anti-knackists are in this station, but the captain isn't one of them. He'll keep them in line, because he knows now that if he doesn't, I will."

Binder nodded. "Got it."

"Where are they?"

"Like we planned. Near the railroad, in four inns, one to a ship's complement, and one from the little boats."

"Do you know which one Eliza Nutbutter is lodging in?"

"Yes," said Binder. "But *you* shouldn't."

"I need to meet with her. To talk quietly at a private table."

"Only one of the inns has private tables, and she isn't in that one."

"Good," said Alvin. "Nobody can say they saw me go to her inn."

"I'll bring her to you."

Eliza walked calmly into the common room—sauntered, really—and scanned the room. She spotted Alvin at his table. He did not watch her walk over, sure that, knowing Eliza, she would put on a show of being a woman with only one thing on her mind. Better not to be seen looking at her.

She slid onto a chair opposite, not beside Alvin. And Alvin so far forgot his courtesy that he did not rise for the woman who was sleeping with five or so men in Crystal City, including Calvin.

She smiled at him. "You asked me to come."

Alvin finally looked at her. Yes, pretty indeed, bosom a tiny bit—just a *tiny* bit—showing rounded above her neckline. A little frightened, because she had thought he would be *her* target, and now he was acting like a man who wanted to assert control. She knew the type and avoided them.

"You attract attention when you want to," said Alvin.

"Not *yours*," said Eliza.

"No, not just that," said Alvin. "You have a power about you, a presence that captures the room, as if you had rung a gong."

"Not sure what a gong is," she said.

"You know exactly what a gong is," said Alvin. "You ring it whenever you want, and everybody pays attention, waiting to see what you're going to do. Or say. Or command."

"Alvin, sir," said Eliza sweetly, "I do believe you're describing yourself."

"Without the prettiness, I certainly am. I need to get this whole company to Crystal City. You know the way."

"By *train*."

Alvin just looked at her.

"It'll cost a fortune."

"You can pay for the passages easily out of what's in your fuligin purse," said Alvin.

Her hand reached involuntarily for her neckline.

"I already knew where you keep it," said Alvin. "First place a highwayman would look, by the way, because for such a man, the looking is worth more than the finding. Well, not more than the amount *you're* carrying.

"Why are you talking so clearly?"

"So that you'll understand my words," said Alvin.

"And so will every pickpocket in the room."

"I would appreciate your help," said Alvin.

"Paying everybody's passage on the train?" she asked.

"You could afford it, but I won't extort any money from you. I'll buy all the passages. You provide me with a list of all the Irish folk in these inns, all the ones wanting to go to Crystal City. There are some without knacks who won't want to go all the way to Crystal City when the best-paying jobs are here. Make sure they know that going west is optional, but the safest course. Group them as families. Include on your list the ages of everybody unmarried who looks to be under thirty years of age."

"I see why *you* didn't want to do it. You don't like being slapped."

"They will listen to you. They'll carry out your orders."

"Why am I now suddenly your unpaid clerk?"

"First, I know perfectly well that whenever any money passes through your hands, you keep a small portion to make it worth your time. So you are *not* an unpaid clerk. Second, I need a new, full census of the group, to replace the one that was made before we left Ireland."

"To keep my hands occupied with counting people instead of money?"

"So I'll know if anybody is kidnapped."

Eliza laughed. But Alvin didn't.

"Is there any actual danger of that?" Eliza asked.

"Watch the children especially, boys as well as girls. Have their parents keep them together. With rope or ribbons, but *together* at all times."

"I've never given orders to a living soul."

"Then this will be a delightful new experience for you."

"New. Experience. But I sincerely doubt that I'll be delighted. Nor will anyone else."

"I will," said Alvin. "Here is my standard of success. If everybody on that list is present in Crystal City, alive, when I get there, then you will have earned your pay."

"It's demeaning to have to take my pay through embezzlement."

"But it's what you always do."

"Not *officially*. Make me an offer."

"Keep a tally of what you steal from me, and when I get to Crystal City, I'll see if I can afford to pay you more than you already took."

She squinted her eyes. "Is this all to punish me for making the beast with two backs with your precious little brother?"

"Isn't he completely my equal as a Maker?"

"I've seen no evidence."

"He has many gifts, and they're getting better. Keep him away from your reproductive system—I mean with his *knack*. He has at best a feeble understanding of anatomy."

"He wouldn't dare," said Eliza.

"He hasn't opened any doors you didn't open to him."

"How do you know so much?"

"I don't have my wife's incredibly powerful knack with heartfires, but I can look into people quite near to me, and see some or much of their immediate future and immediate past."

"So you've watched me and Calvin—"

"I don't watch such scenes," said Alvin. "Your modesty is pretty near intact with me."

"'Pretty near.'"

"You're near, and you're pretty."

"Do you really think I am?"

"The whole world speaks your praise," said Alvin.

"And quite a few other things under their breath."

"Will you lead my people home?"

She cocked her head—saucily, not coyly. "You're not much of a Moses if you don't go yourself."

"People from the press, a detective agency, and several people with a New England agenda are following me constantly. If I separate from the main group, you may be much less bothered by such gnats and weasels."

"Without you to protect us—"

"Oh, Eliza. Be serious. All you have to do is persuade yourself that you're escaping from Philadelphia—"

"By train—"

"Fastest way out of town. And your destination in this escape of yours is Crystal City, where you already have a home and several paramours, some of whom actually love you."

That distracted her a little. "Is Calvin one of them?" asked Eliza.

"Sometimes he thinks so. Sometimes you think so. That's better than many couples do."

"And am I in love with Calvin?"

"You have never been in love with anyone, Eliza. Not yourself, none of your lovers, and I can't see deeply enough to know if you loved anyone in your family."

"I still have some secrets?"

"Till Margaret sees you next."

"She promised that she'd never spy on me."

"She doesn't think of it as spying. It's . . . getting acquainted."

"How can I shield myself from her?"

"If you find a way, let me know. Every now and then I'd like to be able to surprise her with something."

A server came to them and Alvin graciously paid for Eliza's evening stew. And her beer. There were German immigrants bringing a better grade of beer than anyone brewed in America. This inn was stocking some of the best of it.

When the server had left with their order, Eliza said, "Don't read anything into this." To which Alvin immediately replied, "That is definitely a command for me to read a lot into what you say next."

"As you please," said Eliza. "I have had my eyes on you, but not for a moment did I think you had your eyes on me."

"Why would I gaze at you more than my first few glances? Once I knew who you were, I conceived of a use for you."

"All men do."

"The use that I've just proposed. Leading my people west to my city."

"While you do what?"

"Visit family and friends in Vigor Church."

"A side trip? I'd like to come."

"I'm not letting you anywhere near my older brothers."

"I was thinking of your father."

Alvin shook his head mildly. "Do we have a deal?" he asked.

"I lead these Irish to Crystal City and help them get settled in?"

"Margaret will help you. And many other women and men. It's a large influx of new citizens all at once, but we can handle it."

"Feed them?"

"Margaret has doubtless counted all the heartfires, and is laying in provisions and vittles for them all."

"Why aren't you having *Margaret* lead them from here to Crystal City?"

"She isn't here," said Alvin,

Her eyes brightened and she touched his arm. "Exactly the point I've been trying to make," said Eliza.

With this innuendo about her ambition of seducing Alvin into adultery, she felt a sudden desperate need to breathe. She panted, but it didn't satisfy her. She coughed. She drank some beer out of the mug of a man at another table.

Then, suddenly, she could breathe.

She had always been able to breathe, during the whole thing, nothing obstructed her airways. And yet she had been tortured at the lack of air. Though her lungs were full.

"So you threaten to kill me?"

"At no time were you in any physical danger," said Alvin. "I picked this up a few years ago. Your body doesn't tell you to breathe when you run out of good air. It tells you to breathe when you build up too much bad air. It builds up until you breathe it out. If you can't get rid of it, you think you're going to die, see?"

"Did you think that was funny?"

He looked her right in the eye. "Not at all," he said. "But it will sound funny later, when I tell Measure and Margaret."

She reached out to slap him. He didn't move. Her hand simply didn't connect with his cheek.

"I really don't like being slapped," Alvin said.

"And I don't like feeling asphyxiated."

"Then don't ever, ever think of seducing me again."

"I couldn't anyway," she said.

"You could make any man you wished for discover a strong desire for you."

"Except you."

"Let's not try to get around that exception, ever again."

"Or I suffocate with lungs full of air."

"It's a lonely, desperate death," said Alvin. "One I wouldn't wish on anybody."

"You've never killed anyone that way?" she asked.

"You had plenty of good air the whole time."

"I think you *are* the devil, Alvin Smith."

"You're just jealous, because *you* wanted to be the wickedest person in Crystal City."

Eliza perked her head. "They're calling the all-aboard. That means that—"

"I've traveled by train before, Miss Eliza."

"You haven't ridden *everything* yet." Then she flounced away before he could catch her double entendre. If he ever did. He was *so* sweet and naive. But the asphyxiation had been terrifying. She would have nightmares about that. She must never provoke him in that way again.

Except flirting and innuendos were such a habit. She was bound to forget and he'd make her go through this whole thing once more.

He thinks of me as a leader. He's going to go off and leave me in charge, instead of John Binder or Father Luke, or—well, Measure, obviously. Why not his brother Measure?

Oh, it was Measure's family, too. They both wanted to visit home.

She could see two routes through this whole thing. She could make a big show of being boss of the Irish, but actually do a wretched job. Everybody would resent her. Then she could laugh at Alvin and say, "I told you, it's not my knack." Trying to fail makes failure your standard of success.

Or she could try her best to be a mild but firm leader of the group, listening to wise counsel and trying to build consensus. She knew how it was done. She'd seen it done several times. It had simply never crossed her mind that it was a skill she ought to develop. But now if she failed, it would be a real failure, not accomplishing something she really wanted to do.

Calvin wasn't really in love with her. Even there she was a failure. And she would fail at leading hungry terrified Irishfolk. And when she finally got to the Mizzippy, Crystal City wouldn't be there. She would have to get them all back on the train and go back to where she had taken the wrong train and catch the right one. If there *was* a right one.

This is what played through her mind all night. And yet she awoke feeling rested and alert. Ready for a difficult day of thinking about what *other* people wanted and what other people *felt.*

24

"I DON'T HAVE to be an experienced pilot for this stretch of the Mizzippy to get you safely upstream," said Calvin.

"Ever since that Red Prophet put a curse of fog on the river, *ain't* no Mizzippy pilots no more."

"Wouldn't matter if there were," said Calvin. He almost corrected himself to "if there was," but right now pretending to be "just folks" wouldn't put him in good stead. "I haven't memorized a stretch of river, going up and down it fifty times. I can *see*, first time through, whether there's a sandbar or rock or island."

"Through the fog."

"My knack doesn't care about no fog," said Calvin. "Test me if you want. All I know is you folks put on a jim-dandy show, and the people of Crystal City are starving for shows."

"You got all them knacks in Crystal City," said the captain with a smirk. "Why don't you all knack yourselves up a show?"

"*Is* there a knack for putting on shows?" asked Calvin.

"How would *I* know?"

"Do *you* have such a knack?" asked Calvin.

"I got me no knacks!" said the captain vehemently. "I'm a Christian!"

"You the kind of Christian who looks to murder anybody who *has* a knack?" Calvin kept his voice calm and maybe even a little cheerful.

"That kind ain't Christian," said the captain. "And I don't kill folks, unless they die laughing from a comedy."

"How many shows can your company put on in a row?" asked Calvin.

Horatio Hubert Hubbard, the captain of the ship—and, apparently, head of the HHH theatrical company—got a suspicious squint in his eye. "How many other people have you pitched this proposal to?" he asked.

"None," said Calvin.

"None that said yes, anyway," Hubbard scoffed.

"None," said Calvin. "Because their steamboats all run by burning wood or coal as fuel. I am of the opinion that the Red Prophet's curse is to keep fuel-burning machinery off the Mizzippy."

"Our boat runs on machinery. Didn't you see our paddlewheel?"

"I know how it works, and your only fuel is human sweat." Calvin put his open hands flat on the table. "I'm not going to copy your design and go into competition with you."

Hubbard looked a little bit relieved, but still doubtful. "Says you."

"Says me. Test me. Cover my eyes, put me behind a wall, and see if I can't warn you before you step on anything or bump into anything. Try me."

By now the grizzled showboat captain was intrigued. "You've got such a line of patter," he said.

"I'm not selling anything, to you or anybody," said Calvin, wearing his most honest face and detecting easily that Hubbard was halfway to believing him. "It's my knack."

Hubbard rolled his eyes. "Wish I had a greenback for everybody who's bragged on his knack."

"If it's no more than brag, you'll find it out. But keep this in mind. My name is Calvin Miller. My older brother was seventh son of a seventh son. But then the oldest son in the family died, so when I was born I was *also* a seventh son."

"Calvin," said the captain. "Rhymes with Alvin."

"Could have been worse. They're Bible-readers and they could have named me Achitophel or Jehoshaphat."

"You could lose teeth trying to pronounce those names."

"And break your fingers or your brain trying to spell them," said Calvin with a smile.

Hubbard gave a little smile in return.

"You know who my brother is," said Calvin.

"I know who you want me to *think* your brother is."

"Test me."

By the time the test was set up, there was a bit of a crowd. The HHH Showboat had played in Paducah last night and was supposed to chug back up the Hio River today, heading for Carthage, the biggest city on the Hio. If they stayed a second night in Paducah, they'd do a different show, and everybody wanted to see it, if only to ridicule it, because some people think that's how you show you're smarter than everybody. Of course, thought Calvin, I *am* smarter than everybody, so I don't have to ridicule it.

Then he thought of his sister-in-law, Margaret, and realized that it was stupid to brag on himself inside his own head. And Margaret wasn't the only person smarter than him. But Alvin wasn't one of them, Calvin thought bitterly. Why does he let people walk all over him? It's going to get him killed someday.

Calvin sat behind a stack of crates, with the captain on the other side. "It's not a test if you just stand there," said Calvin, loud and clear.

"Ha! If you could really see you'd know that I was walking to and fro!"

Calvin could only sigh. "Well, I suppose all these lookers-on saw you moving when I said you weren't, so—"

The onlookers protested loudly. "He wasn't moving at all!" "Such a liar!"

"I am *not* a liar," said Hubbard. "I am an actor."

"Maybe we should test *you*!" called out one of the fine citizens of Paducah.

"Walk around. Do stuff," said Calvin. "You'll prove I'm a liar pretty quick. Unless I'm not a liar."

The captain covered his eyes with his hands. Maybe he could still see a little, maybe not. Didn't matter. Calvin could sense with his doodlebug what Hubbard was doing relative to his surroundings. "Crate in front of you, don't fall. . . . I know you can smell how close you are to the water, so I'm tempted to see if you'll fall in the water just to prove I'm a liar." And so on until the game was boring. "Are you ready to have a serious conversation with me?"

The crowd murmured their insistence, and Hubbard came around the crates and shook Calvin's hand. "So you have a useful knack. It still means nothing—I'm not taking my boat on that cursèd river."

Calvin sat down on a crate and the captain sat beside him. Calvin looked at the crowd and smiled. "Show's over for now, but I bet Captain Hubbard here wants you to come to *his* company's show tonight."

"Only a nickel a person," said Hubbard.

"You sell yourself short," said Calvin, doing the arithmetic in his head.

"I sell hard liquor to the people at the show," said Hubbard. "The nickel is just to show they have earnest money."

"You sell other things, too," said Calvin, but then quickly began explaining how this showboat ran without burning anything.

"I burn through the muscles on some good strong men here," said Hubbard.

"You're from Hio, you can't legally own slaves."

"They're all freedmen. I buy them as discards because they're too old, too cantankerous, too stupid, or too smart to make a good slave. I ask for a year on the boat after I free them, and then they can go their way—with a set of huge, strong muscles to recommend them to future employers."

"Or terrify them. 'Hello, sir, do you want to hire a dockworker who can tear you in half with his bare hands?' "

"I'd like to see that," said Hubbard.

"No you wouldn't," said Calvin. "I wish I could *un*see it." Of course he had never seen any such thing, but it made a good story.

Hubbard leaned in and, still with a smile, said, "Who told you how my steamless steamboat works? Because I'm going to show him how his headless body works."

"I just looked at it, my friend. It's plain to see—if you know how to see *deeply* enough. Using human labor to run those bellows pumps and make the paddlewheel turn—ingenious."

"I was tired of getting cheated by colliers."

"As good a reason as any."

"The paddlewheel is still machinery."

"Not to the Red Prophet and his family," said Calvin, hoping he didn't get quizzed any further, seeing as how he didn't know a thing about the Prophet or his family. That's where Alvin's power comes from, Calvin figured. The Red Prophet puts ideas in his head.

Hubbard nodded. "How good *is* your knack? Can you keep my boat from sinking?"

"Never tried," said Calvin. "Depends on how many and how big the leaks are."

"Got no leaks in my boat! That's my livelihood."

"I mean whatever new leaks the Red Prophet might put in the boat."

Hubbard stood right up. "You said that you—"

"I said I could keep us from bumping into rocks and sandbars and islands. I didn't say I could fend off any Red magicking."

"So you don't have the Red Prophet's permission."

"I'm hiring you, because you have the best chance of not running afoul of his curse."

"Aroint thee!" cried Hubbard. "Aroint thee, get thee hence!"

"Shakespeare?" asked Calvin.

"You know the bard?"

"He died a bit before I was born," said Calvin. "But I know the Puritans hated him when he was alive, and they never want a play of his performed again."

"On *my* boat we do whatever plays I want," said Hubbard. "Just with a different title and with my name up as author."

"I'm guessing you didn't ask for permission, either," said Calvin.

"He's *dead*," said Hubbard.

"Not when you're playing his characters on stage, he's not," said Calvin. So easy to flatter this man.

Hubbard stood a little taller, gave a little bow with his head and shoulders, then sat back down. "Tell me what you do if there *are* leaks."

"Fix them," said Calvin. "And if I can't do it fast enough, I'll pay you in gold for the price of a new boat."

"What about my actors who drown? How can you replace *them*?"

"Captain Hubbard, I *know* I can save folks from drowning. I've done it about a hundred times, and besides, we're never getting more than twenty feet from the righthand shore."

"Stabboard," said Hubbard.

"We're not at sea and you never were a sailor. No need for port and starboard here. It's left and right. Upstream on the Mizzippy, the safe shore is the righthand shore."

"*If* there's a safe shore."

"Do we have a deal?" asked Calvin.

"You ain't even *pitched* a deal."

"You go up and put on shows for the folks of Crystal City," said Calvin. "You charge what you charge, you make what you make, you take it home and divvy it out with your cast and your crew."

"We don't divvy," said Hubbard.

"You keep it *all*?" asked Calvin.

"They draw off funds whenever they need them," said Hubbard. "I don't steal from my people. And can't nobody else steal from them, either."

Calvin wondered how much of a stash Hubbard had built up over the years, and where he kept it.

Not my business. It's between him and his people. And between him and the law—if there *was* any law out here so close to the Mizzippy. Outlaws couldn't get over the river—or if they did, none of them came back to tell about it. But they could cluster up in the miles of woods where nobody wanted to farm—except the people of Crystal City, because they knew the Red Prophet had no quarrel with them.

And they could fish in the Mizzippy, long as they kept their feet dry. And if they fell in, they could climb right out, no harm done, no body parts falling off or huge catfish swallowing your leg. Calvin had tested those boundaries himself.

"You're going to put me on the Mizzippy and not pay me no *premium*?" asked Hubbard, disgusted.

"If all goes right, which it will," said Calvin, "you'll be making money from a city of people, bigger than that hogtown Chicago, who've been hoping for a show for a long time. You charge them what you think the market will bear, and you should make a good showing, financially."

"Financially," muttered Hubbard. "Boat underwater, cast and crew all drownded."

"Won't happen that way," said Calvin. "And why do you say idiotic things like 'drownded' when you have the words of Shakespeare in your mouth?"

Hubbard spoke very quietly. "But soft. What light from yonder window breaks? It is the east, and . . ."—just realizing—"Juliet is the sun!"

It was so quiet, not bombastic like the way the French performed in Paris, or the actors in the Crown Colonies. Perfectly natural. A young man in love, just realizing how much in love he is. He was talking to himself; he was talking to the love of his life; he was speaking so quietly that nobody could hear him.

Hubbard had a knack, yes sir. He could talk soft and yet everybody could hear him. It meant he didn't have to shout every word like other actors did.

"If you fell in the water and whispered for help," said Calvin, "I bet boatmen from Carthage would leap onto their rafts to rush down to save you."

"I have the good fortune of knowing how to project my voice without shouting."

Calvin didn't bother to call it a knack. Hubbard already knew that Calvin knew. As much as admitted it. This man just might decide to stay. What use could I make of him? A town crier that nobody realizes is shouting? A voice on stage saying, gently, whatever savage thing Calvin wanted him to put into people's thoughts?

Hubbard isn't a bad man, so I'll have to persuade him that he's doing good. But that's how you get good men to go bad. The worse it is, the nobler you make him feel about it.

"How soon can you give it a try with me?" asked Calvin.

"You promised Paducah a show tonight," said Hubbard.

"First thing in the morning then?" asked Calvin.

"Have to talk to the cast and the crew," Hubbard said. "I don't put their lives at risk without asking."

"They were all there at the dock today," said Calvin. "They all saw what I can do."

"What they can't see is whether that's *all* you can do."

The show that night was filled with excitement. The audience because they were getting a second show, and with a lower cost of admission tonight. Hubbard and his people because they were going to go up against a Red curse and try to trick their way through it, but if Calvin was the real thing, it should go all right. And Calvin because—because he was doing something Alvin wouldn't even *think* to do, and doing it better, and nobody was going to be hurt by it because it was *all* good. Like watching that middle-aged man play Romeo as a youth and believing in it. All good.

Calvin didn't watch that second show in Paducah, however. He lay down on the floor of the pilot's box and sent his doodlebug out of himself and into the water of the river, working his way from the wharf out in a straight line for the turning of the stream. He was moving rapidly upstream, but felt no resistance from the water.

The only resistance came when he was hugging the right bank of the Mizzippy and he came to a tangle of tree roots, trunks, and logs that stuck out like a nose into the stream. The steamboat could never get past *this*, thought Calvin. So his bug moved away from the righthand shore and out toward the middle of the Mizzippy. *That's* when he felt resistance. His doodlebug was moving slower and slower until it wasn't moving at all.

Stopped in the river. Calvin felt it like an icy worm inside his chest, making it harder and harder to breathe, getting colder and colder. And then he was moving faster than he could have imagined, back to the right bank and fifteen feet into the mud of that shore. In utter darkness.

All right, Mr. Prophet, Calvin said inside his mind. I won't venture away from the right bank again. And thank you for letting me make as much progress as I already have. Thank you for stopping your curse at the midpoint of the river. Now may I please get back into the water so I can finish clearing a channel along the east bank?

No answer, of course. The Prophet probably didn't even know who it was that he just spanked. Or maybe the Red Prophet didn't even know that it had happened. Maybe it was like a jack-in-the-box, you just wind it and wind it and then *pop!* Like a bit of machinery. So any White man's doodlebug would have been repulsed the same. Other people had knacks involving doodlebugs—the river was set up so that *any* doodlebug could get only so far before getting repulsed.

Calvin began to move toward the river, through the mud. He knew that for Alvin, there was no darkness underground. Alvin explained how he just always knew where he was and what he was surrounded by. Soil, with fallen leaves and the hulls of long-dead nuts. Then a layer that was often damp or even wet with underground moisture, and then bedrock, the solid stone that supposedly wasn't no barrier to their doodlebugs. Speak for yourself, Alvin.

Calvin got his bug down to bedrock and then scooted along just above it till he could feel the mass of earth above him make way for something fluid and relentless in its motion. He rose up then into the river, located the right bank, and then returned to the tangle that had moved him out into the Mizzippy. He found where and how the mass was stuck to the shore, and then loosened a log here, broke off a root there.

Then, like a floating island, the tangle slipped gently and silently into the flow of the river. Calvin pushed it toward the middle of the stream as far as he could, and then trusted that it wouldn't fetch up on the right bank again.

His doodlebug went swiftly again, looking for obstructions that might block the upstream progress of that human-powered steamboat. The distance wasn't all that long before he came to a wharf that he recognized. He lifted his bug to the surface and saw in the east the rising towers of the water-blocks, shimmering in the last rays of the sun. The riverbank was clear all the way from Paducah to Crystal City. His job was done.

He was so exhausted that he thought he must have been all night in dredging and clearing the right bank. But when he struggled to his feet, he wasn't even sore. He hadn't been lying in that pilot's box all night. He could hear a chorus singing a cheerful ditty that he didn't recognize. And then the rushing, crashing sound of applause. The show had just ended.

When he came down from the top levels of the boat he realized that it hadn't even been *that* long. The audience was crowded to the three bars along the sides of the seating area, ordering things to drink and eat. Calvin mingled with them, annoyed that his actual body couldn't move among people as fluidly as his doodlebug could move through water and wood and rock.

He heard what folks was ordering and he was pleased to know that Captain Hubbard was earning money hand over fist. The comedy had put people into a good mood, a convivial mood, and they had whiskey spilling down their throats as fast as the bartenders could fill their glasses.

Then the boat whistle tooted—right as the last customers were getting their last drinks—and they all went back to their seats. Or to somebody else's seat, didn't matter, they knew there was chairs enough for all, cause hadn't they been in them during the first two acts of the play?

The curtain was drawn up again, and there stood the actors and actresses, all in their foolish cumbersome costumes and their heavy, unreal-looking makeup. The voices began, talking louder than real people ever talked, but immediately getting the audience laughing again. The whiskey and corn liquor and barley beer all helped the audience have a wonderful time laughing at the foolish folks on the stage.

When the show ended, Calvin was asleep on the backmost chair and had to be wakened by one of the actors, an old woman with makeup caked on her face to pretend she was a smooth-cheeked girl, or a young lady, anyway. With perfect diction she said, "Are you not the Smith boy who's supposed to pilot us up the river?"

Calvin growled, "That *smith* is my brother, but I'm Calvin Miller, seventh son of a seventh son, every bit as smart and knacky as my brother, as anyone can tell you."

"Well, your nap didn't cheer *you* up very much, did it?"

Soon Calvin stood in front of the cast, them in the audience chairs, him on the stage. The fine folk of Paducah had gone ashore, the sober ones helping the drunks to get home. It was just him and the show people, along with the few members of the boat's crew who could be spared to attend.

"The sun's only just gone," said the man with a hero's voice. "And there's a big moon. We've got us a magical pilot, don't we? One who can see through solid objects? What's to stop us from going upriver tonight?"

"You don't got you a magical pilot," said Calvin. All fell silent, looked at him.

Captain Hubbard looked vexed. "But you promised us to—"

"I promised to clear the way for your boat to go upstream as far as Crystal City. You'll know the place when you see it, because on the brow of a hill no more than half a mile from the wharf, you'll see the Crystal City."

"What does *that* look like?" asked a skeptical-sounding woman, whose costume and demeanor showed that she must play a prostitute. If she was in the play at all. Calvin hadn't been with a prostitute since Paris, and then he was too young to know what he was doing.

But no, he had work to do. "When you see something that makes you say, 'That has to be the Crystal City,' that'll be the Crystal City. Tie up your boat to the wharf and put down your gangplank."

"And you'll be with us," said the captain.

"I'm with you *now*, and I'm telling you that twenty feet out from the shore you'll have clear passage, with a deep enough unobstructed channel that you'll have no delays or difficulties. Twenty feet out from the shore. Can you pilot your vessel well enough to maintain that distance?"

Hubbard scoffed and several cast members said things like, "The captain can do it. The captain can steer straight as a clothesline."

"Will we see you there in Crystal City?"

"If I choose to be seen," said Calvin. "But I keep my word. Twenty feet from the shore. If you get as far as fifty feet away, the Red Prophet's curse will either shove you back or sink you straight down."

"Is that twenty feet from the shore to the righthand edge of the boat?" asked a querulous old man—who Calvin soon realized was not as old as he looked. "Or to the middle of the boat? Or to the lefthand side, which we can't do, because the boat is wider than twenty feet."

"I'll go with you across the confluence of the Hio and Mizzippy, and then I'll go ashore," said Calvin.

"That's pretty time-consuming, putting out the boat and rowing to the shore and back."

"A Maker like me doesn't need your boat," said Calvin.

True to his word, Calvin made sure they stayed within the channel he had cleared, until they got within the twenty feet of the Mizzippy shore—measuring from the righthand side of the riverboat.

"So far so good," said Captain Hubbard. "But if you've sent us into a trap, good sir, I'll—"

"You'll do nothing to me," said Calvin. "You can't hurt a Maker who isn't willing to be hurt." He knew that this was true of Alvin, but not of Calvin himself. His self-healing took concentration that he didn't think he could muster up if he had a musket ball somewhere in his body. But it's better to let them think he could *not* be harmed than to suspect that he could.

"But you've set no trap? Come with us, Calvin Miller, so we know your channel will continue true."

"If you stay where you're supposed to be," said Calvin, "your upriver voyage will be smooth. On horseback, I'll be in Crystal City before you get there, ready to greet you at the end of your completely smooth, uneventful voyage upriver."

"You think a horse can go faster than my boat?" said Captain Hubbard.

"Not downstream," said Calvin. "But there's a limit to how fast your engine can drive this boat against the currents of the mighty Mizzippy. I said smooth, not *easy.* And you actors better use the time to make sure you know all the speeches of all the plays you're going to put on for the good folk of my Crystal City."

"*Your* city?" asked a middle-aged woman. "I thought it was Alvin Smith who made those crystal stones."

"He's not the only one who put crystal blocks into the city walls," said Calvin. "He just features in all the notices about it."

"Don't leave us!" cried out a child's voice—which Calvin saw came from the mouth of a youngish woman.

"If you need me, I'll help. I'll watch your progress every step of the way." If he did *that*, he wouldn't be able to concentrate on little things like steering his horse on the wild roads between Cairo and Crystal City.

Calvin walked out of the theater and onto the deck two stories up from the water. They all followed, and not quietly. He ignored the questions being hurled at him, and went to a gap in the gunwale where a stairway led down to the deck below. But he swung his leg over the railing of that stairway, and then the other, so he was standing with only his heels on the deck and his hands gripping the gunwale, and then he stepped out into the air.

Well, properly speaking, he sort of jumped. But it's hard to jump from your heels, and he only had to leap far enough not to hit any part of the boat below him. He succeeded in that task, but when he reached the water he just knifed right in. Not a hint that he had been trying as hard as possible to solidify the water enough that he could walk to shore. *That* would get stories about Calvin Miller—no, Calvin *Maker*—spread all up and down the Hio.

Instead, his feet touched the bottom of the river, and then he walked to shore, holding his breath. Twenty feet is a long way to hold your breath underwater. But he did it, and when he walked up the shore and his head cleared the surface of the water, he made sure *not* to gasp in a visible way. Let them at least share the rumor that he could breathe underwater. And as he dried his clothing—an easy thing to do—let them also think he could walk through water and *not* get wet.

Then Calvin walked into the thick undergrowth near the shore and disappeared from their view. Then he jogged, in his now-dry clothes, to the place where he had already placed a pair of horses.

Come on, boys, he whispered to them in his mind. You are the wind tonight. Show me how fast you can go.

25

ALVIN HAD CHOSEN a route through the woods that he knew would offer Greensong all the way to Vigor Church. But soon after crossing the Hio, Measure veered off from Alvin's path.

It brought Alvin to a stop. He knew Measure could be part of the Greensong, but he hadn't known that his brother could find his own way through the music of the forest and meadow.

Alvin followed Measure then, instead of the other way around. It didn't take long to see where Measure was leading him. Alvin had intended to visit only Vigor Church, since that's where both he and Measure had grown up. The town of Hatrack River? Alvin had been born there, and their big brother Vigor had died near there. It was where Alvin served his apprenticeship, where he made the iron plow that he turned into gold.

The place meant little to Measure—it was just a place where a few things happened long ago. He didn't know anybody there. But *Alvin*—this was his second home, he knew this place and most everybody in it. He had lost more loved ones here than Measure had. In Hatrack River, Alvin had killed a man who needed killing.

When they both slowed down and walked along the main road through town, Alvin could finally say, "I thought we were going to see our family in Vigor Church."

"We are," said Measure. "I just thought we should go the right way."

"How is this the right way?"

"It's the road we followed, on our way to settling in at Vigor Church. It passed through here, and then Father made us build covered bridges over every rushing stream or trickling brook. Some bridges a bare eight feet long, some spans of near thirty feet. You were a baby. You didn't know what was going on."

"It must have delayed you considerable," said Alvin.

"None of those rivers was going to tear another family apart just cause it happened to be in flood," said Measure.

"So you think we should go along the road, go through all the bridges you built."

"It's been a few decades, and some of the bridges might need repairs."

"They might," said Alvin.

"And you know Hatrack River as your hometown, your prentice town, your journeyman town."

They walked through Hatrack River without talking much, and Alvin didn't even turn aside to visit the roadhouse where his wife had been born and lived for most of her childhood, looking out for Alvin even when he was off in Vigor Church. It was to Hatrack River that a runaway—a flyaway—slave had brought her newborn half-White baby, so he wouldn't grow up in slavery. The effort of it, the magic of it, had worn her out. She died the night she got there, but she knew her baby would be safe. They named him Arthur Stuart, after the King in the Crown Colonies, and he grew up with Alvin as . . . what, his brother? Yes, for a while, but also something more like a father.

He also chose not to enter the roadhouse because here was where Old Peg Guester had been the midwife who delivered Alvin into the world, and then had been like a mother to Alvin during his apprenticeship. When slave catchers came to bring Arthur Stuart back into slavery, they murdered Old Peg Guester because she resisted them. And Alvin, in a rage, killed the man who did it. It was purest justice, but Alvin knew he shouldn't have taken revenge that way, he knew that the law would have been a better course. But when he walked past that roadhouse, his memories all came together in a jumble, and tears streamed down his face.

And then they were out of the town, and they used the Greensong to carry them quickly from bridge to bridge. All of them were still functioning, still secure, though the roofs of some needed repair, and Alvin took the time to seal them the way he had sealed all the boats before leaving Ireland. These bridges would last until workmen had to remove them to replace them with wider bridges for wider roads, and then they wouldn't be his family's memorial to Vigor anymore.

Only the town that they had named for Vigor would remain as a memorial, and Alvin was pretty sure that nobody outside of Vigor Church had any idea that the place had been named for a man, not for the virtue.

Because the Greensong made them so quick on the road, and because the bridges needed so little repair, they reached the outskirts of Vigor Church about noon the next day. Alvin was glad to see how Measure's eyes grew more vibrant as he drank in the sights familiar from childhood. Of course Alvin remembered his own childhood, but for him that had been a perilous time, with the Unmaker causing every form of water to try to kill him.

And it was while Alvin lived here that the great massacre at Tippy-Canoe Creek took place, and Measure had been near kilt by the officers of the White army who had come to slaughter the men, women, and children of Prophetstown. Alvin had managed to save Measure's life and restore him to strength and health, but it took more skill than Alvin actually had. He had been required to force himself to learn things that he had not known how to do.

They approached the town from the high hills, and there wasn't a man working in the fields that Measure did not know, every one of them glad to see Measure, and eager to invite him to supper or tea or to stay the night. "Off to see my folks," said Measure, and that was answer enough. They knew they couldn't give him hospitality when his family was waiting.

All the same, it was a somewhat triumphant return, as it should be. Everyone knew that Measure had taken no part in the massacre at Tippy-Canoe, but when the Prophet Tenskwa-Tawa laid a curse on the town, that they had to tell an honest account of the massacre to every traveler who came to Vigor Church, Measure lived the curse with them, though he had done nothing to deserve it and the curse probably had no force with him. He was part of the town; he bore their punishment and shame with them, until the Prophet lifted the curse a few years before.

Measure was part of this place, and the people knew him and loved him and were genuinely glad to see him.

Alvin knew perfectly well why almost nobody spoke to *him*, or included him in their invitations. He was in some ways the opposite of Measure. He was the one who had used his knackery to help the Prophet, and Alvin was seen as part of the implementation of that curse, though in truth the Prophet needed no augmentation from Alvin. All the same, Alvin had gone to war alongside Ta-Kumsaw, Alvin and the Prophet were good, close friends, and the tales they heard and the tales they flat-out made up about Alvin's knacks during his childhood there made him a figure of awe to the children of the town, and their parents as well.

Alvin and Measure thought of stopping by the homes of several of their brothers and sisters, but no. They had to see their parents before anybody else, that was only right and proper. So they walked by their father's mill and straight to the side door—the family door—of the house. They shouted no greeting, just came through the door and stood in the family parlor, waiting for someone to notice them.

Even though the parents were the only permanent residents of this big old house, it was not a quiet place. There were sounds of children running, shouting, arguing, crying, laughing—all from different parts of the house, or just outside. And of course it was one of the grandchildren—Alvin's and Measure's nieces and nephews—who noticed them.

"Who are you?" demanded the boy—who couldn't have been more than eight.

Measure pointed at the door the boy had just come through. "We came through the family door, same as you."

"Well you got no right," said the boy—not angry, just stating a fact.

"I got a right if I'm family," said Measure.

"He's got a right if he's your Uncle Measure," said Alvin.

"He don't live around here," said the boy.

"I'm here, and I'm alive, so for at least these few moments I most certainly *do* live around here," said Measure.

"You talk like a doctor," said the boy. "The doctor ain't from around here."

"You talk like a hog-caller," said Alvin. "Smell like one, too."

The boy's eyes went wide with outrage. "You're the pig!" he shouted.

"If I'm the pig," said Measure, "then you're the pig's nephew!"

That stopped the boy. He looked back and forth between Alvin and Measure.

"Now do you believe we're family?" asked Alvin.

"I don't believe nothing coming out of your pig mouth," said the boy.

"Well, I do believe that *he's* family," said Measure.

"I'm glad to see that stupid arguments are in our blood," said Alvin.

"Who you calling stupid!" But the boy must have realized he was out of his depth, so he ran back outside.

A minute later, two girls running down the stairs happened to notice them standing around and they stopped cold. One of them, maybe fourteen years old, said, "You're too good-looking to be related to *us*. Who are you?"

"Now how can we resist a challenge like that?" asked Measure.

"I'll have you know that Measure here is accounted the ugliest one in the family," said Alvin.

"He looks too much like my father to be ugly," said the girl.

"Would your father be Wastenot or Wantnot?" asked Alvin, because he knew that the twins looked like Measure and vice versa.

"Wantnot!" said one of the girls, and "Wastenot!" cried the other.

"How can you even tell?" asked Measure. "I don't think either of them could possibly be the father of such pretty girls."

"They're not," said the voice of a woman in the doorway from the kitchen. "They're mine, so it's my fault that they're sassy."

"Eleanor," said Alvin, and strode into her embrace, spinning her around as if they were dancing. "Where's Armor?"

"On a long errand," said Eleanor. She looked at Measure. "Measure," she said, "why are you gallivanting around with a worthless chipmunk like this?"

Measure said, "I don't think your girls are sassy, Eleanor. But I worry that they might be just a little flirty."

"Oh, that's right enough," said Eleanor. "And they flirt their way into having half the boys in town follow them around like a cat as thinks you got a fish in your pocket."

"It happens I do," said Alvin, slapping his pockets and reaching into some of them—the ones he knew were empty. Until he got to the pocket with his one gold coin. "Oh, not a fish after all."

"Some folks can't help turning everything they touch into gold," said Eleanor, laughing. "Let me tell Mama you're here."

"Where's Pa?" asked Measure.

"Where else? In the mill."

"I didn't see the water wheel turning, or even any water in the mill race," said Measure.

Eleanor laughed. "Having grandchildren around changed Pa's ways a little. There's always children swimming in the catchment pool, so if Pa runs the wheel all the time during harvest season, the pool empties out and the children can't swim."

"So he turns the millstone by hand?" asked Measure.

"He only opens the millrace to turn the wheel when he's got something to grind," said Eleanor. "Go, see Mama, she'll be so happy."

Measure laughed and came to Eleanor and gave her a hug, then headed upstairs where he knew his mother would be doing the mending while there was bright daylight coming into the sewing room window.

Alvin, though, stayed near Eleanor. "You got no hexes outside the house."

"Not my house," said Eleanor. "You just try getting gunpowder anywhere near *my* house."

"You and Armor-of-God moved back."

"We woke up one morning and both of us agreed that it was stupid to be paying rent in Carthage when we had a perfectly good house of our own back home."

"So what does Armor do for a living now?" asked Alvin.

"Helps Pa in the mill," said Eleanor. "He's not a young man."

"Which, Pa or Armor?" asked Alvin.

"Still a brat, I see," said Eleanor.

"How else would you know it's really me?"

That evening, at supper, Alvin sat near the head of the table, where Father and Mother always sat side by side—not that Mother sat for very long at a time, what with checking on things in the oven or on the stove, so it seemed that most of the meal was cooked or baked or boiled *during* dinner.

Alvin looked around at his older brothers, and those of his sisters who lived close enough to travel home for this spur-of-the-moment family celebration.

"Do you mind my asking what the occasion is?" asked Alvin, "My sense of the calendar has always been weak."

"Your sense of the clock, too," said Measure.

"Everything takes longer," said Alvin. "I always thought that as I get *better* at things, they should take less time."

"When you get better at things," said Father, "it's usually because you're doing them slower."

"And better," added Measure.

"*Now* you have crucial advice for me?" Alvin said to Measure, pretending to be joking.

"We're together a lot," said Measure. "Life is better when we don't spend all our time together bickering about which of us is better suited to give advice to the other."

Alvin once again took the census of his siblings and their spouses. It took a big board to hold all their plates, and a lot of jostling to find a place to sit around the table. Then it dawned on Alvin what he was looking for. "Where are my nieces and nephews?"

The others looked at each other. "Have you noticed how crowded the table already is?" asked Father.

"My introduction to one nephew and two nieces was . . . extraordinary. They were charming."

"They all are," said Eleanor. "Remarkable creatures. Some of my hexes are to keep them out of my house."

"There's no room for them at table, when we're all together," said Matilda. "So we feed them before or after—usually before, because they're not the most patient people."

"People?" said Eleanor. "Matty, dear, you exaggerate."

There was laughter then, because everybody knew that they all adored the grandchildren.

Alvin, though, was feeling painfully left out. "I thought I'd get a chance to know them."

"Stay a week and you'll be able to tell most of them apart," said Wastenot.

"Except us," said Wantnot.

"I can't stay longer," said Alvin. "I have urgent business."

Measure added, "We really didn't have time to come here, but Alvin insisted."

Alvin thought of the baby girl who died. He thought of young Vigor. What would it be like for his boy Vigor, if he lived here, where his cousins were available all the time?

No. Margaret was where she belonged, and Vigor belonged *with* her. But in his heart, Alvin belonged here. He had lost so many years with his family, during his apprenticeship in Hatrack River, becoming a smith. The three niblings he had met had delighted him but also saddened him. He could have liked them, but there was no time.

"You forget, Alvin," said Matilda. "While you've been city-building and Irish-saving, our children have been growing up. My oldest now has a child, so I'm a—"

Mother interrupted. "Who cares what *you* are, Matilda? I'm a great grandmother, and that tops you all."

"A title you only hold *because* I'm a grandmother," said Matilda.

Mother looked at Alvin conspiratorially. "Please don't hurt her feelings by pointing out that being a grandmother is small beans compared to being a *great* grandmother."

They all laughed, perhaps more than the jest deserved, but Alvin felt his heart swell with memories of all these people at earlier ages. Quarrels, teasing, silliness, rivalry between brothers and sisters. Joy. This is what life is for, not traveling and bullying weaker men, no matter how malicious and small-minded they are. Instead of collapsing the bishop's floor, why didn't I find another hundred knackles to save?

He thought of "knackles" because he had just heard Wastenot say it. "Knackles?"

"We need to call them—us—something besides 'people with knacks.'"

"None of us liked 'knackers' because that's a person who does unpleasant things to dead animals," said Beatrice, aiming the comment at Wantnot.

"The animals don't mind," said Wantnot. "So it's only unpleasant to squeamish girls."

"I have a child older than you," said Mary.

"You do not," said Wantnot.

"If you'd get wiser as well as older, my children wouldn't ask me, 'What's wrong with Uncle Wantnot?'"

"None of your children thinks there's anything wrong with me, except that there's an extra one of me."

Wastenot chimed right in. "An extra one of *me*. You're the spare."

"Spare!" said Wantnot in exaggerated outrage.

Alvin interrupted in a calm, low voice. "Are you really working as a knacker?" he asked Wantnot.

"People around here are too squeamish to do the whole job of butchering," said Wantnot. "So they pay me, *not* the extra, to get the odd bits ready to be boiled down for glue or feed. It's not my *main* work."

"To my everlasting shame," said Wastenot, "he's mostly a lawyer."

"I'd rather be called a knacker!" declared Wantnot. "I only help people draw up wills so they can disinherit the children they don't like and punish them even after death."

"So, still a knacker," said Wastenot. "Cutting off the odd bits of families."

"He farms," said Anne. "Like everybody else."

"He ducks out on farmwork," said Beatrice, "to pursue his other jobs. All of them just hobbyhorses, rocking and rocking and getting *nowhere*."

"Let me guess," said Alvin. "You've had this discussion before."

"We don't have discussions," said Wantnot, "because the others can't deal with my legal arguments."

"None of which is ever to the point," said Elizabeth. "Such as, how many people in Vigor Church have anything to bequeath to their families in the first place?"

"Let me ask all of you," interjected Alvin. "Why do you still live here? Why don't you come to Crystal City?"

Silence at the table.

Mother and Father looked at each other. Then resumed eating.

Alvin slapped the table and stood up and stepped away.

"Alvin," said Measure.

"Temper," said Mother.

"I'm not angry," said Alvin.

"Even as a child you always said that," said Eleanor. "Especially when you were *obviously* furious. Which you proved by picking a fight with whichever brother would whip you most easily."

"Some of you have at least visited in Crystal City," said Alvin.

"I live there," said Measure.

"You live nowhere," said Father, "just like your little brother. Gallivanting."

"I don't have a little brother named Galli—"

"Vanting," said Father.

"Crystal City," said Mother, "is a place for visions and wisdom and understanding."

"And you're opposed to that?" asked Alvin.

"Sometimes you're compelled to understand more than you want to."

"How can you not want to understand *everything*?" said Alvin.

Dead silence.

Mother weeping.

"Mother, I'm sorry, I—"

"In the walls of Crystal City I saw nothing but your death, Alvin," she said. "How long could I bear to stay there, seeing that?"

"You never told me—"

"I won't tell you now, either," said Mother. "It's nothing you would lift a finger to prevent, anyway."

"You think I *want* to die?" asked Alvin.

"It doesn't matter if you want to or not," said Father. "Sooner or later, you're going to do it. I just hope that I'm already dead before you do."

Alvin rounded on his father. "Has she told *you* what she saw about my death?"

"She doesn't trust me to keep *any* secret," said Father. "And I don't want to know."

"So you're hiding from knowledge," said Alvin.

"No," said Father. "She's hiding from ceaseless reminders."

"What would Vigor Church do for a miller if Pap left?" asked Beatrice.

"Stomp the grain right off the chaff by holding a dance on the threshing floor," said Anne.

"Why not be an angel," said Wantnot, "and dance on the head of a pin?"

"Is this what you came for?" asked Father.

"I came to see my family," said Alvin.

"Your family already lives in Crystal City," said Mother, "and I reckon your Little Peggy doesn't like it that you didn't come straight home."

"She understands."

"But she doesn't *like*," said Measure. "You already know that."

"She's the one you owe your happiness to now," said Mother. "Why are you *here*?"

Again, silence, because the question was too serious to deflect with wisecracks.

"He's here," said Father, "to say goodbye."

Mother burst into tears. The sisters looked at each other and all saw tears running down the others' faces.

The boys just looked baffled. Including Alvin.

His mother was crying. And his sisters. Mother had seen his death and fled from it.

Alvin walked to his mother, knelt by her chair, pulled her down to press her face into his shoulder.

She pulled back. "Alvin, do you have any idea how bad your shirt smells?"

Alvin was sure Mother was trying to lighten the mood, but she didn't have the tone of sass that *everybody* else in the family had by second nature. So there were only a few titters, and none of the crying stopped.

"I didn't come here to attend my own funeral," said Alvin.

"Nobody's going to cry at your funeral," said Wastenot.

Wantnot began, "What he means—"

"It has been thirty years since I needed you to translate for me," said Wastenot.

"He means," said Wantnot, "that before we let anybody kill you, we'll be dead first."

"No," said Alvin quietly. "I don't know what manner of death the walls of the city proposed, but even if somebody kills me, even if you know who, my life is not one whit more important than any of yours. Nobody dies for me, do you understand?"

"Not your decision," said Measure.

"Nobody. Dies. For. Me."

"I do," said Measure softly. "I will."

And now it was Alvin's turn to weep. *Was* this what he had come home for? To find out that his family still loved him, even though most had refused to live in Crystal City?

Alvin and Measure set out the next morning, hoisting their knapsacks over their shoulders, protesting to Mother that she didn't need to send them food for a week. Apparently, however, she did.

"Strong boys like you?" said Mother. "*Big* boys? You need a lot of food, and carrying those bags is no harder than carrying the wind at your back."

"We're walking toward the southwest," said Measure. "Wind's going to be mostly in our faces."

"Good," said Mother. "You need challenges in your lives."

There was no answer to that, except a conversation that would keep them from setting out till the next morning. So they laughed and thanked her and thanked everybody for everything ever.

Wastenot piped up at once. "You even thank us for the time we put you in a sack and—"

Wantnot elbowed him.

"I already got two elbows of my own, Wastenot, but if you want me to break yours, I know how."

Measure pulled Wastenot back from his twin, and Alvin placed a hand on Wantnot's chest to restrain him. Not by force—the twins were not small men—but by requesting, reminding.

Last goodbyes were said, and then laster ones, and then the lastest ones, and Measure and Alvin set off down the road.

"Want to go past Prophetstown?" asked Measure.

"Prophetstown isn't there anymore. Just a killing field where a lot of good, harmless people were slaughtered."

"I was there, too," said Measure.

"They broke every bone in your body to *keep* you from being there."

"And you did a second-rate job patching me back together. I still get twinges whenever the weather changes."

"You can go see that bloody ground if you want," said Alvin. "I don't mind waiting in that copse of trees up yonder." He pointed to where an old man was picking things out of the grass.

Measure chuckled. "You knew he would be there."

"Not the slightest idea. But long as he's there, I got things to say and things to hear."

Measure strode off in a more northwesterly direction, while Alvin hiked on up and sat himself down next to a grizzled old man wearing homespun and deerskin.

"Don't have much to add to your book," said Alvin.

"I hear you crossed the ocean in a leaky bathtub," said Taleswapper.

"If I'm in a bathtub, it don't leak," said Alvin.

"Folks get along with water pretty good these days," said Taleswapper.

Alvin laughed. "You talk like you think you was born around here."

"People was ignorant and talked strange all over England. I just picked up the accent of my people here in America."

"You picked up the hill country accent around Hatrack River," said Alvin.

"My people, like I said."

"Am I your people, Taleswapper?" asked Alvin.

Taleswapper put a hand on Alvin's knee. "Alvin, I've known you pretty much your whole life."

"Ain't over yet."

"Your whole life so far. But I'm not writing any more about you in my book."

Alvin tried to guess at what that might mean. He was going to die right away? He didn't matter anymore in Taleswapper's book?

"Because I got no book anymore," said Taleswapper.

That took Alvin aback.

"I'm not fixing to live forever," said Taleswapper.

"You're in good health," said Alvin. "I checked as I was walking up."

"Clean bill of health," said Taleswapper. "Good to hear. Though I've eventually got to die of *something*."

"Heart stoppage," said Alvin. "And then your brain runs out of blood and it stops, too. That's what everybody dies of, no matter what brings it all to a head."

"I gave my book to someone else," said Taleswapper. "A certain young man of your acquaintance."

Alvin's thought immediately raced to the single worst person to receive Taleswapper's precious book. "Not Calvin, tell me it's not—"

"Not Calvin," said Taleswapper, chuckling. "I don't want to read the kinds of stories he'd probably put down. Not that he ain't a good boy."

"He isn't a good boy," said Alvin.

"So far, he's made some questionable choices now and then. But let's not criticize. You're the one who put Calvin's paramour in charge of bringing the Irish knackles to Crystal City."

"On the train. Couldn't trust her to drag her own fingers across the Atlantic."

"Can't trust her now, either, can you?"

"Let's just say people got to have a chance to show you who they are," said Alvin.

"Or who they want you to *think* they are."

"Taleswapper, I've already learned all your lessons."

"All but one," said Taleswapper.

"Then lay the last burden of your wisdom upon me, Taleswapper."

"You were born wise, wise enough to recognize your own foolishness when you noticed it," said Taleswapper. "I knew right away you was a Maker, I lived to see it, I rejoiced. But what kind of boy would have such power, how would you use it?"

"You've seen."

"Well done, Alvin Maker. So far, well done."

"Thank you," said Alvin quietly. "But you said one more lesson."

"You've done mighty works," said Taleswapper. "You've saved many lives, you've taught mighty teachings and you've learned lessons God teaches only to his noble and great ones."

"I didn't know you were speaking for God now," said Alvin.

"Only to you, cause you don't listen to hardly anybody else," said Taleswapper. "It don't matter how much time you got left. Forty days or forty years."

"Those my choices?" asked Alvin.

"No matter how long of life you have left, boy, hear me quick and hear me deep: Spend what time you have, as much as possible, with those who have cause to expect you to love them."

Alvin's voice caught in his throat. "I couldn't save my baby."

"It ain't about saving," said Taleswapper. "In the end, it's about how much love you gave and how much love you were given."

"I had work to do, Margaret knew it, knows it, wanted me to do it."

"Last lesson. Here it is."

Alvin waited.

And waited.

"I'm not sure I'm understanding what-all you're saying," said Alvin.

"Haven't said it yet cause I was looking for the words."

"I can wait."

"If you could wait, you wouldn't have interrupted my thinking. Now hush, boy."

Alvin hushed.

Time passed. Alvin wondered if he was going to have to sleep here.

"Here's my lesson. You don't know how long your life is going to be, but I can tell you one thing: How long your work is going to be."

"My work *is* my life."

"Not anymore," said Taleswapper.

"Is my end that near?"

"Don't have your day marked on my calendar. Don't want to, either. Let the new keeper of the book make a record of it."

"If it isn't Calvin—"

"It's someone closer than any of your brothers except maybe Measure. It's your constant companion. It's the boy who knows how to speak in your voice."

"Arthur Stuart," said Alvin.

"When I gave it to him, he said, 'Now I got to learn me how to read.' I said, 'Reading's no good to those as don't know how to think. And feel.'"

"Arthur Stuart's a good choice," said Alvin. "And he reads better than anybody."

"I know it," said Taleswapper. "Your work is done and my work is done. Don't mean we're dead. But it means your work and my work have to be continued by other hands."

Alvin nodded. "Don't know who can protect my people as well as me—"

"Protect?" asked Taleswapper. "Not your job, not your concern."

"Will they be safe?" asked Alvin.

"Not for a second, my boy," said Taleswapper. "But nobody's ever safe, in case you didn't notice. They're ready to make their own safety, and shelter in someone else's. If you thought all the armies of three nations were gathering to destroy Crystal City, what would you do? Stand and fight? Take your enemies apart? Move mountains from there to here, from yon to hither?"

"Don't know if I could," said Alvin. "Don't know if I'd want to."

"So what's your better plan, if it was still your responsibility?"

Alvin thought a while. Figure out a way to confuse the ground around Crystal City? Make it impossible to find?

Kind of defeats the purpose. It can't be a refuge for knackles if they can't find it to take refuge there.

Lead them to find a new place? Where? Between Quebec, New England, Crown Colonies, Mexico, there wasn't an inch that one nation or another didn't think they owned.

And then he thought of the most obvious safe place he could hope for.

"You think he'd let us?" asked Alvin.

"Don't know."

"Should I go ask him?"

"Not your job anymore."

"What do I do then?" asked Alvin.

"Tell Margaret I sent you home like she asked me to."

"Does Margaret know about those visions my mother saw in the wall?"

Taleswapper was walking down toward the mill, toward Alvin's childhood home. He was a thin man, but he didn't walk away from good food if it was offered. And Mother would offer.

Arthur Stuart. Nobody understood what Alvin was trying to do as well as Arthur Stuart did.

But why not Measure? Measure's prepared, he really *is* my brother, he . . .

Not my job now.

When Measure came up the hill to meet Alvin, he looked around. "Already gone?" he asked.

Alvin answered, "Already at my place at table, eating the sad little scraps of food you know that Mother will probably find for him."

"So, probably the best meal of his life?" asked Measure.

"You know he ate at our table more than once, years gone by."

"When we were poor, and had precious little to feed him."

"It's Taleswapper. He knows what we had, he knows what we shared, it was a feast to him."

"What did he need to say to you?" asked Measure.

"He said I was done. My work. Done."

"That's just crazy talk. The hard part's just beginning."

"But *my* part of the work is done."

"He doesn't get to decide that!" said Measure.

"He didn't decide. I didn't decide. It's just . . . time."

"Well, *I'm* not taking over your job."

"No, you're not."

"You don't think I'm ready," said Measure.

"I think you're the readiest man in Crystal City."

"But not my job."

"Don't know. Taleswapper thought he knew, and he's a clever man, but if Arthur Stuart is ready to step up—"

"Arthur's just a . . . just a lad."

"Older than I was, by double, when I cut a stone out of the rock without hands."

"Which *he* cannot do. And I cannot do."

"Good thing we don't need a stonecutter, then, isn't it?"

"Alvin," said Measure. "How can you let it go so easy?"

Alvin shook his head. "Trying to let it go," he said. "It isn't easy."

"That's what all the goodbyes were about last night," said Measure.

"Probably. I didn't know why. I just had to see Mother and Father again. And the sisters, and—"

"*That* work isn't yours anymore, either, is it."

"They don't need me to teach them a thing. They taught me all they could. Father showed me how a man controls himself, and doesn't let himself get sucked into wickedness."

"All we need now is Reverend Philadelphia Thrower, to tell us what God, or the devil—"

"Unmaker."

"Wants us to do," said Measure.

"Thrower had a job to do," said Alvin, "and he hasn't done it yet."

"Not for lack of trying," said Measure.

"I'll go home to my wife and you go home to yours," said Alvin. "We can stand up taller, because we no longer have to carry such a burden around with us."

"*My* burden wasn't all that heavy," said Measure. "Don't know if I want to give it up yet."

Alvin smiled. "Let's get home."

Measure followed Alvin into the Greensong, and it took only two days to reach the watchpoint on the eastern road. Crystal City would be glad to see them.

26

ELIZA SAT IN the chair nearest the wall, so she could disappear. This wasn't a meeting that she wanted anyone to remember her attendance at. The trouble was that for so many years, every aspect of her bearing had been bent toward attracting attention. Favorable attention. Delighted attention. And even as she tried to do *nothing*, she saw every man in the room turn his gaze toward her a couple of seconds at a time, and no one looked disapproving. Not even the Scottish minister, whose presence here nobody bothered to explain. Which meant everybody else knew, and she was left out.

Why was she here at all? Why had Calvin dragged her to a place where her very presence would mark her as his paramour, his leman, his *girl*? And he refused to tell her what the meeting was about, only this: Sometimes everybody has to do their part.

Well, what's *my* part, Calvin? What makes me the only woman in this room? Who decided? Not me.

Eliza did not like it when other people made decisions for her. Or dragged her along without telling her why. It made her quite angry, and she got angrier the longer the meeting went on without making any sense at all.

The problem was that when Eliza was angry, it made her more beautiful. It brought fire to her eyes, a quickness of movement, color to her cheeks, and a sharp, sharp wit.

I am not going to say anything. I'm not even going to think of things I might have said if I were going to speak. This is not a good time for me to blurt something, considering that I have no idea what's going on.

Calvin was being quiet, too, so she knew it was something really important—so important that Calvin *wasn't* trying to put himself at the head of it.

The Scottish minister was talking. "Surprise is worthless," he said. "He's very quick. As a child he was quick, and now he has so much more knowledge . . ."

So the Scottish minister knew him as a child. Him. They did keep speaking of "him" without saying his name.

"Will the angel come in person?" asked a man, one of the ones who had ridden into Crystal City in a carriage from Wobbish. "We were told there was an angel."

"Do you think angels come at my beck and call?" asked the minister, irritated. "He came to *me* unbidden, and has never come to me afterward at my request, but rather when he had a use for me."

"This would be a pretty good time for that," said another man, who had come by stagecoach from Carthage, along with a few sour-looking men.

"If you think an angel's going to do this for you, then you understand nothing," said the minister. "We are the tools of angels, not angels *our* tools."

The minister really was flustered.

"Why do you need us at all?" asked the fellow from Wobbish. "Can't you get close enough to—"

"No," said the minister.

"You expect *us* to—"

"No," said the minister, and he stood up and walked over to the fireplace, which, on a cool night like this, had no fire in it or even a speck of ash. Not a cookfire, then.

Calvin's voice tore Eliza out of her reverie about fireplace ash. "What Reverend Thrower is reluctant to tell you is that he *tried*, many years ago, it was his task alone, and he failed. He couldn't do it, not to a child."

"You don't know what you're talking about!" said Thrower. "You were just a baby."

"A walking, talking, stone-throwing, spy-on-the-preacher baby, yes sir," said Calvin.

"I don't know what you think you saw—"

"I saw you with the knife, and when you went into the room it wasn't with you. You came out to get it, and when you went back in you were empty-handed. You don't have either the heart or the courage to do it, so you turn to these men here, hoping that they'll have what you lack—a killing instinct, a merciless heart."

"I'm a man of God," said Thrower. "I can't have a merciless heart and still do my work."

"I thought *this* was your work," said the man from Wobbish. "You're setting us up to get kilt."

"He won't kill you! If he was going to kill anybody, it would have been the Bishop of Dublin, and all he did was drop him through the floor. He doesn't kill."

"Sounds like an innocent man," said one of the thuggish fellows from Carthage.

"There *are* no innocent men," said Thrower.

True enough, thought Eliza. Just men who haven't fallen yet.

"And he knows you, so you can't come into his sight," said Calvin, "or he'll be warned."

"None of us know him," said the man from the Crown Colonies. "He tore apart our social order and stole many of our most valuable servants, but none of us knows his face."

Eliza wanted to ask, Then how do you know it was him? Silence, she told herself. Listen.

"I know how you'll know who he is," said Calvin. "When he gets here, he'll go home to his wife and family, but then he'll be sent on one errand only." Calvin turned and used his arm to call their attention to Eliza.

"What are you talking about?" asked Eliza. "Why are you pointing at me?"

"He'll want to talk to *her*, to learn about her train ride bringing all the Irish with her. They are *close*, for him to trust her on such an errand."

"If they're so close, why will she help us?"

"Because she can't help herself. She *will* talk to him. She'll try to kiss him and he'll refuse. But she won't let go of him because—"

"Why!" demanded Eliza. "You know I don't love any man."

Calvin recoiled just the tiniest bit, because her words stung him.

He does care about me, poor boy.

"He's already come to town tonight. He's already walking up to the door of his house, along with his brother, Measure," said Calvin.

"Your brother, too," said a man.

"Measure hasn't noticed me in my whole life," said Calvin. "I don't count him as a brother of *mine*."

"So what do we do?' asked the bossy man from the carriage. "Take him somewhere? Hide him?"

"Never mind," said Calvin. He stood up from his place at the table. "You're too stupid to do the job."

The bossy man began to bluster, but the big man from the stagecoach laughed. "Don't you remember what he *is*?" he demanded. "You don't take him, you don't bind him, you don't do anything to him, because he can unbind your bindings, he can take *you* exactly when you think you're taking *him*."

And now Eliza understood, as she must have understood from the start, but couldn't believe Calvin would meet with men like these to do—to plan the murder of Alvin Maker.

"Our only hope," said Stagecoach man, "is to kill him before he knows he's being killed."

"What's the fun in that?" asked one of Stagecoach's henchmen.

"There's no fun in this, not for any of us," said Stagecoach. "Nor is there a speck of gold beyond what our sponsors have already paid to help us get here tonight. But each of us can carry home with us one of the magic crystal blocks from the wall of the city."

They all fell silent. "Is that a sure thing?" asked one.

"If you complete your task," said Calvin, "the walls won't hold together. You can pick the blocks up from the ground like fallen petals."

"Only bigger and heavier," said a man.

"Not as heavy as you might think," said Calvin.

"I heard *you* could make crystal blocks, too," said the man from Wobbish. "I heard you had all the same powers."

Now was the moment Eliza could not contain herself any longer. "Calvin makes the blocks out of water, they show some kind of life inside, like a newt or a lizard running around, but just the shadow and the shape of it. No clear visions. Calvin claims he can do everything Alvin does, but he's always second-rate." It was, she knew, the cruelest thing anybody could say to or about Calvin.

But Calvin bore it. So great was his hatred of his brother that he would not allow himself to be distracted. "My crystals aren't as good as his crystals," he said. "Or I'd just make you some and send you on your way."

"So the reverend is too merciful to kill him, and you can't kill him because—"

"Because he's my brother," said Calvin.

"Because Calvin loves him," said Eliza.

"As if you'd know what I do and do not love," Calvin said scornfully.

"And you won't even be there to watch," said the Wobbish man.

"If I'm there, people will wonder why I didn't stop you."

"I wonder that right now," said the Wobbish man. He drew out a pistol.

The ball rolled out of the barrel. It was only the size of a pea, not a snug fit the way it was supposed to be.

"I can do," said Calvin, "what *he* can do."

"You're saying, don't try to shoot him," said the carriage man.

"I'm saying, don't even think of what you're going to do until you do it. Knives will be best. Stab him enough times, and he won't be able to repair the damage quickly enough."

"And he won't kill us?" said Stagecoach. "Because he surely could, if he could play that trick with the pistol ball."

"Not a trick," said Calvin, picking up the pea-sized ball from the floor and tossing it to the man. "Not a trick. He's a Maker, don't you understand? The world is too small to hold a Maker. He's too powerful, he takes away other men's power and freedom."

The Wobbish man said, as if he had said it before, "Alvin Miller Junior got no respect for any man's knack except his own."

The meeting broke up soon enough, and then Calvin walked Eliza back to her cabin. "Why do you think I'll help you kill that good man?" she said.

"Oh, don't be stupid," said Calvin. "They *can't* kill him. He's quicker than all their knives. I wager not one will even nick his skin."

"Then what is this for?" asked Eliza.

"Because I will be the one who shouts the warning, so he has time to soften their knives or whatever he might choose to do."

"You plan to *save* your brother from a murder plot you arranged yourself?"

"This way, I know who the killers are and when they'll strike."

"And what will happen to all these men you fooled?"

"Whatever Crystal City thinks to do with them."

"No," said Eliza. "You plan to use your Maker powers to kill them all. Because if any of them is taken alive, he can name *you* and all the part you played in this."

"I hadn't thought of that," said Calvin. "So if I have to silence them, I reckon that's on *you*."

"Oh, Calvin, your stupidity and carelessness and vanity—I'm not responsible for those."

"But you'll help me get out of a jam."

"Why will I do that?"

"Because you were at the meeting. Because everybody knows that you are my—"

"You are my paramour?" asked Eliza. "If you think anyone who knows *you* will imagine that I came up with any of your mad antics, you are the only one who believes it. Nobody blames anybody but you for the things you do."

"You don't love me," said Calvin. He didn't look crestfallen, but in fact he was hurt by her display of disloyalty.

"I said that I don't love any *man*. You're still a boy, Calvin."

He sat down on the edge of her bed, looking angry, looking sad.

Since Eliza clearly had the upper hand, she went on. "You never told me that your plan included the murder of your brother—who is, in truth, a good man."

"And I'm not?"

"So you desperately try to prove."

"I'm not plotting anybody's murder. Alvin *cannot* be killed. These men want to kill him, and, when they make their attempt, they'll be exposed."

"Alvin *can't* be killed?"

"He heals himself too quickly to die. And he can immobilize or disarm any enemy, even at a distance. Who can kill him?"

"Poison?" asked Eliza.

"Do you think that little gang of killers would use *poison*? They'd probably end up spilling it, or accidentally adding it to their own soup."

"Meaning that you have no preparation for poison, no way of countering it."

"Alvin can destroy poison in his own body or anyone else's."

"What you're saying is that Alvin is the real thing, and the idea that you can do *everything* Alvin does is all brag. Or wish. Or hope."

"I learn more every day, and I have Alvin's example to guide me into my self-training."

"How is that working out?" asked Eliza.

"Because Alvin did it, I knew that it was possible to heal my own broken bone. So when I fell from a roof and broke my ankle, I was able to manipulate the bones back into place and knit them together."

"I'm impressed. Did anyone else see this miracle?"

"What's to see?" said Calvin. "It happened inside my leg."

"Which leg?"

"The one that got broken," said Calvin.

Eliza smiled at him. "You're not a kind person, Calvin. You have a lot of malice stored up. But I won't betray you and your little plot, Calvin. Because I'm quite confident that, in the end, you'll betray yourself without anybody else's help."

"You are not just an observer here, Eliza. These men don't know who Alvin is, not by face. So you will have to greet him with a kiss."

"Will I? Have to?"

"And he will push you away. No other man would push *you* away, rejecting the kiss."

"I'm slightly flattered," said Eliza.

"Not only can I heal my own broken bone, I can dissolve anyone else's. One bone, perhaps. Or two. Or ten."

"Why not all of them, and leave me in a puddle on the floor?"

"Shall I demonstrate? Pick a bone you don't think you'll ever need again."

"I believe you, Calvin," said Eliza. "Just as I believe you stupidly threatened a person on whose loyalty you depend."

"I don't count on anyone but myself."

"But Calvin, you aren't reliable enough to be counted on."

Calvin smiled in a way that he clearly thought would be enigmatic. Then he kissed her cheek.

27

IT WAS AFTER supper when Margaret opened the door to find Calvin's paramour Eliza there. Margaret graciously invited her in, with the good manners she had learned from Mistress Modesty so many years ago. "Always treat your enemies far more kindly than they deserve, more kindly than they would ever treat you. It confuses them."

Soon they were sitting at the small table in the nook just off the kitchen, sipping a decent-quality tea, brewed in the pot, not in the cup. "Enough small talk," said Eliza at last. "I know I don't have to tell you anything, because you've seen it all in my heartfire."

Margaret sighed and smiled a little. "I always hope that people will forget what my primary knack is, because when they remember that I can see into heartfires, they try all the harder to shut me out, which nobody can do, or they try to avoid me entirely, which is also impossible within the bounds of Crystal City. All the crystal blocks intensify my insight, and I know what I need to know."

"You know what you *think* you need to know, but what you actually need to know often eludes you, Mistress Margaret."

"That might be so, but if it is, *you* wouldn't know it," said Margaret, with sweetness rather than disdain.

"I came here," said Eliza, "because I did not trust you to see all that you needed to see. I did not know when Calvin dragged me to that otherwise-all-male conversation that they were plotting to murder your husband."

Margaret nodded. She appreciated the fact that Eliza was getting straight to the point.

"Calvin also decided that I would be useful as the judas in the scene—that I should point out who Alvin is by trying to kiss him, and then be heartbroken and run away when he rebuffs me."

"Calvin knows a great deal less than he thinks he knows," said Margaret.

"Don't we all," said Eliza.

"I know a great deal more than *you* think I do," said Margaret.

"But you don't know all," said Eliza.

"I see many future paths, but have no way of knowing which, if any, will come true."

"Jonah's dilemma," said Eliza. "He preached to the wicked people of Nineveh and to his *shock* and disappointment, they repented and ceased their warlike ways, avoiding the punishment of God."

"For a while," said Margaret. She was surprised that Eliza knew *any* Bible story. Most people heard "Jonah" and said "whale."

"You don't know how things will turn out," said Eliza.

"I know how I hope they will turn out," said Margaret, "and as far as I can tweak the present, I have a hope of arriving at an acceptable future."

"I set my cap for your husband as soon as I knew him to be a man of power—and a kind and clever one, too."

"What's not to desire in that?" said Margaret, suppressing her desire to slap the woman. She did not need to hear a would-be rival praise her man.

"Many men have turned me down, but only one has done so without even a flicker of wavering. Men desire me, Mistress Margaret, but not Alvin."

"I know him better than you," said Margaret. "Of course he was attracted by your charms. But Alvin has the ability—the hard-won ability—to dissimulate his passing feelings. Only when he has decided to *allow* himself to feel something does it show in his mien and his behavior."

"I suppose I'm relieved to know that he is not unaffected by my attractions."

"But when you come to kiss him, what if he and I have decided that he should kiss you back, with eagerness, with passion."

"I would enjoy that," said Eliza. "I imagine that you find his kisses pleasurable. Why wouldn't I?"

"But you will know it means nothing," said Margaret.

"Maybe not to him."

"Let me make it clear. When Alvin wants a woman to feel . . . strong feelings toward him, he can do it without laying a hand on her. He can please you more than that shallow child you've been fornicating with."

"By now I believe that common law has slipped into our liaison and made him legally my husband."

"Sorry. You have six more years to go. If you can stand it."

"I can stand it very well. Because one of Alvin's knacks that Calvin *has* learned to emulate is the ability to introduce emotions in a woman, feelings that he believes she wants to have."

"Is he right?" asked Margaret. "Do you want to have those feelings?"

"I bear the burden of Calvin's clumsy love with much patience and, yes, some pleasure."

"If I can help it, Mistress Eliza, you will *never* have the chance to place your judas kiss upon Alvin's hand, his cheek, his forehead, or his lips."

"That's what I was hoping."

Margaret then saw, to her surprise, that she had *not* understood Eliza as fully as she thought.

"You came to warn him."

"These men seem harmless enough, and I can't see into their heartfires the way that you can. But I believe that to a man, they hate Alvin Maker with every fiber of their being. I believe that they all have murder in their hearts. They know that if Alvin sees them coming—sees the pistol before it is aimed—then no bullet will ever emerge from that pistol. Or musket, or rifle. They hope to get him in a jovial, relaxed setting and then, without warning, without wrath, simply insert knives into his body in many fatal places, most especially his throat and his heart."

Margaret had seen their desire, of course, weeks ago. But Eliza's certainty that they were planning on murder and thinking of ways to surprise Alvin so completely he can't heal himself fast enough, that was something she had not foreseen. Sometimes her insights into heartfires were complete, so she knew a person better than he knew himself. But sometimes she found that there were many paths opening up into the future. She had to pick one to follow. One to heed.

"I see several futures," said Margaret, "and not one of them is certain to take place."

"I'm sure you don't want Alvin to die with many knives in him."

Margaret smiled. "You don't know how many metal pieces can be inserted into him, or how brief a time it would take him to heal completely."

Eliza cocked her head. "Calvin said that *his* control over the natural world is nearly complete."

"Calvin brags without a lick of truth in what he says," said Margaret. "I knew him long before he knew me."

"And I know him now, in ways that you do not," said Eliza. "If you don't believe my words might have value, I shall not waste your time any further tonight." She arose from her chair and, like a thoughtful guest, she carried her cup and saucer into the kitchen and set them near the dishwashing tub.

Margaret followed her into the kitchen. "I'll wash, you dry."

Eliza accepted by putting on an apron and washing her hands. Margaret waited patiently for these ablutions and then began to hand wet dishes to Eliza for drying.

Margaret thought, wouldn't it be nice to have a knack that could dry off water-soaked dishes without getting a towel so damp that it could no longer dry anything.

And then she thought, as she always did, that her life would be poor indeed if she had to swap knacks with anybody. Even Alvin's. Her knack was knowing; his was doing. She would never trade.

As if her thought had summoned him, Alvin walked into the kitchen unannounced. "I hope you didn't save any of the tea for me. It's too expensive and it tastes like sawdust soaked in cow's urine." A typical greeting, because Alvin well knew how distasteful she found his humor when it delved into bodily excretions.

Eliza piped up, as if to make sure Alvin noticed her, "How many other things have you tasted after soaking them in cow's urine? Is there a significant difference between bovine urine and pig urine? And what about bull urine?"

Margaret had long since learned that showing her irritation at discussions of bodily functions only guaranteed that Alvin would conclude that his remarks were very funny, and therefore needed to be repeated often. So her answer had to be as sassy as his jest.

"That is a decoction I have never tried myself, my love," said Margaret as her husband bowed to kiss her forehead. "But since we keep a cow, feel free to take a bucket, collect what she discharges, and I'll soak whatever you want in it."

"You have comforted my soul," said Alvin. Then he turned to Eliza. "And *you* brought the Irish without losing a one, and sheltered them, fed them, governed them. Did you like it?"

"Everybody with a complaint believed it to be the most urgent business in the group. I stopped them from mobbing me by instituting a rule that they can only talk to another actor as part of a genuine scene."

"Are they all in a play?" asked Alvin, ever playing the naive country boy.

"When they came to me for judgment they were," said Eliza.

As she answered, Alvin headed into his study to find something better to drink than nasty sophisticated tea. Meanwhile, the ladies walked into the parlor and sat down to converse.

Margaret interjected, "Did that happen often?"

"There were many small disputes, and some more serious accusations. As a general rule, when I said the right things it got them back in their seats in a better temper."

"Alvin will not be surprised to hear it," said Margaret.

"He isn't hearing it now?" asked Eliza.

"He left the room. He's not a spy."

"Is that what *you* are?" asked Eliza.

"Not by choice, by nature. Alvin can see heartfires a little, but he has to be trying to see. He doesn't garner anywhere near as much information as I do. It's in our natures."

"I always thought my knack was getting away with things. Or maybe just getting away. I have been remarkably unpunished all my life."

"Now you think your knack is, what, leadership?" asked Margaret.

"I know you and Alvin rule this city," said Eliza, "and I don't covet an ounce of your authority. I'm no threat to—"

"I know you're not a threat," said Margaret. "You kindly came to give Alvin warning of a very serious plot against him."

"Thank you," said Eliza.

"What do you think should happen now?" asked Margaret.

Alvin walked back into the room, still wearing traveling clothes and carrying a half-empty duffel bag. "Your opinion does not interest me, Eliza," said Alvin. "Nor yours, at this moment, my love. These conspirators want to kill me because I'm a Maker, a knacksman with powers that frighten them. Until I built this foolish city, the United States left knackings alone. But now stories are spreading about the Crystal City, with Alvin Maker at its head, protecting it, teaching powerful knacks to all the people."

"Of course such stories are spreading," said Eliza.

Alvin dropped his duffel and sat down on a chair, his long legs sprawling out under the table. "If I leave, if people are absolutely convinced that I'm gone, then this will just be a town of people who have knacks."

"It will still scare them," said Margaret, "with or without you."

"Much less without me."

"Perhaps," said Margaret.

"Where in the world can you go?" asked Eliza. "You won't be able to resist helping people that nobody else can help. You'll expose your true identity with every rescue."

"I know a place," said Alvin, "where I will be unseen and undiscovered as long as I like."

Eliza shuddered. "The grave?" she asked.

"I'm not playing a game of riddles," said Alvin. "I'm going to cross the river and live with Tenskwa-Tawa and his people."

"I heard they kill any White who crosses," said Eliza.

"They don't—they don't kill any of them. They send them back."

"That's all?" asked Eliza.

"What, you want old war stories to come back? Hacking people's scalps from their head? Shooting whole families, women and children included?" asked Alvin.

"I thought that was how Reds waged war," said Eliza.

"Bring them a war, and they'll fight it," said Alvin. "They used to treat wars like football games between towns. The teams fight over a ball, one of them wins, and nobody has to die. The pinnacle of courage was to ride up to an enemy so closely that you can tap his back or his shoulder with your riding crop."

"Reds use riding crops?" asked Eliza.

"They call them coup sticks. Reds fought whole wars with no killing."

"Reds fought games with no killing," corrected Margaret. "But they fought bloody wars with lots of widows and orphans. Whites didn't bring brutal warfare to this continent. The Irrakwa are all civilized and Christian now, but they were horrid to their enemies. Torturing them to death with burning brands, to see how much pain they could bear in silence."

Eliza shook her head. "Why are you telling me this?"

"Because if there weren't a fog over the Mizzippy," said Margaret, "there would be warfare between Whites and Reds at such a scale—"

"There *is* fog over the Mizzippy," said Alvin. "So that war will not happen."

"And you plan to cross the river and put yourself at the mercy of savages," said Eliza.

"I'm at the mercy of savages on this side of the Mizzippy, too. Isn't that what you came to warn my wife about?"

They sat in silence. Several times Margaret wanted to thank Eliza for her well-meant visit and escort her to the door. But instead she sat and gazed steadily at her husband. "Will your family cross the river to join you?"

"Would you leave Crystal City without your guiding light?" Alvin asked in reply.

Margaret laughed. "Didn't you put Eliza in charge of the trainfuls of Irish folk to give her the experience so she could become mayor of the city when you go?"

Eliza almost fell off her chair.

"Don't exaggerate your surprise, my girl," said Margaret. "You knew Alvin was preparing you for something."

"I didn't actually know *what*," said Alvin. "It just felt right to put you in charge so you could see if you had any skills other than getting out of town."

Eliza chuckled. "Apparently you're going to try to take over *my* knack, by going west over the river."

"Because west *under* the river would mean holding your breath for a long time," said Alvin.

"He jokes about it," said Margaret.

"If I cross the river, it will be because Tenskwa-Tawa sends me a canoe, preferably with a couple of rowers."

"How will he know you want to cross?" asked Eliza.

"He'll see it, in a dream or a cloud or a fog or a whirlwind," said Margaret. "Alvin learned to create solid blocks of water from the Red Prophet, so in a way, Tenskwa-Tawa is the father of Crystal City."

"Ironic," said Alvin, "since he hates cities so much."

"When will you go, then?" asked Eliza. "Across the river?"

Alvin reached down and picked up his duffel, set it on another chair.

"Tonight?" asked Margaret, a little mournfully.

"Waiting around for the right time only means less chance of success."

"Should I write that down?" asked Eliza.

"Why bother?" asked Alvin. "Tell ten people in Crystal City and it will be repeated by all."

"Do you have to go?" asked Eliza.

"I'm supposed to say that," muttered Margaret.

"Don't you know how much we need you here?" asked Eliza.

"Don't you also need me to stay alive?" asked Alvin.

"Nobody can kill you," said Eliza. "Calvin said so. You turn gun barrels into butter and powder into flour."

"Swords into plowshares," murmured Margaret.

"I can't turn gunpowder into flour," said Alvin. "It would take me so long I'd die of old age before the job was done."

"But you can melt the barrels of their guns. You can melt their blades."

"Don't tempt him," said Margaret. "Do you think he *wants* to leave me tonight? And he does like showing the amazing things that he can do."

"Well, am I supposed to *hate* having people see my handiwork?" asked Alvin.

"If he shows that their ordinary weapons can't kill him," said Margaret, "they'll find another way."

"And on that cheerful birdsong," said Alvin, "I'm on my way."

"Won't you take someone with you?" asked Margaret.

"I don't want to bother anybody this time of night. And the others will want to ride horses, while I can travel by shank's mare."

"Arthur Stuart isn't asleep now, you know that boy hates going to sleep."

"He's a man now," said Alvin. "He would come, so would Measure."

"And Verily Cooper, and John Binder, and . . . *anybody* you asked," said Margaret.

"Don't send anyone after me," said Alvin. "By the time they get up in the morning, I'll be on the other side of the river."

"This keeps sounding like death," said Eliza.

"Will you kindly shut your yap?" said Margaret, in the gentlest of tones.

Eliza knew she had no right to offer an opinion, and so, for once, she did not defy authority and refuse to remain silent. She truly had nothing to say.

"Make sure you show up tomorrow," said Alvin. "Or whenever they decide you should kiss me."

"Word will spread that you're gone," said Eliza.

"Just don't pick someone else to kiss, in case they really don't know what I look like," said Alvin. "Don't want some unlucky stranger to die in my place."

Alvin walked over to Margaret, kissed her lovingly—something Calvin had never done with Eliza—and then strode to the door, opened it, and went out into the darkness.

"I'll go now," said Eliza.

"That would be best. I think your business here is done."

Eliza laughed. "Mayor of Crystal City?"

"Stranger things have happened," said Margaret. "And if the future bends in that direction, I believe you'll do the job splendidly. Just as you did on the trains."

Eliza went out the door that Alvin had left unlatched behind him. She did not look for him on the road, but walked straight back to the Crystal towers of the city, through them, and on to her place.

28

WORD SPREAD THROUGH Crystal City like fire through a dried-out cornfield. Margaret was used to this. She didn't tell anybody, Eliza swore she wouldn't and kept her word, and Alvin himself was closed as tight as a rich man's purse.

But he was seen walking west through town, toward the river. Since he had only just come back from going to Ireland and to his family's home, everybody expected that he wouldn't travel anymore for a while. But he was walking with his long, determined traveling stride, which they had all seen before, sometimes because he was setting out across town, and sometimes because he was walking to Philadelphia or Camelot, and sometimes because the ocean was too close and he refused to be walled in, so he was going to sail across it even though everybody knew water had been bad luck for him as a boy.

So neighbors were confabulating and speculating all along the road, and people from the high ground of the Crystal City started coming down to see what Alvin Maker was about to do. This time he didn't turn around to tell them to go back home. Maybe he hadn't even seen them or sensed their heartfires or maybe he just didn't care.

How long did Crystal City have to do without its founder? Calvin Smith had his powers but they all knew he was an envious braggity boy with an eye for women—dare we say ladies?—who were no better than they had to be. And Alvin had done the crazy thing of putting Calvin's current bedmate in charge of the Irishmen, which was like putting a hen in charge of the foxhouse. Or so the gossips said.

When it became clear that Alvin wasn't going anywhere but the riverside wharf, people began to back off. The fog over the Mizzippy was mysterious and fearful. Nobody let their children near it, saying either the fog would reach out and suck them in, or some Reds would come out of the fog and cut their hands off. Margaret had no idea how such an idiotic threat could come about—there was no history of Reds cutting off hands even when Whites and Reds were at war. But pretty much all the mothers in Crystal City made that threat to keep their children away from the Mizzippy fog.

Alvin was still fifty yards from the wharf when there began to be music. There shouldn't be music coming from the river, specially not dancing music.

Alvin stopped right where he was and looked downriver, because that was where the music was coming from. Then Alvin started sauntering on toward the wharf. He wasn't in no hurry now. He just kept looking downriver for the source of that music.

And then it hove into view, a bright-colored riverboat, all decked out in banners and bunting, with splendidly dressed women and men at the second-story railing. They were waving. And then they were singing, though nobody on shore could make out the melody or the words. Alvin reached the shore just as the riverboat was running out its gangplank to let it come to rest on the dock.

At once two biggish men ran down that bridge carrying heavy ropes in their hands, with loops already formed at the end. They set them over the bollards and then snugged them up, so the gap between the boat and the wharf was fully covered by the heavy cloth pads along the side of the wharf. Cushions. Pillows just like on a lady's settee.

The rope men stood aside, presumably for somebody more important to come on down. But Alvin was quicker. Light as a deer he bounded up the gangplank and nearly ran into an in-charge looking fellow.

"Captain," said Alvin cheerfully. "We never thought a boat would dare come up the river."

"I never thought so either," said the captain. "But we were invited by a young gentleman who said he was—"

"My brother," said Alvin.

"So you are—"

"One of Calvin's older brothers. I can see he did a good job of joining the boards to the keel of your boat, and all the other places where it needed doing. A thorough job. I'm proud of him."

"So the boat really can't sink?" asked the captain.

"Any boat can sink, if you fill it up with water," said Alvin. "I'm Alvin

Smith—a journeyman smith, to tell the truth, though I created what I thought was good enough to be a masterwork. What are your plans on this upriver Mizzippy voyage?"

"Your brother allowed as how the people of your gleaming city could use a little harmless entertainment. In the afternoon, a show that will please the children, a combination of 'The Pied Piper of Hamelin,' 'Rumpelstiltskin,' and 'The Emperor's New Clothes.'"

Alvin tilted his head. "You planning on putting your emperor on stage naked?"

"Oh, no, sir, none of our actors would even *think* of acting onstage without clothes. The emperor is wearing underwear. Long johns. With the fanny flap buttoned up tight."

"And your evening show?" asked Alvin.

"I ask your advice. The tragical story of *Hamlet* has a ghost in it, and lots of swordplay and practically everybody dies. *Macbeth* is also by the glorious bard of Avon, and it has witches and more ghosts than *Hamlet* and several foul murders."

"Cheerful," said Alvin.

"The bard could be a bit morose. But perhaps your citizens would prefer a comedy? We have *Twelfth Night*, *Much Ado About Nothing*, *As You Like It*, and *The Comedy of Errors*, about twins who each think their brother is dead, and when they both happen to be in the same town, people recognize the wrong one, including the wife."

"Sounds hilarious," said Alvin.

"But we haven't done that one in a while."

"Maybe between the afternoon show and the nighttime show, your actors can study up on their speeches."

"So you want *The Comedy of Errors*?"

"No," said Alvin. "I want *As You Like It*, because I think the fancy of pinning love poems on trees will amuse and inspire folks to be more romantic and loving."

The captain had never thought of *As You Like It* as having such an effect. "*As You Like It*," said the captain, "seeing as you like it."

Alvin shook hands with the man, making sure that the onlookers ashore saw him do it.

"There's the matter of payment," said the captain.

"No, no, we won't charge you for docking here."

"I meant—"

"Charge my people what you usually charge at a city this size," said Alvin. "They have their share of coin to spend as they will."

"Your brother led me to believe—"

"Calvin leads many people to believe many things, to my frequent regret but never to his," said Alvin. "My wife, Margaret Larner, will see to it that you don't lose money by coming here."

"How long you want us to stay?"

"How many different plays do your actors know how to perform?" asked Alvin.

"Not sure at the moment, cause the number fluctuates."

"Show all the plays you got in you, Captain," said Alvin. "And then another couple on top of that."

"Yes sir," said the captain.

"I'm walking around to the other side of your ship now," said Alvin.

"It's not quite as decorated as this side, but—"

"I won't be disappointed," said Alvin.

The people watching from the shore saw Alvin shake hands with the captain, and saw them jawing a while, and then watched as Alvin walked, not to the gangplank, but around the front of the boat and then along the far side, out of sight.

The whole troupe came singing and dancing down the gangplank, including one fellow in a bear suit. Or maybe a woman. Now they could make out the words of the song, it was full of brag about how they was the finest theatrical troupe on the river.

John Binder said to Margaret Larner, "I reckon they're the onliest theatrical troupe on *this* river."

Margaret replied, "I think they usually work the Hio and a few of its tributaries. Whatever is navigable."

"What possessed them to come up the Mizzippy? They get run out of every town on the Hio?"

"Calvin promised them good payment if they came upriver. And he sealed their boat against leaking."

"What's the plan, then?"

"The showboat puts on shows, and the people of Crystal City will pay for some fine entertainment."

"How do you know they'll do a fine job?" asked John Binder.

Margaret laughed. "Because every single one of them thinks they're the best actor or singer or dancer in the company."

"They can't all be right," said John Binder.

"Logic is with you, but human nature is not. They're all in competition to be the audience's favorite. They'll perform better than they know how."

"You're full of paradoxes, Miz Larner," said John Binder.

"Full twice over," said Margaret. "But I try to let them out only one at a time, so they don't confuse the common folk."

Alvin stood at the gunwale, not far from the paddlewheel. But instead of trying to puzzle out what kind of knack was propelling the boat, he decided that if Tenskwa-Tawa didn't know he was coming, there was no reason for Alvin to await a canoe that might never show up.

So he swung his leg over the gunwale and lowered himself until his boots touched water. Alvin had walked on water before, but it took a great deal of concentration and he had other things on his mind. So he lowered himself without a splash into the river, then lay on his back in the water and began to swim west through the fog.

After only a few strokes, he heard the soft plashing of paddles expertly used to drive a canoe forward. Alvin spoke as he swam. "If you were this close, why didn't you call to me on the boat?"

A few moments of silence, and then, "If we shout to you, we shout to all."

"You could have splashed louder, with your paddling," said Alvin. "I would have heard and waited for you to reach me."

"You reached us here," said the Red in the canoe.

"You could have spared me from getting wet," said Alvin.

A silence. Then, one Red spoke to the other—but in English, so Alvin would definitely understand. "Did *you* mind seeing him all wet in the water?"

"It did not cause me pain," said the other.

"Does this mean," said Alvin, "that you're not going to help me get into your canoe?"

Again a pause, and one Red said to the other, "Helping Whites get up into canoes from the water causes many a canoe to turn over."

"Our cargo should not get wet."

"White man in the water, we cannot lift you into the canoe."

Since they knew precisely who he was, and Tenskwa-Tawa had sent them, Alvin was getting impatient with this game. So he opened a seam in the bottom of the canoe and let water squirt upward onto the paddlers.

They didn't say anything, but a few grunts convinced Alvin that they were trying to stop the leak.

"May I help?" asked Alvin.

"Yes, please," said one of the men.

Alvin reclosed the seam and sealed it tight. Then he caused the water in the bottom of the canoe to evaporate quickly.

"Why did you do that, White man in the water?"

"Why should I be the only one soaking wet in order to amuse the onlookers?"

"We'll pull you into the canoe," said one of the Reds, grudgingly.

"I would just tip you over," said Alvin.

"We can do it. We do it many times."

"I know," said Alvin. Then he rolled over in the water and began a powerful crawl stroke across the river, leaving the canoe behind him. He could hear them paddling frantically to catch up.

Alvin realized that if they returned to the Prophet with an empty canoe, after a dripping wet Alvin came alone out of the river, they would lose prestige and trust. Alvin didn't intend to tell on them, but there would be no way *not* to tell if he went to Tenskwa-Tawa wet and alone.

So when he reached the western shore, he found a grassy bank and sat down to take off his boots. He didn't want to have to buy a new pair, so he drew much of the water out of the leather so the boots would remain supple. Then, lying in the grass, he dried his clothing until there was no sign they had ever been wet.

He heard them arrive upstream of him, and he got up to go meet them. They had the stern solemn faces of Reds trying to hide shame.

"I enjoyed the swim, lads," said Alvin cheerfully.

They looked him up and down, seeing that he showed no sign of having been in the river.

"Tenskwa-Tawa knows all that happened," said Alvin. "But I didn't tell him. I haven't gone to see him yet."

"He's the Prophet, he knows," said one of the men.

"I don't think he'll be angry," said Alvin. "Time was that he, under a different name, played a prank or two of his own."

"What was that name?" asked the younger one.

"If he wanted you to know," said Alvin, "you would know."

"He doesn't tell us his secrets."

"But he sent you to fetch me," said Alvin. "He trusts you well enough."

"We didn't fetch you," said the older one. "We refused to take you into our canoe."

"A bit impolite, but I didn't mind." Clearly they didn't understand "impolite." Alvin said, "I like to swim, and as you can see, I might *get* wet, but I don't *stay* wet."

They seemed somewhat mollified, but when they reached the Prophet, standing among a group of young buffalos, they hung back.

"Will it bother your friends if I come to you?" asked Alvin, indicating the buffalos.

Tenskwa-Tawa smiled. "I don't want them to get used to the smell of White men. They might lose their caution around you."

"White men don't all smell alike."

"Some worse, some better. Swimming didn't get you any cleaner."

"Wasn't trying for clean. I was trying for fast."

"What's the urgency?" asked the Prophet.

"There's a plot to kill me in Crystal City."

"Why? What did you do wrong?"

"Lots of things, but they wanted to kill me already. Reverend Philadelphia Thrower."

"You send them to school to learn about your God and Jesus and the Spirit, but they come out of that school wickeder and stupider than they went in."

Alvin didn't know enough about clerical education to know if the Prophet's words were accurate.

"You want to come and take shelter here among us?"

Alvin stood and looked at him.

"Could you live as a Red man?" asked Tenskwa-Tawa.

"I have before," said Alvin, this time in Tenskwa-Tawa's own tribal language.

"No, no," said the Prophet. "Your accent is too raspy and whiny."

"It's as good as your English."

"I speak English like the King," said Tenskwa-Tawa.

"You probably do," said Alvin.

"You may take shelter here," said the Prophet. "You may be one of us."

"I didn't finish," said Alvin. "What I ask is much larger than that."

Tenskwa-Tawa looked at him in silence. He didn't need to be told.

"All of them? Because some are very bad people."

"They have knacks. If I'm not there to protect them, their enemies will come down on them like a tornado and fling them everywhere and melt the Crystal City."

"Make another."

"Let me bring them to an enclave. A reservation, perhaps. Not the best land, but land they can farm and grow enough to live."

"They will want to go back to Philadelphia."

"Some probably will, of course. City people like city life."

"They cannot cross the river eastward, once they cross to this shore."

"They know I have crossed and come back."

"You are Alvin Maker," said Tenskwa-Tawa.

"They are my people."

"They are not all trustworthy."

"I will keep them within bounds."

"So you take them from Crystal City, full of vision beyond horizons of time and space, and you will fence them into a patch of land?"

"They'll be alive."

"How long, Maker, till they forget to be grateful."

"Some of them, they will never forget."

"And some of them will be grateful half a day," said the Prophet.

"I'd give *those* folks about fifteen minutes of gratitude before they start sowing discord again."

"Why bring them with you?"

"Was every Red you gave sanctuary to on this side of the river completely trustworthy?"

"Different people, different culture."

"Were any of your people wicked?"

"I work with them. I try to teach them."

"Me too," said Alvin. The Prophet seemed to accept this, but Alvin wondered if it was true. He had helped them develop their knacks and maybe learn new ones. Working on power, but spending precious little time on virtue.

"I will choose the land for them," said the Prophet.

"We will choose together."

"I already chose. Far west, in the mountains, there is an undrinkable salt lake, and a river into it from a better lake, where fish live. The land is good. You would not displace any Reds because that land is holy to them, they do not live there."

"They won't like *us* living there, either," said Alvin.

"Will that place be good for your people? It's a long walk across the prairie and the mountains."

"We can do it, because we have to."

"Great need does not confer great strength," said the Prophet.

"It doesn't stop people from complaining or arguing, either, but it does help them keep going."

29

IN THE WATERSPOUT on the Mizzippy, Tenskwa-Tawa led Alvin into the whirlwind and they rose up within the eye of the storm. Just as he had done, when he first taught Alvin how to see.

This time, Tenskwa-Tawa was so at ease with this ability of his that he was able to choose what Alvin saw. It was a flat plain between high mountains, with a large lake at the northwestern corner. Must be the salt lake.

"There's the salt lake," said Tenskwa-Tawa, gesturing toward the only lake they could see.

"Thick grass, no trees," said Alvin.

"You people cut down all the trees wherever you go. This will save you time."

Alvin pointed. "There's a tree."

"Cottonwood. Not good for much, not even cotton," said Tenskwa-Tawa.

"The way folks name things," said Alvin.

"You want to know the name of that lake?"

Alvin could see the Prophet's delight in what he was going to say.

"In every Red language, it's called the Great Salt Lake."

"Sounds like the name goes with the thing."

"You want to know the name of that valley where your people will live?"

Alvin didn't need to answer, since Tenskwa-Tawa was going to tell him no matter what.

"Great Salt Lake Valley."

Alvin gave a little hoot of laughter.

"But you will build the Crystal City there?" asked the Prophet.

"Already built it here."

"Going to leave it behind. Can't carry it across the plains and the mountains."

"Think I can't make a wagon big enough?" asked Alvin.

"I think you can't find tall enough trees to let you make that wagon."

"Not in that treeless valley."

Red Prophet silently moved their viewpoint to the middle of the valley, facing east. These were high, rugged mountains, and between them, heavily wooded canyons.

"Look at the trees in those canyons."

Alvin looked.

Tenskwa-Tawa said, "Try not to cut them all down at once."

"We'll cut what we need and no more."

"Whites need so much more of everything than Reds."

"We live a different way."

"You clear land where a thousand things grow, and you plant only one thing."

"Easier to harvest that way."

"White boy Maker has an answer for everything."

"Not answers. I got none of those. But ideas? Guesses? I think of those all the time. Most of them worthless, but my mind keeps trying to deliver the goods."

"We speak truth to each other?"

"Always," said Alvin. "So far, anyway. You planning to lie to me?"

"I do not tell you all that I know. But you would be angry if I don't tell you this."

"Go ahead. I wouldn't want to be angry."

"A plot to kill *you* carried you across the river, to find a place for you and the people who trust you."

Alvin waited.

"Finding you gone, their assassination plan has given way to a plan many argued for in the first place. Kill all the witches. They have almost a thousand men gathering in three places around Crystal City."

"Is this going to be a massacre, like Tippy-Canoe?"

"My people bore the slaughter. Yours will not. They will use their knacks to defend themselves."

Alvin thought about some of the knacks. Many would be utterly useless against an enemy. But there were firestarters among them, some who could start fires a ways off. He himself had trained a couple of earthshakers. One of them had opened a crack in the Earth—a deep one. Alvin had made him close it back up, but he couldn't. It took the other earthshaker to help him get it closed.

If I were there, I could melt all their weapons unfired so the knackles wouldn't have to expose how terrifyingly powerful they could be. A couple of soldier-swallowing clefts in the Earth, and he didn't think many of the thousand-man army would stay anywhere near Crystal City. Fires popping up in all their ammunition, so their powderhorns blew up on their hips? Everybody would throw away their ammunition as they fled.

Then the word would get out. We went to drive the witches into the river or into the ground, but they had such terrible powers. They did this and this, and that and that. Some of the stories would be true. All of them would be believed. How could an elected government ignore such a general panic? There would be no refuge of freedom left—except across the river, with the Reds.

They want us to leave. *I* want us to leave. So just let us sell our farms, buy or build wagons and rafts to cross the river, and you'll never see us more.

Tenskwa-Tawa said, "Think of your Bible. Moses finally frightens Pharaoh into letting the Israelites go. But how soon does he change his mind and send his chariot soldiers after them?"

"It was too dangerous to let all those Israelites go into the lands of Pharaoh's enemies," said Alvin. "He was afraid he would face them in battle, when they were armed and trained. Better to kill them all now."

"The only Reds left in the East are the Irrakwa and Cherriky. The ones who chose to live White. They are doing very well. But Whites remember when there was war between our peoples. When you have gathered all your knacky people in the West, far from the river. Your enemies don't know where you are. You could be building an army with knacks *and* cannons, ready to cross the Mizzippy with a million bitter and angry Reds beside your knacky Whites."

"So withdrawing all my people across the Mizzippy won't work for long."

"Long enough, maybe. As long as you and I are both alive, nobody can cross the river to harm us."

"You're getting old."

"And you're in constant peril. How long will we both live?"

"Do you have a plan?"

"I am not leader of my people after I am dead. You are not Alvin Maker after you are dead. There will be leaders after us."

"But we're so good and wise." Alvin didn't know if Tenskwa-Tawa would hear his ironic tone.

"There will be good and wise people after us. The future is in *their* hands."

"Suppose that your protections on the river fail, and New England, the Crown Colonies, and the United States all combine in one vast invasion."

"They all despise each other."

"Not as much as they despise Reds," said Alvin. "And not as much as they fear and hate knackles."

"So you try to build your knackles into a trained army, able to withstand assaults. You bring your army to the water's edge, and when they attack across the river, you will sink all their boats and suffocate all their officers, before any sets foot on the shore."

"What will you Reds do?"

"We will kneel and bear it. We have taken an oath to live in peace."

"Then let us protect you."

"A noble thought. Do you know the best thing you can do to protect us?"

"What?"

"Stay on your own side of the river and don't take refuge among us."

"Then we will all die."

"But *we* won't. Why should my people shoulder the burden of *your* people's safety."

"You're right. It's wrong of us to take refuge among you. But that's our only alternative to destruction, isn't it? What do you see in this wall of water?"

"What do *you* see."

"Weeping. Everybody I love, weeping."

Tenskwa-Tawa nodded. "I have seen that, too. But what do they weep for?"

"Their defeat at the hands of these thousand men you spoke of. The hundreds of Crystal City men who died in defense of their families."

"There are so many reasons for people to weep," said the Prophet. "Gratitude for a prayer answered. Honoring the victories of great men."

"Standing beside your baby's grave," said Alvin. Then, breaking down a little, he said, "I'm not like you Reds. My emotions spill out too easy."

"We feel everything that you feel," said Tenskwa-Tawa. "Maybe more.

But we choose to show our feelings with hands, feet, bows, arrows, hatchets. Or our tender feelings we show in the privacy of tepee or hogan or wickiup or counselhouse. Or alone, where only the Great Spirit can see. But in our silence, we feel everything all the more sharply for not being able to show it."

"I have not forgotten the battle at Tippy-Canoe," said Alvin.

"Those were my people," said Tenskwa-Tawa. "I knew every one of them by name, even the children. I knew them and I loved them all." Then, to Alvin's surprise, Tenskwa-Tawa broke down in tears, in sobs, gripping Alvin's shoulders and almost hanging from them. The waterspout was slowing, there were fewer visions, then none, as they sank down toward the river. Just before they touched the water, Alvin said, "Walk with me, my friend," and he made the water solid beneath their feet as they supported each other to the shore.

The reports came in all night. Alvin had only just left, and the angry mobs were already forming. Oh, some of them pretended to be under military discipline, but by all reports there was no difference between the mobs in their brutality and hatred and fear. There were three credible reports of murders by the mobs, and one report of an old man who shot the leader of one mob and then saw them club his old wife to death, a senile old lady who didn't even remember her husband's name. Clubbed her to death before they set him on fire.

Fighting back only makes things worse, the message was.

The leaders of Crystal City came together in counsel all that long night of raids and killings and terror and grief. At one point, Calvin Miller even showed up. Eliza went to him and remonstrated loudly enough that it was disrupting the meeting.

So Margaret went to them, calmed and quieted Eliza, then led Calvin out of the building. "Calvin, only a few of us know of the part you played in the conspiracy to kill Alvin—"

"I would never—"

"Yet you did," said Margaret. "And the men behind these mob attacks are the same ones you broke bread with."

"That's right, I know them, I should be in there to advise—"

"Hush Calvin. Listen to yourself. Who would listen to advice from you, even if it was wise? Some of those men inside are already thinking about kidnapping you—"

"And I'll be declared not guilty in the trial, because I never laid a hand on Alvin, and their little plot evaporated when he crossed the river."

"Calvin, you poor naive child, there's not a man of them who is thinking of putting you on *trial*."

Calvin covered his face with his hands. "You warned me, Margaret."

"I don't think I did. You stopped listening to my advice years ago, so I stopped giving it."

"You cut way back on the advice, but you didn't *stop*."

"Alvin loves you. He has already forgiven you for the foolishness of that plot. Here's the message he told me to give you: 'I *can* be killed, brother, if I receive so many wounds so quickly that I can't heal myself fast enough.' "

"That's like Samson telling the secret of his strength to Delilah."

"Except Delilah played him false," said Margaret. "Nothing requires you to do the same."

The door opened and Measure leaned out. "Margaret, we need your counsel right now."

Calvin clung to her for just a moment. Then he let her go into the house, while he stayed outside and kept explaining to himself that none of this was his fault.

30

ALVIN WOKE FROM a very comfortable sleep on a buffalo robe. Another had been spread over him by Becca, Tenskwa-Tawa's sister-in-law. The great Ta-Kumsaw's wife. Who had just poked him with her toe.

Alvin knew her at once—she had been the keeper of the American Loom. "How can you be here?" Alvin asked.

"I retired. I've woven enough in my life. You've met the boy who took my place. And my daughter Wieza weaves for everybody west of the Mizzippy, and north of the Great Lakes. Maybe a fifth as many threads as *I* had to weave."

Alvin chuckled as he got out from under the buffalo robe, fully clothed, of course, with his knives where they belonged. By appearance he could be a Red of Tenskwa-Tawa's tribe. Except the part about being White. Under a tan, under the normal amount of grime from having swum the river and not bathed yet. So, not all that white.

"Well, Becca, I'm right glad to see you. And now I don't have to fear what you'll discover in your weaving."

"Never anything to fear. Life is life. Yours has been a good one. Crossed the ocean and back. Ireland. The boy hardly knew what to do with your thread, until you assembled those people and brought them across the ocean."

"Now he's fit me back in?"

"He fit you with the Irishmen, and then fit the Irish into the small riverside location of Crystal City. Then Wieza insisted that *that* one had to be woven into the west, not the east."

"I'm . . . I really am happy to hear that. It might mean that maybe I'm making a right decision."

"Just remember, Alvin. When you're faced with important choices, there are many wrong choices but there might be many right choices as well."

"And you won't advise me."

"I don't have any advice. When someone learns something believable about their future, something they don't want to have to face, they go out of their way to get as far as possible from that terrible future—only to find out that everything they did to avoid it is exactly what caused it to come to pass."

"I've read *Oedipus Rex*. Not in the original Greek, of course."

"Oh, I enjoy talking with you, Alvin. I've missed you. So has my husband. But I was sent to waken you because you have visitors coming."

"And they are?"

"Well, first, there's your brother."

Alvin lay back down on the buffalo robe and pulled the other over him.

"Not *that* brother," said Becca. "The one who's a little taller than you. Oh, yes. Measure."

Alvin got out of bed again. "Who's with him?"

"You'll know them when you see them. I'm too old to memorize lists of names of people I've never met."

Barely saying a goodbye, Alvin jogged away from his tepee and headed for a patch of undergrowth where the local Red men directed their urine. Any plants that urine was going to kill were dead already.

Then he ran on, feeling the Greensong, which was welcome this groggy morning. He reached Tenskwa-Tawa, and to his surprise, Ta-Kumsaw, the great military leader of the Reds, was with him. They greeted with a tight embrace. They had been in battle together. Alvin had healed him, or he would have died that day. And he was the brother of the Prophet, so he was Red royalty twice over.

"Some other people are here, you oblivious scoundrel." It was Measure speaking.

"I saw you two days ago," said Alvin.

"A month's worth of trouble has come since then."

Alvin looked at Arthur Stuart. Definitely a man now. I shouldn't treat him at all like a boy anymore. It sets a bad example for others.

John Binder spoke up. "Alvin, the army of those assassins, about a thousand men, they're harrying inside the boundaries of Crystal City."

"Just on the edges, so far," said Verily Cooper. "But three people are already killed, and orchards chopped down, barns burnt, fields burned over. And the hatred from their mouths. Everyone is terrified, because the mobbers taunt them about how it's too bad Alvin Smith isn't here to save them."

"It's the one thing the mobbers and knackles agree on," said Measure.

Arthur Stuart spoke up. "Obviously, they want you to come back and lead them and, of course, save them."

"Among all their knacks," said Alvin, "and common sense, they've got all they need to fight off a thousand."

Verily, John, Measure, Arthur, Ta-Kumsaw, and Tenskwa-Tawa looked at each other, saying nothing.

"People cannot fight," said Ta-Kumsaw, "if they do not know that they are well led."

"I've never led anybody in battle," said Alvin.

"You were with me and saw *me* lead," said Ta-Kumsaw. "Warriors from many tribes, some of them enemies forever until then."

"As I remember it, we lost that battle," said Alvin, "and you were killed."

"I had a friend who bandaged me up," said Ta-Kumsaw.

"They don't understand why you left," said John Binder. "They know you can't be killed, bullets don't touch you, you can stick your enemies' feet to the ground—"

"I *can* be killed," said Alvin. "I hope you all know that."

"When you left and these troubles started," said Verily, "they still trusted that you were working for their good. What can we tell them?"

Alvin looked at Tenskwa-Tawa and Ta-Kumsaw.

Ta-Kumsaw said, "Because he would do anything for a friend, my brother Tenskwa-Tawa has granted permission for all the citizens of Crystal City to cross over the Mizzippy and live in the West."

"Far in the West," said Tenskwa-Tawa. "A good land with no regular residents. Reds and Whites should not collide, as long as we respect each other's boundaries."

Measure laughed.

"It's White people who have broken all the treaties," said the Prophet, "settling in lands they promised would belong forever to the Reds."

"Oh, I'm sure you're right," said Measure. "But on the other hand, I haven't met any tribe of Reds who act like they know what a boundary *is*."

Ta-Kumsaw spoke up. "Every tribe has young men who have no way of gaining honor and fame except in battle, counting coups, slaying, bringing home women and children to serve the tribe, grow up to be part of the tribe. That is how young men have always earned the honor of the tribe."

"They would raid an isolated settlement," said Tenskwa-Tawa, "but instead of counting coups like honorable men, the White settlers fired muskets and rifles at these young raiders. When some of the warriors were killed or wounded, the young men were outraged. They began to kill for revenge, and then in later raids, they started out killing, to put all the musketmen out of action."

"And your leaders couldn't rein them in?" asked Verily.

"And *your* leaders couldn't keep White families from settling in our lands?" asked Tenskwa-Tawa.

"This is the kind of thing that drove us to war in the first place," said Ta-Kumsaw. "We couldn't even punish those young raiders, because we needed their skill and experience in our wars with the Crown Colonies and the United States."

"But now the Mizzippy stands between them and you," said Alvin.

"I will not live forever," said Tenskwa-Tawa. "It is my responsibility—*our* responsibility—to prepare our people for war, when the fog dispels, when the White soldiers cross the river to take revenge on us."

"Revenge for what, after all these years of peace?" asked Arthur Stuart.

"Memories of wrongs done to us are long," said Ta-Kumsaw. "The same is true of your people."

Arthur thrust out his palms to block those words. "Not *my* people," said Arthur Stuart. "*I'm* not White."

"You're half White," said Tenskwa-Tawa, "and that's the half that you've lived in through most of your life. And whatever color you are, Arthur Stuart, you are not Red."

"So if we settle by the Great Salt Lake," said Alvin, "what happens when the war you foretell begins. Do you start by slaughtering our people?"

Tenskwa-Tawa and Ta-Kumsaw glanced at each other.

Ta-Kumsaw said, "To leave you deep in our country would be dangerous, if you decided you were more White than you were grateful to us for your sanctuary."

"Ta-Kumsaw and I discussed this," said Tenskwa-Tawa. "I said that you would never turn on us, and so your people wouldn't either."

"And *I* said," answered Ta-Kumsaw, "that you can't erase the loyalty your people have to their country, their state or colony. At the very least, some of your people will slip away and join the Whites, serving as scouts."

"Like me and my brother," said Tenskwa-Tawa, "you will not live forever. Who will lead your people after you are dead? Will he keep the covenants we make here?"

Verily stood up. "We're wasting time here. We're not making decisions about twenty years from now. We're talking about tonight, and tomorrow morning. The mobs will be back, larger in number because we offered no resistance so they think it's safe to burn out the witches."

"Just knowing you're back in Crystal City might make them think twice," said John Binder.

"How can they think twice if they haven't thought once?" asked Arthur Stuart.

"Is this invasion of our city being controlled by someone?" asked Measure.

"It has to be," said John Binder. "The attacks began at the same time, from every point of the compass."

"What did Margaret say?" asked Alvin.

"We . . . didn't talk to her. We left so early this morning," said John Binder.

"The person who can tell us most about who our enemies are," said Alvin, "and you didn't ask her?"

The Whites all looked embarrassed. But not Arthur Stuart. "I talked to her," he said.

They all looked at him, surprised, maybe even annoyed. But not Alvin—he looked pleased. "Did she give you any message for me?"

Arthur Stuart looked down at his feet. "She said to ask you to forgive her, but sometimes she knows too little and sometimes she knows too much, but she can't give you any guidance about your decision."

"What decision? Which decision?" asked Verily Cooper.

"Whether Alvin should stay on this side of the Mizzippy or not."

"What do you think she wanted me to do?" Alvin asked Arthur Stuart.

"All the years you known me," said Arthur, "and all the years you known your wife, and you want me to *guess* what she secretly wants and doesn't choose to tell me? Can *you* do that?"

Alvin smiled wanly. "No sir, I cannot."

"Nobody can," said Measure. "If Arthur told you, Alvin, would you do what she wanted, or the opposite?"

"Is this how White men give counsel?" asked Ta-Kumsaw. "You all tell each other what you don't know, which is everything, because what you do know is nothing. Alvin, you need better counselors."

"Can we offer him better counsel?" asked Tenskwa-Tawa.

"As long as you're on this side of the river," said Ta-Kumsaw, "you will not be killed."

"Do you *know* this?" asked Alvin.

"How can a man know what has not happened yet?" asked Ta-Kumsaw.

The Prophet smiled. "Ta-Kumsaw, don't you know that when Margaret looks into the heartfires, she sees some of the future? Not all, and maybe not much, but *something*. And Alvin can do this a little, too."

"If you can see the future," said Ta-Kumsaw, a little disgusted, "why do you look for counsel?"

"I didn't ask these fellows to cross the river," said Alvin.

"But you needed to know what was happening to your city. To your *people*," said Verily Cooper. He looked at Tenskwa-Tawa. "Could *you* have told him?"

"Can't tell what I don't know," said the Prophet.

"Isn't it a prophet's *job* to know?" said Verily.

"I am called the *Red* Prophet for a reason," said Tenskwa-Tawa.

"So you can't tell us anything because we're White?" said Verily.

"I can't find out anything to tell you because I'm *not* White," said Tenskwa-Tawa. "If I knew the outcomes of all your choices, I would tell my friend Alvin. I would tell him what he *should* do, if I knew it. I would tell him what I *want* him to do. If I knew it."

"None of us are prophets, Red or White," said Measure. "We have to decide like ordinary human beings—not knowing how anything will turn out."

"Alvin," said John Binder, "the people are frightened. I don't have to see into their heartfires to know that they feel like you have abandoned them—to save yourself. *I'm* not saying that, but it's being said on every side."

"Is anybody trying to organize the people to fight back?" asked Alvin.

"Is that what you want us to do?" asked Measure.

Alvin thought about this for a while. Maybe three minutes of silence, which can feel like forever if you don't have the power to end it.

Alvin tried to imagine the likely outcomes. If the knackles fought, they might well defeat these mobs. But most of them would go back and get more men to pick up weapons or torches and return, this time with more determination to kill and conquer.

If the citizens of Crystal City killed any of the mobbers, they wouldn't tell their neighbors that *they* had killed knackles first. No, they would say that the witches killed innocent passersby, because with Alvin Smith to lead them, they were going to rampage throughout the country, killing whoever and wherever they wanted.

It wouldn't matter whether they used their knacks to protect themselves or not—the mobbers would *say* that they had. They'd invent stories of the terrible magic the witches used against them. Word of these outrages would spread much farther than Noisy River or Wobbish country. There'd be militias called up as far as Carthage City. It was possible that even the Irrakwa and the Cherriky would send warriors. Reds feared witches as much as any White.

It took Alvin only a couple of minutes to think through these ideas. Then he tried to think what would happen if he went back across the Mizzippy. Word would spread mighty fast, but the people would want more than his presence. He would have to go out and confront the mobs. One of them, anyway. He would have to melt their guns, fasten their feet to the ground, and that would be only the beginning, because disarming and immobilizing them wouldn't make them change their minds about wanting to drive the witches from the east bank of the river, and might persuade many that all the witches would have to die.

I can't be everywhere at once, thought Alvin. When I'm in the north, they'll come marauding and murdering in the south and east. My presence will not make the citizens any safer. It might provoke even more murderous action, drawing on militias from farther away.

"My friends," said Alvin, "I don't see a path that leads to peace or safety for anyone."

"Except if you stay here," said Verily. "That will mean safety for *you*."

"Verily," said Alvin. "You held the plow with me. You helped me choose and mark this place."

"I did," said Verily. "Did we do that in order to have it all end in rivers of blood turning the Mizzippy red?"

"We did that because the plow demanded to be used, and our people needed a refuge."

"It began that way," said Verily, "but it's no refuge now."

"I didn't *flee* here," said Alvin. "I didn't know the mobs would strike when I accidentally dodged their conspiracy to kill me. I came here to find safety for us all. A land in the West, surrounded by mountains, a good soil, with water in the canyons. We can irrigate and grow enough crops to feed us all. A thousand miles and high mountains between us and our enemies. Would they remember us when they couldn't see us?"

"We'd be the monsters in every story that people tell their children to scare them into staying in bed and obeying during the daytime." John Binder shook his head. "But as long as they couldn't cross the river, killing us all won't be their highest priority. They're already fixing to go to war between the United States and the Crown Colonies over the matter of slavery. That will keep their minds off of us for a while, I think."

"Do you *know* this?" asked Ta-Kumsaw.

"I know how to hold people together, when they want to be held, and I can feel them break apart, I can feel their fear and hatred."

"So there will be war in the East?" asked Tenskwa-Tawa. "What if one side or the other begs you to join in, with all your knacks, to save their cause?"

"How could they ask us, if they can't find us?" asked Alvin.

"We would let them through. We would lead their delegation to you so they could beg for your help, and you could say no directly to them."

"Would we say no?" asked Arthur Stuart. Alvin knew that he was thinking of his mother, who had died to save him from slavery. Freeing slaves would mean much to Arthur.

"We're talking about twenty years from now, again," said Verily Cooper. "More of our people will be murdered today. *Today.* Not in twenty years."

Measure spoke up, and his voice demanded their attention. "If they all go to war against us, it will unite them in hatred and fear of us. It might preserve the peace between North and South for a while."

"So we should be slaughtered to save the lives of the people slaughtering us?" demanded Verily.

"No one in this gathering is your enemy, Verily," said John Binder.

They could all see the rage boil up in Verily. But as he looked into John Binder's eyes, his temper waned. "You're right, of course, John. My anger at our enemies should not be turned on my friends."

John Binder smiled and touched Verily's arm.

Alvin had not understood the power of John Binder's knack. A tear came to Verily's eye, as his heart softened toward the men around him.

"I have an idea," said Arthur Stuart. "Put Eliza in charge of the defense of Crystal City."

"Maybe I should," said Alvin.

"Nobody in the city has any knowledge of war," said Measure. "She'd be as good a bet as anyone else."

"Ta-Kumsaw knows the ways of war," said John Binder.

"We'll not drag Reds into a war among White men," said Alvin. "Whatever happens is in our hands."

Measure said, "Alvin, we don't know how they'll react if they know that you've come back. They're afraid of your knacks."

"What will Calvin be doing with *his* knacks?" asked Verily. "Is he your enemy, Alvin?"

"I don't know what he wants," said Alvin. "But I know he's my brother."

"He may be your brother," said Tenskwa-Tawa, "but he will never cross the river to this side."

"That's good," said Measure. "Alvin, will you come over the river with us, just to see what our enemies do? We can make better decisions then."

"I don't want to use my knacks to kill anyone," said Alvin.

"Then don't," said Arthur Stuart.

"If I cross the river," said Alvin, "will I stand alone against the foe?"

"Never," said Measure. "I'll be with you, always."

"I know you will," said Alvin. "But what about you, Verily Cooper? John Binder?"

"I know I'll do whatever you need me to do," said Verily Cooper.

John Binder nodded. "I'd swear an oath," he said, "but if my love for you isn't enough to hold me by your side, can an oath rescue my courage and honor?"

"I believe them," said Tenskwa-Tawa.

"So do I," said Alvin.

Arthur stepped into the middle of the group and faced Alvin. He's as tall as me, thought Alvin. And he's barefoot, while I'm in boots.

"Alvin," said Arthur Stuart, "if you cross that river, you'll die. It will be your death. Don't you see that?"

"Of course I do," said Alvin. "Because nothing but my death will satisfy them."

"The whole city will stand with you against them," said John Binder.

"They'll want to," said Alvin. "But we can't control what our enemies will do, or what they *can* do."

"Don't cross the river," said Arthur Stuart.

"Can I keep myself safe, Arthur Stuart, when my people are dying or being driven from their homes?"

"I refuse to live in a world without you in it," said Arthur.

"He's not dying, he's just crossing the river," said Verily Cooper.

"Are you sure there's any difference between those two things?" demanded Arthur Stuart. "No, you're not. I love Alvin Smith more than all the others put together. Do you understand that? I can't ask for his death."

"That's not what we're doing," said John Binder.

"Do you *know* that?" asked Arthur Stuart.

Alvin reached out his hand and rested it on Arthur Stuart's shoulder. "My brother, my friend," he said to Arthur Stuart. "Come away with me for a few minutes."

The others stayed where they were, as Alvin led Arthur over toward the river.

"Don't treat me like a child," said Arthur Stuart. "I'm as wise as any of them, because none of us know the outcome of anything."

"I've already made up my mind, Arthur. I wanted to talk to you about something else."

"What, then?" asked Arthur Stuart, wiping tears away from his eyes.

"No matter what happens," said Alvin, "they will not relent. The only safety for our people is on this side of the river, and farther west, among the mountains, by that salt lake. I'm not sure what Tenskwa-Tawa saw, but before he mentioned that place to me, I had already seen it. In the walls of the Crystal City I have seen it many times. But I never saw myself leading them."

"That proves nothing," muttered Arthur.

"I saw *you* at their head."

Arthur said nothing.

"And when I saw you in that vision, my heart was at peace. Because you can complete the work we've begun here."

"I can't build the crystal blocks," said Arthur Stuart.

"You haven't tried," said Alvin. "But it doesn't matter. Building another Crystal City will not be your purpose."

"What, then?" asked Arthur.

"A city of peace," said Alvin. "Where no one will be poor, because everyone shares gladly."

"So you want me to build a city for angels, is that it?" asked Arthur.

"Yes," said Alvin. "You can lead, you can teach, but they can only become angels if they want to be."

"Are you talking *literally*?"

"I don't know where God goes to recruit his angels. Let's just say, the land, the cities you build in the West, they'll be established to bring the pure in heart from everywhere, to live together in peace."

"Why is this suddenly my job? You haven't prepared me for this."

"Yes I have," said Alvin.

"Nobody will obey me or even listen to me."

"Yes they will," said Alvin.

"Do you *know* that?" asked Arthur Stuart.

"I have enough faith in you to leave my people in your hands."

"You expect to die," said Arthur Stuart. "You've decided to go back, and you expect to die."

"My heart is as calm as a summer's morning," said Alvin.

"As long as your heart is beating, I don't care how calm it is," said Arthur Stuart.

"The people want me back," said Alvin.

"Because they're afraid," said Arthur, with disdain.

"They're right to be afraid. Everything and everyone they love is in jeopardy. Do you remember what that's like?"

Tears streamed down Arthur's face. "You know I never really knew my mother. She died without my knowing her."

"And yet you think of her every day."

Arthur looked away.

"And you loved Goody Guester like a mother," said Alvin, "and you lost her at the hands of a murderer. So are my people *wrong* to be afraid? Are they wrong to value their loved ones more than they value me?"

"I'm not ready to leave you yet."

"Yes, you are," said Alvin. "Stop thinking about me, and think about how to organize a migration across the Mizzippy. With luck, you won't have to acquire a whole fleet of boats. There are three people in the city who can make water freeze. Together, maybe they can freeze the Mizzippy hard enough to drive wagons over it."

"Can't you just make us a bridge?" asked Arthur Stuart.

"You need to get them to accomplish this migration together, depending on each other."

"You do it," said Arthur.

"If I can, I will. But I still need you to plan it. I'll have other things on my mind."

Arthur Stuart smiled wryly. "What do *you* have to worry about?"

"Nothing," said Alvin, "because my legacy is in your hands. If my life has little value to my friends"—he gestured toward the others—"then it has even less value to me. I just want to spend that last coin of mine to purchase a future for my people. I have chosen the best man I know to be their leader."

"Measure," said Arthur Stuart.

"What about him?"

"He's the best man you know," said Arthur Stuart.

"He'll be busy," said Alvin.

"You grownups are always busy."

"You're one of us now." Alvin clapped his hand on Arthur's shoulder and started the two of them returning to the others

"Whatever you said to him," said Ta-Kumsaw, "you made a decision."

"How soon can you launch canoes to take us back to the eastern shore?" asked Alvin.

"The canoes are waiting at the river's edge," said Ta-Kumsaw.

"You knew what I would decide."

"Everybody knew it," said Ta-Kumsaw. "Only this one had the courage to say it outright."

"How did you know?" asked Alvin. "*I* didn't know."

"The Maker is the one who is part of what he makes," said Ta-Kumsaw. "Isn't that the rule?"

"And I'm part of Crystal City," said Alvin.

The goodbyes were brief as the Whites all returned to the shore. Alvin looked at the Prophet and his brother up on the bank, watching the canoes launch. His heart was full of love for them. So much of his life had been shaped by them. They had been true to him, and kind. They were his friends, and they would keep their oath to save his people, if it was possible.

But they can't save me.

Then they came out of the fog, three canoes paddled by silent young Red warriors—or farmers, or herdsmen, or hunters, or all those things. There was some splashing, because Verily and John hadn't had as much experience with canoes as Alvin, Measure, and Arthur.

Alvin was the last out of his boat. He bade a silent farewell to the Red paddlers, who solemnly acknowledged him.

Then Alvin turned toward the wharf, where a large, powerful man was standing. "Alvin, you son of fools with all the wit of your ancestros!"

"Mike Fink!" cried Alvin. "Does the Hio even flow when you're this far away?"

"I told it to keep up its work till I got back," said Mike.

By now Alvin was on the shore, then up on the wharf, and Mike wrapped him in a huge embrace. Alvin thought of Davy Crockett and his bear, and wondered if the bear would have been a match for Mike Fink.

While Mike held him, the riverman spoke softly in his ear—softly for *him*, because there was no chance he wasn't heard by the other men gathered on the wharf.

"That boy told me you're expecting to die," said Mike.

"He spoke out of turn," said Alvin. "I'm not giving up any time soon."

"You can say that again," said Mike, "because while I can still draw breath, no harm will come to you."

"That's a comfort," said Alvin, "because if you ain't been kilt yet, you're never going to die."

31

"THIS HERE WOMAN says she knows your brother."

Calvin sneered. "Everybody knows my brother."

"She says that Alvin was sweet on her."

"A ridiculous lie," said Calvin. "She might believe it, but it doesn't mean it was ever true."

"She says he put a baby in her."

Calvin laughed. "Would her name be Amy Sump?" he asked.

"So you *know* who she is!"

"She and her family have been trying to sue my brother for paternity and breach of promise. My brother wasn't even in the same state as her when she got herself pregnant."

Amy's eyes flashed. "He can walk like the wind! He can go through walls! He don't even have to be in the same continent as me. He came into my room when I was dressing—"

"Stop that," said the calm man on horseback. "We're not in court."

"I used to be a pretty, slender young thing," said Amy.

Calvin chuckled.

"Enough!" said the man. "We're here to serve papers on Alvin Smith."

"And all you found was me," said Calvin.

"For all I know, you *are* him."

"That's not him," said Amy.

"Since your star witness has just exonerated me from the crime of being Alvin Smith, could your brutes let go of me now?" asked Calvin.

The leader nodded, and the hands that had dragged Calvin out of the inn let go of him.

"He's got knacks, too!" cried Amy. "He's a witch, too!"

Calvin shook his head. "If you think my brother's a witch, why do you want him to be the father of your bastard? The lad must be what, ten years old?"

"You have no right to interrogate her," said the man.

"And you had no right to drag me away from my dinner," said Calvin. "What's your authority?"

The man held up a folded paper. "A summons."

"You can give it to me, and I'll serve the paper on him as soon as he comes back to Crystal City."

"He's back," said the summoner.

"Then you know more than I do," said Calvin. "Mostly when people go over the river, they never come back."

The summoner's horse stamped and moved to the side a little. The men on foot also shuffled their feet or took a step left or right. Or back. Nobody stepped closer to Calvin.

"Do you have any so-called 'knacks'?" asked the summoner.

"Nary a one," said Calvin. "I was a great disappointment to my family, and to myself, I must add. I *wish* I had me a knack, but is wishing a crime now?"

"Alvin's brother, and no knack at all?"

"I'm the runt of the litter. Anybody who knows me can tell you."

"I heard you call yourself a seventh son, too."

Calvin laughed. "You never knew a man to brag about things he cannot do? You've never been on the river, have you. Yes, I've bragged like that. I've also said I'm hung like a horse."

"Enough!" shouted the summoner. "We came all the way from Carthage City to serve these—"

"You're a liar," said Calvin, as sweetly as those words could be said. "*You* may have come from Carthage, but the men with you, they've been lurking around Crystal City for days. You hired them after you got here."

"I hired nobody," said the summoner. "These is volunteers."

"What are they hoping for? To hang Alvin Smith, or get at his golden plow?"

"Ain't no golden plow," said one of the brutes.

"The first true thing that's been said here today," said Calvin. "Never was a plow, still doesn't exist, because even Alvin Smith can't turn iron into gold."

"I know it exists," said the summoner. "Makepeace Smith saw it himself."

"Makepeace Smith only wanted to keep Alvin on as his apprentice past his time."

By now, everybody from inside the inn had spilled out onto the dooryard, which had been incompetently cobbled fairly recently, and was as likely to send you to the ground as keep you out of the mud. The inn's customers considerably outnumbered the summoner's crew. "You've done your business," said the innkeeper from the door. "You assaulted one of my guests without provocation, and—"

The summoner waved his paper again. "I have a summons to serve! From Carthage City!"

"Carthage?" asked the innkeeper. "You got no jurisdiction here."

"You a lawyer?" asked the summoner. "Jurisdiction is a pretty fancy word."

"Whatever you imagine your authority to be," said the innkeeper, "I sent a runner to the city the minute you dragged this man out of my public room, and your authority, if you have any, will end when the deputy arrives and we charge you with assault and unlawful detainment and any other damn felony we decide to lay against you. These are my witnesses!"

The whole company from the inn's common room murmured or growled their affirmation.

Calvin found that he actually felt very happy right now. It hadn't often happened in his life that a group of people were on his side.

The sound of hoofbeats not far off intruded into the silence of the standoff.

"Here they come," said the innkeeper. "Sounds like ten or a dozen, and they'll be men trained to shoot from the saddle."

The summoner wheeled his horse. Amy Sump's horse followed suit. The men on foot turned around and jogged toward him, followed him as he trotted his horse away.

Calvin turned and walked up to the innkeeper. "You were an uncommon good friend today."

"Nobody abducts a body from my common room," said the innkeeper.

Other guests were going back in, sidling past the innkeeper, who still stood in front of the door.

The horses came closer, and then they were in the road just beyond the dooryard, where the summoner had been only a minute or two before.

"Thanks for coming, lads," said the innkeeper.

"Deputy's not here," said one of the posse, "but we decided not to wait for him."

"That was well done," said the innkeeper. "Man claiming to be a summoner from Carthage City was fixing to take this fellow to jail. I said he got no jurisdiction here."

"A lawful summons from a Carthage judge has legal force throughout the United States," said one of the posse.

"You a lawyer?" asked the innkeeper.

"I happen to have that honor. Verily Cooper, Esquire, at your service, sir."

"So he *did* have a right to—"

"He had no right to do anything to Calvin Miller," said Verily. "He only had the right to serve his summons on Alvin Smith in person, and no authority to use any kind of force to do it."

"Well, then, he exceeded his authority. Dragged this man—"

"Calvin Miller," said Verily.

"And now his dinner's gotten cold, I bet," said the innkeeper.

"Then you might give a thought to going inside and getting Calvin Miller a fresh hot serving of . . . whatever you're serving. Thank you for looking after one of our citizens."

"My pleasure. By the way, Mr. Cooper, I have a knack myself."

"I'm glad to hear it," said Verily.

"Sure ain't a knack for cooking," said the last of the guests as he went inside.

"Then why do you always ask for seconds?"

"As an act of Christian charity, to keep someone else from eating it."

Members of the posse chuckled at that.

"What's your knack, Mr. Keeper?" asked Verily.

"I have a way with iron," said the innkeeper. "Not a powerful knack, but I think that summoner is going to find that his mount has a nail worked up into the quick."

"You pushed a horseshoe nail deeper into the hoof?" asked Verily. "What did that horse ever do to you?"

"It carried a Carthage summoner into my dooryard," said the innkeeper.

Verily chuckled. "Well done, sir, and I hope the horse recovers soon."

"I reckon he will," said the innkeeper.

"With a knack for iron, sir," said Verily, "why do you keep a roadhouse?"

"Cause who would look for an iron knack in an innkeeper?" The innkeeper smiled. "Thanks for coming so quick, on only the word of my boy."

"We wouldn't be worth much as defenders if it took us an hour to show up when a mob is causing trouble."

Calvin stood in the dooryard, with only the posse for company.

"Calvin," said Verily.

"Mr. Miller to you, Mr. Cooper," said Calvin.

"So be it, Mr. Miller," said Verily. "What are you doing out here on the fringe of the city?"

"I was eating my dinner before I carried on my journey."

"Where are you headed?" asked Verily.

"To the place where I will conduct my private business," said Calvin.

"Margaret Larner told me something about your business of late," said Verily.

"That woman is such a gossip," said Calvin.

Now it was the posse that murmured and growled.

Calvin turned to them, holding his hand out to his sides. "No need to get angry. If a man can't tease his sister-in-law, there's not much freedom left in the world."

"Do you want a ride back into the city?" asked Verily.

Calvin was pretty sure that Verily knew perfectly well that Crystal City was *not* where Calvin wanted to be about now, with Alvin back from across the river. "Why, I'd gladly ride behind any of these gentlemen here."

Verily held out his hand and pulled his foot out of the stirrup. Calvin raised his foot into the stirrup, took hold of Verily's forearm with both hands, and leapt up onto the horse's back just behind the saddle.

"You're a fine leaper, Mr. Miller," said Verily. "Is that a knack of yours?"

"I'm an athletic sort of fellow," said Calvin. "But I have enough knacks for my needs."

Alvin sat on the settee in his own parlor for the first time in months. He had a copy of the *Crystal Times* open, but he was reading only about three words in ten. Margaret came in, set down a tray of cold cuts and rolls, and sat down beside Alvin.

"You spread a nice meal for such short notice, Miz Larner," said Alvin.

"You look like a man who's missed too many dinners, Mr. Smith," said Margaret.

"I didn't think to come back over the river so soon," he said.

"I know. But the people have been clamoring. Panicking. A few have left on the train, some with wagons on the north road."

"How many?"

"Eight families, but if you hadn't come back, it would have been more and more all day."

"Maybe leaving is the wise thing to do," said Alvin.

"Could be. How did it work out for *you*?"

Alvin rolled his eyes and took a bite of the bread with mustard and cabbage and a fine fat sausage.

"That should put some meat on your bones," said Margaret.

"Don't know about that," said Alvin, with his mouth full, "but it's putting pork in my belly."

"Talking with your mouth full—"

"Makes a muddle of chewing *and* talking," said Alvin.

"You should know that a summoner came with papers to arrest you and take you to Carthage City."

"An actual summons? Not a pus of assassins?"

Margaret smiled at Alvin's term. "A pus of assassins," she echoed.

"Seemed like the right word," said Alvin.

Margaret changed tone. Business now. "We're not making a public announcement of the funeral for the three slain yesterday, because we think that might invite a raid on the mourners."

"Wise choice," said Alvin. "And yet I imagine every soul in Crystal City is planning to be there."

"Armed to the teeth," said Margaret.

"Not so wise."

"Unarmed people are so much easier to massacre, if that's what our enemies have in mind."

"Is it?"

"No," said Margaret. "They will come demanding a conversation with *you*."

"A friendly chat right here in our parlor," said Alvin. "Serving papers on me?"

"They *have* papers, if they get a chance to serve them. Alvin, I'm glad you came back. You are the heart and confidence of these people."

"People who are almost all blessed with knacks," said Alvin, "yet they depend on me to protect them."

"Yes," said Margaret. "They do."

They both bit into their sandwiches and chewed in silence for a moment.

"Don't smack your lips," said Margaret.

"She said, with her mouth full."

Margaret chewed a few more times and then swallowed. "A foolish consistency is the hobgoblin of little minds," she said.

"Emerson again?" asked Alvin. "Just because he wrote it elegantly doesn't make it wise."

"It became wise the moment *I* decided to quote him," said Margaret.

"The last time you recited that, he went on and on, until he was pointing out how great minds are always misunderstood. His examples were Socrates, Jesus, and other people who were killed for their wisdom."

"Most of his examples were *not* killed."

"But Socrates and Jesus were."

"And Galileo went before the Inquisition," said Margaret.

"I know an inquisitor," said Alvin.

"I know. A good man, helping you save so many lives. Galileo's inquisitors were not so good-hearted."

Alvin sighed. "Margaret, it is my considered opinion that by coming back here, I sealed my death warrant."

Margaret set down her sandwich and embraced him. He was still holding his sandwich, and took another bite.

"Your wife hugs you and you don't even stop eating?" asked Margaret.

"You said I was too thin."

"Alvin, I don't know what to tell you. Your heartfire is dark to me. Befogged. I catch glimpses but I don't know what causes what. You might die, yes, but that has *always* been true of your heartfire."

"What does it mean that you can't see clearly?"

"It means that I can't see clearly. My knack is not as reliable as yours. Sometimes I can't see anything. Right now I can't see anything useful."

"So when I need guidance the most . . ."

She hugged him tighter. "You don't need guidance from me," said Margaret. "You always do the right thing."

Alvin rolled his eyes.

"I heard you roll your eyes," she said, her face still pressed against his shoulder.

"I don't always do the right—"

"You always do a good thing. *A* right thing, when there is no *one* best thing."

"You're saying, I should do what I think is best."

"I don't have to say that. When have you not done that?"

"I want to be there for little Vigor to grow up with a father. I want the baby you're carrying right now to know my face."

Margaret pulled away from him. "I'm pregnant?" she asked.

"You didn't know?"

"You've only been home from Ireland a few days," said Margaret.

"Well, we couldn't have made that baby before I went to Ireland, or you'd be swoll up like you were toting a watermelon by now."

"Swoll," said Margaret.

"Do you want to know if it's a boy or a girl?" asked Alvin.

"I'll know soon enough," said Margaret. "This is happy news."

"Yes, I needed something good."

"When did you detect my pregnancy?" she asked.

"When I got home today, twenty minutes ago?" said Alvin.

Margaret picked up her sandwich. "I need this now. I'm eating for two."

"Three," said Alvin.

She stared at him a moment. "Are you saying—"

"Twins," said Alvin. "I couldn't *not* tell you it's going to be twins."

"Alvin, this is our future, you and me, sitting together, thinking about—talking about—our children. Letting big events pass by us without even stirring a wind."

"They're going to have that war no matter what we do," said Alvin, thinking of the big event they had been trying for years to prevent. "I'll be just as happy to have our people west of the river when it erupts."

"You know which side you're on," said Margaret.

"I'm against slavery, period," said Alvin. "But that doesn't mean these knackles need to be involved. If their knacks make them an asset on the battlefield, the enemy will target them particularly."

"I'm glad we're going into the wild Western lands," said Margaret. "The place you describe sounds lovely. Grassland, soon to be farmland, steep mountains as a wall against the world, water coming from the canyons to be spread across the fields and orchards."

"When I saw it in the walls of the city," said Alvin, "before I knew where it was or what it meant, I thought, Now that's a land God made for people that he loves."

"But that can be said of all the Earth," said Margaret.

"I know, he loves everybody, but *I* love my people, the ones he endowed with powers—usually gentle powers, not useful in combat. Useful in peace."

"Speaking of combat, Calvin is coming to our door. Don't let him in. Please."

"He's my brother," said Alvin.

"Please," said Margaret. "He wishes you were dead."

"As I said, he's my brother." Alvin got up and went to the front door and opened it.

Calvin stood there, poised to knock.

"Margaret doesn't want me to let you in," said Alvin.

"Amy Sump," said Calvin.

"What about that lying little—"

"Alvin," said Margaret from the other room.

"Well, she *is*."

"I just saw her. Coming into town with a summoner from Carthage City. And a mob."

"That poor, deluded girl," said Alvin. "I think by now she believes her own story."

Margaret came to stand beside him at the door. "She has dreamed and daydreamed and fantasized and lied so much that she really *does* have vivid memories of it."

"Never happened," said Alvin.

"I know, dear. Your heartfire is always clear about the past."

Calvin still stood there.

"The summoner had Amy with him. I think he's now allied with the mobs. He had some thugs with him."

Alvin nodded. "Thank you for warning me," he said.

"I was interrupted during my dinner. I smell food."

Margaret sighed and stepped back, allowing Calvin through the door.

"Thank you, O merciful lady," said Calvin. "May I share in the feast here on the tea table?"

"Just don't take a bite out of *my* sandwich," said Alvin.

"I'll start a fresh one," said Calvin.

While Calvin made his sandwich, Alvin closed the door and hugged Margaret again.

"So they're using the law now," said Margaret.

"They're using everything they can think of," said Alvin. "I think they're pretty serious this time."

"Three of our people dead? Yes, serious."

"Verily's a good lawyer," said Alvin.

"If Daniel Webster comes back to prosecute you, he's more than a match for Verily."

"And Webster is not at all a match for the truth," said Alvin.

Margaret put her hand on his cheek.

"Careful, I didn't shave," said Alvin. It was an old joke between them—no part of a beard grew on his cheeks. "At least they're not trying to extradite me to the Crown Colonies," said Alvin.

"They have no evidence against you there."

"But they think I was part of a slave rebellion," said Alvin. "Evidence won't seem so necessary to them."

"They can't hold you prisoner if you don't want them to."

"I'm not worried about being a *prisoner*," said Alvin. "I've been through that before."

"You have friends. There are hundreds of Irishmen who aren't starving in their homeland because of you."

"I wish I had been able to stop the blight."

"You brought them away from famine and persecution."

"I didn't bring them here to die for me," said Alvin.

"So maybe they won't die. Maybe every one of their lives will be spared, while they bring down all the killers who want your blood."

Alvin turned the talk to something that could actually be done. "Let's get our people as ready as we can to cross the river."

"Now?" asked Margaret.

"It's too late to do it earlier," said Alvin. "Maybe if the mobs think we're leaving, they'll slack off the harassment."

"Murder is not 'harassment.'"

Alvin questioned his own conclusion, as usual. "Or they'll think their tactics are working, and step up the marauding."

"That's what free will is about," said Margaret. "Not knowing in advance the outcome of your choice, and making it anyway."

"Get Eliza to help prepare the Irish to move West."

"To walk across the prairies and climb over the mountains? How do they get ready for that?"

"Wagons to carry a few belongings, seed for planting, food to eat along the way, tools."

"Wagons," said Margaret. "They're expensive."

"And we have almost no money in the city coffers," said Alvin. "Time to make some more gold?"

"Don't even joke about it. If they think we have a hoard of gold, there'll be no holding them back."

"They sent a summoner," said Alvin. "That's better than an army."

"The summoner *recruited* an army," said Calvin, his mouth full, though he hadn't finished making his sandwich.

"Please don't eat all the sausage," said Margaret. "*We* haven't finished eating yet."

"You let *him* talk with his mouth full?" whispered Alvin.

"I haven't given up on you yet," said Margaret. "Him?" She shrugged.

Calvin spoke again, his mouth not full, but his sandwich ready to eat. "You ought to experience it, her giving up on you, Alvin. It's so peaceful."

"He has very good hearing," whispered Alvin.

Margaret silently mouthed the words, He wants you dead.

32

As soon as word started spreading about the time and place for the funeral, people drifted to the large meadow nestled in the ell of the western side of the tallest Crystal tower. It was only three stories high, so Alvin didn't think it was much of a tower. But it was the tallest thing in the city, and what else would he call it? Crystal Mound? Crystal Cabin?

Alvin was sitting on the ground beside the row of plain wood coffins. This had become a custom in Crystal City, when anyone died. A plain coffin, but Alvin would place a small globe of crystal water in each coffin. Not that the coffin's resident would have much use for it. But it bound the dead to the living, and Margaret had told him that this custom meant much to the mourners.

He stayed low so he couldn't be seen from the edges of the crowd. He had Arthur Stuart trying to count, or at least estimate the size of, the crowd. Not that it mattered. Attendance was not obligatory; staying home meant nothing bad or good. He just wanted to know, and Arthur was willing to count.

The sound of horses, and maybe something on wheels. The thought came into Alvin's mind: A cannon?

No, a wagon.

John Binder, who was standing by one of the coffins, said, "Looks to be about forty mounted men."

"And a wagon," added Alvin.

"A jail wagon, it looks like. Tiny windows with bars."

"They think I'm coming with them."

"Are you?" asked John Binder.

"I want only three of them to come here to me."

John Binder didn't have to spread the word. He simply used his knack to get the people at the edge of the crowd to part just enough for mounted riders to come through in single file. When three riders had passed, the people closed up and there was no longer a way through.

The three riders noticed, but their leader kept on coming, not looking back. He didn't think he needed more than his two companions. Or maybe he didn't need anybody but himself.

"Crowd's almost three thousand," said Arthur Stuart from his place on a low branch of a tree at the edge of the meadow.

"Is that all?" asked Alvin.

"I didn't know we had that many citizens," said John Binder.

"We have more," said Alvin. "More than twelve thousand, including the Irish. Margaret counted heartfires."

Arthur Stuart dropped down from the tree, landing on his feet, and quickly bounded over to Alvin, just as Mike Fink pushed his way close to Alvin, and stood between him and the riders.

"Give me a chance to see who I'll be talking to, Mike," said Alvin as he rose to his feet.

Mike nodded and took a half step to one side. Alvin figured that was good enough. Mike Fink could only feel good when anybody who came after Alvin would have to go through him—something that not many men had been able to do, even when he wasn't protecting Alvin.

The first rider stopped, but did not dismount. "Alvin Smith?" said the man.

"I'm listening," said Alvin.

The man focused his gaze on Alvin. "The one they call the Maker," said the man.

"I don't know what they call me," said Alvin, "but yes, I'm a Maker."

"I've come to serve papers on you," said the man. "I have to deliver them into your hand in order to fulfill my duty."

"Here I am," said Alvin.

Reluctantly, the man dismounted from his horse. He wasn't decrepit, but he was old. A White man, and from his accent, he came from the south.

Verily Cooper had reached the same conclusion, and blocked the man's way to Alvin. "Crown Colony papers have no power here."

"I'm not from the Crown Colonies," said the man. "I'm a citizen of the United States, and this summons comes from a judge in Carthage City."

Verily looked at the folded paper the man held out, but did not touch it. The authority of the paper, written on the outside of the paper, confirmed what the man had claimed.

"May I pass?" asked the man. "Or are you resisting my service of a summons?"

"Not at all, now that I know it really is a summons."

"I told you it was."

"But you haven't told me who *you* are."

"Does my name matter?"

Verily cocked his head, but did not move.

"My name is of no import," said the man. "But I am an officer of the Property Rights Crusade."

"Ah," said Verily. "So you're a slavery man."

"I'm a property rights man," came the answer. "But I was only a humble farmer before one of my slaves stole herself and her baby from me."

"Twenty years ago," said Alvin.

The man looked startled. "Twenty-two."

"Cavil Planter," said Alvin. Then he turned to Arthur Stuart. "Arthur," he said. "Let me introduce you to the man who raped your mother and became your father. Cavil Planter, your son Arthur Stuart."

"My stolen property," said Cavil Planter.

"You know that slave catchers long since determined that Arthur Stuart is not the runaway slave you were searching for." Alvin smiled.

"I know who you are and what you can do. I know you interfered with the identification."

"I'm sure what you meant to say was that you suspect that I interfered," said Alvin. "Else that might be taken for slander."

"By all means, hale me into court for that offense," said Cavil Planter.

Planter walked up to Alvin and Arthur Stuart.

"You named him for our glorious Monarch," he said. "Mockery on top of theft."

"Are you here to try to retrieve Arthur Stuart? Because that's a fool's errand," said Alvin. "That will never happen."

"Be that as it may," said Planter. "Here is the summons."

As soon as Alvin took the paper out of his hand, Planter made as if to return to his horse. But now Verily Cooper and Marty Laws, who, like Verily, was a witness of the golden plow, blocked his way. Marty said, "Mr. Planter, perhaps you could stay to explain this summons to us."

There was obviously no "perhaps" about it, so Planter turned to face Alvin again.

"I'm not a scholar," said Alvin, "but I *can* read. This summons isn't about Amy Sump's ridiculous charges."

"I did not say it was," said Planter. "What would I have to do with that?"

"Nor does this summons say anything about stolen property," said Alvin.

"You boast about this half-Black fellow being my son, and then deny that he's my property."

"What father buys and sells his children?" asked Alvin.

"Are we going to have *this* discussion *now*?" asked Planter.

"I'm scanning this paper, and nowhere on it do I see myself being charged with any crime."

"The summons is for you to appear before the judge in Carthage City on the first day of November this year."

"With no mention of why," said Alvin.

"You're summoned as a material witness," said Planter.

"And that's enough to take a man all the way to Carthage?" asked Alvin.

"Or to cause him to be arrested for failing to appear," said Planter.

Alvin nodded. "I'm not going anywhere until I see a charge against me, Mr. Planter."

"I do have an arrest warrant for you," said Planter. "It names the charges against you. But I decided not to give it to you in the midst of this mob."

"These are peaceable citizens," said Marty Laws, "gathered solemnly for a funeral."

"If I had served you with an arrest warrant, Mr. Smith, would they have remained so peaceable?"

"Yes, they would," said Mike Fink, stepping right up to Planter, "because after I had torn your warrant, your summons, and you in half, there would have been nothing for the folks to be upset about."

Verily shook his head. Mike Fink saw it and took a step back.

Verily said, "I believe Mr. Fink wishes to clarify, lest his remarks be taken as threatening an officer of the court."

Planter answered, "That is most gracious. I wonder if Mr. Fink would say that in his own words."

Marty sidled up to Mike Fink. "An apology for the misunderstanding is in order now, Mr. Fink."

"You're actually a real lawyer, like Cooper here?" he asked.

"Wills and civil complaints need lawyering, as well as criminal trials," said Marty. "Your apology and clarification?"

As Alvin well knew, Mike Fink was not dumb, and understood exactly what was required. He straightened up. "Mr. Planter, I apologize that my words were so vague as to be misunderstood as a threat against your person or any of the legal papers you brought. I mean you no harm, and will be happy to escort you safely back to your cavalry."

Planter said, "That's all I ask. But I'll be on horseback, so I won't need an escort who is on foot."

Alvin spoke up. "Give me that warrant, please," he said.

"Which of these men is your attorney?" asked Planter.

"They both are," said Alvin. "But Marty's got a more even temper."

Verily winced.

Planter took another paper out of his jacket and offered it to Marty Laws.

Marty took it, opened it, read it. Fury showed on his face. "These charges are ridiculous. You'll never even get an indictment on this."

"We already have the true bill of indictment," said Planter. "Keep reading."

"They expect to take you to Carthage City in that prison wagon," said Marty.

Verily took the warrant from his hands and read it quickly. "Treason against the United States," he read. "Forming an unauthorized militia without proper authority. Obtaining a city charter under false pretenses. Kidnapping children in Ireland and transporting them to the United States."

Marty touched Alvin's wrist. "Now is a perfect time, Alvin, for you to exercise your right to not testify against yourself."

"I cannot say anything to these charges except that they are none of them accurate," said Alvin, now speaking in his educated voice.

"And yet you are indicted for all these crimes, and you are under arrest, now that your attorney has been served with the warrant."

The murmuring in the crowd was growing louder, as people near this conversation relayed to others what was happening.

"Now we'll see how peaceable these people are," said Planter. It occurred to Alvin that maybe this evil man was so filled with self-hatred that he wanted the crowd to make him a martyr to his wretched cause.

"They're very patient and peaceable," said Alvin. "All they need is an explanation." Alvin beckoned to the captain of the showboat. "Can you repeat what I say now, so everyone in the crowd can hear?"

The captain nodded, and Alvin began.

"My fellow knackles and citizens of Crystal City, do not be concerned. Our conversation here has been nothing but civil, and it will continue so."

From Planter's slight shift of position, it seemed he might have been about to register a protest.

"I have been arrested, and I have been served a summons. The summons first, which requires me to appear before a judge in Carthage City on the first of November."

Planter now raised a hand to make a gesture and to say a word, which Verily's hand on his arm prevented him from doing.

"Since the summons was served first, I announce my intention to comply with it, and travel to Carthage City by the assigned date."

"But you are under arrest, sir," said Cavil Planter, as quietly as he could.

The captain said, "Now Mr. Cavil Planter, the process server, reminds Alvin Smith that he is under arrest."

"I agree," said Alvin. "I am most certainly under arrest. But the highest court in Crystal City issues me a temporary release under my own . . ."

"Recognizance," said Verily Cooper.

"Recognizance," said Alvin.

"The highest court in Crystal City?" said Planter. "Any court in this place is illegal, since the charter was obtained by fraud."

Verily held the open warrant up for Planter to read. "You are not a lawyer, sir. The legality of the charter of Crystal City is a matter to be determined by a court of law. At present, Crystal City has a charter, and its highest court still has the authority to nullify this warrant. But the court has elected to honor the warrant, but merely allow the arrestee a period of free movement to get his affairs in order. He will present himself before the Carthage City judge in fulfillment of the summons and the arrest warrant."

The captain now relayed Verily's words to the crowd. No doubt many people assumed that Alvin would use this stay to escape to safety, but Alvin dispelled that notion entirely. "I give you my solemn oath," he said, "that I will appear in Carthage City on the first day of November. In the meantime, I assure you that I will not leave the boundaries of the city in any direction, by land or by water. But all of this cooperation I offer is contingent."

"Upon what, sir?" asked Planter.

"That the harassment and marauding of Crystal City stop right now."

"Cease forthwith," said Marty Laws.

"If any damage, violence, mayhem, or terrorizing is done to any citizen of Crystal City, then my cooperation is withdrawn and I will appear only in defense of the people of Crystal City."

"You are under arrest, sir!" Planter insisted.

"If your people continue their unprovoked attacks on the citizens of this city, my retaliation will be swift and sure. And unlike Mike Fink here, I believe my threat is absolutely clear, and *will* be carried out, if we are given cause."

Planter was about to express even more outrage, but at that moment, the saddle on Planter's horse slid to one side and fell to the ground.

"Too bad," said Mike Fink. "Looks like you're going to need me to clear people out of your way while you lead your horse. I'll carry your saddle for you. Fair enough?"

Whether Planter thought that it was Mike Fink's knack or Alvin's that loosened the saddle and made it fall, this demonstration of power was a healthy reminder, apparently, of who Planter was dealing with.

Witches.

Planter took his horse by the bridle and led it in a turn, with the crowd falling back out of the horse's way. Meanwhile, Mike Fink picked up the saddle and took his place in front of Planter.

The other two riders also turned their horses. And the parade proceeded, led by Mike Fink. The crowd opened before him, and while the looks directed at Planter were far from friendly, nobody raised a hand or said a word against him.

As soon as the parade got through the last of the crowd, where the rest of the troop—and the prison wagon—awaited them, Mike Fink dropped the saddle and took Cavil Planter by the upper arm and propelled him toward the jail wagon.

"What are you doing? Where are you taking me?"

"To the place of honor in this assembly," said Mike Fink. Planter was now resisting, but Mike Fink dragged him along like a bratty toddler who refused to walk. "I need this wagon opened," said Mike Fink loudly.

Nothing happened. Nobody spoke.

Until Cavil Planter said, "It isn't locked."

"I will not believe that until I hold the key in my hand." He looked at one man after another. Finally, one of them dismounted and handed Mike Fink the key. "You'll see it isn't locked, sir," the man said.

Mike dragged Planter to the door and pulled it open. "Why, it really *wasn't* locked," he said. "In you go, Mr. Planter."

"I will not!" he shouted, as Mike Fink lifted him from the ground and gently placed him supine within the jail wagon. Then Mike Fink closed the door of the jail wagon and, quite ostentatiously, locked it. "Yes, Mr. Planter. You thought this was the proper conveyance to carry the mayor of Crystal City two hundred miles along rough roads. So how can you complain if you, a mere immigrant and slave rapist, are conveyed by the same means?"

Mike turned to the members of Planter's troop. "I assume there is another key back in Carthage City?"

Several nods.

"It will occur to you to break Mr. Planter out of this wagon as soon as you're out of sight from Crystal City. But that's your mistake, my lads. *Nothing* is out of sight from Crystal City. The very walls will show everything that you do, all the way back to Carthage City, and if this prison wagon is opened before you get there, you won't have to deal with Alvin Maker, you'll also have to deal with the rip-snortingest, strongest, meanest, and most malicious varmint between the Appalachees and the Mizzippy. And that's me, when I'm riled up. Don't even imagine that you'll be too far for me to get to you. I know there's a passel of you, but only a couple or three of you at a time can get near enough to fight me, and I fight three men at a time just for exercise." The men did not seem to doubt his brag.

"Also," Mike went on, "the only reason I don't gouge out eyes and bite off noses and ears when I fight these days is because Alvin asked me not to. But I'm sure he'll forgive me for making an exception in this case, so we can find out if any of you can *possibly* be made uglier."

They looked at Mike in horrified fascination.

"If any of you doubt me, I'll take on any three of you just for fun, right now."

"Just for fun?" asked the man who probably thought he was the toughest in Planter's troop.

"Well, it'll be fun for *me*," said Fink. "Not so much for you, what with losing body parts."

"We have guns," said another man.

"Do you now?" said Mike Fink. "That's just an oversight. Please drop all your weapons and ammunition on the ground. If you don't want to, I can assure you that Alvin Maker can make you very sorry, even at a little distance."

When all the guns and ammunition were on the ground, Mike led the horses pulling the wagon around in a wide circle, so it ended up on the road back out of town. "Remember to tell folks back in Carthage that you not only met Alvin Maker, but you also met the wildest, toughest, meanest bobcat-strangler on the Hio and six other rivers west of the Appalachees."

"And that would be you?" scornfully asked the man who had previously seemed inclined to want to test Mike's offer to fight any three of them.

"Ask me that question again," said Mike Fink, "and in three seconds I'll have you off that horse with both your eyeballs popped and squishy, with my thumbs in your sockets."

The man wheeled his horse and moved to the front of the caravan, right ahead of the jail wagon. Cavil Planter was gripping the bars on the back of the wagon, weeping but making no sound.

"Remember, folks, I ain't got me a knack, so nobody used any kind of witchery against you! You tell the truth about that, and I won't have to come after you and kill you."

The troop rode off. Mike Fink watched until they were gone.

Only then did Mike notice that the showboat captain had followed him to the edge of the crowd, and while Mike was shouting his brag and his threats, the captain was relaying every word of it to the whole assemblage.

So the crowd definitely cleared a path for Mike, and made sure that he knew they approved highly of his words and actions.

Meanwhile, back at the coffins, Alvin said, "Can we begin the ceremonies now? We want everybody to get home in time for supper."

While everyone took their places, and the families of the slain citizens came forward to lay flowers on the coffins, Marty asked Verily, "Who *is* the supreme judicial authority of Crystal City?"

Verily, without smiling, gestured toward Alvin. "It's in the charter. The mayor is the supreme justice of the peace in Crystal City."

"He had the authority to override the warrant?"

"Did they obey him?" asked Verily. "Then he had the authority."

33

WHOEVER WAS IN charge of the marauders, they apparently had iron control over the so-called mob. The harassment stopped. Well, the burning and stealing and beating and terrorizing stopped. Every day, somewhere around the fringes of Crystal City, a few riders would come along one of the roads or traces and then stop in front of somebody's house, looking at it. Mothers called their children inside from the yard. Usually a man came out with a musket or blunderbuss or shotgun and stood there watching the riders. Before long all the neighbors were out in their dooryards or on their porches, also armed. But not a shot was fired. And after a while, the riders would go back the way they came.

On both sides, the message was received. We're not done with you knackles, the marauders were saying. We won't let you run over us unscathed, said Crystal City. But the truce held.

Margaret was having meetings most every day, folks from this group or that, coming to confer with her about practical things like where and how to get a wagon or at least a cart to pull their belongings along by hand. How much flour and lard or oil to prepare. How to get a horse when they had little money.

Eliza was having her own meetings, organizing the Irish into small companies of ten families, with someone in charge of each. Several of the groups were headed by a woman, and in each case it was a woman so formidable that no sober man would dare to complain about being led by a female.

Arthur Stuart was organizing all the other knackles into companies. He didn't push his luck the way Eliza had. All his companies were headed by men. He had men hewing wood and setting it out to season during the months they had.

All these preparations for the exodus across the river were done pretty openly. A few of the people tried to sell their farms or shops to people from outside the city, but the offers were so low they couldn't even buy a spavined nag strong enough to pull a dogcart. Several knackles offered to trade a completely furnished house for a horse, and a few half-decent folks, knowing they were cheating the witches but willing to let them gain *some* value from their possessions, agreed, and many of the horses they got in trade were good enough to make the journey.

With a couple of others, the knackle couldn't help commenting, "We'll be eating this one before we get very far," to which the outsider said, "Yours to do with as you please, as my new house here will be for me to use."

Nobody bought or traded for any of the shops, though some made a deal for the shop's stock. "No point getting a shop in a town that pretty soon isn't going to have any people in it," said one outsider. "Where's my custom, where's my trade?"

Crystal City had been prosperous, trading up and down the Noisy River country. But there was no trade now, when the people needed it most. The shopkeepers couldn't get credit, so their shelves had emptied out, with no new stock to fill them.

Alvin took no part in the selling, buying, building, stocking. He talked a couple of fellows with a knack for wheelwrightry into making the best wheels they could out of wood that was still too green to be worked properly. "Can't promise they'll hold up," said one of them. "Will they carry a family's supplies over the river?" asked Alvin. "You didn't ask me to make a boat, Alvin. You asked for wagon wheels."

Mostly, though, Alvin went about talking to folks about their knacks, how everybody needed to help. About the Good Samaritan, and how everybody going into the West was going as the Crystal City, not a bunch of strangers or rivals. It wasn't exactly preaching. Alvin was just letting them know what was expected.

He deflected questions. When will we leave? How will we cross the river? Are you sure the Reds won't massacre us just like Tippy-Canoe? I'm no hunter, Alvin, how can I feed my family?

"Well, that's what Arthur Stuart is working on. I heard him say something about every company having a couple of designated hunters to try for a deer a week, or a buffalo every couple of weeks."

"I never et buffalo," said one woman. "And I sure never roasted it."

"From what I hear," said Alvin, "it roasts up pretty much like beef, except a little tougher. Make sure you bring your best teeth." That got him a laugh, because it was a joke he only made to people as *had* teeth.

What they didn't know was that when he visited each family, he looked at whatever they had in the way of a cart or wagon, and strengthened and sealed all the joints, and made the axles and hubs work smooth. Wherever rats were trying to get into the food, Alvin got them to move away, out of the city limits, because they couldn't afford to share their supplies with varmints. Nobody even noticed that rats weren't a problem this fall, after the harvest. Too busy being afraid of the marauders, afraid to go off into untracked wilderness.

"Will there be stout?" asked more than one Irishman. "Lager? Beer?"

"Well, that's a good question," said Alvin. "Do *you* know how to brew it?"

To those who said yes, or maybe, or more or less, Alvin said, "We've got a few barrels of barley grain and a bag or two of hops. Think you can work with that?"

They said yes, and it seemed that they were much relieved. Here they were in this good rich land where there was plenty to eat, no famine, no blight—but Irishmen had to know they could have a pint now and then. Besides, Alvin was relieved that *none* of them asked about making good whisky. Maybe they knew that a bit of beer wouldn't hamper them on the journey, but a serious whisky drunk would lay them out and slow down the whole caravan.

Alvin had a good talk with Arthur Stuart. "I'm not fit to do this, Alvin. You better be there all the time to back me up."

"I'll try," said Alvin. "But you've been doing a splendid job so far. People seem content and nobody's grumbling about anything they might fancy you done wrong."

"They don't want to complain to *you*."

"Who else can they complain to? Margaret tells me that nobody is harboring resentment or disdain for you and your efforts. You chose your company captains well. But here's something you might not have thought of. You get to the other side, you need to get inland a ways and make a camp. Build log cabins or sod houses, because when winter comes, these wagons ain't going nowhere till spring."

"Cabins?"

"We got so many people as know how to build cabins you'll not even need to put anybody in charge of it. When spring comes, you don't all go at once—there wouldn't be enough pasturage for the horses on the way. You space them out, a couple of days between companies, and following traces a couple of miles apart."

"We don't know the land," said Arthur Stuart.

"Then it's a good thing Tenskwa-Tawa won't ask any of you to scout out your own paths. You'll have Red guides. Good men you can trust. In the walls of the city, I've seen there are times you'll have to lower wagons over an escarpment by ropes, and then pull them up the other side of the ravine. Hard work, slows you down, but in the spring there's no hurry—you don't want to get to the mountains when they're still deep in snow."

Arthur nodded. He listened, he took everything in. He knew that Alvin was telling him everything he could, but he couldn't tell what he didn't know. Arthur Stuart also refrained from asking, And what will *you* be doing while I'm supervising the migration? He knew Alvin would be doing what was needed, as he always did.

As long as he didn't do something insane like going to Carthage City to turn himself over to the authorities. Arthur Stuart knew Alvin had given his oath, but if he and all of Crystal City was over the river before that day, what were the mobbers and murderers going to do about it?

Another thing Alvin did was have little Vigor with him every chance he could. Sometimes he'd hoist the boy on his shoulders, but other times they'd walk together as Alvin taught him to hear the Greensong and move with it. Alvin couldn't guess what knack the boy might have, if any, but he could hear the Greensong as long as Alvin was with him, and so when it was just the two of them, both walking, they could get all the way around the city in half an hour or less.

It was mid-October, and the city was readier than Alvin had expected to make their journey. Arthur was starting to nag him, and Verily and John Binder, too, that he needed to get things moving so he wasn't still in town on the first day of November. Alvin just smiled.

Measure never plagued Alvin about such things. Alvin hadn't told him what he was going to do, but he figured Measure already knew. He had eyes and a brain, and he didn't let himself get distracted by what he *wished* would happen.

And Measure, too, had his three children with him pretty much all the time. He knew.

Calvin knew nothing, except that he hated the idea of being left behind.

"Not my choice," said Alvin. "Tenskwa-Tawa said that if you made the midpoint of the river, you'd fall out of whatever boat you were in, and have to swim back to the east bank."

"What does he have against *me*? What did I ever do to him?"

"He doesn't trust you," said Alvin.

"Why not?" demanded Calvin. "What you mean is *you* don't trust me!"

"Well, of course I don't trust you, Calvin. I'd have to be six kinds of stupid to trust you."

That seemed to sting, and Calvin recoiled. "Haven't I told you everything I found out from the conspirators?"

"I'd rather you hadn't known any of the conspirators, or what they were planning," said Alvin. "But that's water under the bridge, so to speak. Stay behind here and make a good life for yourself. Marry. Have children. Keep them safe."

Calvin was bursting to say something else. Alvin waited until Calvin was ready to say it. "When they find out I'm a Maker, they'll want to kill me the way they want to kill you!"

"First, you're an *apprentice* Maker," said Alvin. "Second, they won't know anything about your knacks unless you go bragging on them or showing off the things you can do."

"Can't do much."

"Next to me you're the most powerful man in this country," said Alvin.

He could see how gratified Calvin was to hear him say it.

"Study. Learn the human body, the diseases, the injuries, and practice healing people. Healing them from ten feet away, or on the other side of a wall, or the other side of a field. Without them knowing that it's you doing it."

"I don't know how you *do* it, Alvin."

"I didn't know how to do it till I figured it out," said Alvin.

"I'm not you," said Calvin miserably.

"You'll be glad of that after I'm gone," said Alvin.

"All I ever wanted was to be like you," said Calvin.

"You're my brother and I love you," said Alvin. "But never, not once in your life, have you *ever* wanted to be like me, except in my knacks and skills."

"What else is there?" asked Calvin, truly baffled.

"The other things I've tried to learn. I've got no knack for wisdom or generosity or patience, I have to work on those things all the time and I'm still not all that skillful at them. Work on those things, too, Calvin, and you'll have a happier life."

"They'll kill me as soon as you're gone," said Calvin. "The leaders of this mob, they know me, they know what I can do."

"They have no idea what you can do," said Alvin.

Calvin rolled his eyes.

"*You* have no idea what you can do," said Alvin.

"Why aren't you angry with me?" asked Calvin. "Why don't you hate me?"

"You're my brother," said Alvin. "And it was hard being my younger brother, with gifts of your own, and all the attention was coming to me. I know how you suffered, I know how it rankled. Why would I hate you, when you always came down on my side, in the end."

Calvin looked away for a few moments. "You're taking my girl with you," he said.

"Come now, Calvin, you're not a child. Eliza is not and never was your girl. She's fifteen years older than you and her domicile has been occupied by so many boarders and renters that she barely knows who's inside her from one night to the next."

Calvin's face flashed with anger. "I love her, Alvin, and I won't have you—"

"Speaking the truth about her? How do you think I know this? I'm not Margaret, I can't see deep into people's heartfires. I know what Eliza herself has told me."

"I mean it," said Calvin. "I love her."

"I don't doubt it," said Alvin. "I also don't doubt that once she's over the river, and you're back here, both of you are going to find people to love. With any luck, one each, so you can start families."

"If she's pregnant, the baby's mine," said Calvin. "What about that? Don't I get to know my own baby?"

Alvin shook his head. "She's not pregnant."

Calvin started leaking tears. "I wish she was."

"She's old enough that there's a fair chance she never *will* get pregnant, by anybody, Calvin."

Calvin embraced his brother and wept onto his shoulder.

"You're taller than I remembered," said Alvin.

"I was just thinking how you weren't half as big as I thought."

The two of them chuckled, still in their embrace.

The horse had been approaching for some time. From the east.

Alvin pulled away from his brother and saw that the rider was Verily Cooper. Calvin started to walk away.

"No," said Alvin. "Stay."

Verily dismounted and took a few steps to get his legs working right after much riding.

"Who did you meet with?" asked Alvin.

"Cavil Planter is still humiliated and furious."

"He's always been furious. He's done so much wickedness that it eats him up all the time."

"Did humiliating him help?" asked Verily.

"I didn't tell Mike Fink what to do. Planter must know that."

"Planter hardly spoke, but his eyes were flashing anger and resentment at everybody."

"Who's really running the show in Carthage City?"

"Is that where you were, Verily?" asked Calvin.

"Had to talk about terms," said Verily. "Don't want Alvin getting murdered on his way into town."

Calvin was stunned. "You're going?" he asked. "To Carthage City?"

"A man ought to go wherever he's wanted," said Alvin.

"They want you dead," said Calvin.

"I have no doubt of it."

Verily shifted his weight. "They promised to let your people alone. Perfect safety, no interference."

"You believe them?"

"I believe them, but that doesn't mean I believe their underlings will comply with a treaty like that."

"Do they know we're emigrating?" asked Alvin.

"Nobody even hinted at it. I don't think they know, no matter how many spies they send in."

"They must have seen the wagons," said Alvin.

"People who *aren't* crossing the river make wagons, too," said Verily.

"Who's running the show?" asked Alvin.

"You know who's running it," said Verily.

Alvin waited.

"Philadelphia Thrower is the one giving orders, the one they report to, but you know who's *really* running things."

Alvin nodded.

"Dammit," said Calvin. "Why did you have me stay if you aren't going to let me know what's going on?"

"Reverend Thrower," said Alvin, "believes he is the servant of a powerful angel, or maybe Christ himself, I'm not sure what lies the reverend has been told."

"But he's *not* serving an angel, is he?" demanded Calvin.

"God has better things for his angels to do, I hope," said Alvin. "No, the being who has appeared to Thrower many times, urging him to kill me, to destroy all my work right down to the ground, it's . . ." Alvin couldn't, for a moment, bring himself to say it.

"The Unmaker," said Verily. "The enemy of all creation."

"The Maker is opposed by the Unmaker," said Calvin.

"Seems appropriate," said Alvin.

"And Reverend Thrower has *seen* this creature?" asked Calvin.

"He's seen whatever the Unmaker wanted him to see. He's sure he's on the Lord's errand."

"So he's trying to kill you *innocently*?" asked Calvin.

"Such a good question," said Alvin.

"Not innocently," said Verily. "He *thinks* he believes that the angel he sees is from God, and he's on the Lord's side. But in his soul, Calvin, he knows that he's serving the father of lies."

"Then why doesn't he stop?" asked Calvin.

"He has no importance in this world," said Verily, "except what he gets from following the Unmaker."

"So it's the Unmaker directing the marauders, the assassins," said Calvin.

"I doubt any of them know it, except Cavil Planter. But yes, they're all acting out the Unmaker's plan."

"If he makes a plan," said Calvin, "isn't that a kind of making?"

"It is," said Alvin. "But what none of his followers know is that the Unmaker never *tells* his plan to anyone, because the ending of it all will be the utter destruction of all the Unmaker's servants."

"You'll defeat him?"

"It doesn't matter. The Unmaker's promises are all lies, he has no loyalty, he has no gratitude, he has no honor."

Calvin stepped back to think about this.

Another horse was coming, this time from the direction of Crystal City. It was John Binder and Marty Laws, plodding along on horseback.

"Those were the best horses you could find?" asked Verily.

"We figured Alvin would be walking, and so would we," said John Binder. "Walking with him, we cover ground pretty nicely. And the horses are needed here to pull wagons."

"Neither of those beasts could even pull a plow," said Verily.

"You and Alvin are the ones who know about plows," said Marty. "Or so I've heard."

"And there's a difference," said John Binder, "between pulling a wagon over the ground and pulling a plow *through* it. These horses will do their work well enough."

"They will," said Alvin. And he knew that they all knew that if the horses had anything wrong with them, Alvin had just healed them and made sure it was well done.

Out of the nearby house came its owner, on foot, with children draped all over him, or so it seemed. Measure's wife Delphi came out and scolded the children mildly back into the house. She embraced Measure and kissed him and he swung her around in the air twice and set her down on the porch of their house.

"So Measure is coming too?" asked Verily.

"He's coming with me, yes," said Alvin. "But you have work to do here, and I want you to stay and see to it."

"If everybody else is going," said Calvin, "what work does Mr. Cooper have here?"

"He's got the deed to every piece of ground in Crystal City that hasn't already been sold or traded, and he's going to make sure that every deed is properly recorded in the capital."

"So we're coming back?" asked John Binder.

"I imagine that someday this land will be worth something," said Alvin.

"With the Crystal City sitting on it?" said John Binder. "It's a wonder of the world."

It was Verily who explained. "The Crystal City is coming down. It'll be kind of a flood, as it all turns to ordinary water and flows away."

"So . . . nothing where it was but a slurry of mud," said Calvin.

"All the crystal blocks I made," said Alvin. "I think you know how to undo them."

Calvin protested. "I don't even know how to *make* them properly, let alone unmake them."

"You'll figure out how to unmake mine, and you'll figure out how to break up your own. Unless you think our enemies should find a few dozen crystal blocks lying about."

"I'll break mine first," said Calvin.

"So Calvin's staying," said Verily, "with an important and difficult job to do. And I'm supposed to protect the knackles' property rights here, if I can."

"If you can," said Alvin.

Verily waited. Then said, "You're taking Measure with you."

"Yes," said Measure.

"And John Binder," said Verily.

"He couldn't stop me if he tried," said John Binder.

"If he asked you to stay, you would," said Verily. "And Marty?"

"I'm not here just because I'm so pretty," said Marty Laws.

"So you *will* have a lawyer with you," said Verily.

"Somebody's got to speak up to the judge in Carthage City."

That's when they heard a kind of rushing sound, and then saw Arthur Stuart just emerging from the woods on the other side of the road, slowing down. Alvin was pleased to know that Arthur Stuart could hear the Greensong well enough to have such speed.

Alvin held out his hand to Arthur Stuart, who took it, then tried to throw Alvin to the ground. He succeeded, but ended up sitting on his buttocks in the road himself. The two sat in the dirt of the road, laughing.

"I want to go with you," said Arthur Stuart.

"You've got work to do," said Alvin.

"I don't want to do that work. I've been all over this continent with you, Alvin. Why are you going to shut me out now?"

Measure helped Arthur to his feet, while Verily did the same for Alvin. "Arthur Stuart," said Measure, "you know that you have a role to play."

"It's not a play," said Arthur. "It's real life."

"And in real life, you should have all the people and wagons across the river before we get back," said Measure.

Arthur Stuart looked as if he wanted to say something—something angry. But he calmed himself. "There's no changing your mind on this, Alvin Maker, you fool."

"You're the keeper of Taleswapper's book now," said Alvin. "You can't come with me."

Tears were streaming down Arthur's face. "Will I ever see you again, Alvin?"

"Well, I don't know," said Alvin, "but I can't think why not. Meanwhile, you have my greatest work in your hands."

Arthur Stuart looked puzzled.

"Crystal City," said Alvin. "The people are the city, not the crystal blocks. I'm giving over my city to you. Protect the people, hold them together."

"Holding them together is John Binder's job!" said Arthur Stuart.

"Usually it is," said John Binder, "but Alvin asked me to go with him."

"You and not me," said Arthur Stuart.

"Arthur," said Alvin, "seeing as how you know the way back to Margaret's house, would you be so kind as to take Calvin by the secret way back to the Crystal tower. He has work to do there." And then, to Calvin, "When you dissolve the blocks, make the water flow off to the south instead of going right to the river. The last thing we need is for the approaches to the river to be a sea of mud, to mire all the wheels."

Calvin nodded gravely.

"Measure," said Alvin, "would you take these horses down to your house and ask your wife to watch over them till somebody comes from the city to bring them back."

Measure immediately and wordlessly took the horses' leads and showed them the way down to the house, where he loosely tied them to the porch railing.

Alvin looked at Calvin and then at Arthur. Arthur Stuart held out his hand, and Calvin took it. "You know how to hear the Greensong, don't you," said Calvin.

Arthur nodded.

"I've tried," said Calvin.

"Maybe this time you will," said Arthur. Then the two of them, holding hands, jogged off into the woods, speeding up as they went.

"I wish you hadn't taken my horse, Alvin," said Verily. "I've got a lot of riding to do, getting up to the capital."

"I know," said Alvin, "but Margaret is already planning for you to take the buggy. *She* can't drive it anymore, and you'll want to ride with a roof to keep off the rain."

Verily smiled. "I should have known that you'd prepare things right."

"I know you, Verily," said Alvin. "You'd always rather drive than walk or run or ride."

"I'll cut a wider swath in the capital if I come in a buggy," Verily said. "You chose right."

Measure walked up from the house. "Well, Alvin, I figured, why wait for somebody from the city, when Verily here can ride his horse and lead the other two."

"That sounds like a good idea," said Alvin.

Verily grinned. "Which is your way of saying, that's what you were planning all along."

"I'm not good at making plans," said Alvin. "That's why I try not to make any."

In a few minutes, Verily was down at the porch, untying the horses. He mounted his own, and began to move his little equine parade out to the road, about fifty yards closer to the city than the men surrounding Alvin.

"Four of us?" asked Marty Laws. "Is that enough?"

"It's more than they'll want me to have," said Alvin.

"That doesn't answer my question," said Marty.

"I don't know what 'enough' would even mean," said Alvin. "I know that I want the four of us to go to Carthage City together. And you seemed willing to go."

Alvin didn't have to join hands with anybody. He led the way, and Measure brought up the rear, and between the two brothers, the other two were swept up in the Greensong and in a few moments they ran like the wind, without the forest or farmland causing them any delay or difficulty. In Ireland, Alvin had learned to find the Greensong in farms and fields, not just in woodland, and so despite the cut-down trees and single-crop fields, the land was still alive enough to carry them along.

They were halfway to Carthage, Alvin reckoned, when he called a stop to void their bladders and get a drink.

As they were reassembling into their single file, Measure asked, "I reckon you already said goodbye to Margaret."

"When she told me where to rendezvous with everybody, with Verily especially, we said our goodbyes then. And little Vigor, too. Though he's not so very little anymore."

"It's a hard thing to say goodbye to children," said Measure.

"It's easier to say goodbye when you're leaving them at home with their mother, than when you're standing over their grave," said Alvin.

"I didn't forget your daughter, Alvin," said Measure.

"Neither did I, and never will," said Alvin. "I wasn't rebuking you. I was just thinking on all the loved ones I'm leaving behind here."

"Well, if I'm on your list of loved ones," said Measure, "I'll be right behind you all the way."

And soon the four of them were running through the forest, the Greensong giving them the rhythm and music of their path. Alvin wondered if this was his last journey with the Greensong. Then he silently mocked himself for sentimentality. If it was, it was. If there'd be more, then there'd be more. Nothing he did right now would make any difference. So he emptied his mind except for the Greensong, and led them even faster through the forest.

34

ALVIN AND HIS companions emerged from the forest and the Greensong in farmland north of Carthage City. Alvin had made it a point to pass the city first, so that they would be coming in from the northeast, not at all the direction they would be expected to arrive. Not that he thought they would not be noticed, but he wanted them to be surprised, discommoded, maybe even confused.

The four of them walked into town on a well-used and heavily trafficked road, so that lots of people saw them. Nobody challenged them, though—why should they? It was not threatening to have four strangers heading into the biggest city on the Hio. There must be a thousand people a day, from every direction, even across the river, coming to Carthage for some business or other. Shopping. Looking for work. Aiming to steal or defraud. Seeking vengeance or looking for love. That's what cities were for, to attract people to live together in close proximity, where there were more opportunities for good or ill.

They were in a main square, with a couple of churches and a couple of banks marking the four sides.

"The two main religions of Carthage City," said John Binder.

"I don't know as how there are many Christians here," said Measure.

"Well, however many there are," said John, "they probably got a lot of Methodists and Episcopalians."

"Each of them not quite sure whether the other kind is even Christian," said Measure. "And they're right to wonder."

"Christian doesn't mean Christlike," said Alvin. "It just means they aspire to follow him."

"I stand by my words," said Measure.

Alvin looked around, past the immediate buildings, but saw nothing helpful. So he led them to a bank. "You might want to wait out here," said Alvin. "Four of us might look like a bank robbery."

"Four unarmed men?" asked Marty Laws.

"Are we really unarmed?" asked Measure. "Being witches as we are."

Alvin walked on up the stairs into the bank. It announced itself to be the Third Bank. Rivers only had two banks, thought Alvin. But the city has three, apparently.

Measure followed him in, but waited by the door. Alvin went to a man at a desk. "Sir," he said.

"You have to talk to a teller first."

"Here you are, sitting back, looking at nothing, writing nothing, neither adding nor subtracting," said Alvin. "And I have the simplest of questions, which you can answer easily."

The man sighed and sat up.

"You aren't going to open an account?"

"Not enough money to do that," said Alvin.

"What's your question, then?" asked the man, sounding weary.

"I've been told that I'm under arrest," said Alvin. "I was hoping to find a sheriff or a marshal or a constable. Or a judge—I'm supposed to appear before a judge tomorrow."

Now the man had come awake. "Heard you were coming," he said. "If you're Alvin called Maker."

"I'm mostly called Alvin, or Alvin Smith, or when I was a boy, Alvin Miller."

"Who's the man at the door?" the banker asked.

"My brother," said Alvin. "I think he wants to make sure I don't get into any trouble."

"You're under arrest already," said the banker. "What more trouble do you want to *be* in?"

"If you could point me to—"

"If you're out walking around when you're under arrest, that makes you an escapee."

"Do escapees come and look for the sheriff?" asked Alvin. "Just tell me where to go, and I'll go there, and you can go back to keeping your chair warm, or whatever you was doing."

"Go out the front door, sir," said the banker, "and cut across the square and go around the far side of the Episcopal. Down a block, turn left, and the sheriff's office is there."

"And the jail?" asked Alvin.

"I'm sure the sheriff will be able to tell you the way," said the banker.

"You've been very helpful," said Alvin. "Thank you, sir."

"What I heard," said the banker, "I didn't expect you to be so polite."

"But I *did* expect you to be helpful, as you *have* been, so good day to you, sir." Alvin walked to the front door of the bank. Measure held the door open for him, and they both walked out.

"I imagine," said Measure, "that he's already rushing around, sending messengers to every law enforcement officer in Carthage."

"Well, if folks want to put themselves to all that trouble, I can't stop them and I don't even care to try."

They reunited with John Binder and Marty Laws, and together they followed the banker's directions.

They found the sheriff's office—a modest building, only one story, but the sign was clear enough, even though "sheriff" was spelled "sherrif."

John Binder chuckled. "Maybe your wife, Alvin, could do some good improving the education of folks in Carthage."

"Just the sign painters," said Measure. "And spellings are still settling out these days. Maybe Noah Webster says it should be two Rs and one F."

As they approached the door, it was flung open, and the two windows were flung up and open, revealing six muskets or pistols pointed at them. Moments later, a dozen armed men came around the sides of the building, also pointing weapons at the four travelers.

"Hands up!" cried a nervous looking young man.

"Oh, you can't be the sheriff," said John Binder.

"I'm Deputy Fiddler," the young man said. "Sheriff Wiley is out scouting around the boundaries of the city."

"Looking for us," said John Binder.

"We came in from the northeast," said Measure.

"Trying to evade being taken into custody," said Fiddler, darkly.

"Well, now," said Alvin, "This is October thirty-first, and so I'm not due to appear before the judge until tomorrow."

"You are under arrest already, by a warrant served on you back in—"

While Fiddler paused to try to remember the date, Alvin said, "I remember it well, but the summons to the judge was served first."

Marty Laws stepped forward. The guns were suddenly aimed at him.

"I'm Mr. Smith's attorney," he said. "We already settled this with the process server. We're here to fulfill Mr. Smith's promise, a day early."

"Marty," said Alvin. "I don't like having a bunch of guns pointed at you. Or me either."

As he finished speaking, hot molten lead dribbled out of the barrel of every gun. It took a few moments for the posse to realize what was happening.

"That's better," said Alvin. "Nice of you to unload your guns like that. Much safer for everybody now."

The men examined their weapons in consternation. Some of them reached for powder and ball to reload.

"Oh, you don't want to do that," said John Binder. "The molten lead is already setting up now, and if you load those guns, they'll just explode in your faces."

"We don't want anybody getting hurt," said Alvin.

"Witchery," said one man, and several others echoed him.

"I think trying to keep people from getting hurt is more like Christianity than witchery," said Measure. "But suit yourselves."

Alvin said, "You have a place where we can sit out of the sun while we wait for Sheriff Wiley?"

"And aiming guns at us," said Marty Laws, "is technically assault, which violates about six different laws. If you think Alvin is under arrest, then it's your duty to keep him safe until our arraignment."

Measure said, "Al, I think I'm going to go see about renting us a couple of rooms for tonight."

"I think only one room, if it's a big one," said Alvin. "Don't want us splitting up."

"You're going to spend tonight in jail," said Fiddler.

"It's nice of you to offer us free accommodation," said Marty Laws, "but incarceration isn't justified until after we meet with the judge tomorrow."

"It's jail for all four of you, if you don't stop giving me sass," said Fiddler.

"How can I stop giving you sass, when you keep talking crazy?" said Marty Laws. "There's been no warrant issued for the rest of us. And I'm Mr. Smith's attorney. Do you generally incarcerate the *attorneys* of persons under arrest in this fine city of democracy, law, and order?"

An older man from the posse spoke softly in Fiddler's ear.

"That's right," said John Binder. "You're getting good advice now, and it'll be easy to follow it."

There was something in Binder's voice that made it sound as if they were all comrades in a common cause. Alvin had seen Binder's knack at work before, but this circumstance was unusually difficult, and Binder was handling it deftly.

"You're lucky nobody shot you all dead on your way into town," said Fiddler defiantly.

"You had no idea there'd be four of us, or what Alvin Smith looked like," said Marty Laws. "So are you saying that you folks are prepared to murder us without due process of law? Especially when three of us aren't under any kind of legal charge at all? You sound like a murderous bunch of rapscallions, if you don't mind my saying so."

"I do mind, and if you don't—"

"Are you, completely unarmed as you are, going to threaten us?" asked Marty Laws.

"Some people take longer to understand a situation than others," said Alvin, beginning to enjoy himself. "Mr. Fiddler here, he's a mite simple, so he doesn't grasp things quick."

Fiddler was furious now, but the other men inside the office drew him back inside, and they all set down their ruined weapons. The older man who had spoken to Fiddler before now stepped forward. "Deputy Fiddler here is my son," he said. "He's always been impetuous, but he's only trying to protect the citizens of Carthage, as he's sworn to do."

"You have my solemn oath," said Alvin, "that we will not harm a soul in Carthage, particularly if you drop this silly idea of arresting my friends and incarcerating us before we appear before the judge tomorrow at . . . ten? When can we—"

"Oh, the judge will be there the moment you show up," said old Mr. Fiddler. "I suspect the judge is already there, awaiting word about your arrival."

"Then you ought to go tell him we're here and we'll see him tomorrow at a time of his choosing," said Marty Laws. "So long as he chooses no earlier than ten o'clock in the morning."

Old Mr. Fiddler nodded toward a couple of men outside in the street, who set down their useless weapons and took off at a jog up the street.

"Now if you don't mind, it looks like my brother has found us lodging for tonight," said Alvin.

Measure was shaking his head. "Nobody wants to rent to us. They think there's going to be a gunfight or something."

"A wizards' battle!" exclaimed Deputy Fiddler.

"Can't have a wizards' battle," said Measure, "lessen you find some wizards. We're just citizens of a city in Noisy River, one of the sovereign states of this federation. The charter of that city has been reaffirmed by the state legislature a couple of weeks ago."

"You mean the den of witches and abominations called Crystal City," said another man.

"I see you're a Christian," said John Binder. "I appreciate your warning that such awful things might be found in our city. We just came from there, and the only abominations were a few thousand bats, who mostly keep our city free of flies and mosquitos. But when we go back, we'll try to find if there are any worse abominations around."

"Don't bandy words with us!" cried Deputy Fiddler

"What my son means," said old man Fiddler, "is that we'd like to ask if you would care to sleep in our spacious city jail, a couple of blocks away."

"With the door left unlocked?" asked Marty Laws.

"We'll offer you the upstairs suite," said old man Fiddler. "I hear that a lot fewer rats get up there."

"What I'm wondering about," said Measure, "is whether your jail also serves a nice dinner for its guests."

Silence was his answer.

Old man Fiddler spoke up again. "We generally rely on the friends of our prisoners to bring meals to the jail for them."

"You don't have a budget for meals for the incarcerated?" asked Marty Laws.

"We do," said old man Fiddler. "But we can't spend any of it without Sheriff Wiley's signature on the paper."

"You Carthaginians are mighty devoted to papers with words on them," said Measure.

"We accept your kind offer," said Alvin. "And two of my companions will go out and find a public house or inn that serves a worthy dinner for four hungry men."

"And you'll bring the food back to the jail," said Deputy Fiddler.

"Only if the innkeeper will also bring us chairs, a table, and all the dishes and utensils we need, with a tablecloth and napkins," said Measure. "Otherwise, all four of us will go to the inn and dine there, before returning to the free upstairs lodgings you so kindly offered us."

Once again, Deputy Fiddler seemed about to explode; again, his father calmed him with a touch on his shoulder. "We will fully comply with the law, Mr.—Smith?"

"We're brothers, but I still use my father's name, Miller," said Measure.

"Mr. Miller, then," said old man Fiddler. "We will not discommode you or disturb you. We ask that you not damage any more of our equipment, that's all."

"Damage?" said Measure, looking at his three companions.

"I don't know what he's talking about," said John Binder. "We didn't damage anything."

Alvin shrugged. "Folks are always blaming us knackles for causing things we had nothing to do with."

"You're saying you didn't cause our balls to melt and drip out the barrels of our weapons?" said another man from the posse.

Alvin smiled, and Marty gave a tiny little hoot of amusement. "We're not responsible for anything that happens to your balls. Every man has to look after his own."

Now it was old man Fiddler's turn to look a little annoyed. "I've spoken respectfully to you, sirs," he said. "I don't deserve to be ridiculed with such crudity."

John Binder said, "Oh, I see now, yes, I believe you misunderstood the meaning of our attorney's words. He referred only to musket and pistol balls."

A couple of the men huffed, but since the four men from Crystal City were all innocent and reassuring, what could they do?

A dozen of them followed then along the street toward the jail. Along the way, they passed a tavern. There were cheerful sounds coming from within.

"This place have good food?" Measure asked old man Fiddler.

"I think so," said Fiddler.

"And the customers are kind to strangers?" asked John Binder.

"As long as the strangers are gentlespoken," said Fiddler.

Alvin got to the door and turned around to address the throng. "I think we have money enough to buy dinner for only the four of us. If the rest of you want to dine here also, I'm afraid you'll need to pay for your own meals."

Only old man Fiddler and his son seemed interested in following Alvin's party inside. The others drifted away, while the tavernkeeper found a table for Alvin's group and another for the Fiddlers. John Binder made it a point to walk over to the Fiddlers' table and say, to old man Fiddler, "We appreciate your patience and forbearance, sir. We don't have money to pay for meals for all the men who escorted us here, but we would be glad to pay for your dinner."

"In a pig's eye," said Deputy Fiddler.

"If you reconsider," said John Binder, "just tell the tavernkeeper to add your meal and drinks to our bill."

Old man Fiddler thanked him, and Binder returned to Alvin's table.

"Well done," said Alvin.

"I'm counting on you to make the prison cots comfortable for us," said Measure to Alvin.

"When did your bed become my business?" asked Alvin.

But they all knew that Alvin would do exactly what Measure asked.

They were just finishing up their meal when Sheriff Wiley came into the tavern. He was a man with a lot of strut, but Alvin could see that he was restraining himself. Probably because he would already have heard about the molten bullets and ruined gun barrels. He came to their table, and after taking John Binder to be Alvin for a minute, there were handshakes all around.

"Please sit down and eat with us," said John Binder.

The sheriff considered for a moment, and pulled up a chair and sat.

"I hope you'll have someone guide us to the courthouse tomorrow," said Alvin, "for my appointment with the judge."

"It should be the very judge who issued the summons and the warrant," said Marty Laws. "We want to make sure he knows we complied with his orders as if they were completely lawful."

"They were," said Deputy Fiddler from his nearby table.

"We have taken them at face value," said Marty Laws, "and complied with every particular."

"The food here is pretty good," said Alvin, his mouth full. Then he chewed and swallowed. "I apologize," he said. "My wife would be dismayed to see me talking to our guests with my mouth full."

The Fiddlers and Sheriff Wiley looked confused.

"My wife says that refined people in Philadelphia, Paris, and London make it a point not to speak with their mouths full of food," said Alvin. "But I'm glad if you weren't offended by my faux pas."

Again, they all looked baffled. But since Alvin's tone was quite mild and pleasant, they didn't take offense at the French words. Foe paw? Meaningless.

The dinner lasted through drinks of cider and beer—no hard liquor, they needed their wits about them—and several of the posse joined them for those libations, though Marty reminded the tavernkeeper that these men would pay for their own.

After the meal was finished and the bill was paid, the tavernkeeper looked at Alvin suspiciously and said, "These coins aren't going to disappear or melt or something after you leave, are they?"

Alvin smiled. "Since you aren't aiming to shoot us with those coins, I can assure you they'll remain solid and inert." He loved stymying bossy men with the fine words Margaret had taught him when she was still his teacher and not his wife.

Meanwhile, to avoid rankling them, John Binder quietly explained what "inert" meant.

"Why didn't he just say that?" murmured Deputy Fiddler.

"He said *exactly* that," said John Binder, "using the exact right word."

"Ain't a word if nobody else ever heard of it," said another of the posse.

The jail wasn't far away, and Sheriff Wiley and old man Fiddler led the way to the upstairs cell. Wiley unlocked the heavy door and pushed it inward. The room was larger than Alvin had expected, and there were four cots. Had the number been augmented while they dined?

Sheriff Wiley was about to relock the door from the outside when he dropped the keys. He bent down to pick them up, but he couldn't seem to get a grip on them and kept dropping them.

"I reckon we'll sleep well enough without locking our door," said Alvin.

After the four of them were alone in the room, and Measure verified that Alvin had done a good job of making all the cots firm and soft enough, Alvin asked Marty Laws and John Binder to take turns singing a few songs before they slept. Alvin enjoyed Marty's sweet tenor, and John Binder's rumbly bass had real strength to it. Alvin and Measure didn't mind that Marty and John mostly knew hymns and other religious songs. It's not as if songs from Philadelphia had much currency on this side of the Appalachians, but everybody knew the common church songs.

After a while, when Marty claimed he was about sung out, they blew out the lantern and went to sleep. Without any words, they all took their turns being awake and on watch. Nobody came to disturb them, though Alvin was aware of the heartfires of several men who watched the jail from outside. It was all right with Alvin that his enemies seemed to have a healthy respect for his abilities. Maybe that respect would translate into nobody getting attacked or hurt.

35

As far as he knew, Arthur Stuart had everything as ready as it could be, short of actually calling the companies to muster and moving everyone out toward the river. At that point, of course, he would have to decide between hoping the Prophet had a hundred canoes big enough to carry wagons to the far shore, or giving the order to plunge the wagons into the water and cross the river on the bottom. "How long can you hold your breath?" he would ask each householder. They would say something, and he would say, "Hold it longer." Then they would all drown and float down the river.

In the meantime, he had absolutely nothing to do. Everything had to wait until Alvin came back from Carthage City.

Except that Arthur Stuart did not believe Alvin would ever come back from Carthage City.

In this morose frame of mind, with nothing left to do that needed doing, Arthur Stuart thought of going to Margaret's house and . . . and what, grieve her more? She knew even better than he did how dangerous Alvin's trip to Carthage was. Why did she let him do it?

As if anybody could stop Alvin from doing anything he decided had to be done. Or, for that matter, persuade him.

Oh, he had seen Margaret talk him into accepting many an idea that he at first rejected, but that was with matters of learning and logic. She was his teacher, long before being his wife. But when it was a matter of his purpose, his plan, he had often seen it: They would argue it, chew at it, sometimes for hours, sometimes for weeks. But in the end, Margaret always agreed to help him accomplish his aim, reach his goal.

As she had helped with this one. As Arthur Stuart was helping, too. Whatever the mad plan was.

He would not go to Margaret, because she would persuade him to be content, and even though he could never, never be content with this, he would *act* content. He would acquiesce and nobody but Margaret would know how much he hated being compliant.

Only she could see into his heartfire. She already knew. He did not have to waste her time convincing him of what he already knew. Alvin knew what was right. His plan was the right plan. His plan would *create* a better, stronger world.

Even if he wasn't there to enjoy it.

Because he was a Maker. Not really even a leader. A Maker.

Alvin, you stubborn man, the Maker is the one who is part of what he makes. Now you're making something that you cannot be part of because you'll be dead. The Unmaker cannot endure a world that has you in it, and you're handing him—it—the victory. Giving him that very world.

Because he had nowhere better to go, Arthur Stuart found himself entering the Crystal tower, though he had no reason to be there. It wasn't going to show him anything that he didn't already know.

He wandered idly among the halls, barely noticing whatever the walls were showing.

"You know what I'm trying to do here, don't you?" demanded a voice. Calvin Miller. What *was* he trying to do?

"Actually, I don't," said Arthur Stuart, turning to see Calvin sitting cross-legged on the floor, a single crystal block before him. Calvin's hand was resting on the block—which seemed as solid as ever. Oh, yes. Something about Calvin taking the Crystal tower apart so that the enemies of knackles wouldn't be able to use it to *see* anything.

"It's no use," said Calvin. "I was thinking that I couldn't dissolve these things because they were made by Alvin, and how could I unmake anything of his making."

So it wasn't taking the tower apart, it was taking the water-blocks apart, turning them back to water.

"You do know that if you succeed, all the water in the tower will come crashing down on you," said Arthur Stuart.

Calvin looked at him disdainfully. "Why else do you think I chose this spot, in the center of all the blocks, at the bottom?"

"Not sure that's what Alvin had in mind," said Arthur.

"I don't care what Alvin 'had in mind,'" said Calvin. "I know what *I* have in mind. Except how can I destroy Alvin's greatest work?"

Arthur heard this and knew it was wrong. Deeply wrong. He thought a while. And said, "This is not his greatest work."

"He told me that himself," said Calvin.

"No he didn't," said Arthur.

"You weren't there," said Calvin.

"He told you," said Arthur, "that Crystal City was his best work. The hardest job he ever succeeded at. That's what he told *me*, anyway, and he's not the kind who says one thing to me and another thing to you."

Calvin looked up from the block and met Arthur's gaze. "That's what I just said, except that you're right, he would never call it his 'greatest' work, because he didn't think greatness applied to anything he ever did."

"Don't you see the difference?" said Arthur. "He wants you to take down the Crystal tower, the crystal blocks. Those are *not* Crystal City."

Calvin stared at him. Thinking? Enraged? Motionless, anyway.

"He assigned you to take the actual crystals apart, Calvin. He charged *me* with keeping Crystal City together. Those are not contradictory."

"The people," said Calvin. "These shortsighted, foolish, gossipy, mean-spirited, confused, childish, self-destructive fools. The 'city,' as if that is an actual thing."

Arthur Stuart knew the answer, but he knew Calvin knew it, too.

And after a few moments of silence, Calvin said, "If he gets himself killed in Carthage—"

"When, not 'if,'" said Arthur.

"And if I figure out how to tear these blocks apart and release the water in them, the Crystal City will still exist, because it's the stupid people."

"It's the good people, the kind people, the ones who use their knacks for bettering the lives of other people."

"Have you met anybody like that?" asked Calvin.

"Yes," said Arthur Stuart.

"Name one," said Calvin, who then immediately corrected himself. "I mean, besides Margaret. And—why not?—you."

"And?"

"Measure," said Calvin. "Self-righteous, disdainful—"

"Kind, loyal, supportive, loving Measure," said Arthur Stuart. "A man worth three of either of us."

"And John Binder," said Calvin. "Annoying as he is, always so *nice* and soothing."

"His knack," said Arthur Stuart.

"Never worked on *me*," said Calvin.

"His knack was never to compel, only to invite. You've been invited, haven't you?"

"Only constantly," said Calvin.

"But you refuse."

"I *want* to be part of it," said Calvin. "Part of the city. I want it."

"You want to be in command of it," said Arthur Stuart. "I don't."

"Which I suppose is why he put you in command, and put me in charge of breaking what can't be broken."

Those words struck Arthur Stuart with real force. "He wouldn't have asked you to do what can't be done," said Alvin.

"And yet he did."

"No, no, we're both thinking of it wrong. Alvin never tries to Unmake *anything*."

"What else would you call it?"

"Don't you see, Calvin? He doesn't want you to tear down the tower or break apart the crystals."

"That's kind of what he *said* he wanted me to do."

Arthur Stuart knelt down to be on the same level as Calvin. "Cal," he said, "he doesn't want you to Unmake the crystals. He wants you to *make* them into *water*."

Calvin stared at him. "That's the same . . ."

"Maybe," said Arthur Stuart, "you need to get out from under the whole tower before you make it into water."

Calvin smiled wryly. "The Maker is the one who is part of what he makes."

"The Maker is *not* the one who deliberately drowns himself in a flood of his own making," said Arthur Stuart.

Calvin's hand was still on the block that lay on the floor in front of him. "To make these things, it took a tiny trace of the Maker's blood, and then a strong will to get the water to bind together using that blood, and become larger, and solid, in the shape of a block. But what is the shape of water?"

"Whatever you tell it to be."

"Does it take new blood?" asked Calvin.

"I don't think you have enough blood in your body to turn all these blocks back into water. I'll offer mine, as far as it goes, but I can't fulfill Alvin's instructions if I'm a bloodless, desiccated corpse."

"So I use the blood that's already incorporated in the blocks. Alvin's in most, mine in a few. Yours in none."

"I once offered Alvin some of my blood, and he said, 'It's the Maker, not his friend, who is part of what he makes.' "

"Alvin doesn't want me to serve the Unmaker," said Calvin.

"Never," said Arthur Stuart.

"*Make* them into water," said Calvin.

"Shouldn't we get out from under the main tower, Calvin?" asked Arthur Stuart.

"Yes, yes, you're right. It won't work if my plan is to have the water unmake *me*."

Arthur Stuart realized something. "Because the Unmaker is *never* a part of his own unmaking."

Calvin reached up a hand. "I've been sitting here a long time, I'm not sure if my legs will even work."

Arthur Stuart took Calvin's hand and pulled him up into a squat, and then to his feet, standing tall. About Arthur's height.

"A minute before I try to walk," said Calvin.

"I've got all the time in the world." Which was Arthur's way of saying, Take your time, but don't take forever.

Still gripping Arthur's hand, Calvin took one step. His hand pressed and pulled on Arthur, trying to use him to keep his balance. Arthur cooperated, until he was embracing Calvin, and Calvin was embracing him in order to maintain his balance.

"Keep holding on," said Arthur. "Your balance will come back to you."

"You hope," said Calvin.

But even in saying those dismissive words, Calvin's strength and flexibility returned, his *balance* returned, and he let go of Arthur Stuart's strong but exhausted hand.

Together the two of them walked toward the egress, Arthur Stuart always close by in case Calvin stumbled, which he did, several times, but never fell because Arthur was right there.

Outside the building, there were several passersby who saw them. Maybe they wondered at these two longtime rivals helping each other. Maybe they didn't know or even care what was going on.

Calvin sat down on the sheep-mown grass, though no sheep were close by today. Did they know there was going to be a flood?

"So how do you make water out of a block of crystal?" asked Calvin. Arthur Stuart knew he wasn't really asking him. He was asking *himself.*

"Can you find the blood traces?" asked Arthur Stuart.

There was a nearby block on the grass. Arthur and Calvin both looked closely at it. A thin bead of red appeared on top, then began to glide down the face of the block. It never grew. It reached the edge and then dripped off the tilted block into the grass.

"Water," whispered Calvin.

The block shape was instantly gone. Instead, water splashed and gurgled, running over the meadow along the downward slope leading to the river.

"I need to channel it toward the south, not the river," said Calvin.

"Then do it," said Arthur Stuart.

The ground heaved slightly under them as the slope began to guide the water to the south. Another jolt and Arthur Stuart could see that between the brow of the hill and the pathway down toward the river, there was now a slight ridge of earth that would channel any water away from the river.

"I think that does it," said Arthur Stuart. "But if you could do that, why haven't you ever done it before?"

"I didn't know I could do it," said Calvin. "I never tried. I never *thought* of doing it."

"You live and you learn," said Arthur Stuart.

"I don't think it would be wise of me to bring the whole thing down at once," said Calvin.

"It's your job, to do as you see fit," said Arthur.

"I'd feel safer if you weren't here," said Calvin. "I mean, I feel that *you'd* be safer."

"I am of the same opinion," said Arthur.

Calvin looked at him oddly.

"What?" asked Arthur.

"For a moment there . . ."

Arthur shrugged.

"You sounded like him," said Calvin.

Arthur laughed. "You don't know my knack, then?"

"Didn't know you had one," said Calvin. "I mean, I never gave it a thought. Of course you have a knack."

"For a while I lost it," said Arthur. "When Alvin changed me. When he made it so the slave catchers couldn't identify me anymore. But in the years since then, little by little, it came back to me, as strong as ever."

"Your body remembered itself?"

"Maybe," said Arthur. "But I figured it was Alvin that remembered how I was, and over time kept trying to give me back my knack without making me identifiable to the catchers again."

"You never asked him?"

"He was ashamed of having lost me my knack. And it was all a long time ago, when I lost it and when it came back. Might have been my own body remaking itself. Or Alvin. Or some angel, for all I know. Or myself, in a dream, knowing more than I knew that I knew."

"It's all pretty vague," said Calvin.

"Just when I think I know how knacks work," said Arthur Stuart, "something happens that doesn't fit, so I have to tweak my ideas a little. Or a lot."

Calvin nodded.

"It's the way of the world," Arthur said. "It works, whether we understand it or not."

"What works?"

"Breathing. Walking. Sleeping, waking, dreaming, hoping. Illness, health, anger, peace, love. So much magic in the world," said Arthur Stuart.

"Sometimes it seems to me that nothing is actually real," said Calvin. "Things are just as everything and everybody agreed to make it all work together, but it could all change its mind, a little, a lot, and then there'd be a new set of rules."

"And then we have to figure it all out again," said Arthur.

"And whether we're coming to understand how things are, or whether things *are* as we come to imagine them to be . . ."

"Listen to us, philosophizing like old professors," said Arthur Stuart.

"Oh, we know *way* more than any professors anywhere," said Calvin.

"I don't know about *that*," said Arthur.

"*We* have known a real Maker," said Calvin. "We've seen things change, impossible things."

"Blocks of liquid water that you can build with," said Arthur.

"And crystals that can be turned into water," said Calvin. "Run along now, Mr. Stuart."

"I imagine things will go swimmingly for you now," said Arthur.

Calvin laughed at the pun.

And at that moment, for the first time he could remember, Arthur Stuart thought he saw why Alvin loved Calvin, despite all that Calvin had done. Alvin's brother, so close to being a Maker, was like anybody else, trying to figure out his place in the world, if he had one. And at this moment, he had found *something*. A way to be.

Calvin got up and started back toward the entrance to the tower.

"I hope you're not going inside again," said Arthur Stuart, tagging along for the present.

"I don't know *what* I'm doing. Do I have to be touching a block to change it? I don't know the rules."

"*Make* the rules," said Arthur.

"Oh, obviously," said Calvin. "Everybody knows *that*."

They stood beside a wall near the entrance. Even on the outside of the structure, there were visions in the crystal blocks. A movement in one block caught Arthur's eye. It was one he thought he had seen before. A man walking away from a building in a faraway city. A large man, a strong one, grizzled and creased and craggy. Mike Fink. Walking away from the city and out toward the woods, where someone was waiting for him.

Me, thought Arthur Stuart. He's coming to me. Disappointed, hurt, grieving, weeping. Mike Fink, coming to me.

And suddenly it became clear to Arthur Stuart. "Well, Calvin," he said. "I've got to go see a man about a cow."

Calvin waggled the fingers of one hand in farewell.

With that, Arthur walked away, upslope a little, and then down the slope the other way, toward the town.

It didn't take him long to find the man. Mike Fink had realized that Alvin was gone, and he went to the only person he could be sure would know where he was. Margaret Larner.

Mike was sitting on the top step of the front stoop of the house.

"Miz Larner isn't home?" asked Arthur Stuart as he approached.

"She's home."

"She won't talk with you?" asked Arthur.

"We had a talk," said Mike. "She told me to trust Alvin and not try to find him."

"You know where he is," said Arthur Stuart. "There's no mystery about that."

"Carthage City. Keeping his word to that damnable slaver," said Mike.

"So why are you just sitting here?" asked Arthur Stuart.

"Even if I could find a horse willing to let me ride her," said Mike, "I don't know the way and it would still take a couple of days to get there."

"What do you think you could do if you got there in time?" asked Arthur Stuart.

"Save his damn fool life," said Mike Fink.

Arthur held out his hand. "Then let's go."

Mike hesitated. "You can take me into the Greensong, like Alvin?"

Mike got up from the porch and let Arthur Stuart lead him. Arthur felt like a pebble dragging a boulder along behind him.

But as they walked, Arthur Stuart felt the Greensong tugging at him, and he let the melody of it, the harmony, flow into him, through him, until it ran like his own blood through his arteries and veins, away from his heart, then back again, with every beat of his pulse.

"Good Lord," muttered Mike.

They were in the Greensong. And Arthur Stuart started running, pulling Mike along, and they both began running as lightly as deer, Mike right along with Arthur, and they were surrounded by green on every side, and the branches and briers parted for them, and the ground came up easy to their feet, with no obstruction to trip on.

The world moved around them rapidly, faster and faster, as the miles fell behind them.

Alvin wouldn't want me to do this, thought Arthur Stuart. But I'm a free man, and so is Mike Fink, and maybe we can make our own plans sometimes, not just follow what Alvin tells us to do or not do. Maybe we can save that good man in spite of himself. Did he ever think of that?

36

"AM I THE only one as wants breakfast?" asked Measure.

All three of the others had been sound asleep. John Binder and Marty Laws stirred at once, but Alvin remained absolutely still.

Alvin's stillness lasted until the others were nearly dressed. "Come on, Alvin," said Measure. "We're not going to go eat without you, and the rest of us are hungry."

With a sigh, Alvin rolled over and spilled himself onto the floor, guiding his feet into his boots, pulling them on.

"You're going to put your trousers on *over* your boots?" asked Marty Laws.

John Binder looked again. "He slept in his trousers," he said.

"I don't like changing clothes to no purpose," said Alvin. "Why take them off if I'm just going to put them back on in the morning?"

"So they don't look slept in," said Marty.

John Binder smiled. "Marty, your clothes always look slept in."

Meanwhile, Measure laughed. "Well, gentlemen, it looks as if Alvin found him an all-night laundry and clothes-press."

John Binder sighed. "Alvin, you've got these fabulous powers, and you use them to press your trousers?"

"My shirt, too," said Alvin. "And make them shed their road-dust and sweat-stains. And my bootsoles repair themselves to my specifications. I'd say that's a right demanding set of accomplishments for my knackery."

"Didn't clean *my* clothes," said Marty.

"You didn't ask me to," said Alvin.

"As if any of us would ask the Maker to do our laundry," said John Binder.

"What if I did it wrong?" asked Alvin. "Don't want to be liable for any weaknesses in your apparel down the road."

"We going somewhere on some road today?" asked Measure.

"We've got a good while till we come before the judge," said Alvin. "Nothing in that paper required us to come at ten in the morning. And by whose watch, anyway?"

"I think I'm the only one with a watch," said John Binder, pulling it by the fob out of his waistcoat.

"Alvin keeps the time ticking in his brain day and night," said Measure. "Waking and sleeping."

"Do not. I'm just a good guesser." Alvin made a point of looking at the window. "Some morning clouds, but it'll be a right sunny day."

"What time is it?" asked Measure.

"Half past seven," said Alvin.

"Which you knew without looking," said Measure.

"Do you know what I found out by looking?" asked Alvin. "There's no bars on that window. Just a counterhung sash. No locking mechanism, no blocks, it's just a regular window."

"I hope you don't plan to escape that way," said Marty Laws, looking out and down. "This is a right high window, and the ground below it is paved with cobbles so if a body jumps, they'll split their head."

"Or break every *other* bone in their bodies," said John Binder. "No way to jump out and hit the ground running and get away."

"Alvin can do it if he wants," said Measure.

"But he doesn't want," said Alvin. "You think I'd run away, and leave you three here for the mob to vent their anger on?"

"Right now, we aren't even locked in. We just open the door," said Marty, "go down the stairs, and go on our way."

"To the tavern for breakfast," said John Binder.

"Taverners don't know how to cook an egg," said Alvin. "They always break the yolk and wind up scrambling the eggs, like any lazy, incompetent parlor maid what got assigned to breakfast because the cook was sick."

"Where do you think we should eat, then?" asked Measure. "Plead with some hens to lay us soft-boiled eggs this morning?"

"If there's one group that knows less about cooking eggs, it's hens," said Alvin.

"Where, then?" said John Binder.

"Why don't we set out on *my* morning errand, and see if we come upon breakfast along the way," said Alvin.

It's not like any of them had any reason to disagree, beyond the impatience of hunger.

Alvin had his waistcoat on, but no tie or collar.

"Don't you feel naked?" asked John Binder.

"I been naked," said Alvin. "This is different."

"No collar?" asked Marty Laws.

"Collars are all scratchy," said Alvin.

"It just makes you look like a condemned man," said John Binder.

"The noose works best when there's no collar in the way," Alvin agreed.

"I imagine you've made a study of hangings," said Marty.

"Just common sense," said Alvin. "If I ever seen a hanging, I'd remember, I think."

They weren't ten steps out of the jail building when a huge creature bounded up and threw its arms around Alvin.

"You didn't think you could get away from your bodyguard, did you?" By the voice, they all knew it was Mike Fink.

"Thought you was up between lakes," said Alvin.

"Heard it was time for you to go to Carthage to get arrested," said Mike. "No way that was going to happen without me beside you."

"Didn't Margaret tell you—"

"Margaret told me some nonsense about you not wanting me put at risk. And I told her, my being at risk was the life I chose for myself."

"And she told you to stay in Crystal City."

"Because she told me *you* told her to say that. If you got instructions for me, Alvin, tell me to my own face."

"If you're here," said Alvin, "I won't have a free hand to do the things I must."

"My being here is *why* you'll have a free hand," said Mike Fink.

"Mike, if anybody wants to get to me, what do they need to do first?"

Mike Fink thought a bit longer than the others would have found necessary. "I reckon if I was them, I'd say, kill that big man as is always looking after Alvin Smith, so we can get to the Maker without any of *us* getting kilt."

"That's my problem, having you here, Mike," said Alvin. "I don't want anybody getting kilt to save me from what nobody can save me from."

"Then why did you come here?" demanded Mike Fink.

"Because my promise to come bought my people time to get their wagons and their companies and prepare to cross the Mizzippy."

"Without boats," said Marty.

"Won't need boats," said Alvin.

"Wings?" asked John Binder.

"A sudden hard freeze," said Alvin. "Solid ice, roll the wagons right across."

"Then you need to be back there," said Mike Fink. "To freeze that river."

"There are two good freezers in the city," said Alvin. "One among the Irish, one among the folk we brought up from the South."

"Why haven't I heard of them?" asked John Binder.

"We didn't need their knacks until now. And Calvin will strengthen whatever they freeze."

They all fell silent at the mention of Calvin.

"Why do you go on picking people to lead who never led anybody before?" asked John Binder.

"Everybody has to do everything for the first time, once, anyway," said Alvin.

"But *Calvin*," said John Binder.

"Calvin isn't leading, because he's not crossing the river," said Alvin. "He'll know that the two freezers can't reach far enough or make it thick enough, but he can help them reach, and so he will."

"Miz Larner told me you like to pick people she warned you against trusting," said Mike Fink.

"I don't pick them *because* she warned me."

Measure gave an abrupt little "Ha!"

"I pick them because I don't know as anybody's ever given them a chance to show their character," said Alvin.

"Calvin's shown his character about three hundred times so far," said Measure.

"Calvin's never shown his own character," said Alvin. "You'll see. He knows more than you think. He *is* better than you know."

"I'm trying to figure out," said Measure, "how Mike Fink got here so quick."

Mike looked away.

"Greensong," said Measure. "And since Alvin and I were here, it had to be Arthur Stuart."

Mike's blush gave it away. "I bet he's back in Crystal City by now," said Mike.

"He's waiting right where you left him," said Alvin, "at the forest edge."

"Why?" asked Mike Fink.

"To take you back to Crystal City by the same road you came on."

Mike looked defeated. He also looked angry. "Who says you always get to have your way?"

"It's not my way," said Alvin. "I don't *have* a way. Things don't go by my plan. I just make the best of what comes up."

"And this . . . asinine thing is 'making the best'?"

"As far as I can figure it out," said Alvin.

"Start your figgering over at the beginning, then," said Mike Fink.

"Done that many times," said Alvin. "I even crossed the river, but some of my friends came to tell me I needed to come back."

"We didn't know you'd accept a summons and a warrant and show up here, which is like the northernmost bit of the slave-owning South," said John Binder.

"I made the best deal I could for my people—with the Prophet and with his wicked counterpart, Cavil Planter."

"You got the time you needed. Why did you keep your word?" demanded Mike Fink.

"Because it was *my* word," said Alvin. "Now if you'll excuse me, Mike, I need to find us some breakfast and go to a place in Carthage that means something to me, before I go see the judge."

"You inviting me to breakfast?" asked Mike Fink.

Alvin was already walking down the road.

"No, he's not," said Measure. "He's inviting you to go to Arthur Stuart and get him to guide you home."

"My home is wherever Alvin is, when he needs me," said Mike Fink.

"Your home is wherever he needs you to be," said Measure, "and he's told you where that is."

Mike Fink burst into tears. Big and mean-looking as he was, it still wasn't incongruous, the tears streaming down his face. Like a big disappointed toddler.

He turned away, not so much to hide his tears as to get started walking back to where Arthur Stuart was waiting.

This moment had been foreshadowed multiple times in the crystal blocks of the tower. It was always known that Mike would come, and that Alvin would send him away. Did that mean they were on the right track? wondered Measure. Or did it mean that they had been warned again and again not to let this happen?

Back at the forest edge, Arthur Stuart saw Mike approaching and ran to him, embraced him, let him weep into his shoulder. "You knew this was coming," said Arthur Stuart.

"Knowing ain't liking," said Mike Fink.

Arthur pulled away from the larger man. He was weeping, too.

"Can we still run with the Greensong even when we're both all blurry with tears?" asked Mike Fink.

"Let's find out."

Alvin and his companions walked a couple of blocks up the road from the jailhouse when they came upon a woman hanging clothes on the line. "A right nice day for drying clothes," said Alvin.

"From your mouth to God's ears," said the woman.

"You think God minds how quick your clothes dry on the line?" asked Alvin.

"God minds the little sparrow," said the woman.

Alvin laughed a little. "Goodwife," said Alvin, "I reckon I smell bacon from inside your house."

"That's my daughter," said the woman. "She's cooking, that is, not *being* cooked. She's making up breakfast for her da."

"All that bacon and all them eggs, just for one man?" asked Alvin.

"For me, too, and her, and the little-uns."

"The little-uns are two boys, twins, thirteen years old, am I right?" asked Alvin.

"How did you know?" she said.

"Just seemed logical," said Alvin. "Just like I figure you got enough breakfast in there to add four hungry grown men, without depriving anybody of anything they wouldn't've et anyway."

"I don't think we have that much extra," said the woman.

"Goodwife," said Measure, "when Alvin Maker says you got enough, you got enough."

The woman mouthed the words "Alvin Maker" and then she looked over to see that Measure and John Binder had already put three sheets on the line, with good, secure-looking pegwork. "You set to finish this basket's worth?" she asked them.

"Think we can manage it," said Measure.

"But how will you eat if you're doing my work?"

"We'll be in before you say grace over the food," said Measure. "We don't aim to miss such a good breakfast."

The woman harrumphed, but it was partly amusement, almost a laugh. She walked away from her basket of laundry and walked inside.

Three quarters of an hour later, the man of the house, the daughter, the twin boys, and the goodwife herself had eaten to satiation, as had their four guests from the jailhouse. "Alvin promised us he'd find us a better breakfast than anything in the tavern," said Marty Laws.

"They don't know how to cook an egg," said the daughter.

"But miss, *you* sure enough do," said John Binder.

Alvin rose from the table. "Madam," he said, "I think I can say that even if this turns out to be the last breakfast I eat upon this Earth, it could not have been better."

"Let's all pray that it's *not* the last!" said the daughter, a little outraged.

"Oh, we been praying," said Measure. "But the breakfast was as good as my brother said."

"And we had Alvin the Maker as a guest at our table," said the husband. "It has been an honor, sir."

Alvin knew but did not say that he had paid for the breakfast by clearing up the arthritis in the man's knees, straightening up the stoop in the daughter's posture, and taking out the cancer in both the goodwife's breasts, long before it could grow dangerous and spread throughout her body. The twins had nothing but a bunch of scrapes and scabs, but Alvin healed the skin without leaving any scars. It seemed to him the least he could do.

It was only another couple of blocks till they came to Alvin's real destination. The roads all came together in a circle going around a steep cone of earth rising up like an arrow.

"What is that?" asked Marty Laws.

"It's a Red mound," said Measure. "Seen them all across Hio and Wobbish."

Alvin walked across the road, jumped the low fence, and started to climb the mound. The others joined him. It was steeper than any Red mound any of them had seen, yet it wasn't hard to climb.

"Have you been here before?" asked John Binder, when they were gathered on the top.

"Not with my body," said Alvin. "But I saw it from Eight-Face Mound. In fact, you can't help but see it, since it's visible from there no matter which face you climb and no matter which way you face."

"Sounds impossible," said Marty Laws.

"Sounds miraculous," said Mcasurc.

"It's just the way of the Reds with the land," said Alvin. "Not that this was built by any of the Reds that live around here now. This is near four thousand years old, older than Eight-Face Mound, though not by much. The Reds who built it didn't speak any language that's being spoken now. From this mound, these people ruled an empire that went all the way to the mountains and across the Mizzippy to the mountains on the other side."

"How do you know all this?" asked Marty Laws.

"I saw it all, years ago, from Eight-Face Mound," said Alvin. "This was all built before Rome started up their empire. Before Alexander conquered half the world."

"Why didn't they build in stone, like the Egyptians?" asked John.

"Why didn't the Egyptians build in soil, like these folks?" asked Measure.

"I reckon what the Egyptians had instead of soil was sand," said Marty.

"They had *good* soil, those Egyptians," said John Binder. "Floods of the Nile River brought good fresh soil every year, so they could grow crops of grain—barley, I hear, since they drank beer prodigiously."

"You had a good education, I reckon," said Alvin.

"I read me a book once," said John Binder.

"I guess it don't take much to get educated," said Alvin.

"Why did you bring us here?" asked Measure.

"I wanted to complete the vision," said Alvin. "Because when I was on Eight-Face Mound, I saw myself standing here. With my brother Measure and two other men whose faces I couldn't make out at the time."

"You saw *yourself*?" asked Marty.

"And, apparently, I saw you, too," said Alvin. "And now, my friends, I think we got plenty of time to find the courthouse and go inside by ten o'clock. Why keep the judge waiting, if we don't have to?"

When Alvin and his companions entered the courthouse, he was not surprised to hear a cry of "There he is!" and hear the scampering and pounding of feet on the heavy plank floors. At once hands were all over Alvin's arms, shoulders, the back of his neck—but the hands immediately slid off, like butter on hot bread.

"I'm a mite confused," said Alvin after this had gone on long enough. "It's my name on the summons, and here you are gripping my companions, who aren't charged with anything, who came along as my attorney and some friends, and yet you're treating them like criminals."

"You know we can't get any hold on you," said one of the men.

"Of course not," said Alvin. "I'm an innocent man. So are my friends. We got here in time for me to present myself to the judge at ten in the morning on the first of November, and you seem to be trying to make me late."

"We are charged," said the leader, "with making sure you appear in court."

"I see. Did you escort us all the way from Crystal City? No? Did you escort us from the jail where we spent the night? No? Did we enter this courthouse a little early, without the slightest compulsion from any of you?"

"We have our orders!"

"Weren't your orders to see to it we got before the judge?"

No answer.

"We're heading for the courtroom, if you'll just tell us which one is his. There seem to be four courtrooms in this building."

"Two of them are still empty," said the leader. "Haven't needed them yet. There's a civil case under way in courtroom three, and the judge is waiting for you in courtroom four."

"So courtrooms one and two are the empty ones," said Measure, as his guards let him go.

"We started with three and four because they're on the north side of the building. Way cooler on a sunny day."

"That's sensible," said Alvin. "You got sensible folk here in Carthage."

Now Alvin and his friends were all free. Marty Laws took his place beside Alvin and they walked into the courtroom together, the other two following right behind. Marty led Alvin up to the front of the aisle, so that the defense and prosecution tables were on either side of them.

The judge glowered at them. "I thought I sent men to fetch you."

"And here we are," said Marty Laws. "Fetched."

"Are you mocking this court, sir?" asked the judge.

"I certainly am not," said Marty Laws. "We came a good long way from the shores of the Mizzippy to comply with your material witness summons, sir. I think that shows our respect for this court."

"Who are *you*?" asked the judge.

"Martin Laws, Your Honor, attorney for Mr. Alvin Smith, who is standing beside me."

The judge looked at Alvin. "Are you the one they call Alvin Maker?"

"Can't rightly say, Your Honor," said Alvin. "I was born Alvin Miller, Junior, and then I became a journeyman smith, so now I'm called Alvin Smith. Others may call me whatever names they choose, but I came here for a summons that has my name as Alvin Smith."

The judge raised his gavel. "I hereby stay the material witness summons against Alvin Smith." He brought down the gavel.

"Why thank you, Your Honor," said Marty Laws. "We'll be on our way, then." He started to guide Alvin to turn around.

"Hold where you are, sir," said the judge. "There's the little matter of the arrest warrant for Mr. Smith."

"But that arrest warrant doesn't actually charge him with anything," said Marty. "Without any charges, how can my client even be arraigned? He has to be charged with *something* before he can plead."

"Whatever the charge is," said Alvin, "I plead not guilty, on account of I done nothing wrong." Alvin was pouring on the hick country boy attitude, because it would be better if the judge thought he was too dumb to be a threat to anybody.

"Mr. Laws, please instruct your client to be silent until he is directed, by *me*, to speak."

"Just hoping to save time," Alvin muttered.

The bailiff brought a piece of paper to the judge, who glanced at it and looked again at Alvin. "Alvin Smith, or Alvin Miller, Junior, as you have styled yourself before, this court charges you with resisting arrest, interfering with officers of the law attempting to obey a court order to bring you before this bench, and doing so by means of so-called knacks, which it is illegal to use against law enforcement personnel, doing their sworn duty."

Alvin thought this through, realizing that these charges all pertained to what happened not ten minutes ago, outside the courtroom.

Meanwhile, Marty Laws put on his most innocent face. "Your Honor, were these the charges for which my client was placed under arrest back in April? Because *if* these things happened, they happened in the last quarter hour. What have the charges been from serving the warrant until now?"

"What the original charges were is irrelevant," said the judge. "These are the charges for which your client is being arraigned right now."

"With respect, Your Honor, how can my client be charged with resisting arrest when he came into this court of his own volition?"

"Is there a motion in there somewhere, Mr. Laws?"

"Since I was present for the alleged events, I can personally affirm that the men who accosted my client and his companions, including me, never identified themselves as being officers of the law. So as far as we knew, we were being set upon by bandits, and we had no reason not to resist them."

"So you stipulate that you did indeed resist them," said the judge.

"I stipulate that we submitted to them, did not harm them, and complied with their instructions, without raising a hand of violence against them," said Marty Laws.

The judge looked at the squad of constables or whatever they were, and some of them sheepishly nodded.

"Well, apparently there's a circus in town, and these are the clowns," said the judge.

"They've been sober gentlemen throughout our acquaintanceship," said Alvin.

"I believe your client is speaking," said the judge.

Marty again gripped Alvin's arm and urged him to keep still.

"The arguments you have brought up are not appropriate for the arraignment. All such matters can be addressed at the trial."

"Trial? Has there been a true bill of indictment?" asked Marty Laws.

"Done last April," said the judge.

"And what were the charges upon which my client was indicted?" asked Marty Laws. "His *future* outrages?"

"It was a sealed indictment," said the judge.

"The defendant still has a right to—"

"Not if the court has reason to believe that witnesses before the grand jury are likely to be intimidated or harmed should their names be revealed."

Marty took a step toward the bench. "On what grounds does the court suspect my client of intimidation of witnesses!"

"The grounds that he has powerful knacks that can strike down his enemies from far away."

"What enemy has he ever stricken down? Your Honor, I mean."

"You are coming near a charge of contempt of court, Mr. Laws."

"And what is the penalty for that?" asked Marty. "Hanging? Drowning? Flogging?"

The judge brought down his gavel. "I hereby cite you for contempt, Mr. Laws. You will be held for three days in Carthage Jail."

"Your Honor," said Marty. "Would that be the very jail where we are already boarding?"

The judge consulted quietly with the bailiff. "The same," said the judge.

"I will serve my sentence with great penitence for having behaved in such a way as to cause Your Honor to feel that I was disrespectful to the court."

"Shut up, Mr. Laws. Your sarcasm is likely to add to your sentence for contempt."

"Sarcasm?" cried Marty Laws in outrage.

The gavel came down again. "Silence. This court did not assemble to hear your complaints and feigned outrage, Mr. Laws. Alvin Miller, Junior, or Alvin Smith, whichever alias you are using today, do you understand the charges against you as I listed them—a long, long time ago?"

"I understand them, and I plead—"

"You have not yet been asked to plead, Mr. Smith."

Alvin waited.

"Mr. Smith or Miller, to these charges, how do you plead? Guilty or not guilty?"

"Not guilty, Your Honor."

"There will be no bail in this case," said the judge, "since I have been assured that the defendant has a habit of escaping custody and evading arrest."

"I got no money anyway," said Alvin.

The gavel struck again. Marty again forcefully whispered to Alvin, "Don't go off the script."

"The defendant will be escorted to Carthage Jail where he is to be confined until his trial, for which the date of November fourteenth has been decided." To Marty, the judge said, "This will give you nearly two weeks to prepare your case."

"I look forward to receiving all of the depositions and interrogatories that have been sworn against my client," said Marty Laws.

"There are no documents at present," said the judge, "but as they are prepared, copies will be sent to you in jail."

"Can we expect to be fed while imprisoned?" asked Marty Laws.

"Yes," said the judge. "But not at the expense of the City of Carthage. You have companions with you?"

"Yes, Your Honor," said Marty, stopping Alvin from answering directly. "They can acquire food in the city and bring it to the jail."

"I hope they can eat with us, and sleep in the room with us, as they did last night," said Marty Laws.

"Of course. But the door is to be locked at night."

Alvin tried mightily not to smile at the idea of a lock holding him in.

The judge might have seen the first trace of that smile on Alvin's face. "The court is well aware that no lock can keep Alvin *Maker* inside any place he wants to get out of. The lock is for your protection, in case outraged citizens try to cause you harm."

"That is very considerate of the court," said Marty Laws. "Has the court any specific information about persons seeking to harm my client?"

The judge gaveled the end of the arraignment without answering. Then he stood up and stalked out of the courtroom through the door leading to his chambers.

We really managed to discombobulate the fellow, didn't we? thought Alvin. It had been so tempting to turn the head of that gavel into taffy, so it would stick to the anvil. But Alvin knew that only he would really appreciate the humor of it, and it couldn't help his case. Not that it mattered, not that his trial would ever take place.

A parade of law enforcement personnel followed them through the streets leading to the jail. The four companions climbed up the stairs and, as promised, the door was locked behind them.

"I think the locking of the door was premature," said John Binder, "considering that we haven't had our luncheon yet, nor our supper."

"At least we have the chamber pot and the cuspidor," said Measure. "Though for four men, I don't know how a chamber pot that size will serve."

"Maybe that's why the window opens," offered Marty Laws. "So we can empty it onto the stones below, every time someone has used it."

"Since nobody here chews tobaccy," said Measure, "I nominate the cuspidor as our urinal, which will make the chamber pot discharge less fluid and splashy on the cobbles."

His nomination was carried by acclamation.

With little else to do, they sang a few songs that they knew—hymns, some of them, and ballads, and anthems. They napped a little as the day got hot—the open window, having no cross-ventilation, did not cool the room much, especially as it was south-facing and there was no shade.

The door was unlocked at five in the evening, and two men brought in four pails, containing "a bean stew with cinnamon in it—a specialty of Carthage City," one of the men explained, a melange of fruits, bread and cheeses, and a watered-down wine of an exceptionally bad vintage. They made the best of this feast, and, as Measure pointed out, "We don't have to pay for it after all."

"Unless they present us a bill upon our release," said John Binder.

They all chuckled, though mirth sat pretty low in their hearts tonight.

"John Binder, you have a good voice," said Alvin. "Do you happen to know the song about the man who keeps helping a stranger, and the stranger turns out to have been the Savior all along?"

"It's a new song, but I liked it right away, so I committed it to memory. If I had a guitar, I could accompany it, too."

"Can't help with the guitar," said Alvin. "But I want to hear it again tonight. I think I need the reassurance of those words."

37

MARGARET WAS ONLY occasionally in suspense about the outcomes of crucial choices. She knew all the things that could go wrong, but usually she could catch glimpses, at least, of how people she cared about would cope, adapt, recover from disaster. And along with that, she foresaw much about people she cared about less.

I am not a very good Christian, she had to admit to herself. She knew she *should* care about all God's children equally. But if that's what God really wanted, why did he put us on Earth in families? Nobody could hurt and annoy you like family members; no one could give you strength and wisdom better than family members.

The virtues of families were spread no more equally than knacks. She saw children playing, and recognized, in their outward behavior and in their heartfires, which children really had compassionate hearts, which were kind by nature, with no disposition toward taunting and tormenting.

And she recognized the torturers, the ones who thrived on other people's fear and grief and pain. Why would this be born in some children, and not others?

I know too much, thought Margaret.

And I do not know enough, because for the past few weeks Alvin's heartfire has shone no light on what is coming. Did this blankness mean that he will die in Carthage, and never come home to me and Vigor and whoever these new babies turn out to be? Or is it just a way to humble me, so I won't get too complacent in my foreknowledge?

This is how Margaret spent most of her nights, or so it seemed. She must sleep at night, because she kept waking up all night. And the moment she awoke, all she could do was fret about Alvin.

Yes, protecting and supporting him was her life's work, and had been since she pulled the caul from his newborn face and allowed him to catch his first breaths. Using that caul, breaking off a pinch of it when she needed to use some of Alvin's power, she had been able to save him from the attempts of the Unmaker to kill him as in infant, as a child. And when he was old enough to protect himself by using his own knacks, she got her training as a schoolteacher and then came to be his teacher, along with the other young people of Hatrack River.

How long was it before he realized that she was the same Little Peggy who had laid hands on his mother's womb and seen that brightness of the light that shone from his heart. She did not even know what a Maker was, when she first formed that word in her mind. A Maker is born.

His ability to see into heartfires was limited compared to hers, but surely he saw from the start of her stint as his schoolteacher that she had been his childhood protector when she was barely older than he was. But then, maybe he also had blind spots about her, as she did about him.

Will he die?

Please bring him back to me, alive and ready to live the peaceful life of a husband and father. *My* husband. My children's father. So long he has belonged to "his people," the knackles who had few other protectors, but now it had to be the time for him to live among his people in the faraway West, near that strange Salt Lake, like a Dead Sea in the midst of the mountains, and I will live with him, and we will be . . . ordinary. We'll have an ordinary life.

Or I'll bury him before we cross over the river.

God, has he been serving you all these years? Have I? Isn't there an end to the sacrifice? Can't Vigor grow to manhood in the light of Alvin's proud and loving eyes? Can Alvin and I grow old together? Is there no respite?

It was already light outside, she could see through the drapes.

When I feel like I've had no sleep at all, how am I supposed to rise up and face this morning?

There was a knock at the door.

Alvin had urged her to keep a maid, someone who could answer the door. And so she had a maid—who began her duties at nine in the morning.

Margaret got out of bed, feeling more energy than she had expected, but less good cheer in the morning than she usually felt. This was not a day of confidence, but it *was* a day of work and works. There would be so many people wondering: Will we cross over the river before Alvin comes home? Where will we get boats? Will the showboat ferry us across, along with our animals? Should we muster a militia and be prepared to defend our city against marauders again?

Two men with the knack of making ponds and puddles and, yes, streams and rivers freeze over in winter. Alvin had mentioned that there were such men, one Irish, one from the South. He had spoken as if she already knew who they were, but how would she? If those were their knacks, there hadn't been much call for freezing rivers during the summer and fall, so they hadn't made much use of those knacks.

It was Calvin at the door. He did not seem to want to come in, so he wasn't here to mooch a free breakfast.

Get your resentment of Alvin's nasty little brother under control. For all you know, Margaret, he's doing his petty, malicious best to be a good brother to Alvin.

But lately, the last few days, really, Calvin seemed to be making an effort. So maybe Alvin had been right to trust him with a few responsibilities. Though perhaps it was telling that his main responsibility was to *Unmake* the crystal part of the Crystal City.

"Miz Margaret," he said, and his humility and meekness were quite believable, along with a shy kind of pride. "I've made sure that the water will all flow south, into the boggy land where nobody lives. So the last part, the main tower, I thought I'd bring it all down at once."

Margaret waited for him to tell her why he got her out of bed to hear this news.

He wants me to watch his triumphant moment. Doesn't he realize how much those crystal blocks meant to Alvin and me? How devastating their destruction will be?

"Can we see it from here? Because I don't want to dress to go out in public this early in the morning."

"If you can see the tower from here," said Calvin, "you can see its fall."

"Well then, Calvin, let me see you fulfill the charge your brother left with you."

He looked a bit crestfallen, and she realized—he wanted me to watch with him as equals, each of us doing our part. Instead, I reminded him that he was only obeying Alvin, and I would be watching *his* work, not *their* work together. I diminished him.

No I didn't. I treated him exactly as his stature in this community deserved. I am respecting his power.

At least he didn't try to make it a huge public ceremony, though he had hinted a couple of times, should they tell people it was going to happen? And she had refused to make it a grand spectacle for the whole city.

She stepped out onto the porch. The two of them rested their hands on the railing, and Calvin leaned a bit against the post holding up the porch roof.

The Crystal tower at that moment caught the first sunlight coming over the horizon. No part of the disk of the sun was visible from the porch, but its light reflected and dazzled at the top of the Crystal tower.

The place of free and open visions for all comers would come down. She thought of the place in—Exodus? Or one of the later books?—when Moses said, "I wish all my people were prophets." That's what Alvin had built out of his own blood and the water of the river. Now coming down.

"You don't have to be touching one of the blocks?" asked Margaret.

"I've learned a lot in the last day. I can sense Alvin's blood in the crystals, because his blood there is still alive. No heartfire—that would still be in his own heart!—but fire nonetheless. Alvin's blood burns and shimmers wherever it is."

"I thought I was the only one who saw that," said Margaret.

"But I had to detect it, call to it, bring it out of the crystal."

"And put it where?" asked Margaret.

"Nowhere," said Calvin. "I will simply hold it, to return to him when he comes back from Carthage. And if he . . ."

"And if he never comes back," said Margaret.

"Then it will be a kind of—what, a reservoir? A bank? A garden of light inside me, and perhaps I can draw power from it, as long as I use it in a way that he would have approved of."

"You've thought of many good things," said Margaret, holding back her grief and, yes, rage that such things could be said so calmly by Alvin's disloyal brother.

Beaming, but trying to conceal his pride, Calvin reached out a hand toward the tower.

The top row of crystal blocks wavered, shimmering, but then disappeared. Margaret imagined that the water they contained was now spilling to the ground around the tower.

"There's less water in each block than you might think," said Calvin.

"Otherwise, it couldn't be carried. Certainly not by one person! So it won't be quite the deluge that Arthur and I feared."

"Arthur and I." That was Alvin's phrase to say, because he and Arthur had been bound up in each other's souls in a way that was much closer and more permanent than brotherhood. It irritated her for Calvin to think of himself and Arthur Stuart as having some kind of bond.

But they *had* a kind of bond.

Don't be angry at Calvin for having the nature of a thoughtless young man.

The second level of blocks shimmered and disappeared, but this time the layer under it was already shimmering. It wasn't immediate, but it was quick, the movement, the melting that progressed down the tower.

Until the tower was no longer visible above the rooflines across the street.

"It's not finished yet, is it," said Margaret.

"About halfway. But it's the same all the way down—you've seen all there is to see," said Calvin.

The visions in the blocks were gone, so she *had* seen all there would ever be to see in these seeing stones. All that so-called "crystal balls" showed was a distorted upside-down reflection of all the light sources playing across the orb. Charlatans could pretend to see profound things in the ball, but those things were not there. In Alvin's crystal blocks, there were real visions, of the true, the possible, the probable, the unchangeable.

But gone. Everyone who wanted to had seen all that there was to see in Crystal City.

Alvin half expected to be wakened by marauders in the morning—or in the small dark hours before morning. But nothing happened. A few heart-fires of sentinels watching, no doubt, to make sure Alvin and his fellow "witches" didn't get away in the night.

He was tempted to walk out of the jail, as he so easily could, lock or no lock, and wander among the sentinels, asking them how their vigil was going. Seen anything? "I don't think they dare stage any kind of jailbreak today," the sentinels would say—not realizing that the person they were talking to was Alvin Maker himself, proving that no jail could hold him.

But he had proven that many times before. Why should he vainly flaunt his powers? He had done nothing to earn them—they had always been there waiting for him to learn how to use them. Possibly he was so knackled because he was seventh son of a seventh son, a mundane cause for all the complication in his life.

Why should I take pride in what came to me without effort or merit on my part? Like pressing my own pants without touching them—it *was* a trivial way to use the powers he had been given. And yet they needed pressing and cleaning and he *could* do it. So why *shouldn't* he?

The light in the window let him know that day had broken. His inner clock told him that the days were indeed shortening.

"Is this Wednesday or Thursday?" asked Marty Laws softly. Alvin opened his eyes enough to see that Marty was standing at the window. He wanted to warn him to come away, he was too easy a target there. But there were no assassins waiting. Maybe the people here *would* wait for judicial process.

Alvin cast off his covers and sat up on his bed. I have a better one than this at home, he thought. Why am I not there?

"Measure went to get breakfast," said Marty. "And John Binder went with him, in case it was awkward to carry."

"And you stayed here to—what, watch over me?" Alvin made his way to the cuspidor and used it, as agreed. He wondered what its capacity was, compared to the bladders of four grown men.

"I stayed here out of sheer laziness," said Marty Laws. "I'm a lawyer, not an errand boy."

"There's much to be said for the profession of errand-running," said Alvin.

"So you can be the patron saint of deliverymen," said Marty. "And I will be the patron saint of nap-takers and sleepers-in."

Alvin tried to remember all the words of the new song John Binder had sung the night before. A poor wayfaring man of grief hath often . . . what? Something . . . on my way, and begged so humbly for my aid. Sued so humbly for relief.

"Can you remind me of the words of the song John Binder sang for me last night?"

"I like to think I'm a singer," said Marty Laws, "but that was a new one to me, and it's got a few stanzas, and I didn't get all the words."

Alvin repeated the words that he remembered from the opening.

"Well, that's a lot better than *I* could do," said Marty. "And you don't have a bad singing voice yourself."

"As Margaret says, my singing is always on *some* pitch, but it's hard to guess in advance what pitch it's going to be."

"I believe the Latin word for that is 'pshaw.' Or is it 'piffle'?" Marty laughed. "You have a right good voice, always on pitch as well as any man who isn't paid to sing."

"I fear that people would pay most generously for the privilege of *not* hearing me sing."

John and Measure returned then, carrying bags with clinking plates inside. Clinking *tin* plates. No nice chinaware for *them* today.

A guard, this time in the uniform of the Carthage Grays militia regiment—one of six regiments in town—unlocked and then relocked the door. "Trying to keep you safe," he said as he closed the door. And Alvin saw in his heartfire that he was sincere—he knew his duty and he would do it.

"The governor sent orders commissioning the Grays to guard the jail and keep anybody from attacking the prison," said John Binder.

"It's nice that we'll know who it is that betrayed us," said Measure.

Alvin looked quizzically at his brother. "Do you know something I don't know?"

"I have always known *many* things that you don't know," said Measure.

"No bickering, children," said John Binder. "The plates aren't much, but the food is hearty and while it won't measure up to *yesterday's* breakfast, it's enough to keep the meat from falling off our bones."

They ate, and talked about various nothings as the whim struck them, though not for a moment did any of them forget the danger they were in.

"Relax," said Measure. "Nobody's going to do anything this morning."

"And you know this because . . ." said Marty Laws.

"Any assassins were being whipped into a frenzy of blood lust last night," said Measure. "They know today is their chance, that somebody might move us somewhere else, or some other militia might be assigned this duty, or maybe they're afraid that an entire Crystal City militia is marching here, armed with knacks and guns to raze Carthage to the ground."

"I hope our militia is staying safely invisible in Crystal City," said Alvin.

"I imagine they're patrolling, not in uniform, to withstand or repel any marauders," said Measure.

"Because that's what you ordered them to do," said Alvin.

"I have no authority in the city," said Measure.

"The great secret is that *nobody* has authority," said Alvin. "Or everybody does. It was something we made together."

"You made the crystal blocks, Al," said Measure.

"Calvin made some, too," said Alvin.

"His showed nothing sensible. Not the same as yours. Not at all."

"Well, I imagine that by now, Calvin has mastered the secret of breaking the blocks open and releasing their water," said Alvin. "Maybe there's no crystal left in Crystal City."

"It'll be sad to get there and not see the tower," said Marty Laws.

Alvin said nothing. The towers were among the least of the things he would not see again in Crystal City. Because now more men were arriving in the environs of Carthage Jail, and these were men whose heartfires were burning with desires that did not bode well for Alvin.

"So the would-be killers," said Measure, "had to get all het up and likkered up last night. They would have been so drunk that some of them slept out in the open, and this morning nobody felt like early rising."

"A few," said Alvin.

"Including, probably, a few who never went to bed last night," said Measure.

"So they won't come at us today?" asked Marty Laws.

"They won't come at us this morning," said Measure. "They won't do it in daylight, anyway. They need to have the disguise of darkness, because not everybody in Carthage is in favor of cold-blooded killings of men who haven't been convicted of anything, and who are officially under the protection of the governor."

"I bet the governor is in on the plot," said Marty.

"Do we even know there *is* a plot?" asked John Binder.

"Yes," said Alvin. "There are a few heartfires out there who were there for the harangues last night. A certain Reverend Philadelphia Thrower was at his oratorical best, and Cavil Planter, always a faithful servant of the Unmaker, and half a dozen others who had their own reasons for being terrified of the knackles."

"Witches," said Marty Laws.

"Murderous sons of Satan," said John Binder.

"And Alvin as the chief among the devils of Pandemonium," said Measure. "That's what Mother always said, when we were growing up."

"About *Wastenot* and *Wantnot*," corrected Alvin. "I was too busy studying to be the perfect son that I didn't have time for mischief. And they never invited me to take part."

After breakfast, Alvin wrote a letter to Margaret, which began normally—his ideas about things they ought to do, changes they ought to make. But soon he was writing about the children—the one they had, the two that were coming, even the one they had lost. Tears bleared his vision once he was writing about the little ones, so his letter went slowly. And he wondered: How will this ever be delivered? Who will be respectful of my last letter to my wife?

Not necessarily the last, thought Alvin. I don't know that. I know what they *intend*, but intending isn't accomplishing. He still had his knacks, and maybe he could save them all. He figured that when they came to drag him out and kill him, he'd make sure the others let them do it. Then, when he had a chance to assess his would-be killers, he could set to work. Not harming any of them, but disarming and disabling them. Arms out of joint, splitting headaches, stumblings and fallings—he knew how to do these things without causing lasting harm. He'd make it clear that they could not harm him. When would they give up, once that had been demonstrated?

Then he heard his own voice in his memory, when he told somebody—who?—somebody, anyway, "You know that I *can* be killed, don't you?"

Why had he said that? Because people had too much confidence that he was in no danger.

So what did he mean when he said that?

There's a limit to how many musket balls I can deflect at once. How many weapons I can destroy at once. How many men I can even detect at the same time. If they all shoot at once, and a bullet hits me, I can heal it—but if six more strike me while I'm doing that, then what? Can I heal them all?

I have to act as soon as they start leading me away from the others, before I can be shot by so many guns at once. That will give me time—

"Oh," said Marty. "I suppose I shouldn't have accepted it, but it's not as if Mike Fink tolerates arguments from lawyers." He pulled a single-shot pistol out of his pocket. "It's loaded and wadded. I figure if Mike Fink was carrying it, then it would be lethal."

"Can't shoot a pistol from the window and hope to hit anything," said Measure.

"I don't expect to fire it at all," said Marty. "Mike Fink told me to take it, not use it. I've never fired a pistol in my life. Never been hunting. Don't own a firearm of my own. So you don't have to persuade me how useless this weapon would be in my hands." Whereupon he handed the pistol, butt-first, to John Binder.

Binder held it, examining it like some incompetent student's examination paper.

"John, I know you've gone hunting and brought home your meat," said Measure.

"I'm just trying to figure how I can make use of two pistols," said John Binder.

Alvin, who had been lying back on his bed, his letter temporarily abandoned, now sat up. "Two?"

"Seems like Mike Fink figured that if he couldn't be here himself, he could leave us with some means of self-defense." John Binder pulled a six-shooter revolver out from under the thin mattress of his cot. He spun the chamber. "Fully loaded, of course."

"I'm surprised he didn't pre-aim them for us," said Marty.

Measure looked at Alvin, raised his eyebrows.

"No, I'm not surprised, I'm not mad," said Alvin. "I've got nothing against self-defense, though I don't know under what circumstances these would be useful compared with muskets and rifles."

"I don't expect they'll bring artillery," said Measure, "because they won't want to have to pay taxes to rebuild the jail."

The others chuckled.

"So, drunk, murderous, and cheap," said Alvin. "That's about right."

"Can you shoot that thing?" Measure asked John Binder.

"I don't think this is a good time for me to try to practice with it. Especially since if I use these as practice bullets, there won't be any more to replace them."

John Binder handed the single-shot revolver back to Marty, but before Marty could get a grip on it, Alvin got the pistol in his hand and studied it. "This should be pretty accurate. The barrel is straight and true, the charge is strong, and the ball will do some damage at close range." He handed the single-shot to Measure.

Measure rolled his eyes and took it. "Was this pistol in such good condition *before* you examined it so closely?"

"I clarified and enhanced it. Made sure everything was clean and lubricated. The normal thing that fellows do with their weapons."

John Binder handed his revolver to Alvin. "You're the one who will need this. Nobody's looking to kill *me*."

Alvin shook his head as he examined the weapon. "I'm not a killer," he said.

"Neither is any of us," said John Binder.

"Shooting with a pistol at people who are trying to shoot *you*," said Measure, "isn't the same thing as using your knack to hurt people."

Alvin didn't seem convinced.

"Think of it this way," said John Binder. "You won't use this to save yourself. You'll use it to protect the rest of us."

Alvin rolled his eyes.

"He rolled his eyes," said Measure. "That means he liked your reasoning."

"It means I rolled my eyes," said Alvin. "Measure doesn't know me as perfectly as he thinks."

"I know you better than you know yourself," said Measure.

Marty gave a little hoot of laughter. "I did *not* know that your big brother could sass you, Alvin."

"I'm too tolerant by half," said Alvin, "but I like his company too much to turn him into a toad."

Marty looked shocked. "Can you *do* that? Turn a man into some other creature?"

"I've never tried it," said Alvin, "and I never will. Bodies are too different. And look at the size difference. Measure would make one huge toad."

"Nice to know I'm untoadable," said Measure.

At about one in the afternoon, John Binder went alone to get lunch. "I'm thinking just some bread and cheese and cold meat. And a bottle or two of—"

"Water," said Alvin. "Clean water. We need to have our wits about us."

"Guess it's better than licking slime off a slug," said Marty Laws.

"You're welcome to do that," said Alvin, "if you can find a slug."

Lunch, which was not a small meal, even if the ingredients were simple, left them a little sleepy. Alvin, who doubted he could sleep, set the tone by lying down and closing his eyes.

"If you're going to pretend to sleep," said Measure, "take your boots off."

"I like them on," said Alvin.

"You're getting your blanket dirty," said Measure.

"It started dirty," said Alvin. "Nobody brought us the best out of their linen closet."

After a few minutes, Marty was snoring lightly. But Alvin knew the others were awake.

"John," said Alvin. "I've been trying to puzzle out the words to 'A Poor Wayfaring Man of Grief.' "

"There's a lot of words," said John Binder. "But they make up a single story."

"Would you sing it for me again?" asked Alvin. "I like the song, and I want to have another try at memorizing the words."

John Binder sang softly, but at some point Marty woke up and all three men listened to John with full attention, even if their eyes were closed.

"These deeds shall thy memorial be. Fear not, thou didst them unto me." The song ended.

"Would you mind singing it again?" said Alvin, trying not to let his emotion control his voice.

"Anybody want to sing with me?" asked John Binder.

"No," said Alvin. "Yours is the right voice for that song, at this time."

Marty Laws had been quite willing to join in, but he smiled a little and lay back to listen to John Binder. Their voices were so different, it really would be a different song.

Nobody was sleeping, when the song ended again. Measure slid his cot under the window and sat on it to read by the sunlight through the window.

"What are you reading?" asked Marty Laws.

"Josephus," said Measure. "A Jew who joined up with the Romans against his own people. But he's the only writer besides the evangelists to even admit that Jesus existed."

"Everybody knows he existed, and still exists," said Marty.

"Spare us a theological argument, please," said Alvin.

"No argument from me," said Measure. "I'm *reading*."

Alvin was adding to the end of his letter to Margaret. He enjoyed misspelling a certain portion of the words in all his letters, because she got just a little annoyed, but also enjoyed the creativity of some of his spellings.

A few men were shouting out in the yard. Couldn't make out any words.

A key was put in the lock. The door opened. It was a couple of court officials bringing a bottle of wine and some plain glasses. The prisoners thanked them.

"Judge Ligon sent it from his personal stock," said one of the men.

"Please tell him how grateful we are," said Measure.

The men left, relocking the door.

"I'm not much of a wine drinker," said Alvin.

"Then don't drink any," said Measure. "I, for one, wouldn't mind a taste of spirits to settle my nerves."

That opinion turned out to be universal, including Alvin. He sipped at his glass and found that it was a pretty decent wine, as wine went.

It was about five in the evening, a little after, when they heard some guns discharging outside on the grounds. Marty rushed to the window and said, "At least a hundred of them, all armed."

"What are they shooting at?" asked John Binder.

"This building. Or, to be accurate, us inside it," said Alvin.

"And they're *missing* the whole building?"

"The lead balls turn into liquid before they hit anything," said Alvin.

"So you're dealing with it," said Measure.

"It's only a few guns at a time," said Alvin. "A hundred men, firing at once? And most of them have two or three guns, fully loaded."

There was a clatter of boots pounding up the stairs.

"Bet they have a key," said John Binder.

Alvin would have tried to fuse the lock shut, but he was too busy dealing with the shots from outside.

The moment the door started to open, Measure pointed his single-shot down into the men gathered there and fired. He didn't know if he hit anybody because at that moment, a bullet from the stairway hit him in the face.

"I'm a dead man," said Measure, surprisingly calm. Then he collapsed on the floor.

Alvin tried to concentrate on the damage to Measure's body and brain, but as he did, Marty tried to open the window to jump out, and a hail of bullets dropped him, still inside the jail.

"Marty's alive," said Alvin to John Binder. "Get him out of the line of fire."

John Binder dragged Marty's limp and bleeding body under one of the cots against the back wall.

Alvin fired all six bullets from the revolver into the crowd at the top of the stairs. They backed off—Alvin had certainly done some damage, though he had no time to assess it. He slammed the door and this time fused the lock shut.

Bullets now were coming through the walls on both sides, and Alvin couldn't even interfere with them anymore. He was too distracted by the death of his brother, the shooting of Marty Laws, the knowledge that yes, indeed, he *could* be killed by a hail of bullets from a trained militia.

If he could draw the fire to himself, maybe they would spare John and Marty. The window was still open, and Alvin leapt to it, started climbing out, stopping several of the bullets coming at him. But a score of bullets made it into his body.

He started falling out of the window. "O Lord my God!" cried Alvin, and fell.

He was not killed or much injured by the fall. But the bullets were having their way, despite his best efforts to mitigate the damage, to hold onto his blood. He drew himself to a sitting position against the wall of the jail and then so many bullets took him that he could no longer do anything to save himself, because he was dying, and then he was dead.

When the firing stopped, John Binder assumed the worst. But there was no time to grieve. Alvin had given him charge of Marty Laws, so John Binder kicked open the door, then gathered Marty into his arms and hurried down the stairs, past the bodies of several men who might or might not be dead from Alvin's revolver.

At the bottom of the stairs, he found what he was hoping for, a door down into a cellar. No, a dungeon—it was fitted out with some manacles at the walls. He carried Marty down and the two of them huddled in shadow, as John tried to stop Marty's bleeding and dress his wounds. From the location of the bullets, John concluded that Alvin had somehow managed to stop much of the bleeding—or Marty would have been already dead.

Outside the jail, a couple of men made as if to mutilate Alvin's body with swords, knives, or hatchets. But others angrily stopped them. "He won't care," one of the hatchet men said.

And one of the others said, quite fiercely, "This man was a Maker. Show some respect."

The men with savage hearts soon went away, sulking. The others gathered up Alvin's body, and somebody brought around a wagon. When Alvin was in the wagon bed, other men brought down Measure's body and laid the brothers side by side.

Only a few men, among those who were not handling the disposal of the bodies, saw something whipping around the jail building, flying so fast that its shape could not be identified. But if it was a bird, it was a white bird, except that there was flame in it, too. And a couple of the men thought that it wasn't flying at all, it was running, clinging to the vertical walls the way roaches or lizards do.

But the men who saw it did not speak of it, not even to each other, until decades later, when a couple of them were finally willing to admit that they had been at Carthage Jail that day.

"I don't know what it was," said one. "Some monster. Moving so fast, clinging to the wall, so fast."

And the other one said, "I don't care what it was. I just knew that it hated me. And it was triumphant."

38

After bringing down the Crystal tower, Calvin had spent the rest of the day checking with all the companies to make sure that the captains knew whether all the wagons in their group were ready to go.

"Don't know *where* they'll go," said one, late in the afternoon, "what with not being boats and they can't fly."

"But are the wagons ready to roll," said Calvin, pretending, rather badly, to be patient.

"If they aren't, it's a little late to do anything about it," said the captain.

"Take me to the wagons with problems."

They ended up visiting all the wagons in that company, and Calvin tweaked boards and axles, hubs and wheels, making sure that all the moving parts moved and the solid parts were so fused together that nothing could make them come apart short of an axe. He inspected the horses, but since none of them had broken bones or problems with their hooves, there wasn't much Calvin could do for them. He wasn't half the healer Alvin was. He could find and remove stones and nails from hooves. He could trim the hooves without having to use any tool but his mind. And if a leg had been broken, he could have set it good as new. But otherwise, the horses had to look out for themselves.

Besides, even if he could heal horses from injury and illness, Calvin wasn't going with them.

Why would I even *want* to go with them, he asked himself. Permanent exile among the Reds in the trackless deserts of the mountain country. A salt lake—so you grow beans that are already salted before they go into the pot? Farming was not Calvin's dream for his life, and he couldn't imagine there'd be any work for a man like Calvin any time soon.

Not that Calvin knew what his life's work was going to be.

"Thank you, sir," said the captain. Calvin said his goodbye and started walking up the road toward Margaret's, because he didn't have patience enough to hear the man say, as he inevitably would, "Why, you did that up proper just like Alvin would've done."

I did it up proper the way *Calvin* would have done it, because I *am* Calvin, I'm *here* in Crystal City, and I did it myself without any help from Alvin or anybody else.

Margaret's place was up ahead on the left when he heard a wail from inside that near tore his heart out. Calvin ran, and not waiting to knock, burst into the house and found Margaret fallen on the parlor floor, two other women standing by wringing their hands, and the parlor maid bringing in a ewer of water and a glass for Margaret to drink from.

Calvin knelt beside her. "He's gone, isn't he," Calvin asked.

Margaret, unable to stop sobbing, managed a nod.

"Do you need anything," Calvin asked.

Margaret whispered fiercely, "My husband back."

Calvin rose to his feet. "Can you ladies help Miz Larner to her bed chamber."

"I don't know if we're strong enough to—"

"She'll walk. Just be with her to steady her. And to help her get into bed."

Margaret allowed herself to be pulled to her feet.

One of the visiting ladies asked Calvin, "Does she do this a lot?"

"Do what?"

"Suddenly faint and burst into the most insane weeping—"

"I thought you would have guessed. Margaret always has her eye out for Alvin's heartfire. She knows where he is, she knows that he's safe."

"But then why would she—"

"Until today. A few minutes ago. When Alvin's heartfire went dark and then disappeared."

The matron hurried away to join the others in Margaret's bedchamber.

Was it Calvin's job now to spread the word that Alvin would never come back to his city? Or, with the tower gone, *was* it still Alvin's Crystal City?

With Margaret's needs being met, Calvin went out into the dooryard and then up onto the macadam road. He needed to do *something*, but the only meaningful job for him he had already done.

Calvin spotted a fast-moving deer. No, it was a boy and a—a big dog? Coming right toward him, but not on the road.

The boy was a beanpole, and far from being a lad, it was Arthur Stuart. What Calvin had thought to be a big dog was Mike Fink, who was tall enough when he wasn't standing beside Arthur Stuart.

I need to have Alvin check my vision, when I can't tell these two from a boy and a dog.

Not asking Alvin anything now.

Tears came to his eyes.

But he also felt a strange exultation deep in what Calvin hoped was a soul. I'm the Maker now.

No I'm not. Never.

Arthur Stuart had them moving right fast, right out in the open. Calvin had always thought Alvin's Greensong required trees, but here with only cornfields and weeds and bushes, Arthur Stuart was maintaining the Greensong.

Alvin and Mike Fink came up to Calvin, and Arthur Stuart was already talking. "We left them in the jail, upstairs, in decent shape. There was talk in Carthage about the trial being hurried up."

"Won't be a trial," said Mike Fink.

"We don't *know* that," said Arthur Stuart. "People sometimes get struck by an inexplicable wave of human decency."

"I gave a couple of pistols to Marty Laws and John Binder," said Mike Fink. "Didn't want them to face their enemies unarmed."

"You did well," said Calvin, since Mike Fink seemed to expect some kind of comment.

"Well, I got to go talk to Margaret," said Arthur Stuart, starting to move along the road.

"Don't do it," said Calvin. "She might be glad to know you're back, both of you, but she's in no shape for conversation."

"What happened?" asked Mike Fink instantly.

"About fifteen minutes ago," said Calvin, "she gave a cry and fell to the floor weeping."

Not even a second, and then both Mike and Arthur burst into tears themselves.

"If I had been there," said Mike.

"Then your heartfire would be gone, too," said Calvin.

Arthur had got his tears under control. "Should I hurry back to bring his body home?" he asked.

"Who you asking?" said Calvin. "Mike? Me? How would either of us know what you should do?"

Mike said, "Lessun they kilt Measure and Binder and Laws, too, they'll see to bringing Alvin home."

"This is going to destroy Measure," said Calvin.

Arthur Stuart shook his head. "If Alvin's dead, Measure's dead, too."

"You don't know that—" said Calvin.

"I know it," said Arthur. "Measure is with him. Measure is gone."

Calvin wondered if Arthur Stuart really knew something, or just thought it was logical for Measure to be at Alvin's side.

"I noticed the tower's gone," said Arthur Stuart.

"I took it down this morning."

"Pity," said Arthur Stuart. "I could have used a good long look at the walls."

"Alvin told me to take it down, and Margaret stood beside me watching as the tower collapsed."

"I'm not criticizing, Calvin," said Arthur Stuart. "I know Alvin didn't want to leave the Crystal tower behind when we cross over the river."

"I think," said Calvin, "that Margaret will want to see you now."

"I think so too," said Arthur Stuart.

"It occurs to me," said Calvin, "that most of us didn't die in Carthage this afternoon. Most of us are still here, looking for something to do."

"I know what to do," said Mike Fink. "I'll find out who kilt him and I'll kill them. I'll kill them all, bury them, then dig them up so I can kill them again."

"Please don't," said Calvin.

"None of your business," said Mike Fink.

"If you go into Carthage a-killing folks, they'll put together an army and come here before we can get over the river. How much mercy do you think they'll have on us witches?" asked Calvin.

Mike Fink looked at Arthur Stuart.

Arthur nodded. "Calvin's thought it through exactly right, Mike. We have to show everybody that *we're* not going to turn this into a war."

"I reckon they're hoping that all the folks with knacks will go home and hide their knacks like they always did before. That's what they wanted, was to erase everything Alvin accomplished."

"If we're peaceful," said Calvin, "if we leave our houses and streets and the water tower, the fields and drainage channels, and the bulk of our stores of corn, they might be content to let us pass into the mysterious Red lands without any harassment or marauding."

"The Reds won't want me in their lands," said Mike Fink.

"Mike," said Arthur, "folks take one good look at the size of you and *nobody* wants you in their lands."

Mike Fink laughed and slapped Arthur on the back. Arthur didn't flinch.

Arthur is stronger than he looks, thought Calvin.

And then the next thought: Arthur is *more* than he looks to be in every way. In a country where Blacks and mixups are usually slaves, Arthur looks Black and there's slavers who want to take him back into the slavery he was born to. Yet he doesn't look like a fugitive or an ex-slave. He has something of the bearing of Alvin himself—not surprising, given all the time they spent together.

Alvin left Arthur in charge of the migration into the Red lands. And for the first time, Calvin realized that leading the migration would certainly lead to Arthur Stuart becoming Alvin's successor as the leader of the knackles.

But *I'm* the only living Maker. How can anyone else claim to inherit Alvin's mantle?

Arthur Stuart walked swiftly down toward Margaret's house.

"Do you think . . ." began Mike Fink. "I mean, I don't think she'll want me intruding at a time like—"

Calvin gestured for him to follow Arthur Stuart.

Mike Fink jogged down the slope. Calvin imagined that in the neighboring houses they had to be wondering if it was an earthquake.

Calvin almost followed.

I already saw her, in the first moments of her grief. Let them have their own moments with her. If Margaret wants me, she knows where I am.

Calvin wandered toward the business district of Crystal City, the shops and offices. Not that he had any office there. There was nothing in Crystal City that showed any mark of Calvin's having lived here.

There was a coffee shop. No, a tea room. Right downtown. Calvin wasn't much for either tea or coffee, but this seemed like a good fall day for a hot drink.

He was halfway through his second cup of coffee when Eliza showed up in the doorway with a meek little man behind her. What in the world was Eliza doing with a man like *that?* Calvin beckoned to her and she led her little accessory through the room to his table.

"Sit, please," said Calvin.

"I've missed you," said Eliza.

By now Calvin routinely disregarded any of the sweet things she said. He knew that she was following a script in her mind. How to keep the boy happy. Well, the script worked. Insincere as he knew she was, it warmed his heart.

It also warned him to be on alert.

"My friend here," said Eliza, "is—"

Calvin held up a hand. "No, wait. I want to meet you, but I have to tell you what happened in Carthage this afternoon."

"In Carthage?" asked Eliza, suspicious.

"Alvin was killed," said Calvin.

"He can't be killed," said Eliza.

"Or so we thought," said Calvin. "I thought you should know. Before we went any farther with . . . whatever this is."

"It's an offer to help sir, unless the plan is over," said the man. "With Alvin gone."

"We're going to try to fulfill all of Alvin's plans, as far as we understand them," said Calvin.

"So you speak with authority today," said Eliza.

"I speak as I always have," said Calvin.

She caressed his cheek. "I've missed you, Calvin. I think I'll need to listen to you with different ears now."

"Those ears are very becoming to you," said Calvin.

"You're studying gallantry, is that it?"

"You make a man *want* to be gallant," said Calvin.

"Oh, you garter snakes, always wanting to writhe around in a ball," said the man.

"What would you know about snakes, being from Ireland?" asked Calvin.

"This is Lot McEddy," said Eliza. "He can freeze things."

"Ah," said Calvin. "Have you ever seen garters in a mating ball?"

"I have," said McEddy. "They were the first snakes I saw in my life. Quite an impressive sight. I was told they weren't poisonous."

"They're not," said Calvin. "But they look very much like coral snakes, which are *very* poisonous, of a testy disposition, and corals form mating balls just like garters."

"So I shouldn't assume I'm looking at a garter snake," said McEddy.

"It's always wise to treat every snake as if it had venom enough to kill you and your unborn children," said Calvin.

"What a wonderful herpetology lesson," said Eliza.

Calvin looked at her with mock wonder.

"I've read books, you know," she said. "And I once had a friend who was a snake scientist."

"And lizards," added Calvin.

"'Herpetologist.' It sounds like a religion," said Eliza. "I'm a baptized Herpetoligist."

Calvin gave Eliza a smile, and then turned to the Irishman. "You freeze water," said Calvin to McEddy. "Fresh or salt?"

"Fresh water is a good deal easier. If the Mizzippy counts as fresh."

"It counts as not briny," said Calvin. "How thick can you make your ice?"

"Right to the bottom of the stream. Only I've never tried anything as deep as the Mizzippy, so . . . I don't know."

"Why are we sitting here watching you drink a cup of cold coffee?" asked Eliza. "Don't you know where the Mizzippy is? Let's go and find out the answers to your questions by observation."

"Now?" asked McEddy.

"It *is* almost dark," said Calvin to Eliza.

"There's a moon," said Eliza. "I saw it myself. Up there. Shining."

"I believe you," said Calvin. "Let's go."

Calvin had to slow down his walk because McEddy was a man of careful steps. But in due time they stood on the wharf where the showboat was still tied up.

"Let's give it a go," said Calvin.

"What should I . . . do?"

"Freeze the water about a foot thick from here to the far side of the Mizzippy."

"With all this fog, how will we know if I get to the other side?" asked McEddy.

"We'll send Eliza out on the ice to test it," said Calvin.

"We will not," said Eliza.

"Alvin said. He said that you could maybe help me," said McEddy.

"Maybe," said Calvin. "I can see what you do, and try to join in and make it stronger. But at first I might make it more difficult, before I understand what exactly you do."

"Enough with lowering expectations," said Eliza. "Build us some ice. A different kind of crystal." Eliza smiled cheerfully.

"A crystal highway," said Calvin.

McEddy sat down on the dock and closed his eyes. Under the dock the water stopped moving. There was a thin layer of ice on top now, and it grew wider and thicker. In about ten minutes, the ice was thick from the shore to about ten yards out into the river. Calvin thought now that he understood what McEddy was doing.

He was mistaken, as he proceeded to melt McEddy's ice in the attempt to extend it.

"Close," said McEddy. "But you're doing this when you mean to do that." And the ice re-formed.

Together now, Calvin and McEddy threw their ice bridge across the river, well beyond the fog in midriver.

And then they were at the limit of their influence over the ice.

"How long does it last?" asked Calvin.

"It's not magic, it's really ice," said McEddy. "So, in freezing weather, it can last days. In July, it can melt in half an hour."

"It's November, so . . ."

"So the wagons get halfway across," said Eliza.

"There's another freezer, one of the Southerners," said Calvin.

"Who?" asked McEddy.

"I have no idea. Just like I didn't know about *you* till Eliza brought you."

"Alvin didn't tell you?" asked McEddy.

"I'm not sure he knew he was going to die before he could reveal the location of the golden plow," said Calvin.

"Is there a golden plow, then?" asked McEddy.

"There was."

"You saw it?"

"Not directly. But I watched as several other men saw it and examined it. In the end they signed affidavits," said Calvin. "They're men of good and sober reputation."

"No alcohol involved?"

"Well, *I* was full of beer," said Calvin.

"You were still a child," said Eliza.

"My version makes me more manly," said Calvin.

"Why don't you two just get married?" said McEddy.

The two of them laughed. "Shall we go in search of the other freezer?" asked Calvin.

"I bumped into Mr. McEddy here," said Eliza, "and he asked what I was doing, and I said, looking for a way to freeze the Mizzippy."

"I had to offer to help the lady in distress," said McEddy.

"That would have been my highest priority, too," said Calvin.

"In Ireland they would have killed me for making that ice," said McEddy.

"Lots of ways to die in Ireland." Which made Calvin think of Alvin. Lots of ways to die even if you're unkillable.

"Nobody needs more than once," said McEddy.

"Gotta point that out to Mike Fink," said Calvin.

"I think I've seen Mike Fink. Big fellow. Is he *your* pet?" asked Eliza.

"My friend," said Calvin.

"Why haven't you assembled the wagons?" asked Margaret as soon as she got to the dock, where Calvin stood with McEddy and Eliza.

"Oh, Margaret, have I done it wrong?" asked Calvin with exaggerated regret. It's how he always acted when Margaret expressed doubt about something he had done. Pure sarcasm, a quick surrender before she even knew she had attacked him.

Margaret held her tongue.

"I thought that before we got the horses out pulling wagons, we should make sure we can extend the ice bridge all the way across," said Calvin.

"We don't need a bunch of wagons stuck out on the ice, I suppose," said Eliza. As if she thought she were a part of anything. Margaret did not even look at her.

"Are you helping them?" Margaret asked Calvin.

"I do what I can."

McEddy spoke up. "Madame Larner, he's a great help. And so is Grampus."

He was referring to the old Black man standing at the back corner of the dock. Margaret walked to him and offered her hand. He seemed reluctant to shake it.

"Is something wrong?" asked Margaret softly.

"I don't know what to do with Lady Larner's hand."

Margaret took his hand between both of hers.

"But you an't wearing no glove," said Grampus.

"I believe it's rude if I shake your bare hand with my glove," said Margaret. "Please be at ease. We need your help, and I'm grateful you've come forward."

"I used to turn a bayou all froze," said Grampus. "The children loved sliding around on it. And when I melted it, all the fish in it was frozen but they cooked up fresh."

"It sounds like you made good use of your knack," said Margaret.

Grampus took his hand back, looking puzzled. "Black folks got no knacks," he said. "We got spells and such." He reached into his capacious pocket and pulled out what looked like a wad of mud. In fact, it *was* a wad of mud.

"It's my mud charm from the bayou," he said. "Why make a new one iffen I can just bring this?"

"Are those sticks in it?" asked Margaret.

"Not just any sticks," said Grampus. "Tiny dowsing rods. All working together." Grampus reached the mud charm down into the Mizzippy water. "Sorry I have to do mine all at once," Grampus said to McEddy and Calvin. "I don't know how to hook onto somebody else's ice, you got to hook onto mine."

In forty-five minutes, Calvin pronounced the bridge complete, and McEddy agreed.

"Can I cross it first?" asked Grampus.

"Why not?" said Calvin. "Alone, or you want someone to lean on."

"Miss Peggy right for this," said Grampus.

"Miz Margaret Larner is always right," said Calvin.

"No need to correct him," said Margaret. "I like thinking back on the years when I was known as Little Peggy to anybody who knew me."

With Grampus leaning on her, just a little, Margaret moved out onto the ice.

Calvin wanted so badly to follow. But he knew he wouldn't make it far if he tried. So he waited on the dock for them to start coming back, figuring it would be a long wait, at Grampus's pace.

When they were back on the dock, Calvin asked, "Did you see him? The Prophet?"

"I did," said Margaret. "He seemed very pleasant and welcoming."

"You told him the wagons were coming?" asked Calvin.

"I knew my assignments," said Margaret. "I told him first thing in the morning they'd start arriving. He said he knew right where he was going to help them set up their first camp."

Calvin waited.

"You want his answer," said Margaret. "Well, he said no. He said it wasn't his decision to block you from crossing the river."

"Whose idea was it?"

"Apparently the River has a mind of its own. It won't let you cross."

"The *river* won't let me," said Calvin. To him it sounded like the Prophet was dodging responsibility for his own decisions.

"This is making you unhappy," said Margaret. "I'm only telling you what he said. If you want a different truth, ask someone else who was at the meeting."

"Who else was at the meeting?" asked Calvin. "Besides Grampus."

"I didn't learn all their names. But to a man or woman, they heartily welcomed us for Alvin's sake. They were grieved to hear of his death, but I think they already knew."

39

When John Binder drove the wagon up to Margaret Larner's door, it had three bodies in it, two dead and one dying. John picked up Marty Laws and carried him down to Margaret's porch. By the time he got there, Margaret was already at the door.

"Bring him inside," said Margaret.

"He's in a bad way," said John Binder.

"Lay him on the settee," she said. "Don't worry about the blood."

"All dried by now. Don't think there'll be any staining."

"Has he been conscious?" asked Margaret.

"Back at the jail, yes. But on this ride? I believe one of the men who helped me with loading this wagon has a knack, though he'd never tell that to anybody. I think he put Marty to sleep, deep enough that the jolting of the wagon never woke him."

"I hope it doesn't turn into the sleep of death," said Margaret.

"There are two bodies in the wagon, ma'am, and I don't know where to take them."

Margaret nodded. "You did well to bring them here, John. I've got a few men working in my garden. They can carry the bodies inside. What you need to do for me, John, is find Alvin's brother Calvin and ask him to come here. He has much of Alvin's knackery, and it may be he can help Marty."

John Binder doubted it, but he strode out into the dooryard and then up onto the road. He was loath to walk away from the wagon, with the horse not looked after and the bodies not being watched over. He suspected that there would be those—not citizens of the city, but outsiders—who would want to do some kind of defilement to the Maker and his brother.

A two-horse buggy came jouncing up the road—somebody needed to smooth it, thought John—and came to a stop beside the wagon with the shrouded bodies. Verily Cooper stepped down from the buggy, then reached up to help his wife, Purity, to join him. They walked to John's wagon and looked at the two bodies. Measure's body did not show any wounds, though John Binder knew if they uncovered his face they would see how it had been destroyed by a single shot at point-blank range. Alvin's body, though, was obviously riddled with bullet wounds. Clothing blood-soaked. His heart must have kept pumping right to the end.

What would this mean to Verily Cooper?

"I should have been there," said Verily.

"So that we could have three dead bodies in this wagon?" asked John Binder.

"You don't know that," said Verily.

"The two founders of Crystal City, Alvin Smith and Verily Cooper," said John. "Your name is known. What brings you out on the road today?"

"Margaret assigned us an errand," said Purity.

"And advised us not to discuss it," said Verily.

"John Binder was at Alvin's side," said Purity.

Verily conceded her point. "When we've all crossed over the river into the Red lands, there'll be lots of knack-wielding folk left in the United States and the Crown Colonies. We're assigned to go to the President and ask him to allow us free access to the river at Crystal City, so that we can help them get away into the west."

"The President of *what*?" asked John Binder.

"The United States," said Verily. "I know, why would he see a humble English barrel-maker like me? But I'll be speaking for many. Including Alvin, now he can't speak for himself."

"If Margaret sent you, it's because she's seen into the man's heartfire and she sees that a good outcome is at least possible," said John Binder.

"Or she's seen that some other good thing will happen because of our errand," said Verily. "Or some awful thing will be avoided."

"Verily, you have as good a right as anyone to see Margaret Larner before you go. But I wonder if, having received your instructions, you might go on your way without interrupting her? Preparing your husband for burial—"

"Yes, you're right," said Verily. He led Purity back to the carriage. "John, please give Margaret my love and condolences." He helped Purity climb back in, then joined her on the seat from which he would drive the horses. "Tell her we're about her business."

"It's only fair to tell you," said John Binder, "that Margaret plans to bury them with a simple ceremony as early this morning as possible, so that the people can still get across the river before dark."

Verily nodded. "I can trust Margaret to see to it that Alvin and Measure are decently laid to rest. Seeing them here like this—that's all I needed. I know they're gone. But Purity and I will shed our tears on the road to Philadelphia."

"You do know there's a train that goes right there," said John Binder.

"Not everybody loves going that fast," said Purity, shuddering.

"Goodbye, John Binder," said Verily. "Hold this city together even after they move out of their fields and farms and shops and schools and leave them all behind."

"I'll do my best," said John Binder. He had no idea if Verily heard him, because he started the horses moving before John could speak.

Margaret's workmen came around the house just then. They were husky men, and they each carried a body, as if they weighed nothing. Well, with the soul gone out of them, maybe they *were* lighter.

"You can go now," said one of the men to John. "We'll look after the horse for you."

John thanked him and walked along the road into town. Where would Calvin be? His own house? Eliza's place?

He found Calvin at the dock, with a couple of men who had made a strip of ice about three yards wide leading out into the river.

"Does it reach all the way?" asked John Binder.

The others turned to him, looking startled. Two men, yes, one Black, a fellow called Grampus, and the other an Irishman that John Binder hadn't had many dealings with. McEddy, thought John. He almost never forgot a name.

Calvin did not look surprised. As Alvin would have, he must have sensed the approach of John's heartfire.

"You took them to Margaret's house," Calvin said.

"I did," said John. "And Marty Laws, bad wounded but still alive."

"And not a scratch on you," said Calvin.

"Not a scratch on my *skin*," said John Binder. "Savage wounds in my soul."

"I have no doubt," said Calvin. "As mine. They were my brothers."

"I know," said John Binder.

"I mean, everybody thinks I was nothing but trouble, and Measure was his *real* brother. But I grew up with Alvin, and Measure looked after me, too. It's my childhood you brought home in that wagon."

Eliza spoke during a lull, apparently unwilling to interrupt. "Are you talking about the bodies—"

Calvin held up his hand before John Binder had a chance to stop her. "Eliza," said Calvin, "there are some things that will require privacy and maybe even secrecy."

Grampus chimed in, rather boldly. "There be folks wants to harm those fellows."

John Binder appreciated that Grampus was no longer speaking of bodies. Because there were folks who had stood admiring the ice who were now coming nearer. To John's surprise, they addressed him as if he held the authority there. "Do you think that ice track is wide enough for a wagon?" asked one man.

John Binder shrugged. "Looks wide enough to me, but I can't see how wide it is farther on."

"We went for three yards wide. Enough for a train track and more," said McEddy. "But we can always widen it, if needs be."

"I've done me some wagon driving, including a couple of Conestogas a few years ago. Perched up on that driver's bench, you can't see your own wheels. Makes it hard to steer around obstacles."

Grampus nodded. "Needs to be wide enough for the drivers to see safe road on both sides of the wagon."

"If the horses are centered on the road, the wagons will be all right," said Calvin.

"But it's a long way across, if you're fearful of slipping off the road," said Grampus.

"He's right," said John. "There'll be children beside the wagons, and they need walking room. Women, too. We don't want to add to the weight, putting them up inside."

Calvin nodded. "I see your wisdom. But let's not try to widen this path until we're ready to start driving wagons onto it."

"I wonder," said McEddy, "if we don't need to start the road over here, where the bank is low and eases into the water. There's no way to get the wagons over the dock without a three-foot drop."

"Another good bit of counsel," said Calvin. "Tomorrow we'll freeze the route you just described, so the wagons can move smoothly onto the ice."

"Ice is slippery," said John Binder.

Calvin nodded. "Wheels aren't good on ice, but every company has at least one knackle who can keep the wheels from skidding to the side."

"So many with the same knack?" asked John Binder.

"Different knacks can help keep the wheels from slipping," said Calvin. "What I thought of, I tried to solve in advance."

"Good work," said John Binder. He saw Calvin recoil slightly, and realized: He doesn't want my praise or encouragement. What he wants is Alvin to praise him. "I think Alvin would be more than satisfied."

"You have no idea," said Calvin, "what all I've done. I appreciate your desire to encourage me, but I'm not discouraged. I'm just . . . ready. Readier than you might think."

"I know what you can do," said John Binder.

"I don't even know what I can do," said Calvin.

"Apparently you're finding out, and in so doing I believe you are fulfilling Alvin's trust in you."

Calvin nodded and looked out into the fog. John Binder was pretty sure that his words had done Calvin no good whatsoever. Alvin's death might well devastate him more than anybody.

But John Binder also suspected, though the thought made him ashamed, that Calvin might also be secretly rejoicing that now, finally, people needed his knacks.

"Calvin," said John Binder, "Miz Margaret asked me to invite you to come help with Marty Laws."

"What does he need?"

"The bullets out of him and the wounds healed," said John Binder. "I think he has a sucking wound in his chest. Alvin was able to help him some before he died, but not much. Kept him from bleeding out, I think that's all Alvin had time and thought to do. What he really wanted, I think, was to save Measure, but Measure was beyond saving. Shot in the head."

Calvin nodded.

"Can you come?"

Calvin looked startled, as if he hadn't registered that Margaret wanted him to come *now*. He got to his feet. "Will you walk with me?" Calvin asked John Binder.

"Indeed I will, though my legs are still stiff from sitting on the wagon seat from Carthage to here."

"That was fast passage," said Calvin.

"I believe that the remnants of Arthur Stuart's path were still active. I think that, walking, the horse covered more ground than any horse could do galloping. As if every step were five."

The two of them walked up the slope, where the Crystal tower should have loomed ahead. But there was nothing there. Even the water had already flowed down into the bog south of town. And the grass was growing where the crystal blocks had been, as if sunlight had been reaching the grass the whole time the tower was there.

"John Binder," said Calvin, "I'd be grateful if, while we walked, you could find breath to tell me all that happened."

"I can tell you all I saw and heard," said John Binder, "but I wasn't a witness to anything that was done outside the jail."

"Tell what you know and tell what you guess," said Calvin. "You saw, and I didn't."

So John Binder found the breath to tell the tale, though from time to time he had to pause on the road to catch his breath. He said once, "Just a few days in a jail and it robs you of half your limberness."

Calvin nodded. He seemed to be concentrating on something, so John did not resume his story. Then Calvin stopped still, and asked John to do the same. Now John Binder realized that Calvin was trying to do something inside John's body, to limber him up, to ease the pain and stiffness.

"It's kind of you to help me," said John Binder, "but I'm really not injured enough to need—"

Calvin made a shushing sound and John waited silently until Calvin opened his eyes. "Not as good with my doodlebug as Alvin was with his, so it takes me longer and I don't know if I helped."

"You helped," said John Binder. "I'm ready to continue walking *and* telling, if that's good for you."

Calvin took a few steps and John Binder caught up immediately, with no pain in his legs or hips. Calvin always talked as if he couldn't do any healing, but now John Binder understood that Calvin had always been afraid to try to heal, because he knew he couldn't do as well as Alvin, so whatever he did would leave him humiliated. Now, with no Alvin for people to turn to, whatever Calvin could do would have to be enough. Nobody else was known to have healing knacks like his, beyond helping heal the skin under a child's scab, until it could cast off the covering.

They were almost at Margaret's house when John Binder got to the part where bodies were loaded into the wagon, and he skipped the whole journey because here he was. And there was his wagon. But the horse had been led away, presumably to be groomed and fed and watered. And the bodies of Measure and Alvin would be waiting inside.

To John's surprise, the door was standing open and there were two coffins inside resting on sawbucks, nailed shut and wrapped around with iron straps. John figured he was seeing Verily Cooper's knack as a barrel cooper, binding the coffins shut with stout bands that couldn't be cut with a buck knife. Grave robbers, take *that*, thought John Binder.

Calvin stood between the coffins, resting his hands on the nailed-down lids. Calvin leaned toward John Binder and said, in the faintest whisper, "Only stones in these boxes, to make them heavy enough."

John Binder understood at once. They would make a spectacle out of burying these boxes, probably in the city cemetery. The real coffins would be buried somewhere else. Somewhere safe.

Can we carry them with us to the Great Salt Lake? John thought not—such a cargo could not be concealed through all the weeks of the journey. Margaret Larner would decide. Maybe she could arrange for them to be carried back to Vigor Church, to be buried in a family plot, if there was one, or even the town cemetery there, with headstones that let the cognoscenti know who was buried there, but no one else.

Not my job, thought John Binder. No need for me to spin out an imaginary story.

Margaret Larner came into the front parlor and also rested her hands on the box lids. "Someone with a sticky knack," she said, "arranged the contents of these boxes so they wouldn't roll when the boxes are moved."

John Binder tried to think who had a knack like that.

"I could have done that," said Calvin.

"You were doing your duty down at the river," said Margaret. "And now I hope you'll come help Marty Laws get healed up, and then, maybe, to wake up. Whoever put him to sleep was *very* skilled with their knack."

"Sleep heals," said Calvin.

"That's my hope," said Margaret. "He's in the back sitting room."

The place where Alvin met with individuals and small groups. The closest thing to an office he ever had.

"Bleeding?" asked Calvin.

"Stopped before he got here. Blood is dried."

"Heartbeat?" asked Calvin.

"Perhaps," said Margaret, "if you come to Marty, you can answer those questions better than anyone else."

Calvin looked doubtful. "This was never a skill I mastered."

"I've seen you set broken bones," said Margaret. "And stop bleeding. And patch up broken skin."

"Superficial," said Calvin.

"So this time you'll take longer, and get your doodlebug smaller, and move more slowly to find out what's going on. And then, when you understand it, you can repair it. Slowly if need be."

John Binder realized that she was describing to him what Alvin would have done. And Calvin was enduring it from her, getting counsel about what the *real* Maker would do.

And if Calvin could do it, then perhaps he *was* a real Maker himself. Perhaps he was the successor that the people of Crystal City needed, a leader with Alvin's skills.

In the back sitting room, John Binder saw that Calvin was concentrating on the inert body of Marty Laws. John didn't want to interfere, but he had to ask. "Pulse? Breathing?"

"He's doing both," said Calvin. "And he's pissed himself something awful, but that might have happened yesterday, for all I know."

"I'll leave you to your work, then, Calvin. Thank you."

What did I thank him for? wondered John. Maybe . . . I was thanking him for even trying to do what he had never succeeded at before.

John left the room and quietly closed the door.

Margaret was waiting for John by the coffins. "Well?" she asked.

"He's trying," said John, "and I think he might succeed. Anyway, he says that Marty has a pulse and he's breathing."

"So he's still among the living, though not awake."

"If Calvin is a Maker," said John.

Margaret touched her finger to his lips. "What you're thinking about is the succession. But that's out of our hands. The people will choose."

"If Calvin heals Marty, word will spread that there's still a Maker in Crystal City."

"It takes more than astonishing knacks to make a man a Maker."

And she would know. So John did not pursue the matter of the succession.

Margaret quietly led him down into the cellar, and then pushed on a section of wall, which opened like a door. Inside, with a few candles burning, were two more coffins, smaller but still large enough to hold Measure and

Alvin. John Binder was not surprised. If the coffins upstairs were full of stones stuck to the wood, the bodies had to be somewhere. It occurred to John that whoever made these hurried boxes had made them so the smaller coffins nested inside the larger ones. That way, only two coffins had been carried into the house. And only two coffins would be carried out in front of everybody. But there were four coffins.

"Where will they go?" said John softly.

"Here," said Margaret. "In the dirt floor." She pointed. In the flickering, shadowy candlelight, John had not seen that there were two graves already dug—deep ones—waiting to receive their residents.

"So they'll stay here, in your house," said John Binder.

"Where I can watch over them," said Margaret.

John Binder nodded. And then he thought of a problem and said it. "Until you come west with the rest of us."

"I'm not going," said Margaret.

It was unthinkable. John could not keep his consternation from showing on his face.

"The people who are needed there will *be* with you on the journey," she said. "But my work with the city is done. You'll be a shepherd for Alvin's flock, helping them stay together and at peace."

"I'm not sure that my knack is as strong as you hope."

"I know it's stronger than you can even *wish* for," said Margaret, "as you'll learn when it's tested again and again on the journey."

"Please don't tell me I'm going to have to be in charge."

"Of course not," she said. "Your knack works best when nobody knows what it is or what you're doing with it."

John Binder nodded.

"Then Calvin will want to lead," he said.

"Calvin cannot cross the river," said Margaret.

"He thinks he can force his way across, I believe," said John.

"Then Calvin has no idea of the power of Red magic. When the river doesn't want you to cross, you will not take one more step. And if you try to swim past the barrier, the river will refuse to let you float, and he'll have to shed his pride at the bottom of the river, if he wants to rise to the surface and come back to the eastern shore."

"You think he understands that?" asked John.

"Once he's on the bottom of the river and can't float back up, he'll understand perfectly well. Though perhaps he'll have sense enough not to try."

"That would come perilously close to being obedient," said John Binder.

"Calvin still has time to learn many things," said Margaret.

"What will you do here?" asked John Binder.

"Take care of Vigor. Make sure he knows every good thing his father ever did. And when this new one comes, I'll teach her, too."

"Does she already have a heartfire?" asked John Binder.

"Soon," said Margaret. "When the body is strong enough to live, and her heartfire begins to warm her body and fill her to the toes and fingertips."

John Binder knew perfectly well that Margaret was pregnant with twins. But she must have had her own reasons for concealing it. Instead, he had to ask. "Margaret, what *is* a heartfire? Is it the soul?"

"I think the heartfire is where the body and the spirit of a person come together. Quarreling with each other, but also rejoicing in each other. As happens inside all of us. I think that the combined spirit and body are the soul, so the heartfire represents the soul. Or *is* the soul. I have no one to give me instruction on the matter, so all I have are my own guesses."

"They sound better than mine," said John.

"I hope you'll be one of the men entrusted with this secret, who can help me lower these coffins into the ground."

"I am proud and grateful to be invited. Of course I'll help."

"There won't be many of you," said Margaret, "so it will be harder perhaps than you think."

"I'm stronger than I look," said John.

"You look quite strong, so that's good."

"Calvin?"

"Calvin is never to know where his brothers are buried. If I find it necessary, I will placate him with a lie, so he won't keep wondering. Because he knows about the stones, so he knows the bodies are somewhere. If he had anything like Alvin's knack, then he can explore this whole house until he finds them. But I don't think he has the patience and determination to search that thoroughly."

"He might surprise you," said John Binder.

Margaret looked down at one of the coffins. John wondered if that was the box that held Alvin.

"I don't know which body is in which box. It doesn't matter. They will lie side by side in this cellar, with paving stones laid over the whole floor, and crates and shelves of supplies and seeds and tools and stored food. No one would think there was even room enough under the floor to hold one coffin, still less two."

"When did you think of all this?"

"When you arrived," said Margaret. "When you carried Marty into the house. My mind was out with the bodies of my husband and his brother. I knew I had to find a way to bury *something* for all to see, and yet bury them somewhere safe. In this house, I can watch over them."

"Some would think you were inviting them to haunt you," said John Binder, with a chuckle to show that he didn't believe in haunting, though of course, like everyone else, he did.

"I would love it if Alvin and Measure would both haunt me. I miss our conversations already."

John Binder nodded.

"But there'll be no haunting," she said. "These are not restless souls. God will have lots of things for them to do. The afterlife, in my opinion, will be a busy life. This nonsense about playing lutes and singing praises all day long—how quickly do you think God would weary of such time-wasting nonsense. If heaven is joyful, it'll be because there are things for us to do, jobs that *must* be done."

"Is this what Alvin believed?" asked John Binder.

"Right now, Alvin is no longer living by faith. He knows whatever there is to be known, but he won't tell me."

"So you'll watch over his grave by living in the house that stands over it."

"I can't think of a more convenient arrangement."

"When will the other men come to help me wrestle these boxes into the ground?"

"Well, John, as Abraham said to Isaac on the mountain, 'The Lord will provide.'"

"You mean it's just you and me."

"We'll see if we can do it. Notice that both graves are dug with a slope at one end, so perhaps we can slide them down into position."

"Steep ramps."

"But not vertical. We'll slide them and see."

"When?" asked John Binder.

"I don't see any other heartfires coming to join us. Everybody's mind is on the exodus and driving wagons and leading children on that icy road."

"They're all thinking about you and Alvin."

"And whenever they do, their emotions will overcome them and they'll weep and stop worrying."

"I don't think you have any idea how much people love you," said John Binder.

"How sweet of you to say that," said Margaret, "but if there's anyone on God's green Earth who absolutely knows *exactly* how much the people of Crystal City love everybody they love, it's me."

John chuckled. "I don't know how you've borne the burden of such knowledge all your life."

"I haven't borne it all my life. Only up to now. We'll see about the *rest* of my life later."

Because there was a good moon that night, the wagons began assembling near the river long before dawn. Everybody wanted to go into action. They couldn't fight their enemies, they couldn't avenge the Maker's death, but they could do *something*, so they roused their children early and took their wagons and handcarts and formed up wherever Arthur Stuart told them to be. They were remarkably quiet, for such a large assemblage with so many animals and, above all, children.

Calvin watched as Arthur quietly assigned every company its place, and then went about checking everything to be sure nobody had left a barrel of flour behind. I could help him with that, thought Calvin, but he stopped himself from offering. Arthur probably had the whole design already in his head, and the last thing he would need would be someone who kept thinking of ways to "improve" it.

"Do you think the King will come all the way from Camelot to wish us well?" asked Eliza.

Calvin smiled. "Wouldn't that be lovely. Then *he* would think he was in charge of this whole rebellion against his own authority."

"The best conflicts are the ones that can be and *are* entirely settled, peacefully, indoors of one's own house," said Eliza.

"How gnomic of you," said Calvin. "But Alvin did a very bad job of settling the succession before he died."

"Everybody will do their part," said Margaret.

"There has to be one leader," said John Binder. "I know there are several aspirants, but I always thought it would be you, Miz Larner."

"I'm worn out. I've lost heart. Quite literally."

John Binder smiled wanly. Yes, Alvin had been her heart, her life, her purpose, and he was gone.

"Do you think everyone is here?" asked Calvin.

"Have you counted the wagons and handcarts?" asked Margaret.

"We have a decent count, but not a reliable one. For instance, what do we call the people from the showboat who want to come with us?" Calvin shook his head. "I welcome them—indeed, I hope they *all* come. But are they one company, or just one household? Do I make the boat's captain the captain of their company on the road? They have lots of supplies, but they don't have their own wagon, they're sharing it out among whatever wagons still have any room left."

"Very resourceful of them," said Margaret.

"Why aren't you coming?" asked Calvin. "John Binder, have you even asked her?"

"I believe you know the answer," said Margaret. "I'm not leaving my Alvin behind, to go gallivanting across the prairies and through the mountains."

"Calvin," asked John Binder, "are you going to assemble the travelers into a meeting, so you can prove your leadership by telling them things they already know?"

"Well," said Calvin. "That sounds like a good idea."

"If it turns out to *be* a genuinely good idea, remember who suggested it," said John.

"Well, of course, *I* did," said Calvin, grinning.

"So it's going to be like that," said John Binder.

"Quite the contrary. I only wish I were going with you. Once you've left me behind, you don't have to mention my name again. Nobody but Eliza will miss me, or maybe not even her."

"*I'll* miss you," said Margaret.

"In a pig's eye," said Calvin with calm amusement. "We'll *both* be left behind here."

"But with the tower gone, and the people emigrated, there's no reason for you to stay here with the empty city."

Calvin said nothing. Margaret looked into his heartfire and saw the futures he aspired to—being the bulwark of Margaret's life, looking after her and the children. He thought he owed that to Alvin.

"Do you know if Measure's family is staying or going?" asked John Binder.

"They have their own wagon. What they don't have is anything but food and tools and seed to put in it. All donated. Did you know how very *poor* Measure and his family are?"

"Children with such a father can never be poor," said Calvin. "And a father and mother with such children are well provided for."

"A very noble observation," said John Binder.

"Arthur has assured me," said Margaret, "that he will take special notice of Measure's family."

Calvin muttered, "That should be my job."

"Yes," said Margaret, "it should. But for some reason, the river doesn't want to let you by."

This time, what Calvin muttered was unintelligible.

Margaret could only shrug mildly. It had not been a matter of her choosing, whatever Calvin thought.

"Isn't it time to call the meeting to order?" asked John Binder.

"Meeting?" said Calvin. "Everyone knows what to do."

"But everyone knows that it isn't yet time to do it," said John Binder. "Let's offer some counsel, some wisdom, whatever we can dredge up from our wasted hearts."

"Don't fall into the Mizzippy," said Calvin. "Drinking it will make you sick."

"Oh, there's nothing in it but a little dirt," said Margaret.

John Binder took up her challenge. "Let's see. There's also urine and feces from all the water creatures from the head of the river down to here. Plus whatever body parts and fragments have rotted and fallen away from the corpses of all the animals and humans in the river upstream."

"Well, if you're going to let things like that bother you," said Margaret.

"Plenty of dead fish eyeballs, too," said John.

"And the eggs of mosquitos, midges, gnats, and flies," added Margaret, joining the game.

"It's a crowded river," said Calvin. "Let's have this meeting."

The captain of the showboat used his penetrating voice to call them all to listen. Many of the people were expecting to hear the order to move forward. But Calvin stood beside the captain and held up a hand to stay those who were eager to get their equipage onto the ice.

"Here's where we stand," said Calvin. "With Alvin gone, I'm the closest thing to a Maker that we have. I just came here from healing Marty Laws. I drew out from his body enough lead and brass to be the roof of a small shed. And his body is healed. He will be able to walk onto this ice like anyone else. I only wish Alvin had allowed me to come with him. Between us, maybe we could have stopped *all* the musket balls. And stopped up the muskets, too. But Alvin made up his own mind, and gave me no role to play. I don't think he really believed that he could be killed. I think he saw salvation coming, but did not know from where."

Calvin went on, candidly discussing the difficulties of the road ahead. "From the start, we need to be sparing in our meals, so the food will last all the way to the valley. We need to go to sleep early, so that everyone has plenty of time to sleep. Sleep will be precious on this journey."

But after much good counsel, and a few witticisms that won him some laughter, it came down to this. "I believe that Tenskwa-Tawa doesn't understand how tightly our city, our culture, is involved with the presence of a Maker among us. I believe that if several of our leaders go to him and ask him to let me go with you, he'll relent. Eventually. And until he does, why not wait on the other side, near the shore, so that when I do cross over, there you are, ready for me to take, not *Alvin's* place—no one can do that—but the place of an apprentice Maker who can still do useful things, like saving Marty Laws from his injuries, and helping McEddy and Grampus make a bridge of ice that would cross the river all the way. When you get to the valley, who will make crystal blocks to rebuild the tower, the Crystal City? Who among you has *made* such blocks of water?"

And it was clear that he was making sense to many. When he finished, there was applause from many, shouts of acclamation from some.

Then Arthur Stuart came forward to stand beside Calvin. "We've heard from the Maker's brother, and I know he can do all the things he said he could do, and maybe more. But look yonder," said Arthur. "The sun's about to rise above the trees in the east. It's time for us to make our way across the river."

When Arthur pointed to the sunrise, many turned to look. But when they turned back to him, they realized that Arthur was speaking in Alvin's voice. And many would later say that Arthur Stuart wore Alvin's face while he spoke to them, giving instructions on which companies should prepare to come forward, with McEddy and Grampus guiding them onto the ice, so they could widen the ice road if need be. It was Alvin's voice, it was Alvin's face, and in that moment, all who saw this knew that whatever Calvin was, he was not the one to lead them as Alvin would have.

But Arthur Stuart, nobody cared now about his dark skin or his youth or the fact that he was not a Maker of any kind, or at least made no claim to be such. What they knew was that Arthur Stuart had been Alvin's choice, and in this miraculous appearance of Alvin's similitude and the sound of Alvin's voice, they saw a sign that it was Arthur Stuart who was Alvin's true successor, the natural leader of the Crystal City. It was Arthur Stuart whom they wanted to follow into the uttermost West.

"All of you who won't be moving onto the river until later today," said Arthur Stuart, "if you want to, you can come to the city cemetery to see Alvin's and Measure's coffins lowered into the ground in the place they worked so hard to build."

It seemed as if they all intended to come to the burial.

"Measure was not the Maker, but only the Maker's brother. But *such* a brother! Who was more loyal to Alvin than Measure was? As Alvin's older brother, he never resented his younger brother's leadership. And at the time when Alvin sent me away and made me bring Mike Fink back with me, there was a long moment when I stood there, looking at the brothers. And I thought I could hear Measure saying—though he never spoke a word—some of the words that Ruth said to her mother-in-law, Naomi. 'Entreat me not to leave thee, nor to depart from following after thee'—for I think that Measure feared that Alvin would send him away, too, as he was sending me. And in Measure's heart, I still heard these words: 'The Lord do so to me, and more also, if aught but death part thee and me.' "

There was some weeping, soft weeping, for no one wanted to miss any more of the words coming in the voice of Alvin, from the lips of Arthur Stuart.

"But death did not part them, did it?" said Arthur Stuart. "First Measure, as the older brother, took the musket ball that killed him. He even said, 'I am a dead man,' because Alvin had to know that Measure had fulfilled the covenant between them. I don't think Alvin ever decided to die, but John Binder and Marty Laws both attest that Alvin was trying as hard as he could to heal Measure's wound before the life entirely left him. But as Measure himself had said, he was a dead man, and it was not in Alvin's power to raise his brother from the dead, not while bullets still threatened to kill his other companions. Who knows what Alvin meant to accomplish when he rushed to the window and cried out, 'O Lord my God,' and a score of bullets took him there in the window, and dozens more after he was on the ground. Too many, too fast for Alvin to heal himself, and there on the ground outside Carthage Jail he died. The most powerful Maker in the world could not vanquish the Unmaker that last time."

Now the weeping was louder, so Arthur modulated his voice, using the technique that he had seen the showboat captain use to cast his voice directly to the ears of everyone present. They all heard Arthur Stuart say, in Alvin's voice, "How many times the Unmaker tried to kill Alvin from childhood on up, how close he came, how many people he enlisted to try to kill Alvin Maker. And yet he failed—until that very moment outside Carthage Jail. Then the Unmaker celebrated his triumph. He had accomplished his mission! The Maker no longer stood against him, making a mockery of all the Unmaker's brutal, destructive work."

The weeping was silent now. There were growls and grumbles as Arthur talked about the triumph of the Unmaker.

"But the Unmaker's triumph was misplaced. The Unmaker was wrong. Alvin was dead, but his work remained after him. Not the Crystal tower—what was that, but water and a few drops of Alvin's blood? No, Alvin's finest work was *you*. The people of Crystal City, who had worked together in loyalty and love to make a city of harmony and peace, where no one was poor or rich, but all were free to use their gifts, their knacks, and all their other works to sustain each other in harmony." Arthur paused, his arms outstretched as if to embrace them all. Then he went on, his voice even clearer.

"You have gathered here, ready to cross the uncrossable river, to venture into unknown lands, but with perfect confidence because you know these people who will travel with you, you know they have all been touched by the Maker's hand and word and heart. You who have known him—generations of children will rise up and hear your stories and account you a most blessèd generation, because you knew him, you spoke to him, you heard him, you heeded him, and together you built a godly city, a city of vision and hope. When we cross the river, those who hated you and Alvin for your gifts, your powers, your knacks, will think, like the Unmaker, that they have triumphed. But they have lost, they have failed, they are *defeated*, because you are still alive in your thousands, and in a generation, your tens of thousands, to carry his work forward into the future. I am proud that I will be one of you. We will go to the place that Ta-Kumsaw and the Prophet have chosen for us, and we'll make our winter quarters there, and then as spring begins, we will go on westward until we have crossed over the mountains and come down into the green and grassy valley that was shown to Alvin and the Prophet, as the place where *we* will continue to use and celebrate our knacks, to make the desert blossom as the rose, to bring water down from the canyons to water our fields and orchards. Is this not what Alvin wanted?"

Arthur Stuart gestured toward Calvin. "I am glad that Alvin's brother, who is also a seventh son of a seventh son, wants to support his work. I don't know if Tenskwa-Tawa will grant our petition to let Calvin cross the river and join us. But if that be impossible, then can't Calvin stay behind, to gather and guide others with knacks, who want to move to the free land of the Great Salt Lake Valley, where none shall come to hurt or make afraid. Calvin can guide them to the river, and help them cross. Because if the Prophet cannot make the river let Calvin pass over, perhaps he will allow the knackles who still live in hiding to gather up their courage and come to this shore and throw their lot in with the Maker's people. With you. Will you welcome them?"

The answer was a roar of acclamation.

And in that moment, Calvin knew that he would never cross that river. He was not needed in that peaceful land; these were a people who could govern themselves. And in Arthur Stuart, they had a leader they could love and follow.

Did Arthur Stuart think that Calvin had not felt the sly digs when he talked about how loyal Measure had been? Everyone knew that Calvin had *not* been a faithful brother. He was being loyal *now*—when Alvin was dead. But Calvin had imagined that his knacks would make him a leader. He had not realized that it was never Alvin's knacks that gave him primacy and power. It was his heart. His love for these people. His eagerness to teach them, to sustain them in their knacks, to keep them safe from illness, injury, hunger, and their bloodthirsty enemies.

Calvin had never shown even a scrap of such concern for others, because he had never felt any. His concern had always been to jockey for the front position, to "win" a race that no one else was running in—certainly not Alvin. I'm alive, Alvin is dead, but I did not "win" anything. I was never involved in Alvin's true cause. So, dead, Alvin could never be surpassed by such as me.

The life Arthur Stuart had just promised him, he could do that. And he could protect the graves of the Maker and his brother. And he could also look after Alvin's and Margaret's children, and Margaret herself. If anyone or anything threatened harm to them, Calvin could surely stop the threat and destroy the threatener.

That's me, thought Calvin. Destroy the menace that comes against us. I'm not a builder of harmony, but I hope that I'm the enemy of wickedness.

The burial ceremony was simple and brief. Arthur Stuart had already given the funeral oration. So it was in silence that they watched Vigor, along with Measure's children, lay nosegays of wildflowers on their fathers' coffins. Then the wooden boxes were lowered into the ground, and men with spades pitched the dirt back down into the hole, beside and then over the coffins. Then, at Margaret's invitation, as they left they all trod upon the loose earth over the graves until it was packed down, solid.

Then they went back to their wagons and carts, along with Measure's children and widow, leaving Margaret and Calvin there alone.

"I'm not the man you would have chosen for your companion here and now," said Calvin.

"You are exactly the man I would choose," said Margaret. "There was a time when I feared that if Alvin were ever killed, it would be because you betrayed him. But that did not happen. You did everything that Alvin asked of you, and everything I asked. The Prophet won't let you across, I fear, because I think he can't. I think the river made its own rules. But I hope you listened to Arthur Stuart as he outlined a future of nobility and generosity for you."

"All I can promise is that I'll try to do all of that," said Calvin. "As best I can."

"Your best will be good enough," said Margaret.

"I know you buried stones today," said Calvin, "but I do not ask you where their bodies will really be laid to rest, because I don't want to know."

"I think *these* graves will be a good enough memorial. I'll get a stonecutter to make headstones. Or one headstone. A wide one, with both their names. Does that sound right?"

Calvin laughed. "Since when does Margaret Larner ask an ignorant, foolish apprentice for advice?"

"When he is the brother of my beloved," said Margaret. "In whom I have high hopes."

"Put your hopes in Arthur Stuart," said Calvin. "*He's* the one the people chose to follow into the West."

"Where I won't see him again," said Margaret. "But *you* I'll see every day. So pardon me if I have chosen *you* to be the vessel of my hopes."

Calvin bowed, and not sarcastically, for once. "I will serve as best I can."

"As best you can."

"I don't make vows that might not be within my power to keep."

40

Down at the water's edge, McEddy, Grampus, and Calvin were standing together, arm-over-shoulder, working on the ice road. It was now nearly twenty feet wide, and it wasn't glassy, it had frost on it, thick enough to give the metal-rimmed wheels some bite.

Arthur's job was to walk among the wagons, making sure that there were no parties in conflict or distress. There might be some legitimate causes for argument, but in this passage across the river into the forbidden Red lands, Arthur Stuart didn't want any conflicts to disturb the journey. What if, because of a quarrel, somebody tried to turn a wagon or handcart around on the ice and come *back*, past the outbound line of wagons and people? It could be a disaster, if anyone was in such high dudgeon as to forget all responsibility to the rest of the exiles from Crystal City.

He never had to use Alvin's voice directly, in speaking to the people—though he would have, if that's what it took to help calm a conflict. What he found was harmony among the people. Fear, too, of course, and regret for all that they had built and were now leaving behind them. How could they not feel that? But this longing helped bind them together instead of driving them apart. It made them tender-hearted instead of irritable. Arthur Stuart wondered just how much John Binder had to do with that peace, that binding friendship. It could not last forever, but Arthur Stuart sure hoped it could last through this day. He hoped it would outlast the ice.

The sun was above the eastern horizon when Calvin, McEddy, and Grampus walked up from the river's edge to where Arthur waited with the wagons assigned to the start of the crossing.

"It's solid all the way across," said McEddy.

"The frost was my idea," said Grampus.

"A good one," said Calvin.

"Will the ice hold, with all this traffic on it?" asked Arthur Stuart.

"Can't know till we try," said McEddy. "But we'll keep watch on it."

"Can you watch the whole bridge from either end?" asked Arthur Stuart.

Calvin nodded. So did the others.

"It seems to me that it would be wise for Grampus and McEddy to cross ahead of the first company, and then stand watch—or sit!—while the city crosses, ready to heal any problem in the ice. And Calvin, can you do the same from this side? And if there's any reason for us to stop, any reason why the wagons stop rolling, you can warn us, so we stop sending new wagons out on the ice?"

Calvin nodded soberly. "A good plan, to make sure all are safe." The other two nodded.

"Well then," said Arthur, "you've built well. You've *made* well. And now, Mr. Grampus and Mr. McEddy, would you step onto the river road and lead the way?"

"We will," said Grampus. "But first, Mr. Stuart, I have to ask you a question."

Arthur Stuart waited expectantly.

"You look like me," said Grampus, "but I know you're half White."

"I hope I got nothing from my father except a slight lightening of my skin," said Arthur.

"No, no, I'm not accusing you of nothing. But I never seen you make no charm, and yet it seem to me you got you more than one knack."

"I do have some knacks," said Arthur Stuart. "But I had no mother to teach me the ways of Blacks holding power in the world."

"I know a charm or two," said Grampus. "I can teach you."

"I'll gladly learn from you, Mr. Grampus," said Arthur. "When we're well across the river."

"And I can teach you how to think so's you can make up your own charms at need. There's logic to it. Just not White man's logic or, I must say, no Red man's logic neither."

It seemed as if Grampus wanted to say more. But maybe he realized he had too much to say to be able to fit it into the time before the wagons had to get started.

The freezers all walked down to the bridge together, but Calvin stood aside on the dock as the other two stepped carefully onto the ice. It would be bad news if the bridgemakers slipped and fell on the ice, with the first steps of the passage.

But their steps were firm, their strides longer and longer, though they had no desire to run, lest children feel encouraged to run after them, and risk slipping into the river. Calvin explained their plan to Arthur Stuart, when he came down with the wagons of the first company and beckoned each one out onto the ice.

Arthur didn't have to remind them that every walking child had to hold fast to the loops of cotton cord attached along the side of every wagon, at a height a child could reach. Children too small to walk or too young to be trusted to hold on for themselves were bundled into narrow sledges that were tied to a couple of loops each, so they were pulled smoothly along with the wagons, while women kept an eye on them, so no child could fall out and onto the ice without being noticed.

"It's all about safety," said Calvin. "You don't want any accidents on this crossing."

Arthur Stuart agreed. "I had nightmares of this crossing turning into one long emergency of repairing broken ice or rescuing drowning children or women or animals."

"The animals still worry me," said Calvin.

"John Binder is conversing with the flocks and herds, such as they are—we're not bringing a serious number of either, but . . . breeding stock," said Arthur Stuart.

"I didn't know that John's gifts extended to animals as well as people," said Calvin.

"Neither did John," said Arthur Stuart, "until he tried it."

"What Grampus talked to you about," said Calvin. "Your knacks."

By now Margaret was stepping onto the dock, that being the best vantage point. "Pardon me, gentlemen," she said, "but these have been my people and my city for long and long. I won't be crossing this river in my lifetime, I believe, but my heart goes with them."

Arthur Stuart did not really understand why Margaret wouldn't cross over. But whatever her reasons, he was sure they were good ones.

"I don't believe you were finished with the conversation that I interrupted," said Margaret.

Arthur Stuart laughed. "Calvin was just about to ask me a question I can't possibly answer."

"You knew my question?" asked Calvin. There was more than a little doubt in his voice.

"You wanted to know what knacks I have," said Arthur Stuart. "Because I do have a few White men's knacks, things I've learned over the years, things Alvin taught me, or helped me to improve on. But I couldn't enumerate them. They're just things I've learned to do, and when I need them, I do them."

"Like running with that Greensong that I could never hear," said Calvin.

"Oh, Calvin, you and I both know you hear it. You just don't trust it."

Arthur could see Calvin seethe. And in Calvin's heartfire he saw that he wanted to say, Don't speak to me about what I can and cannot hear or see or do.

But it was Margaret who spoke up and answered Calvin's unspoken resentment. "I happen to know more than Arthur Stuart does about the knacks he has. Because it wasn't just from Alvin that he learned. I even taught him to make a few charms that I had learned from free Black women in Philadelphia and other places, before Alvin and I threw in with each other as a full-time career."

"You taught me . . ." Then Arthur smiled. "Those were *Black* charms. I thought it was more like making hexes."

"It's just like making hexes," said Margaret. "Those are the magic of Black people, just as the Greensong is the magic of Reds. Alvin could do them all, as soon as he learned. Nobody made better, truer hexes. Alvin never tried to *be* a Red man or a Black man, but he wanted to learn all he could from anybody, because . . . well, because that's what a Maker does." She made a point of not looking at Calvin when she explained this to Arthur Stuart, because she knew that Calvin would resent a direct sermon from her, but would listen carefully to all she said.

Meanwhile, Arthur Stuart's mind was racing. "I learned Greensong from him," he said, "even though I'm White and Black, with no Red in me."

"Love is the teacher," said Margaret softly. "Who loved you more than Alvin, and who loved Alvin more than you did?"

"You, Miz Larner," said Arthur Stuart instantly.

"No, Arthur Stuart. You and I both gave our whole heart to him. There's no more than that to give."

That was when Papa Moose and Mama Squirrel came down to the water's edge. Each of them was pulling a handcart, and following them was a wagon driven by another man from the bayou country, who knew Grampus well. There was a slight delay because their dozens of children were a little hard to rein in.

"Margaret," called out Mama Squirrel, "is there some spell you can cast on these children to make them cross safely and without making me insane?"

"There is," said Margaret, "and you already cast that spell."

The two women looked solidly at each other, and then Mama Squirrel smiled. "Oh, you are a seer, Miz Larner. You are an oracle. Come with us. Cross over with us. Bring your son and the baby you're carrying inside you. Bring them and become a part of our family. We need you so!"

Arthur Stuart saw how Margaret hesitated, lured by the promise of a family life that had been stolen from her and Alvin while he lived.

But she held to her original decision. "I long to say yes," said Margaret. "But I also know that you need me no more than a one-legged, one-armed man needs a ladder!"

"No, but he needs a second arm and a second leg! You've got both of yours," said Mama Squirrel.

"Oh, don't plague her, old woman," said Papa Moose from the handcart ahead of her. "She knows the way across the river as well as anybody, if she wants to come."

Then, Papa Moose, holding firmly to the two arms of the handcart, stepped out onto the ice and instantly all the little squirrels stopped their madcap antics and lined up in a double file directly behind him. When all the children were on the ice, including those pulled in sledges by older children, Mama Squirrel gave a jaunty wave, then picked up the arms of her handcart and followed the lines of exceptionally well-behaved children.

Their wagon followed her onto the ice. It was heavily laden, for even though no one child would eat more than they needed, there were a lot of children, and the wagon was full of supplies for the journey, with scarcely any seed or tools for work once they reached the valley. Moose and Squirrel knew that others would help them, as had always happened since they set out to follow Alvin north to the Crystal City. That was something that had always been true of Crystal City. No one was poor because everyone's hand was open to the hungry, the widow, the orphan, the homeless, of which Papa Moose and Mama Squirrel had a whole passel, not only from their orphanage in the South, but also orphans and lost children they had picked up along the way, giving a helping hand to all, and a home to those who had no other home.

After the interruption, the people on the dock all watched in silence for a time.

Then Margaret said, touching Arthur Stuart on the arm, "You know, I can sense from Tenskwa-Tawa's heartfire that he's troubled because his brother Ta-Kumsaw is giving orders to the people from the city as if he had authority over them, which as their host in the Red lands I imagine he does. But Tenskwa-Tawa is wondering when the *leader* of Alvin's people will cross over, so that they can get everything organized and move our people west, away from the river, so there's room for all the rest who are coming."

"That's a lot of wondering for you to receive so clear," said Arthur Stuart. "You know that you sensed *exactly* the same thing from him."

Margaret saw Calvin startle a bit and look from Margaret to Arthur Stuart, not in awe, but with curiosity. Arthur Stuart had never told anybody just how much he saw of other people's heartfires. But how could he think that Margaret wouldn't know? Or that Alvin hadn't at least guessed that despite Arthur's fibs, he saw a good deal farther and deeper into people's heartfires than did Alvin himself.

"I think," said Arthur Stuart, "that I should hurry across that bridge and ease the Prophet's mind."

Calvin finally spoke up. "I hope you don't startle any of the women and children into panicking and falling into the water."

"Well," said Arthur, "there's time to tread on the road, and time to run on secret paths beside it."

Margaret laughed. "Don't tell me there's Greensong out on the water, too."

"Not green, no, the plants and animals under the water don't care what's happening on the surface. But Alvin could walk where he needed to, not by freezing the water, but by making it into crystal wherever his feet stepped."

Calvin could not hold his tongue. "It takes blood to make the crystal."

"Well, yes," said Arthur Stuart, "if you want it to last forever. But where he stepped only needed to be crystal while his foot was on it. You should try it, Calvin. I believe it may be well within your knackery." Unlike Margaret, Arthur Stuart had no qualms about reminding Calvin of all he had missed by rejecting Alvin's tutelage for so many years.

But Arthur did not linger to deal with Calvin's resentment. Calvin was a grown man—he should be able to calm himself down, when the provocation was removed.

Instead, Arthur Stuart strode briskly to the edge of the dock and leapt out over the ice that lingered there. When he landed, the ice shattered, because where it wasn't part of the road, the freezers had allowed it to grow thin. But there was no splashing of the water under the ice. Where Arthur's foot landed, the water was solid crystal, and as he ran headlong into the west, some fifteen feet off to the side of the ice bridge, he made no splash at all, and soon was running as fast as ever he had in the Greensong, and the people on the ice saw him doing something miraculous they had never seen Alvin do, and they waved and called out to him. And then, in a step, he was gone, moving far too fast for any conversation.

"I hope none of the children think they can run where Arthur ran," said Calvin.

"They won't," said Margaret. "Nobody thinks they can do what Arthur Stuart can do. Ever since the meeting this morning, he's Alvin to them now."

Calvin laughed wryly, resentfully. "Who knew Arthur could do all these things he does? How is he a Maker also?"

"I believe Alvin once said that he wished that all the people of Crystal City could be Makers," said Margaret. "Dear Measure learned more than most people realized. He met Alvin more than halfway. If Measure had lived, he would have been Alvin's heir, and I think the people would not have been disappointed."

"As they would have been disappointed in me," said Calvin.

"I don't know," said Margaret. "I think that if they had needed you, you would have been what they needed."

Calvin laughed again, this time with real mirth. "You are a wonder, Little Peggy Guester," he said. "You said that with such reassurance that I had to think for a moment to realize that what you said had no meaning at all."

"Well, it *had* a meaning, and it was true, but laugh if you want. Like Measure, like Arthur, there's more to you than meets the eye."

"More, yes," said Calvin. "But also less."

"You would know that better than I," said Margaret.

"Oh, why can't you say 'better than me' like a natural American."

"Because I'm a schoolteacher at heart, and I know all the rules, even the useless ones."

"You're not staying behind just to watch out for me."

"Not that you don't need some watching over, since you have a tendency to make very poor choices at times," said Margaret.

"I don't think loving Eliza was a mistake."

"Neither do I," said Margaret. "She has been surprisingly good for you. But *sleeping* with her, that was silly and unnecessary."

"My body felt otherwise, and my mind agreed," said Calvin.

"I know," said Margaret.

"You knew all along," said Calvin.

Margaret looked at the wagons now moving out onto the ice. The captains of each company were doing their jobs and everybody helped if anything got fouled up.

"Calvin," said Margaret. "Do you think you can do anything about that patch where the wheels are getting mired in mud."

"Do what?" asked Calvin.

"Make the ground a bit firmer there. Perhaps pack it down hard. Or dry it somewhat. Something."

Calvin realized that yes, he could do something about it, and he was angry with himself for not having seen the need and done it. But within a minute or two, as the wagon was manhandled out of the sticking place, what was behind that wheel was solid, smooth, unrutted ground. Nobody else got stuck there.

"I asked my kitchen girl to make a lunch for us both," said Margaret. "Actually, enough for McEddy and Grampus, too, because I didn't know the plan would put them on the opposite side. But I think you're hungry enough to eat all that I don't eat."

"You knew I was sleeping with Eliza all along, but you never showed any anger."

"I never felt any anger toward you, Calvin. I don't talk about it, but my own father succumbed to such allurements one time, with a woman who knowingly participated in his adultery, and yet she became my friend and tutor when I went to her."

"Did you think she might have given birth to a sister or brother of yours?"

"No, Calvin. I had seen enough of her in my father's heartfire to know that she was a lady of grace and wisdom. I was able to become a lady and a schoolteacher because of her. Mistress Modesty, she was called, and I loved her. My father loved her. My mother never knew, because I never told her, and Father broke off the liaison of his own accord. I grew up knowing about *every* adultery in Hatrack River and anywhere else I went. Everybody's secret sins. Calvin, that was too much of a burden for a child, to know how little faith there was in the world."

"So you forgave me."

"You did *nothing* to me that needed forgiveness. Nor did you steal Eliza's virtue from her—she had been giving it away with both hands since she was a slip of a girl, fourteen or fifteen years old, or so she seemed in her own heartfire. Calvin, I know more than I ever wanted to know."

"Did you know that Alvin was going to die in Carthage?"

"When I laid my hands on his mother's belly and saw his heartfire inside her, I saw him sitting dead beside a whitewashed clapboard building, many bullet wounds in his body. But then I was involved with his birth, and when he was born with his face covered, I saw no more in his heartfire than his suffocation. Only after I removed the birth caul from his face and allowed him to draw breath did I see any future for him, and that image of his death never appeared again. So many *other* deaths—oh, the Unmaker was out to destroy him, indeed! And I saw that by keeping his birth caul, I had access to powers he would not learn how to use himself till he was older, and so my task was to use his power to protect him."

"From Hatrack River, you protected him in Vigor Church."

"Until I used the last of his caul. Meanwhile, he mastered many of his knacks by working to keep *you* alive as hard as I worked to save *him*."

"Was the Unmaker trying to destroy me, too?"

"No," said Margaret, "or not that I saw, anyway. He saved you from your own childish recklessness. The more he saved you, the more you thought nothing could harm you. But you grew up and after a while, you were able to save your own life, when you needed to."

"If he had let me be there, I could have—"

"You could have died right along with him. Do you think it's an accident that Measure was killed, and the other two were not? If you had been the brother with him, you would have died, too."

"Did you see that in my heartfire?"

"I saw in Alvin's heartfire that your death was something he was determined not to allow, not while he was alive."

"He loved me," said Calvin.

"There were times when I couldn't really fathom why," said Margaret. "And then I *did* see, and I *did* understand. He saw in you the boy he might have been, without my protection, without your parents' love."

"My parents loved me," said Calvin.

"But you weren't sure of that, were you?" asked Margaret. "Because you saw how they were in awe of Alvin, and they never showed such feelings toward you."

"I have to stay away from you," said Calvin. "You're a witch, and you know too much."

"I am *not* a witch. I'm your sister, and at first for my husband's sake, and now for your own sake, I love you as my true brother. You have enough of the heartfire vision to know that I am not lying to you."

Calvin nodded, and tears streamed down his face. "I know why the river rejected me."

"You're not here because you're *rejected.* You're here because you're *needed.* Do you think that everybody with a dangerous, hidden knack has been found and led across the river?"

"No ma'am," said Calvin.

"Verily Cooper is on his way to Philadelphia to try to persuade the President to allow those isolated knackles to make their way to the river and cross into the West. Who will lead them there? Who will even find them?"

Calvin nodded. But then he went and sat on the edge of the dock, dangling his legs over until they nearly touched the water that had been exposed when Arthur Stuart broke the ice. He did not even react when Eliza walked onto the ice with the knacky people from the showboat and, seeing him, called out and waved. But he heard her. He just didn't want to care.

She had made her choice: She had no claim on Calvin now, nor on Margaret, and certainly not on Arthur Stuart. But she had shown talent for leadership, and liked it, so she might be a great help to the people of Crystal City in their new home, and in crossing the plains and mountains to reach it. Or she might be a thorn in Arthur's side that would challenge him constantly to deal with her in a way that wouldn't exile her from the new city.

Margaret did not stay to watch everyone pass. She was heavy enough with Alvin's last babies that she could not stay without a chair to sit on, and even that would not be enough, not for long. So as the wagons continued to pass, and the sun made its downward way in the sky, Margaret walked back up to her house.

Mike Fink was there, keeping watch at the door. She had found that he was a good man, not cruel at heart despite the many cruel things he had done in his life. She liked him. She trusted him. He would have died for Alvin, but Alvin wanted him to live, and it occurred to her that having Mike Fink watching over her and her children was not a bad thing. She would not be an unprotected widow. They would not be vulnerable orphans. And they would grow up under the protection of a man who had known their father and loved him.

She went inside the house, and murmured, "Come with me" as she passed Mike. Soon they were down in the cellar, standing where they both knew Alvin and Measure were buried. "You haven't had the floor done yet," said Mike.

"I didn't want any of the workmen from Crystal City down here. There are too many knacks, and one might include seeing what's buried under this dirt floor."

"But workmen without knacks?"

"Masons," said Margaret. "Men who can make a solid brick floor, two layers deep, and then a layer of wood on top."

"And who will use this dark and quiet room?" asked Mike Fink.

"You may," said Margaret, "any time you want to come down here. Not necessarily to remember Alvin—I know you won't forget him, but sometimes a person needs time to himself, to think his thoughts and dream his dreams."

"That's right kind of you," said Mike Fink. "For what it's worth, I haven't killed a man since I met Alvin. Well, since very soon after I met Alvin."

"Did he ask you not to?" asked Margaret.

"Well, I knew he disapproved of it, especially because he didn't kill *me* when I came *this* close to killing him. And he didn't take anything from me—not my nose, not an ear, not an eye, nor any other part belonging to a man. I had never fought anyone who did not want to break me somehow. Who merely wanted to stop me from killing *him.* Or that's how I remember it, anyway."

Margaret smiled and leaned her head against his upper arm, his shoulder being out of her reach. "You and I are the only two people east of the river who know what lies in this floor."

"What if people from west of the river someday ask to be able to take his body west and bury it in the new Crystal City?"

"If I know Arthur Stuart, there will *be* no city called Crystal, because that belonged only to Alvin. And if I know Arthur Stuart, he will *never* ask to take Alvin away from me, nor Measure away from Alvin."

"Will you ever marry again?" asked Mike Fink.

"That's two questions, my dear friend. Yes, I'm still of child-bearing age, and my children will need a good father, and other siblings besides each other. So even though I will never find any man to compare to Alvin, I will find a man whose heartfire shows he'll be kind to me and my children, that he'll be able to provide for us, and that he will truly love me. I will marry that man."

Mike Fink nodded.

"You will never be that man," said Margaret kindly. "You will watch over Alvin's children as long as you can, and you will love them for Alvin's sake. Like Measure, you are a good brother to Alvin, and so it will be as Uncle Mike that Alvin's children will know you."

"Uncle Fink," said Mike. "There are already enough Mikes in the world."

"Uncle Fink it shall be," said Margaret.

"Are you going to raise them to talk in that high falutin way?"

"Absolutely," said Margaret.

"Then the other children at school will want to beat them up, and they'll do it, too."

"Not with Uncle Fink walking with them to and from school," said Margaret.

"Damn right," said Mike Fink. Then he knelt by the graves and wept, and Margaret left him there to mourn. Alvin, you left so many broken hearts behind you. But mine is not broken. My heart is whole, because you made me whole for so many years. I still carry your heartfire inside mine, as Arthur Stuart also does. Nobody understands that connection that transcends death, but it's real. You are alive in my heart, and in Arthur Stuart's heart. Your power is no longer in the world, but your love remains.

Ta-Kumsaw greeted Arthur Stuart with a handshake when he sprang up onto the riverbank, still running very fast. At the top of the bank, Arthur Stuart took the offered hand, and thanked Ta-Kumsaw for helping the people.

"Alvin's people," said Ta-Kumsaw. "He saved my life when I was a dead man, and my debt can never be fully repaid. But this will help."

"Have you shown John Binder where the people of Crystal City can camp for tonight?"

"He's already assembling and arranging the first arrivers."

"How did you know he should be in charge? Because I know he would never *declare* it."

Ta-Kumsaw rolled his eyes, not what Arthur Stuart expected a stoic Red warrior to do. "I have a brother who sees who people really are, and he told me that John Binder was holding this great tribe of yours together."

"Then I thank you both."

"Oh, my brother is right beside him. You don't think he'd leave it all up to a White man, do you?"

Arthur Stuart laughed, and since he laughed with Alvin's voice, with Alvin's laugh, Ta-Kumsaw embraced him. "I see that Alvin also had a brother, besides those that God gave to his parents."

Arthur Stuart did not deny it.

"Did he teach you to run on the water, or did you find that road for yourself?"

"Both, in a way," said Arthur Stuart. "This was the first time I actually did it. But it went well, I think."

"I believe Alvin left his people in good hands. And in your case, he did *not* leave things up to a White man."

"Half White," said Arthur Stuart.

"In you," said Ta-Kumsaw, "there is no 'half' this and 'half' that. You are whole, you are one, you are a man."

"Then I may continue doing such Red magic as Alvin taught me?"

"If the living world accepts you, then a Red man can do no less," said Ta-Kumsaw.

Arthur smiled. "It's a long way to the Great Salt Lake," he said.

"And don't get any foolish ideas about taking the salt out of it," said Ta-Kumsaw.

"I don't have any plan to undo the land where we'll live."

"Nonsense. You'll plow under the grass and plant your own grasses, and trees that bear the fruits you like. And you'll find the makings of gunpowder, and make it. You'll find iron and coal because in that land, there is plenty of both. Copper, too, a mountain's worth. It's a place where White civilization can be built."

"I believe," said Arthur Stuart, "that just because a thing *can* be done, does not mean that it *must* be done."

"That eases my heart," said Ta-Kumsaw. "We are both leaders of a great people now, and our people will grow to fill all these lands, and they will learn reading and writing, and they will come to you to buy paper and pen and ink. They will learn deeper agriculture, as I did in my time among the White people, and they will come to you for plows and hoes, and you will trade with them, or, God forbid, give them money for it, and teach them to be rich when others are poor."

"I hope my own people don't learn that themselves."

"My people will traffic with yours, and there will be envy and resentment. My people will come as they come to everyone, expecting to be fed wherever they go."

"My people will feed them as long as they have any food themselves."

"You make bold promises about the future. But I know my people's weaknesses, too. Young men will decide to take what they are not given. They will do it by stealth, and then openly, and then by threat of force. And your people will take their hunting rifles and shoot my young men dead when they misbehave like this, and thus we will have war in the future."

"Because you can't control your people," said Arthur Stuart.

"And because when they are angry at being robbed, you cannot control *your* people, either."

"I will teach them," said Arthur, "to be patient with your young men, and give them freely whatever they take, and never try to prevent them by force."

"You can teach them all you like, but where are the White men who will listen to such teachings?"

Arthur Stuart said, "And you will teach them about White men and their need to own things and have no one take them away. You will teach them to take only what is freely offered, and never what is needful for White colonists to keep and use."

Ta-Kumsaw laughed. "We will both teach our people to behave so unnaturally that your Whites will not act White, and my Reds will not act Red."

"But they will still *be* Red and White, and we *will* have peace."

"When you die all these promises will soon fade," said Ta-Kumsaw.

"Die?" asked Arthur Stuart. "If *you* haven't died, why should I?"

"Let us always remember that our true enemies lie east of the river, not west of it. Your people are feared and hated because of their knacks, and mine are feared and hated because the Whites of the East know that they are living on *our* land, so they believe we must hate them as they would hate anybody who dispossessed *them*."

"But you *do* hate them," said Arthur Stuart.

"I fear them," said Ta-Kumsaw, "because I learned something when I lived among the Whites."

Arthur Stuart waited.

"Here is what I learned. A man might fear someone who has harmed him, because he may harm him again. But a man will *hate* someone that he has wronged, because he knows that he does not deserve to be forgiven."

"That is very wise," said Arthur Stuart.

"That is why we have given your powerful people a good land where they can thrive as they want to thrive, and live as they want to live. You have not wronged us, we have not wronged you, so there never needs to be hate between us."

"That is a good balance," said Arthur Stuart. "I vow that I will teach my people to abide by this law."

"Yes," said Ta-Kumsaw. "It *was* you that I was waiting for here by the river."

"You were waiting for Alvin Maker," said Arthur Stuart.

"And you came, not as his shadow or his echo, but with his heartfire and with his voice."

Arthur Stuart bowed, and then knelt before Ta-Kumsaw. "You are king of this land," he said. "I pledge my allegiance and obedience to you."

"There will be no kings in this land," said Ta-Kumsaw.

"Then be my father," said Arthur Stuart. "The father of my body is a creature of slime and filth. Please take me as your son, and be the father of my heart, and I will obey you as a father, because you have nurtured me as a son."

The people of Crystal City who were just coming off the ice bridge saw Arthur Stuart kneel before Ta-Kumsaw, and whether anyone called it by that name, they understood that the mayor of their city was pledged to the chief man of the Reds. Word of this would spread, and they would understand that no matter what, any lands they had here were Red lands, and they would answer to the Reds for anything they did. They talked about this, and decided they could live with that. The Reds did not have to take them in, yet they opened their wall and let them enter.

The last wagons crossed after it was dark, but there was moonlight, and darkness was no hindrance. The Crystal City settlement consisted of wagons and blankets spread out on the grass, because there was no rain coming tonight. The children slept easily, near their parents but not huddled in any kind of fear. The marauders had been left behind. The people who had murdered Alvin and Measure had been left behind as well. And the Reds were accepting them in peace.

The animals weren't in on any such treaty, but there were enough people with knacks to keep wolves and coyotes at bay, and bar them from taking so much as a lamb or a calf or a foal.

That night as he lay on his blanket under the stars, Arthur Stuart cast out far and wide, looking for all the heartfires he could find. He looked into the heartfires of many Reds, and found only pity for the refugees and acceptance of them in their land for Alvin's sake, because Alvin was a legend of nobility among them. He had been with Ta-Kumsaw in the great war and saved his life. He had healed Lolla-Wossiky of his drunkenness and blindness so he could become the Prophet and teach the Reds. There was no hate there, not tonight.

And he looked into the heartfires of his own people, heartfires that he already knew before they became *his* people. And there, too, there was no malice or fear or hate or anger. No one harbored any ambition of crossing back over the river in order to take retribution on Carthage for murdering the Maker.

Tonight, thought Arthur Stuart, we have something so rare that it is remembered only in legends of a golden age. Tonight we have peace.

I will nurture it. I will make it last as long as the people want it. Long after I die, let them live in this peace. Then we will have fulfilled Alvin's dream by creating the true Crystal City.

Suddenly it crossed Arthur Stuart's mind: There is no reason now for me not to marry, because I will not be haring off with Alvin to the ends of the Earth. I belong to myself now, if I belong to anybody, so it's time for me to have the life that Alvin longed for but could never have except for moments here and there.

She must be somewhere in this company, among the people from the South. She knew that I loved her, and I knew she loved me, and if she hasn't chosen someone else, she will be there for me, and I will be there, at last, for her.

That was the dream in his mind when he fell asleep in the land of the Red man, in the midst of the Crystal City, on the grass of this great land, under this moon and these stars, where he belonged.

Afterword

The Tales of Alvin Maker began with an idea and a poem.

I was taking a graduate course in Elizabethan literature except Shakespeare, which led directly to Edmund Spenser and *The Faerie Queene.* While I had little patience with the heavily allegorical narrative (I prefer my history in prose and plain speaking), I did appreciate the fact that Spenser was trying to do for Modern (Post-Chaucerian) English poetry what Dante Alighieri had done for Tuscan vernacular poetry.

I had already begun to dislike the apparent duty of American fantasy writers to set their stories in a pseudo-medieval England. When Tolkien did it, he was writing a profoundly English epic. But what do American writers have to do with the English landscape, folklore, and culture? Don't we have folklore of our own? We do, along with a history and a landscape that are quite different from those of England.

I wouldn't have minded so much if the traditional fantasy writers had bothered to learn enough about medieval English culture to understand how the society worked. It grates on my nerves when American writers speak of the non-royal peerage and armiger classes as "royalty." No! "Royalty" refers only to direct and near relatives of the reigning monarch. Also, the king and queen are addressed as "your majesty," princes of the royal house are "your highness," and other nobility are addressed as "my lord," "my lady," "your lordship" (or ladyship) or, at the lowest levels, "Sir John" and "Lady Jezebel."

And, to me, the most annoying thing—a fault even with Tolkien's *The Lord of the Rings*—is the fact that gentlemen of property, like Bilbo and Frodo, seem to have no duties apart from making tea, entertaining visitors, reading and writing letters, and gallivanting about on horseback or in carriages. Jane Austen, who rarely makes such omissions, shows her well-to-do gentlemen with very demanding duties in directing the agriculture on their property, caring for the tenants of their land, seeing to the upkeep of their buildings, and hiring and paying employees. Being a prosperous landowner is a full-time job, and those who expend their income on gaming and gambling and other money-losing activities are prone to leave nothing to their heirs but debts and obligations.

When Lobelia Sackville-Baggins finally gets possession of Bag End, Bilbo's and Frodo's prosperous estate, there is no hint that there are tenants and employees to be met with and supervised. It seems, in *The Lord of the Rings*, that Bag End is nothing but the house and its furnishings, with its only staff being Hamfast Gamgee (the Gaffer) and his son, Samwise. Sam is definitely a servant—somewhere between a valet and a batman—and views himself as a minor character in his "master's" biography. But where is the source of Bilbo's money, once he spent or gave away all the treasure he had brought home from his travels and adventures in *The Hobbit*? There's real work to be done, or where in the world does your money come from.

Some fantasy writers broke away from the medieval English straitjacket by writing contemporary fantasy. I think particularly of Megan Lindholm's brilliant *Wizard of the Pigeons*, which profoundly affected me. It simultaneously opened the door to a universe of fresh fantasy milieux, and closed the door for me on urban fantasy itself, since she had created such a gorgeous urban fantasy world that I did not know how I could write urban fantasy without imitating or echoing her.

Besides, fantasy benefits from a sense of being ancestral, a memory of days long past. So I thought, what would an American ancestral story look like?

My first thought was of James Fenimore Cooper's Leatherstocking Tales. Natty Bumppo was definitely not a creature of fantasy, with no magic about him. But he was larger than life, herculean, and gave American history a sense of depth and humanity. Anything earlier than the frontier days of the French and Indian War would not be American history. The Native Americans certainly had cultures, many of them very magical, and a depth of history that is impossible for Anglo-America. But most Americans today don't feel any ancestral connection with the Mound Builders, still less the Aztecs, Mayas, Quechuas, or Olmecs. There are fantasy epics to be written in those milieux, of course, but if I'm setting out to write fantasy in the American past, Natty Bumppo is as far back as I could go.

Until I realized that I had a different past—still American, but both more and less. I grew up as (and continue to be) a believing, practicing Mormon, deeply inside the culture of The Church of Jesus Christ of Latter-day Saints.

Christian historical novels, like biblical fiction in general, have the power of supernatural happenings along with tales of great heroes, both hubristic and humble—or both, like David the humble shepherd, and David the lecherous and predatory king. One of the great beloved novels and plays of the late nineteenth century and well into the twentieth was the story of Judah in *Ben-Hur: A Tale of the Christ.* Jesus was not the hero of the story—he was the god. Every reader in that time period knew the story of Jesus, so that in writing the novel, Lew Wallace did not have to explain. Judah Ben-Hur could cross paths with Jesus several times in the novel, and each time the encounter was memorable and transformative—but not history-making. Jesus touches Judah Ben-Hur and transforms him, but Ben-Hur does not change Jesus in any way, or bend his path even a little.

At that time, in the late 1970s, I shifted a little. It wasn't enough for me to attempt a vernacular American epic. I also had to write a vernacular Mormon epic. The obvious thing was to tell the story of Joseph Smith, a figure with supernatural connections at least as good as those of Achilles or Hercules. But, like Spenser, I knew I could tell the story best as allegory. Nobody would be named Joseph Smith, and nobody would have visions like those of the founding Mormon prophet. Instead, I would take a cue from his name, and make my character a blacksmith. And I would take his name from that of Joseph's beloved older brother who died as a young adult: Alvin Smith.

However, I regarded the Mormon connection as being less important to the story than the American setting. This was to be an American fantasy, not a Mormon one. For one thing, Mormonism has no room for fantasy—there are plenty of supernatural events in the historical lore. No magic added.

When I first set pen to paper, I was still in grad school, though I had already had several novels and other books published. I was comfortable inventing a fantasy universe, though for my initial foray it did not need to be very wide or deep. There was an apprentice blacksmith, still a boy—conceivably, fourteen years old, like Joseph Smith at the time of his first vision. But instead of being concerned about which Christian church to join, Alvin Smith was concerned with making his masterpiece—the work that would prove his worthiness to be called Master.

What would he make? An iron plow is a difficult thing to make, since it is both cast and wrought. That was hard enough. But if I reached into alchemical tradition, Prentice Alvin needed to make a plow that turned iron into gold—but a gold that was not only hard and unmalleable, but also alive, able to move under its own volition, needing no horse or ox to pull it through the dirt.

When in Alvin Smith's life should my story take place? For me, it was obvious that it had to be about the making of his masterwork. And with some idea of how the story would be told, I first wrote the title: "Prentice Alvin and the No-Good Plow."

I wrote the poem, not in contemporary English, really, but in imitation of the dialect spoken in the early nineteenth century. I had already received confirmation of the accents of the frontier when I saw, in one of his letters, that Brigham Young spelt "piano" as "pianna." Which nails down his pronunciation at the time.

I wrote the poem as if it were being told aloud to listeners staying warm near a fire—listeners who spoke a hill-country dialect of English, where it was the accent of the West Virginia Appalachians, of the Ozarks, or of the mountain valleys of Utah.

I knew the rhythms, cadences, and some of the vocabulary of those dialects. I knew the pronunciations—the hard retroflex R, the open O that becomes the open Ah of opera. (See Wayne Booth's wonderful essay, "Farkism and Hyperyorkism.")

There were two competing standards. I could try, as Artemus Ward did, to write down the accent. But this is why Artemus Ward has vanished from the public consciousness, while Mark Twain is still widely read by volunteers. Twain *suggested* the country dialect, but spelled almost all the words exactly as they're normally spelt.

There was only one place where I felt a need to correct a long misconception. In modern English, our present participle and gerund verbs end in "ing." Often, to show that a character is a country hick, writers will have these lower-class people use words like "talkin'," "eatin'," "sufferin'."

But I knew from personal observation that even the most pretentious people elide the "ng" sound into a simple "in" or a nasalized schwa. In other words, saying "walkin' up the street" and "hoppin' mad" does not mark you as a lower-class person—it marks you as someone who speaks modern English, period.

And why *should* people pronounce "ng" at the ends of participles and gerunds? That "ng" is as accurate as spelling "offen" as "often," even though the T is silent in the correctly spoken word.

Those participles were originally written as "and." Had this ending survived, we would write of people "walkand down the street" and "singand a song." But, as languages do, English dropped that D, and the ending began to be a simple nasalized schwa or grunt, with no vowel at all. It should be written as “walkn” and “singn,” because, like the final “le” of “little,” the final syllable of those participles is a vowelless grunt, with the liquid L and the nasal N functioning as standalone syllables. Walkn, eatn, hittn, speakn.

But when writers first tried to write that syllable, they settled on “ing,” to represent a general nasalized sound. Syllables needed vowels, so they used the shortest vowel. And it was *not* a terminal N as in “broken,” “taken,” “beaten,” or even “stone,” “pain,” “throne.”

Alas that we make little to no distinction between the final syllables of “eating” and “eaten,” “beating” and “beaten.” Fortunately, not a lot of past participles take the “en” ending—there’s no “I have often walken there,” nor “I have never callen that number.” Still, the “ing” spelling lingered, even though as a present participle it is almost never pronounced like the “ing” of “ending,” or of “linger,” or of “ring.”

If I had characters in my vernacular language say, “I’m working on that,” should I spell it as it is pronounced—“I’m workn on that”? Or with the condescending apostrophe—“I’m workin’ on that”? I figured that “workn” would look like Polish to American eyes, while “workin’ ” with an apostrophe would seem like the sneering way the educated represent the conversation of the unlettered.

Instead I settled on the “in” ending, no G and no apostrophe: “Laughin and pantin on the ground . . . Frost a-comin on.” The words thus remained completely intelligible, while better reflecting the common pronunciation.

Yes, right, *you* always pronounce the “ing” properly. Maybe you do. But maybe it’s like when I was directing a production of *A Dixie Christmas Carol*, in which someone was supposed to say the name of the North Carolina town Fayetteville. I insisted that the actor say the name of the city the way it is almost always pronounced in Carolinian conversation: “Fettvul,” or even with the “tt” replaced by a glottal stop: “Fe’vul.”

One cast member was outraged. I think she thought I was disparaging the way North Carolinians talked, while I was merely trying to *use* it to get the right feel for the language. “We say ‘Fay-ette-ville,’ ” she said adamantly.

I stopped arguing with her about it and went on with the rehearsal. During a break not ten minutes later, I heard her talking with some other cast members, and she mentioned Fayetteville in passing—pronouncing it as “Fe’vul.”

I don’t remember what we did in performance. I think I changed it to another regional town name, like Danville (“Damvul”) or Asheville (“Ashvul”). What matters is that a lot of people *think* they speak with elevated formality, when in fact they usually speak the more abbreviated and elided vernacular.

I labored over the story of "Prentice Alvin and the No-Good Plow" for several months, until I had worked out the orthography to my own satisfaction, even if to no one else's. Then I submitted the finished poem to a contest sponsored by the Utah State Institute of Fine Arts. In the Long Serious Poem category, it won first place in 1981.

The poem appeared in the August 1989 issue of *Sunstone* magazine, and I included it in my short fiction collection *Maps in a Mirror*. Upon publication, it seemed to me that the poem actually existed, though I have little indication that anybody read it all the way through. For all I know, "Prentice Alvin" was the *only* entry in the Long Serious Poem category that year.

I had no illusions. The audience for long-form poetry in America today is usually the poet and his mother. Even English graduate students feel imposed upon when asked to read any modern poem longer than a sonnet or a limerick. But I loved the character and situation of Prentice Alvin. I didn't want to let the story die on the vine.

That's when I worked it up as a proposal for an American frontier fantasy trilogy: *Prentice Alvin*, *Alvin Journeyman*, and *Master Alvin*. I submitted it to Lester del Rey of Del Rey Books. He rejected it with an explanation that I was violating a whole bunch of rules of fantasy, every single one of which was also violated by Stephen R. Donaldson's then-recent Thomas Covenant trilogy, published by Del Rey. In other words, they weren't rules at all—if the story was good enough, it would transcend the rules.

My goal, as always, wasn't to "get published." It was to get the novel right, and then try to find its audience. It didn't take long to find the right editor and publisher: Beth Meacham, whom I had worked with when she was at Berkley, but who now was at Tor Books, which would soon become the publisher of *Ender's Game* and *Speaker for the Dead*. Beth and I had tried to work out a contract for a science fiction novel based on the Middle English romance King Horn. Beth and her boss, Tom Doherty, made a generous offer on the Alvin Make series. That advance allowed me to quit my job as book editor at Compute! Publications and go back to being a freelance novelist working from home. Alvin Maker changed my life.

The trouble is that the first volume, *Prentice Alvin*, turned into three novels: *Seventh Son*, *Red Prophet*, and *Prentice Alvin*. And in *Alvin Journeyman*, something Alvin didn't do much of was journey. The series was out of hand. I kept hearing from people about the seven books in The Tales of Alvin Maker. Seven? *Five*, I insisted. I figured it was the title of *Seventh Son* that led readers to think of "seven" in connection with the series. And then when *Heartfire* didn't move us more than a micron forward in the story, I realized there had to be six books.

But in book six, *Crystal City*, to bring the series from Louisiana to Illinois and take the story through to its obvious end would have taken a thousand pages, or so I figured. So when I turned in *Crystal City*, without the conclusion of the series, we had to face the fact that despite my best intentions, the Alvin Maker series would be seven books long. Beth was a little cynical about it—did I *really* think I could end it in one more book? I promised that there was only going to be one last book, entitled *Master Alvin*, and I really hoped it wouldn't be a thousand pages long.

Her reply? "I'm an editor. I know how to cut."

The real problem for me was that *Master Alvin* was going to show Alvin as the political leader of Crystal City, as well as its designer and architect. This was analogous to Joseph Smith's time as mayor of the city of Nauvoo, Illinois, a period of time I had already dealt with in my long historical novel *Saints* (originally published under the ridiculously generic title *Woman of Destiny*).

Furthermore, in Joseph Smith's life everything was complicated by the idea of polygamy—which I had already dealt with in *Saints* and in the musical play *Father, Mother, Mother and Mom* (with composer Robert Stoddard). I wasn't interested in doing anything more with these topics than I already had.

So I didn't intend to deal with the entire history of Crystal City and all the betrayals and problems. My task was simple: Alvin Maker was going to die near the end of the book, murdered in his jail cell in the city of Carthage—which, in the Alvin Maker series, is basically Cincinnati. Then his people cross the Mississippi River and move on through prairies and mountains to the Great Salt Lake Valley. Therefore, this final volume needed to show why Alvin Maker, who could have been effectively immortal, placed himself in harm's way and died at the hands of a disciplined military force that had decided to assassinate him.

All I had to show of Crystal City was the condition it was in shortly before Alvin's death—I didn't have to cover the whole thing. All I had to do with polygamy was to ignore it completely, since it had no place in this story. I had to have characters who worked against him, among them his brother Calvin, perpetually envious of his powerful brother.

Master Alvin starts near the end of the Crystal City period. All the development phases have already happened. If you find this intriguing, my novel about it is *Saints*. But *Saints* is a historical novel. *Master Alvin* is a fantasy.

Let me go back now to the early days of writing the series. I wanted the fantasy to rely on the actual beliefs and practices of frontier Americans—only those magical beliefs would actually be true, in the world of the book. I knew that I would be using the idea of knacks, but those aren't in the old folk beliefs. So instead of trying to research frontier beliefs from scratch, I decided to rely on somebody who had already studied that period. Carol Breakstone was a graduate student who knew how to get the information I needed. Only I couldn't tell her *what* I needed; I'd know it when I saw it.

She brought me a few things at first, to see if she was on the right track. But they were the right things. They immediately triggered everything else. First, she reminded me that hexes were displayed on buildings as a blessing or a protection. I knew I could play with that.

Then she told me of the practice of having a seer lay hands on a pregnant woman's belly, to find out things about the coming baby. I turned that practitioner into a "torch," a term of my own invention, and eventually it became one of the most powerful magics in the Alvin Maker series.

I had never heard of a birth caul—a section of the amniotic sac that covers a baby's face at birth, making breath impossible until someone peels it away. Carol told me that the caul was believed to have magical properties pertaining to the child, which opened many doors to me.

I believe that she also reminded me that people believed that a seventh son had powers of healing and other magics. I liked that—but I also thought about a seventh son of a seventh son. *That* would be powerful stuff. All the more powerful if all six brothers were still alive when the seventh son was born.

Carol gave me several starting points, and I ran with them. But there was more than magic required. Just as medieval fantasies needed to depict the details of life, I would need to do the same with frontier life. For this I relied on what I had learned from reading, in my early teens, Conrad Richter's beautiful Awakening Land series: *The Trees*, *The Fields*, and *The Town*. If the "great American novel" could actually exist, I believe that Richter's trilogy has the opening bid and a good chance of winning the category outright.

I had no intention of trying to top Richter's fiction. I only aspired to convey some slender part of the world he created so beautifully. His research and storytelling were so excellent, I did not need more than a handful of sources beyond what Richter and Breakstone brought to me.

I had the magic; I had the daily life. But I was well into the first draft of *Seventh Son* when I realized: If the magical beliefs of the people of that time were true, wouldn't that magical power have altered American history? A magical America wouldn't have had all the same events, and while the prominent people might still rise to fame and influence, they would do so in a different way.

So I started playing games with history. I was taking my changes seriously, but at the same time, I was frolicking through American history, trying to tell a story that was truer than the actual historical facts.

Here's a weird thing that happened: Americans are so ignorant of their own history that many readers didn't realize that the history in the Alvin Maker books was bogus. We actually got one fan letter in which a lady said, "I never knew that George Washington was beheaded." We tried to interpret her words as a joke, but we gave up. She meant it.

Another weird thing: Many Mormon readers recognized elements from Joseph Smith's life, and then followed along as if the whole novel were a one-for-one allegory of his life. It was as if, because they got the Joseph Smith connections, they couldn't see anything else. This is, above all, an *American* fantasy novel, and I'm trying to deal with the pre–Civil War era in American history as truthfully as possible, while playing entertainingly (I hope) with the facts.

You can't find Joseph Smith's life accurately portrayed in the Alvin Maker books. His life was a frame on which I built story and character. But American history was also a frame I built on—and it shaped far more of the story than Joseph Smith did.

One aspect of Joseph Smith's life I kept: How it ended. I told Mormons who asked about the later books in the series, "Come on, you know how it all will end—with Alvin Maker dead on the street of Carthage City, and Arthur Stuart leading most of the citizens of Crystal City west to the Great Salt Lake." They agreed. That was how it had to end.

And in the fall of 2023, I decided it was time for me to follow through and get to that ending. It took me until June of 2024, and then I needed to do a round of revisions, with which my audiobook-narrator daughter, Emily Rankin, was of extraordinary help.

But the whole project began because I wanted to follow in the footsteps of Dante and Spenser, by creating an epic poem about my own people. I originally planned to go back and add more to the poem—later chapters, if you will. But instead I gave up on the verse, for which there is little audience, and just told the story, plain and simple. Or plain and complicated—my plans don't always work.

You have, I assume, now read the entire Tales of Alvin Maker. To coincide with the launch of the series finale, Tor has allowed me to assemble all the outside stories of Alvin Maker. One of them, "Yazoo Queen," was originally the first chapter of *Crystal City*, and now it is back in its place. The other Alvin stories don't have a clear place in the timeline, so we inserted them into the books we thought they were most compatible with.

Now the series is complete. The rumors are not true, of course. Neither Disney nor Universal are planning to open "The Hexing World of Alvin Maker." For one thing, it would be hard to decide how many potentially fatal water hazards to have. And . . . no wands or quidditch.

Just because a story is presented to you as part of a genre, it doesn't mean it has to resemble everything else in that genre. My American frontier fantasy did not spawn a new genre. I don't see many other fantasy writers working in American history. But *I* wrote an American frontier fantasy series, and that's enough for me. It will never have the stature of *The Inferno* or *Faerie Queene*, but I didn't write it to impress; I don't write *anything* to be impressive, and as my detractors would say, good thing.

Being "in fashion" is such a transient thing. Those who seek fame may find it, and they'll find out that it is nothing.

What I wanted for Alvin Maker was readers. And here you are, fulfilling my ambition. I hope the story means something to you. I know that inventing it and writing it has meant a lot to me.

As Tolkien wanted *The Lord of the Rings* to be an epic for the English people, I would be glad if some people thought of The Tales of Alvin Maker as *their* epic, a place where their story is told. It is definitely a place where *I* think my people's epic is told.

Remember that The Tales of Alvin Maker is set in the period of American history just before the Civil War—the war that killed more Americans than any other, and we did it to ourselves. Alvin Maker tried to forestall this terrible outcome. But in the real world, we went to war. We *came* to war, in our own towns, in our own homes. It's part of our story, part of our epic—one we periodically decide to reenact among ourselves.

History can lead to tragedy. Good people die. Good projects fail. Awful people prosper at the expense of better people. That's the world we live in.

And that's the world in which I tell stories. If fiction does anything valuable, I think it's that stories allow you to have experiences that you could not otherwise have. You can experience tragedy without having to live through it. You can see how sacrificing for the good of others makes everything better for all. You can know what it's like to build a community that's good for everyone in it.

I have dreamed of building a Crystal City, a place where nobody has to be poor, because everyone shares their goods with others in need. I don't think such a thing can ever be created by coercive power, by legislation, by confiscation. We build the Crystal City by voluntarily meeting other people's needs when we see them, or when we're asked. When we've given all we can, we give more, if not in money, then in service, in sharing.

The Crystal City is built out of blocks formed with drops of the blood and sweat of the citizens, added to the water of life that flows like a powerful river through and around us all. We work, not to build a private fortune to pass on to our children, but to build up an inheritance for all the people of the City, where all are partakers of the heavenly gift.

We do it one person at a time, by our own free decisions. We cooperate to identify the people in need. We help each other prosper, because only with prosperity will we have enough to share abundantly. The Crystal City can be built wherever there is freedom, love of neighbors, and kindness to strangers.

We don't need Alvin Maker to create these blocks for us. The magic is already inside us. It's already in our blood, our labor, our love. The Maker is the one who is part of what he makes.

 Prentice Alvin and the No-Good Plow 

Alvin, he was a blacksmith's prentice boy,
He pumped the bellows and he ground the knives,
He chipped the nails, he het the charcoal fire,
Nothing remarkable about the lad,
Except for this: He saw the world askew,
He saw the edge of light, the frozen liar
There in the trees with a black smile shinin cold,
Shiverin the corners of his eyes.
Oh, he was wise.

The blacksmith didn't know what Alvin saw.
He only knew the boy was quick and slow:
Quick with a laugh and a good or clever word,
Slow at the bellows with his brain a-busy,
Quick with his eyes like a bright and sneaky bird,
Slow at the forge when the smith was in a hurry.
Times the smith, he liked him fine. And times
He'd bellow, "Hell and damnation, hammer and tong,
You done it wrong!"

One day when the work was slow, the smith was easy.
"Off to the woods with you, Lad, the berries are ripe."
And Alvin gratefully let the bellows sag
And thundered off in the dust of the summer road.
Ran? He ran like a colt, he leaped like a calf,

Then his feet were deep in the leafmeal forest floor,
He was moss on the branches, swingin low and lean,
His fingers were part of the bark, his glance was green—
And he was seen.

He was seen by the birds that anyone can see,
Seen by the porcupines that hid in the bushes,
Seen by the light that slipped among the trees,
Seen by the dark that only he could see.
And the dark reached out and stumbled Alvin down,
Laid him laughin and pantin on the ground,
And the dark snuck up on every edge of him,
Frost a-comin on from everywhere,
Ice in his hair.

Ice in the summertime, and Alvin shook,
Crackin ice aloud in the miller's pond,
A mist of winter flowin through the wood,
Fingerin his face, and where it touched
He was numb, he was stricken dumb, his chin all chattery.
Where are the birds? he wondered. When did they go?
Get back to the edge, you Dark, you Cold, you Snow!
Get north, you Wind, it's not your time to blow!
I tell you, No!

No! he cried, but the snow was blank and deep
And didn't answer, and the fog was thick
And didn't answer, and his flimsy clothes
Were wet, and his breath was sharp as ice in his lung
Splittin him like a rail. It made him mad.
He yelled, though the sound froze solid at his teeth
And the words dropped out and broke as they were said
And his tongue went thick, and his lips were even number:
"Dammit, it's summer!"

With the snow like stars of death in your eyes? "It's summer!"
The wind a-ticklin at your thighs? "It's summer!"

Your breath a fog of ice? "Let it be spring!
Let it be autumn, let it be anything!"
But the edge of the world had found him, and he knew
That the fire of the forges would be through,
That the air would be thick and harsh at the end of the earth
And all the flames a-dancin in his hearth,
What were they worth?

"Oh, you can cheat the trees, so dumb and slow,
And you can jolly the birds that summer's through,
But you can't fool me! I'll freeze to death before
I let you get away with a lie so bold!"
And he laughed as he was swallowed by the cold,
He sang as the ice a-split him to the core,
He whispered in his pain that it wasn't true.
"You can bury me deep as hell in your humbug snow,
But I know what I know."

And look at that! A red-winged bird a-singin!
Look at that! The leaves all thick and green!
He touched the bark so warm in the summer sun,
He buried his hands in the soil and said, "I'm jiggered."
"Oh, blacksmith's prentice boy," said the red-winged bird.
"Took you long enough," said Prentice Alvin.
"Came now, didn't I? So don't get snippety."
"Just see to it you don't go off agin.
Where you been?"

"I been," said the red-winged bird, "to visit the sun.
I been to sing to the deaf old man in the moon.
And now I'm here to make a maker of you,
Oh yes, I'll make you something before I'm through."
"I'm something now," said the lad, "and I like it fine."
"You're a smithy boy," said the bird, "and it ain't enough.
Bendin horseshoes! Bangin on the black!
Why, there be things to make that can't be told,
So bright and gold!"

A thousand things, that bird was full of talk,
And on he sang and Alvin listened tight.
Till home he came at dark, his eyes so bright,
His smile so ready but his mood like rock,
He was full of birdsong, full of dreams of gold,
Dreams of what he'd draw from the smithy fire.
"How old is old?" he asked the smith. "How tall
Do I have to be for hammer and tong?
It's been so long."

The smith, he spied him keen, he saw his eyes,
He saw how flames were leapin in the green.
"A redbreast bird been talkin," said the smith,
His voice as low as memory. "So young,
But not so young, so little but so tall.
Hammer and tong, my lazy prentice boy,
Let's see if they fit your hand, let's see if the heft
Is right for your arm, the right side or the left,
See how you lift."

Out they went to the forge beside the road,
Up and stoked the fire till it was hot.
The tongs fit snug in Alvin's dexter hand,
And the hammer hefted easy in his left,
And the smith had a face like grief, although he
  laughed.
"Go on," says he. "I'm watchin right behind."
The flames leaped up, and Alvin shied the heat,
But deep in the fire he held the iron rod
Till it was red.

"Now bend it," cried the smith, "now make a shoe!"
Alvin raised the hammer over his head,
Ready for the swing. But it wouldn't fall.
"Strike," the blacksmith whispered, "bend and shape."
But the red of the black was the red of a certain bird;
Behind his eyes he saw the iron true:
It was already what it ought to be.

"I can't," he said, and the blacksmith took the tool
And whispered, "Fool."

The hammer clattered against the stone of the wall,
But Alvin, he took heed where the hammer fell.
"There's some can lift the hammer," said the smith,
"And some can strike," and then he spoke an oath
So terrible that Alvin winced to hear.
"I'm shut of you," said the smith. "What's iron for?
To be hot and soft for a man of strength to beat,
To turn the fat of your empty flesh to meat
For the years to eat."

When the smith was gone, poor Alvin like to died,
For what was a smith that couldn't strike the black?
A maker, that's what the redbreast said he'd be,
And now unmade before he'd fair begun.
"I know," he whispered, "I know what must be done."
He took the hammer from the wallside heap
And blew the fire till flames came leapin back
And gathered every scrap at the fire's side
And loud he cried:

"Here is the makin that you said to make!
Here in my hand are the tools you said to take!
Here is the crucible, and here's the fire,
And here are my hands with all they know of shape."
Into the crucible he cast the scrap
And set the pot in the flames a-leapin higher.
"Melt!" he shouted. "Melt so I can make!"
For the redbreast bird had told him how:
A livin plow.

The black went soft in the clay, the black went red,
The black went white and poured when he tipped the pot.
Into the mold he poured, and the iron sang
With the heat and the cold, with the soft and the hard and the
form

He forced. When he broke the mold it rang,
And the shape of the plow was curved and sharp where it
ought.
But the iron, it was black, oh, it was dead,
No power in it but the iron's own,
As mute as stone.

He sat among the shards of the broken clay
And wondered what the redbird hadn't said.
Or had he talked to the bird at all today?
And now he thought of it, was it really red?
And maybe he ought to change the mold somehow,
Or pour it cool, or hotten up the forge.
But the more he studied it the less he knew,
For the plow was shaped aright, though cold and dark:
He knew his work.

So what was wrong with black? It was good enough
For all the hundred thousand smiths before,
And good enough for all the plows they made,
So why not good enough for Prentice Alvin?
Who ever heard of a bird so full of stuff,
So full of songs to make you feel so poor,
So full of promises of gold and jade?
"Ah, Redbird!" Alvin cried, "my heart is riven!
What have you given?"

He shouted at the black and silent plow.
He beat it, ground it at the wheel, and rubbed
Till the blade was a blackish mirror, till the edge
Was sharp as a trapper's skinnin knife, and still
It was iron, black and stubborn, growin cold.
All broke of hope, he cast it in the fire
And held it with his naked hands in the flame
And wept in agony till it was over.
Here was the taste of pain—he knew the savor:
The plow was silver.

All silver was the plow, and his hands were whole.
He knew what it was the redbird hadn't said.
He couldn't put the iron in alone
And expect the plow by itself to come to life.
He took the plow again—it's gleamin bright—
And this time when he put it into the fire
He clomb right in and sat among the flames
And cried in pain until the fire went cold.
The age of agony—he knew how old:
The plow was gold.

The smith, he come all white-eyed to the forge.
"The buffalo are ruttin in the wood,
A hundred wolves are singin out a dirge,
And a doe, she's lickin while her fawn is fed.
What you be doin while I'm in my bed?
The trees are wide awake and bendin low,
And the stars are all a-cluster overhead.
What will a prentice do when his master go?
I want to know!"

In answer, Alvin only lifts his plow,
And in the firelight it shines all yellow.
"Lord," the smith declares, and "damn my eyes,
My boy, you got the gift, I didn't reelize."
The smith, he reaches out. "Now give it here,
That's worth ten thousand sure, I shouldn't wonder,
All we got to do is melt her down
And we'll be rich afore another sundown,
Move to town."

But Alvin, he's not like to let it go.
"It's a plow I meant to make, and a plow I got,
And I mean for it to do what a plow should do."
The smith was mad, the smith, he scald and swore.
"Cuttin dirt ain't what that gold is for!"
And he reached his hand to take the plow by force,

But when he touched his prentice's arm, he hissed,
And kissed his fingers, gaspin. "Boy, you're hot
As the sunlight's source.

"Hot and bright as sunlight," says the smith,
"And the gold is yours to do whatever you like with,
But whatever you do, I humble-as-dust beseech you,
Do it away from me, I've nothin to teach you."
Says Alvin, "Does that mean I'm a journeyman?
I've a right to bend the black wherever I can?"
And the smith says, "Prentice, journeyman, or master,
For what you done a smith would sell his sister,
Been Satan kissed her."

What was Alvin totin when he left?
I tell you this—it wasn't hard to heft:
A burlap bag with a knot of leaden bread,
A hunk of crumbly cheese, and a golden plow.
A map of the world was growin in his head,
For a fellow who knows the edge can guess the whole,
And Alvin meant to find the certain soil
Where his plow could cut and make the clover grow,
The honey flow.

He left a hundred village tongues a-wag
With tales of a million bucks in a burlap bag;
The smith, he swore the gold was devil's make
And therefore free for a godly man to take;
His wife, she told how Alvin used to shirk
And owed them all the gold for his lack of work;
And others said the golden plow was a fake
That sneaky Alvin made so he could gull
Some trustin fool.

The tales of Alvin flew so far and fast
They reached him on the road and went right past,
And many a fellow in many a country inn
Would spy his bag and start in speculatin.

"Kind of a heavy tote you got, I reckon."
And Alvin nods. "The burlap's kinda thin—
Do I see something big and smooth and yellow?"
And Alvin nods, but then he tells the fellow,
"It's just my pillow."

True enough, if the truth ain't buttoned tight,
For he put it under his head most every night;
But country folk are pretty hard to trick,
And many a fellow thought that he could get
A plowshare's worth of gold for the price of a stick
Applied with vigor to the side of Alvin's head;
And many a night young Alvin had to run
From the bowie knife or buckshot-loaded gun
Of some mother's son.

While Alvin beat through woods and country tracks,
Comes Verily Cooper, a handiworkin man,
Who boards wherever there's barrels to make or mend,
And never did he find so fine a place,
So nice a folk nor never so pretty a face
That he'd put away his walkin boots and stay.
It happened that he come to the smith one day
And heard that Alvin had made his golden plow,
And wondered how.

So off he set with boots so sad and worn
And socks so holey, the skin of his feet was torn
And he left a little track of blood sometimes—
Off set Verily Cooper, hopin to find
What tales were envy, and if some tales were true,
What the journeyman blacksmith did or didn't do.
He asked in every inn, "Did a boy with a bag
Come here, a brown-haired boy so long of leg,
About this big?"

Well, it came about that the findin all was done
On a day without a single speck of sun.

Young Alvin, he come down to the bottom lands,
Where the air was cold and the fog was thick and white.
"In a fog this deep you'd better count your hands,"
Said an unseen man a-waitin by the track.
"What could I see if a man had any sight?"
And the unseen speaker said, "That the sun is bright
And the soil is black."

Now Alvin knelt and touched the dirt of the road,
But the ground was packed and he couldn't feel it deep,
And though he fairly pressed his nose to the dirt,
Still the white of the fog was all he could see.
"The soil, it doesn't look so black to me."
And the unseen speaker said, "The earth is hurt
And hides in the fog and heals while it's asleep.
For the tree, she screamed and wept when the beaver gnawed
And no one knowed."

"I'm lookin," Alvin says, "for a soil that's fit
To spring up golden grain, make cattle fat."
And the unseen speaker says, "What soil is that?"
"I'm lookin," Alvin says again, "for loam
That a plow can whittle till it comes to life."
And the unseen speaker says, "A plow's a knife,
And where it cuts the earth is broke and lame."
Says Alvin, "Mar to mend, from the moldrin leaf
Will grow the limb."

"Then go, if you mean to make from the broken ground,
Go till you hear the rushin river's sound,
For there in the river's bight is a dirt so rich
You can harrow with your hand and plow with a flitch."
"Thank you, stranger," Alvin says, and then:
"I've heard your voice before, I can't think when."
"In such a fog as this, so cold and wet,
Your sight's so dim your memory's in debt
And you forget.

For the fog, it goes afore and it goes behind,
Hides what you're lookin for and what you've found,
And the deeper you go, the dimmer it makes your past.
And yet in all the world, this soil is best."
With that, though Alvin tried to learn his name,
The unseen speaker never spoke again,
And at last the journeyman smith went on to find
In the fog, by listenin tight for the river's sound,
That perfect ground.

Near done was the day when Alvin came to the shore
Of the mighty River Mizeray, all deep
And brown and slow and lookin half asleep.
Said Mizeray, "Jes step a little more,
Young feller, and I'll carry you across."
And Alvin, blind as a bat in the fog, he said,
"Don't I hear the rush of a river in its bed?"
But Mizeray, he gave a little toss
And whispered, "Cross."

So again that day young Alvin Maker jedges.
How can he know what's true in a fog so white?
How can he trust what a hidden voice alleges?
He kneels, he touches the soil, he lifts it light,
He crushes it in his hand and it's loose and smooth,
But still old Mizeray's voice can tickle and sooth,
And says, "Come on, step on, I'll carry you
To the only soil in the world that'll ever do,
I tell you true."

Old Mizeray has a voice you must believe.
Old Mizeray has a voice that could not lie.
Old Mizeray, he whispers to deceive,
To draw the trustin step to the edge, to die;
But the voice, the voice is full and sweet with love.
So Alvin, with his fingers deep in the loam,
He wonders if this soil is good enough,

And again he hears the river's whisperin hum:
"I'll take you home."

And now he doesn't know his north from south,
And his fingers search but cannot find his mouth,
And he can't remember what he came here for,
Or if it even matters anymore.
Only the sound of the river callin him,
Only the whine of his fear, so high and thin,
Only the taste of the sweat when he licks his lips,
Only the tremblin of his fingertips,
Their weakish grips.

He stands, but he doesn't step, he daresn't walk,
He puzzles for the key to this hidden lock,
And he knows the key isn't in that hissin voice,
He knows there's another way to make his choice.
The soil he's lookin for, it's not for himself,
It's meant for the plow he carried all so stealthy;
He opens his burlap bag and lifts the plow
And sets it on the earth real soft and slow,
And sees it glow.

He sees it shine, that plow, it shines all gold,
All yellow, and it gets too hot to hold,
And around the plow the fog begins to clear,
And the wind, it blows till the fog is gone from here,
And he sees the soil is humusy and black
Just as the unseen voice in the fog had said;
And he sees the river lap the shore and smack
And if he'd taken that step, now he'd be dead
In the devil's sack.

For Mizeray, down deep, don't flow with water:
The bottom slime is made of the stuff of night,
The darkness reachin in at the edge of light,
Awaitin for the step of a man unwary
To suck him down and slither him out to bury,

Numb and soundless, pressed in the dark of the sea,
Where the driftin dead look up through the night and see
Forever out of reach the earth in her dance,
O heaven's daughter.

And in the tree young Alvin sees a bird
All red of feather, mouth all wide and singin,
And Alvin, he calls out, "I know your voice!"
But the wind-awaker answers not a word.
Enough for him that his breezy song is heard,
And he darts from tree to tree, so coy he's wingin,
And Alvin sighs at the come-out of his choice,
Not altogether sure how the thing occurred,
For the choice was hard.

And while he lies a-restin in the grove,
Up comes young Verily Cooper, shy and smilin.
"Are you the one that they call by the name of Alvin?"
"There's many who's called that name. And who are you?"
"I'm a man who wants to learn what you know of makin.
They call me Verily Cooper; I work in staves,
I join them watertight, each edge so true,
But never a keg I made that was proof from leakin
Or safe from breakin."

Alvin answers, "What do I know of barrels?"
Verily says, "And what did you know of plows?"
And Alvin laughs, and he says, "Ain't you a marvel,"
And up he hops and gives his hand a shake.
"Verily Cooper, there's things in a man that shows,
And here at the river's edge we'll plow the earth
And together make whatever we fix to make
And be the midwives at the barley's birth
And weigh our worth."

So they cut an oak and together hewed the wood
To make the plowframe strong and slow of flex,
And they set the plow in place and bound it good

And never mind a halter for an ox,
For this was a livin plow, of tremblin gold.
And when the work was done, they marked their field,
And side by side they reached and took ahold,
And the plow, it leaped, it plunged, it played like a child
So free and wild.

Verily and Alvin, they hung on;
There wasn't a hope of guidin the plow along.
It was all they could do to keep it to the land;
Other than that they couldn't do a thing.
And at last, with bleedin blisters on their hands,
With arms gone weak and legs too beat to run,
They tripped and fell together on the dirt.
Aside from the blisters, the only thing much hurt
Was Alvin's shirt.

They look, and there's the plow, still as you please,
Gleamin in the sunlight. "How'd it stop?"
Asks Alvin. Verily, he thinks he sees
The truth. He touches the plow, it gives a hop;
He takes his hand away, and it sets right down.
"It's us that makes it go," he says, and he grins.
Now Alvin laughs, a-settin on the ground:
"Maybe it goes a little widdershins,
But it gets around!"

And as they sat there, hollerin and whoopin,
Out come the farmer folk who lived nearby,
To find out what had caused the fog to fly—
And at the same time do a little snoopin.
They saw that the furrow went all anyhow,
And they said, "If you think that's plowin, boys, you're
daft!
Straight as an arrow, that's how a plow should go!"
And the farmers mocked—oh, how the farmers laughed
At that no-good plow.

That sobered Alvin up, and Verily frowned.
"Don't you see that the plow, it cut the earth alone?
We got no ox, we got no horse around!
The plow's alive, and we'll tell you how it's done!"
But the farmers went their way, still mirthful merry,
For they had nothin to learn from any fellow
As young and ignorant as Al or Verry.
And the plow just sat at the head of its crooked furrow,
Hot and yellow.

The rest of the tale—how they looked for the crystal city,
How they crept to the dangerous heart of the holy hill,
How they broke the cage of the girl who sang for rain,
How they built the city of light from water and blood—
Others have told that tale, and told it good.
And besides, the girl you're with is cruel and pretty,
And the boy you're settin by has a mischievous will.
There's better things to do than hear me again,
So go on home.

Poem completed in 1981
South Bend Indiana
Orson Scott Card

Acknowledgments

As the internet age was dawning, America Online aggressively marketed their gateway to the internet, though they hoped that besides coming to AOL for email, they would stay to take part in the content provided. Among that content was an AOL site called Hatrack River.

Readers of the early volumes of The Tales of Alvin Maker were drawn to the site, then largely managed by my good friend and sometime collaborator, Kathryn Kidd. Participants would devise their own characters, along with their knacks and their backstory, and tell brief stories or conduct dialogues in their Hatrack River personas.

The characters were many and very creative. And as they became more real, they started to work their way into the books as reasonably important characters. Any time a novelist gives a character a name, it makes that character loom larger in the reader's mind. Throwaway characters are rarely named; for instance, you can call a character only by their job, like carriage driver, ship's pilot, housekeeper. When they aren't named, they may have dialogue in a scene or two, but the readers know that this nameless character is not going to amount to much in the story.

So when personas from the Hatrack River community started showing up with names, it meant they were going to matter and, perhaps, be memorable.

In *Crystal City*, in Nueva Barcelona we met Papa Moose and Mama Squirrel. These had been delightful characters in Hatrack River, and they became quite important to the story. But Papa Moose in particular, a character devised by Michael Sloan, also contributed heavily behind the scenes.

I have never had the best memory, and, like many other novelists, I have sometimes begun to develop a storyline and then forgot about it, neglecting to bring it to fruition. Knowing I was going to write the final volume, *Master Alvin*, I was afraid that I would leave storylines dangling. So I asked Michael Sloan to reread the entire series and alert me to dangling threads.

He did a superb job, and his report became an important element in my composition of this last volume. I did not find ways to involve all the unfulfilled storylines, but the fact that any of them were brought to fruition is owed to Papa Moose.

He also pointed out inconsistencies and discontinuities, places where one book contradicts another. Not all could be resolved, but the ones that seemed important to me needed to be reconciled, if it were possible.

Many others from the Hatrack River community have stayed in touch with us, even after Kathy Kidd passed away. Many times when I had a question about a character or "fact" from earlier books, I would ask the question online and get answers right away. At first I thought that the online community had extraordinary memories, and perhaps they do. But they also threw themselves into answering my queries with a generous sacrifice of time.

Andrew Wahr, whose persona on Hatrack was named Hobbes, saw my question and decided it was his responsibility to get me the answer at once. He informed his English teacher that he had to leave class because Orson Scott Card needed his help. He went to the school library, plunged into the books, and gave me the answer the same day I asked. He was a great help on this and many other occasions. I hope that English teacher understood that these days, authors can be in close touch with their readers, and the readers, in their turn, can contribute to the content and continuity of the work.

Another friend of ours was and is John Hansen, who created the character of John Binder. When I was deciding who should be in Carthage Jail with Alvin and Measure, it just seemed right that John Binder, who contributed so much to the harmony and unity of the Crystal City, should be one of the four—and that he should be the one to have memorized the words and the tune of "A Poor Wayfaring Man of Grief," a song that moves me so much that I can't sing it; I keep breaking down and falling silent. I knew I could trust John Binder with the singing of that song.

Robert Davis, my new editor at Tor, after reading *Master Alvin*, sent us a note indicating that a certain chapter contained some pretty dark material, which seemed out of character for Alvin. Since I had written that chapter, I was inclined to resist his suggestion.

My daughter, Emily Janice Rankin, has provided great help on my two most recent books, this one and the novel *Reawakening*, the sequel to *Wakers*. With *Master Alvin*, she was reading for continuity and realized that she felt just as Robert Davis had—that a certain event that I had written about at some length seemed out of character for Alvin. Yes, perhaps he would have acted that way, but it made Emily quite sad, and when my wife agreed with her and with Robert, I realized that the incident would have to go.

This is a hard thing to do, not because I was emotionally connected to the events, but because removing a chapter leaves a chasm in the storyline. Emily helped me greatly by bridging that gap so I could keep my attention focused on later events. Emily wrote some new material to fill the gap, and pointed out the one place where I would have to write a lot of new stuff to connect the events. I followed her recommendations and the book is better for it.

No, I'm not going to tell you where the chapter was cut. It was excised for good reason, so why should I defeat the purpose of cutting it by talking about it? Sometimes writers take a few steps in an unproductive direction, and when they retrace their steps and remove the offending passages, those pages are not part of the novel and never should have been. Perhaps some desperate graduate student decades from now will discover an archive copy of the draft prior to the excision and, after careful analysis, will conclude that I was absolutely right to remove the chapter in question. For now, you'll have to take my word for it—whatever flaws this novel may contain, that is not one of them.

Cyndie Munk Swindlehurst has repeatedly taken breaks from her legal career and her other work to help me by proofreading manuscripts that are sent to me by the publisher. Her incisive, logical mind is far more capable than mine to discover contradictions and omissions. When I worked as a professional proofreader, I learned the proofreaders' law: No matter how careful and meticulous you are, some errors will remain uncorrected. But if that happens in this book, I can assure you that it is not Cyndie's fault.

Perhaps more than anyone else, I owe a great debt to Beth Meacham, the originating editor of this series. She believed in me and in this story, and protected each volume. Since I decided to write the first book in a frontier American vernacular voice, the first copy editor misunderstood her role, and tried to correct the style and language to comply with Strunk & White's *The Elements of Style*.

Now, it happens that I regard *The Elements of Style* as the only book that deserves to be burnt in the public square, because it promulgates many of the stupidest fake rules that lead writers into horrible mistakes in their approach to writing. There are no needless words. English sentences often have to end in words that seem to be prepositions but in fact are part of compound verbs. One of the glories of English is that we have a two-word infinitive, and sometimes for clarity and euphony some words have to be inserted into the middle of the infinitive. This does not "split" the infinitive; it fills a gap in the infinitive. There is nothing wrong with "to boldly go where no man has gone before."

When I got the copyedited manuscript, there were dozens of "corrections" on almost every page, since the editor had set herself the task of changing the voice of the entire book. I looked at the monstrously marked-up pages and despaired. I phoned Beth Meacham and said that it would take me longer to correct the edits than it had taken me to write the book.

"Can't you just write stet a lot?" she asked me.

"Beth, even if I made a rubber stamp that said STET, I would exhaust three or four stamp pads of ink and have to ice down my shoulder and elbow every day for a week. I can't do it, Beth," I said. "Instead I'm going to send you a new, clean copy of my manuscript. And when you give it to a new copy editor, could you explain that I have worked professionally as a copy editor and I know the *Chicago Manual of Style* backward and forward? While I'm as prone to error as any other typist, many eyes have already scanned this manuscript and by the time it gets to you, there will be no more than one or two correctable errors every six pages or so. If the editor thinks she's found a second error on the same page, chances are very good that it is not an error at all, but rather a deliberate choice of mine. Especially point out that I know all the rules about commas in formal writing, but my fiction is always written in a very oral style, and commas are placed for rhythm and not by rule. So don't mess with my commas unless there's a real problem with clarity."

In short, I take pride in the quality of my manuscripts and I don't appreciate it when copy editors try to "fix" my style. When the manuscript of *Seventh Son* came back a second time, there were very, very few corrections; most pages had none at all. And the voice of my narrator stood strong and clear. Thanks to Beth, my novels have appeared as I wanted and needed them to be. She has earned her retirement many times over, since she has devoted decades to the protection of many authors' work—but I miss working with her. If only I had finished this book a year earlier, she would still have been my editor for this last journey with Alvin Maker. But I can't write novels any faster than I can figure out what is supposed to happen in them. And even if Beth's hands were not on this last Alvin Maker book, her wisdom and influence are still felt on every page.

Tor continues to be my primary publisher, a relationship that I hope continues. Certainly Tor is making a strong effort to bring out the definitive versions of all the books, so they will include novelettes, novellas, and short stories that I have written and published outside of the confines of the books. I'm especially happy to have "Yazoo Queen" restored to its place as the first chapter of *Crystal City*, and there are many other inclusions that mean a lot to me. This is not a trivial expense, to reprint the entire series with these additions incorporated. Only an extraordinarily committed publisher would go to this trouble and expense.

Tom Doherty set out to create a new science fiction and fantasy publishing company at a time when everybody in the industry "knew" that there wasn't room for another publisher in a crowded marketplace. Tom proved that there's always room for a new publisher who knows how to publish and market books of high quality and large demand. Just as authors try to create works of fiction that will outlive them, so also publishers try to create institutions like Tor that will endure long past their founding. I think Tom Doherty has made history over and over with his achievements in acquiring and marketing good fiction. I am glad and grateful that he included so much of my work since he founded the company. Being published by Tor is as great an honor as any of the awards in the field. It's nice to see "Hugo Winner" on the cover of a book. But to have "Tor" on the spine of book after book is an even grander prize.

As always, I owe most to my wife, Kristine Allen Card, who maintains our lives in good order. Every marriage needs to have at least one grownup, and she is the designated adult in our marriage. My life is a good one because she has been a part of it since our first date in October of 1973.

Not that our marriage has been one endless round of joy. There are two graves in the cemetery in American Fork, Utah, where our son Charlie Ben and our daughter Erin Louisa are remembered. Losing them broke my heart, and it has not healed. But those lost children are also part of everything I write. I miss them terribly, but they are always with us, and Kristine and I see the world differently and perhaps more clearly because they are in our memories.

What I value in fiction, drama, and film are stories of good people doing good. The best stories are not centered around some kind of ersatz "conflict." Rather, the essence of good storytelling is characters who are caught up in the struggle to achieve good ends despite all obstacles and opposition. To achieve victory, the hero does not have to crush his opponent; he does not have to drag the dead body of his enemy around the walls of Troy. It is enough that he has achieved his noble purposes. That is still the only happy ending, even if the hero had to give his life to bring it about.

About the Author

Terry Manier

Orson Scott Card may be best known for his science fiction (including *Ender's Game* and *Speaker for the Dead*), but, regretting the lack of fantasy novels set in the American past, he started The Tales of Alvin Maker, the epic of a powerful mage on the American frontier.

Card was born in 1951 in Richland, Washington, and went to school in Santa Clara, California; Mesa, Arizona; and Provo, Utah. After serving as a missionary for The Church of Jesus Christ of Latter-day Saints in São Paulo, Brazil, he earned degrees at Brigham Young University and the University of Utah, worked as an editor of books and magazines, and wrote plays and audioplays. He lives in Greensboro, North Carolina, with his wife, Kristine Allen Card. They are the parents of three adult children and grandparents of seven.